By Natalie England

Natalie England

This is a work of fiction. Names, characters, places and incidents are either the product of the author's imagination or used fictitiously, and any resemblance to actual persons, living or dead, business establishments, events or locales is entirely coincidental.

The Vine

First Edition June 2024

Published by Natalie England Publishing LLC

Print Cover by Damonza

To my dearest Rich,
for being my best friend
and for inspiring me to dream big.

To my readers,

While I've tried to make this series fun and full of adventure, the root message behind these books is based on depression and the struggles that go with it. Which means that there will be dark moments.

My hope is that you will finish the series to the end, when you can.

That is where happiness is discovered.

Chapter 1

Nobody's been up to Falling Rock. Not since the incident with the hunter last year.

We're not supposed to be up here either, but after the long, cold winter, Caleb insisted we come up to the hot spring for our eighteenth birthday. I just hope Mom and Dad don't find out we lied to them about where we'd be.

I step out of the truck, into the warm summer air, and walk to the ATV trailer hitched to the back. Caleb has already released one of the straps pinning our four-wheelers in place and tossed it to my side. It now lies in a tangled, dusty heap on the ground in front of me.

Bending down, I grip it in my hands and start rolling it up.

While my fingers work through the old strap, my eyes rise to the pine trees surrounding the clearing. I quietly try to summon the same feeling I get every time I smell these pines, but I'm only met with an unsettling feeling.

We shouldn't be here.

I let out a huff of air and stand back up, taking the wound strap with me. I hate that my memories of the hot spring were tainted the day the hunter died. That it became a place not only to be avoided but feared. I toss the wound strap into the backseat of the truck before walking to the trailer's ramp. Wrapping my fingers around the heavy metal, I try to lift it out of its mount, but it doesn't budge.

"Need some help, Alena?" Caleb asks, mocking my weak efforts. He has another tie-down strap in his hands. Setting it on the trailer, he steps to my side and grabs the other end of the ramp. With ease, he pops it out and drops it to the ground, sending a cloud of dust into the air.

I shake my head as he jumps onto the trailer.

Caleb's not afraid of this place like me. He was there that day too, a year ago, when we came to this same hot spring. But he didn't follow Dad when the helicopter appeared over the trees. He knew it wasn't a good idea. Maybe I should've listened to his warnings.

But I couldn't.

Like Dad, I'm undeniably drawn to medical emergencies. It's hard to explain, but I just had to follow the helicopter that day.

I pick up Caleb's strap sitting on the trailer and take it to the truck, then toss it into the backseat next to the other one.

Following the helicopter had led us to a cabin and ultimately the hunter who was lying in the bushes close by. Dad immediately went to work on the man while the helicopter found a place to land. I had dropped down beside him to help. It looked like the man had been attacked by a bear, a common occurrence in these mountains. There was so much blood that it was hard to find the open gashes.

That wasn't the worst part, though. A slash across his throat exposed his airway, causing him to choke on his own blood. The gurgling sound of him struggling to breathe still has me occasionally gagging for my own breath.

I inhale deeply now.

As scared as I was, though, I kept thinking that the man was lucky my dad just happened to be up in the mountains. He's the most experienced doctor when it comes to bear attacks.

What I soon realized, though, was that that man had not been attacked by a bear, and even with an experienced doctor's help, he was never going to survive.

I follow Caleb up the ramp and slide past Jess, who's loading up the four-wheelers with towels and food. She stops briefly to swipe at a couple of defiant strands of blonde hair before proceeding to fold our old towels.

It wasn't hard to convince Jess and her brother, Rick, to lie to their parents and come to the hot spring with us. Jess will do almost anything for Caleb. And Rick, well, if it has trouble written all over it, he'll be there.

Sitting on his four-wheeler next to me, Caleb pulls at my attention. "I dare you to jump off the cliff today, Alena," he says. The breeze softly blows through his brown hair, the only trait we share even though we're twins.

I force a soft laugh as my eyes send a quiet warning in his direction, cautioning him not to go there. While I enjoy this place for the hot spring, Caleb's favorite thing to do up here is jump off the twenty-foot cliff overhanging the river that runs adjacent to the warm water. He's always tried to get me to jump off, but the water freshly melted from the snow on top of the mountain is freezing cold. And I hate being cold.

"Sorry," I say, sitting on my four-wheeler.

Rick leans against the trailer, smiling while tapping my leg. "Caleb told me about the cliff. I'll do it if you do."

I glare at Caleb. I shouldn't be surprised that he's been scheming. But, somehow, I am.

"You're using Rick to get me to jump off?"

A sly, proud smile sweeps across Caleb's face. He thinks he's smart, but as much as I want to prove I'm cooler than Rick, I shake my head. "I'm not going to jump, Caleb," I say before turning on my four-wheeler, allowing the loud engine to end our conversation.

Caleb laughs over the noise and turns on his own four-wheeler before driving it down the ramp. I kick mine into gear and follow behind, bouncing down onto the dirt path. Jess climbs on behind Caleb, of course, leaving loud Rick to ride with me.

"Let's go," Caleb shouts with Jess's arms wrapped around him.

We race up the mountain, traveling through the pine trees and brush. The branches reach out and pull at my swim shorts and tank top. I lean forward in response, trying to beat Caleb to the hot spring.

But then our trail spills into an open clearing. I don't mean to stop. I don't want to stop. But my thumb acts on its own, releasing the throttle completely.

I stare ahead.

There, tucked within the shadows of tall pines, is the old abandoned log cabin. The air is still here, solemn and heavy. There isn't even a single bird or squirrel prancing through the hushed trees. It's as if the place itself is still etched with the horror of the hunter's death.

When we were younger, Caleb and I used to fight over who was going to own this cabin one day. With it being so close to the hot spring, it's been the topic of many conversations.

But I don't think we'll be having that conversation again anytime soon. It's unsettlingly creepy now, with weeds growing wildly over its rotting wooden logs and through the broken windows. The door hangs open on one hinge, with a piece of yellow caution tape still stuck in the crack. It squeaks in a chilling way and reveals the dusty interior where furniture and clothes are scattered all over.

My eyes find their way to the bushes where we found the hunter bleeding to death. I take in a deep breath, trying to slow my pounding heart. When I first saw the hunter, I really thought he had been attacked by a bear. But then I saw the eerie letter S carved into the skin of his shoulder. That's when I knew the man was going to die. Nobody survives an S attack. That's what we call them now: S attacks. The mysterious attacks that have proudly claimed dead bodies all over the world for the past several years. The letter S is always carved into their shoulder with a blade laced with a type of poison. Those who have studied the dead bodies think the poisons are a mixture of several types of venom. But the mixtures are always different—different venoms from different animals, different blends. Since scientists don't know exactly which blend will be used when, or on whom, they haven't been able to create an adequate antivenom.

So those attacked always die.

Unfortunately, we don't know much about those who are targeted either, except that they're always Pepps, the mysterious humans with vines woven into the skin of their arms. Who the Pepps are, though, or why they're being targeted, no one knows.

Bringing my thumb back to the throttle, I inch the four-wheeler closer to the cabin.

What I can't understand, though, is why the hunter was attacked. He didn't possess that vine-like mark. If he wasn't a Pepp, then why did they kill him? And, aside from that, what happened to his son, who was never found?

That's why I'm afraid of this place. Not that the hunter died but that those who killed him were never caught. They could still be lurking around these woods, ready to attack anyone.

Us.

"Alena." Rick taps my shoulder, pulling me from my thoughts. He points in the direction of the hot spring, irritated that we're far behind Caleb now.

Forcing the questions from my mind, I sigh and turn my attention back to the trail in front of us. Maybe there are answers in the cabin that the officials missed. Maybe answers that I can find ... later.

We travel for another mile, and then I hear it: the swishing of the large, cold river.

This spot has been a family favorite for as long as I can remember. Sometimes we bring a tent and camp for a night or two during the summer. I can still see some of the rocks gathered in the familiar circle where we build campfires and roast marshmallows. One time we even came up here during the winter on Christmas Eve when my dad surprised us by wrapping one of the snow-loaded pine trees with Christmas lights. We sang Christmas carols around the fire before leaving on the snowmobiles. It's still one of my favorite Christmas memories.

I see the wide river bank first, with hundreds of perfectly smoothed rocks from years of tumbling in the water. Then I see the steam from the spring, which sits fifty feet from the cold river. Excitement rises in my stomach. The hot spring bubbles out of the ground and travels down a crevice where it mixes with the cold water of the river. Someone long ago dug a ten-foot hole at the mixing point, excavating it just right so it's mostly hot but bearable.

After parking the four-wheelers in the trees closest to the spring, I kill my engine.

"Hey, Rick, let me show you the cliff," Caleb says, winking my way.

I try to ignore his taunting. Rick, of course, jumps off the four-wheeler and follows Caleb and Jess up the dirt path that leads to the top of the cliff. I can't see the ledge from here, but I know it's hiding behind those trees sitting at the top of the hill on my left.

Standing, I grab the stack of towels and walk the opposite way to the hot spring. I can almost feel the steam on my face, when I hear loud, hurried footsteps behind me. The sudden unsettling sound makes me jump, and I turn just as strong hands grip my arms, making me drop the towels. It's Caleb and Rick. They grin wildly on either side of me, quickly sweeping me into a restrained cradle.

"What are you doing ...?" I start, but when they carry me toward the path that leads to the cliff, I panic. "Put me down!"

I push my legs out, trying to straighten my body so they'll loosen their grip, but they're too strong. They hold me tightly, stretching my arms over their shoulders and gripping my legs as they walk up the dirt slope.

When we approach the top of the cliff, I scream out for Jess. She only laughs behind me. "I'm sorry, Alena."

She doesn't sound sorry at all!

I spit out threats—they laugh. I beg Rick—he laughs. I grip their shirts as tightly as I can, determined to take them with me. But nothing stops them. With one last laugh, they both look at each other, then toss me over the edge.

My limbs flail in the air, and my stomach rises as I fall toward the water. For only a moment I cry out, trying to brace myself, but the shock of the icy cold steals my breath right when I meet it. My body slaps the water, sending sharp pains through my side and up my back. Before I've even satisfied the force of the drop, I'm fighting against gravity to come back up. I move my arms frantically, suddenly unsure of how to swim until my face breaks the surface of the water.

I cough violently, trying to get the stupid water out of my nose. Then I try to catch my breath, but I can't. Not when my body is shaking so much. Man, it's *so* cold!

I frantically search for the cliff, gritting my chattering teeth. I spot it, growing smaller as the river pulls me away.

Oh, Caleb is so *dead.*

My body's already painfully frozen. Any movement sends aching pulses through my bones, but I force my limbs to move me in the direction of the closest shore.

I approach the edge of the river carefully, waiting for my feet to brush against the bottom. When they finally do, I push myself farther until I can grip at the rocks with my hands and knees. Unfortunately, the river is stronger than I am. My grip slides right over the rocks, along with my body, like a cloth on a washboard, rolling helplessly. I wail when one slams me in the shin.

But I dig my arms and knees in deeper, using all my muscle strength. Finally, I stop myself from being pulled further and hang on tight. The water rushes into me, smothering my face, trying to loosen my grip. Mustering all my strength against the swift river, I crawl with shaking limbs until I reach the rocky shore. Perched on all fours, I try to catch my breath.

Suddenly, a high-pitched scream breaks through the noise of the river, and I freeze.

Please tell me I imagined that.

My gut starts to churn. An image of the hunter with manmade gashes comes to the forefront of my mind. I'm so distracted by the image that I almost miss the sound of swishing branches close by. My muscles tense, preparing me to run. That is, until I hear a second scream coming from the direction of the hot spring. Definitely not imagined. I should move, but my limbs have suddenly lost all their ability. *What do I do?*

The swishing sound slows, and I hear the crunching of branches. Each sound seems to bind me in some stupid way, weighing me down so I can't move. I'm hopelessly trying to plan some sort of attack, when I hear what sounds like laughter coming from behind the branches. Suddenly, Rick and Caleb step into view, unable to contain their amusement.

"You should've seen your face!" Caleb howls.

It takes me way too long to realize I'm not in danger. When I finally do, my fear quickly melts into boiling anger. *Caleb knew how scared I was to come up here and decided to trick me? And Rick played along?* Glaring at them as dangerously as I can, I rise to my feet, thankful I still have my shoes on, and stand on the rocks.

I'm not sure which one of them I'm going to attack first, until my eyes land on Caleb. He's beet red and practically falling over from laughing so hard.

"*You*!" I snarl low, water dripping from my body. Ignoring the pains in my legs and side, I walk over the rest of the rocks. "I'm going to kill you!" Stumbling, I run toward him. He turns to get away, but not before I clumsily jump onto his back and hold on tight.

"Ahhhh, you're cold!"

"You think!" I wrap my legs around his torso, hoping it makes him even colder. He runs with me on his back through the trees, toward the hot spring, where I see Jess, the culprit who let out the scream, sitting lazily on a sunny rock next to the river. My glare rattles her more than it did Rick and Caleb. A guilty look passes across her face.

"Sorry, Alena."

Ha, she's not sorry. Not yet.

Caleb pauses for only a moment when we reach the hot spring before jumping into the warm water.

The hot water quickly encompasses us, and, even amid my anger, I sigh in relief as the heat begins to counter the cold. Still on Caleb's back, I try to hold him under the water, but he easily tosses me to the side and pops up. Clearing my eyes, I look up, finding Rick and Jess watching me, still laughing.

I generously splash each one of them. "I'll get you all back," I vow.

Then I swim to the deeper end of the hot spring where I can submerge my whole body in the heat.

Holding my breath, I sink into the deep water. My feet touch the bottom of the pit and settle into the mud. My ears pop when I drop to my knees, enjoying the smooth, stickiness on my skin.

Suddenly something brushes up against my leg. I kick my limb to keep it from tickling my skin, but instead of freeing me it wraps around my calf, tying me to the bottom of the spring. I try to swim to the surface, but my leg doesn't budge.

Panic rises in me. I accidently scream in the water, letting out too much oxygen—oxygen I need. I try to flap my arms above me to indicate that I need help, but I'm too deep. They can't see me! I frantically reach down to my leg, feeling something hard and long against my skin. I follow it down to the muddy bottom and yank. It doesn't pull out but somehow continues to move up my body.

My desperate efforts are stealing my energy, and my head begins to fade in and out. Finally, arms grab my torso and try to pull me up out of the water. I cling to them, but the force tears my skin, and I scream again. This time there isn't much air left to expel. My mind fogs and my limbs weaken.

Everything fades away.

Chapter 2

"Lenny." A soft, familiar voice calls to me through the darkness. It pulls me from my sleep, awakening something inside. Something new. Something strange. It spreads within me like black tar, stealing the light and energy from every cell in my body, like a parasite sucking the life of its prey.

I don't want to wake up.

The feeling rises to my chest, my throat, until it reaches my eyes. I begin to cry.

"Lenny!" It's Caleb. He's the only one who calls me that, but only when he's angry ... or scared.

I force my eyes open, squinting into the harsh fluorescent lights. Those lights. I would know them anywhere.

After the incident with the hunter, Dad allowed me to help him in the hospital before pursuing my own medical education. During the endless hours I've spent here with him, I've memorized every inch of the place. Every room. Every piece of equipment.

We're in the hospital. *But why?*

Then I see the invasion of IV lines in my arm. I jerk my achy body into a sitting position.

"It's okay, Lenny," Caleb says. Both he and Mom are sitting to my right, leaning onto the bed, their worried faces somehow matching the discomfort within me.

"What happened?" I ask with a croaky voice. I expect anger to flash across my mother's face. She and Dad threatened to take away our four-wheelers should we pursue the trip to the hot spring when we begged to go. They clearly didn't want us returning to Falling Rock. But looking at her now, her brown eyes are only etched with concern. She places her hand on my arm.

"Alena, I tried to pull you out of the water, but you were stuck," Caleb says. "By the time we were able to free you, you were unconscious. I was so scared. I brought you straight here."

Before I can respond, the door to the room opens and Dad walks in with another doctor. Dr. Brown. It's Rick and Jess's dad. I know him well. Apart from my dad, he's one of the most respected doctors in the high mountains. With so many men making a living off bear hides, both doctors have been needed since the day they graduated from Residency. Our families are practically, well ... family.

The fact that he's here now, though, isn't a good sign. He's usually busy in the hospital. I search their faces, hoping to find the familiar joking looks on them, but they aren't happy. Not now.

I swallow, fighting the knots growing inside my stomach.

"Alena, I'm glad you're awake," Dad says. Pulling a chair to the bed, he sits next to me, across from Caleb, and softly grasps my hand. His look scares me. *What's going on?*

"Alena, what happened in the hot spring?"

I stare at him for a moment, wishing the concern in his blue eyes would go away. But it doesn't. So, I clear my achy throat.

"I was in the water, when something brushed against my leg. I tried to kick it away, but it wrapped around me." I shake my head, still not understanding. I continue to explain what happened. When I get to the part about my skin tearing, I sit up and pull the blankets off my lower limbs. My lungs inhale sharply when I see that the skin on my right leg is shredded all the way to my thigh, exposing long, red, oozing wounds. It begins to throb now for the first time, as if it needed acknowledgement to produce pain. I look at my dad, who has now let his eyes wander to Mom's face.

"What's going on?" I finally demand. My shredded skin is bad but not terrible and definitely can't be the culprit for the fear in their eyes.

Dad finally speaks, but very softly. "It's not your leg we're worried about, Alena." He gently grips something on my left arm. For the first time, I realize my arm is wrapped in a bandage up to my shoulder. I watch as he unravels it. It doesn't hurt, so what could be wrong with it?

He barely exposes my wrist when I see it. Chills ice my spine, and I grab at the bandage, ripping it off the remainder of my arm. I suck in a breath when I see it in full view.

It's a vine woven through the skin of my arm.

It's the mark of a Pepp.

I blink at the vine, sure it will disappear if I close my eyes, but it doesn't. Suddenly, I'm unable to breathe.

Since the death of the hunter at Falling Rock, my fear of those who seek the lives of the Pepps has increased, but deep down inside there was a small amount of comfort in knowing that at least I didn't possess the mark of a Pepp. Now that comfort is gone, like steam evaporating into the air. This vine is a target of sure death.

"Dad." My voice shakes. "What's going on? Where did this come from?" I pick at my arm with my right hand, anxiously trying to remove the invasive vine. But it's buried under my skin.

"Alena, it's okay," Dad says, pulling my hand away to keep me from tearing my skin off. "We're not going to let anything happen to you." I try to see him through my blurry eyes, listen to him through my heavy breathing, but I'm pretty sure he can't keep such a promise.

"Look, we've run several tests on you to figure out what this is doing to your body. We want to make sure this thing isn't hurting you. I want you to listen to what Dr. Brown has to say."

I lean my head back. I can't breathe. Maybe it's suffocating me.

Dr. Brown sits on a short stool at the foot of my bed. "Alena," he says, trying to get my attention. "Will you look at these results with me?"

My throat thickens in fear. But I look up anyway. He's holding a folder in his hand, but before he opens the folder, he studies me. "I've never actually seen a Pepp, let alone been able to assess the mark on their arms. I found some articles from doctors overseas who've evaluated bodies of Pepps who've been killed the past few years. Unfortunately, their research has been limited since the vine turns to dust as soon as it's removed from the body. I wish I knew where the Pepps lived so I could just go ask them about the vine, but, as you know, they stay very hidden. I wouldn't even know where to look. I guess what I'm trying to say is, we have no idea what we're dealing with here and no idea what that thing is doing to your body. I want to assure you that I'm going to do my best to keep you safe, but you need to know this is all new to me."

I grip my trembling hands. We all wish we knew about the Pepps. But we don't. Nobody does, except for the fact that they're sought after and killed.

And now I'm one of them? *What does that even mean?* Did they intend for me to get this vine? If so, why? If not, why was this vine in the hot spring?

Dr. Brown flips the folder open, pulling my shaky thoughts back. I'm familiar with the images that spill out. They're from an angiogram. He lays them on the bed so we can all see them. "We took an MRI first of your arm to get more detailed images of the vine in your body. We were able to see that the vine not only runs through your skin but also into your blood vessels. So, we performed an angiogram to see if it was causing any blockages or damage."

Pointing to the first picture, he says, "This is an angiogram of a normal arm." I examine the picture, with thousands of black wiggly lines running the entire length of the limb.

"Now, this is your arm." Dr. Brown places my picture next to the normal one, and I immediately see the difference. The black lines are less defined, running only along the outside of the vessels. The middle of the vessels consists of just one thick white line.

"You can see the blood, the black border of the vessels, is pushed to the outside since the vine runs through the middle," Dr. Brown explains. "So far, I don't see any blockage or damage, but the amount of space allowing the blood to flow through is not very much."

He moves the pictures of the arm to the side, then pulls out two more. One is a picture of my chest. Dr. Brown's expression now changes from confused to worried.

"The vine doesn't just run through your arm, though, Alena." I search the picture and can see the same distorted blood vessels traveling through my heart. He lays one last picture below them all. This picture is of my brain. "Even if we were able to remove some of the vine, we wouldn't be able to do it without severely damaging your heart or brain."

It's in my heart? A dull pain in my chest starts to grow in response to the news. Even if I don't end up getting murdered because I'm a Pepp, I'll probably still end up dying. I can already picture it, the vine strangling me in my sleep. I lean my head back onto the pillow and close my eyes.

The images of the man from a year ago, slashed and cut up, slam to the forefront of my mind.

"So, what do we do?" I whisper, tears spilling from my eyes.

Dad's sad voice reveals what I already know. "Alena, we need to keep you out of sight. Rand and I will be going up to the hot spring tonight to see if we can find anything. I'm wondering where this vine came from and if there are other vines there. I would alert the authorities, but I don't want to draw attention to you. So, we're going to keep this just between us for now. Got it?"

Dad looks around at each person in the room, quietly demanding their cooperation. Of course, Caleb nods, so does Mom. But what does this mean for me? Keep me out of sight? What about my plans for college?

Dad and Dr. Brown talk about more tests. Mom holds my hand, rubbing it softly while trying to listen. I try to hold on to their conversation in my mind, but I can't. My chest rises and falls much quicker than normal, the pain increasing.

What's happening to me?

Chapter 3

I slouch in front of my mirror, trying to take deep breaths. It's five o'clock in the morning. I should still be asleep. Should be.

I breathe in, trying to control the dull chest pain that woke me up. I went to bed last night with the pain and was hoping the sleep would ease it. Obviously it hasn't.

I feel awful. Just like I have every day for the past two months since the vine attached itself to my left arm.

Lying back on my shaggy beige carpet, I stare at the dim log ceiling above me. *Two whole months* ... of being cooped up in this house.

The fatigue that seems to permanently plague me creeps up inside me now, accompanied by the silly urge to cry. I hate crying, especially when there's absolutely no reason at all for me to be doing it.

On top of the crying, there's this new emotional irritability that I cannot control. It doesn't matter who's talking to me, I can't for the life of me respond to anyone kindly. I can see how much my words hurt others, especially Mom, but no matter how hard I try, I can't stop.

I force in another deep breath and focus on the odd knots in the wood above me. The knots I've memorized since being in here every day.

Will I ever regain control of my life? Will I ever be able to calm down enough to get rid of these stupid panic attacks? Everyone tells me that the chest pain is only a result of the anxiety in my head and I just need to relax, but how could something so painful stem from just my thoughts? I'm pretty sure I'm dying from a heart attack.

I focus my gaze on a knot in the wood that resembles a snail with a very large shell. Mom thinks my emotional struggles are a result of the fear that orbits the vine in me. Because of the vine, I'm more afraid of getting killed.

But Dad's opinion differs. He thinks I'm struggling because I haven't left the house in two months, for my own safety.

Both of their theories about my uncontrolled emotions ring true. I *am* afraid of the vine, and I absolutely hate being stuck inside the house all day. I've lost my friends and have had to give up my college dreams, so it only makes sense that I would be discouraged, but there's something I know that they don't. Something only Caleb seems to believe.

I recall the moment I woke up in the hospital right after the vine attached itself—the life-sucking sadness that stole my energy. It was slightly familiar to me, like the way I felt after witnessing the death of the hunter but worse. Way worse.

I felt it right in the beginning at the hospital, when I woke up, before Dad showed me the attached vine and before I had been locked away for two months—the tar-like darkness that stole the light. It still doesn't make sense to me, but I know this crappy feeling isn't just a result of my circumstances—it's coming from the vine, and every day it gets worse and worse.

Mom has encouraged me to keep talking. At first, I tried. I told her everything about how I felt. But there's nothing I can do about it. I can talk and talk, but I can't change anything. I'm trapped. So now I don't see the point in talking and have since stopped doing so. Mom hates it.

I breathe out and grit my teeth.

I know everyone is trying to be patient with me, but I can see the frustration in their eyes every time I start crying over something silly. I can't say that I blame them. I get frustrated with myself too. I wish I could stop crying, but I can't. Dad has prescribed me an antidepressant. It's helped, but I'm still not me. I'm beginning to feel like I will never be *me* again.

Sitting up, I take off my sweater to expose my spaghetti strap camisole underneath so I can see the vine better in my mirror. As terrible as the vine makes me feel, though, I can't deny its beauty. I've never been more grateful to have obtained my mom's looks: dark eyebrows, long eyelashes, and olive skin. The vine is a perfect complement to my features, twisting and swerving in an attractive unique way. It even brings out the auburn color in my brown eyes.

I run my fingers over the vine for the hundredth time. It's about a quarter of an inch thick in diameter and resembles a dead stick without leaves or bloom. It burrows under the first couple of skin layers, then weaves through my entire left arm and the left side of my neck, reaching almost to my jawline, almost enhancing the narrowness of my chin. From my shoulder the vine travels over to my chest, terminating right over my heart, where a green hole the size of a marble rests. I call it the green eye because whenever I expose it, it just stares at me. I don't let it do that now. Instead, I stretch my arm out, amazed, again, that my arm moves so easily without any restriction from the vine. I can hardly feel it at all.

Dr. Brown has run some blood tests, but they've all turned out normal. Other than taking up space in my blood vessels, brain, and heart, they can't find any clinical changes. Dad didn't find anything at the hot spring either. He took a water pump up there and drained the pool. Then, wearing a protective suit, he closely examined everything. He even brought back samples. But ultimately he found nothing.

Nothing. No other creepy vines. Nothing.

I drop my arm into my lap and look at the mirror. It's littered with the printed articles I've found regarding the Pepps. Researching them is the only thing I've been able to do lately. It's the only thing that's kept me sane.

Some of the articles consist of rare pictures at an earthquake or tornado site where a Pepp is seen avoiding the camera in the background. To me, they look like normal humans, only with a simple vine design on their arm.

But why would they only be seen at disaster sites? I put my sweater back on and notice that it covers most of the vine. *Do they cover their vines in public? Have I actually met a Pepp before without realizing it because they covered themselves?*

Other articles mention that the Pepps have been around for ages and have incredible powers. I found five reports from survivors of a deadly earthquake in the Southern Lands who claim they had been crushed beneath rubble, sure they were going to die. But then, out of nowhere, these *angels* found them, pulled them out, and healed them. All five of them claim to have caught a glimpse of a vine-like mark. I stare at those five reports now taped to my mirror.

Do they have power? Do *I* have power?

There have been other reports from authorities who claim that the power of the Pepps is not used to help or heal but instead causes the natural disasters.

Now that I'm a Pepp, I sure hope it's the five survivors who are right.

There are other articles I found online but couldn't bring myself to print. Old reports from hundreds of years ago, of Pepp bodies found shredded to pieces. These gruesome articles speculate that the bodies were being searched. Cut, torn apart, for the sake of trying to find something.

The source of their power.

The attacks eventually stopped for a while but then started back up only two years ago. *Why?*

I shiver.

Other than those awful articles and what's pinned alongside my mirror, though, I haven't been able to find any other information on the Pepps. The number of questions I have regarding them increases every day with very few answers. *Who are they? Where do they live? What's the purpose of the vine? Why does it make me feel this way?* And *is there a connection between the hunter from Falling Rock and the Pepps*?

My eyes are drawn to the last article, the one with the picture of the hunter's son, Mark, on it. He was the one to call for help when he found his father bleeding in the woods, but then he disappeared. There was a search party sent out for him, but he was never found. Nobody knows if he was taken or killed. I touch his picture. His handsome, strong face both comforts and saddens me at the same time. I want to know what happened to him and to his father.

I hear Caleb stirring in his room, which sits adjacent to mine. I look at my clock—I've been sitting here for an hour now, and he's getting up for school.

Caleb was accepted to a prestigious college out of state in the spring, but he rescinded his application after what happened to me. He decided to go to the one just down the mountain. I hate that he gave up his opportunity to go to a better school for me. But I'm grateful for his company. He's the only reason I've survived this ordeal. He even went back up to the cabin against Mom and Dad's wishes to look for clues but said he found nothing.

Jess and he are still going steady, but I know my condition has been a strain on their relationship since Caleb is so preoccupied with helping me. Both Rick and Jess came over many times in the beginning to check on me. They tried to convince me to go out on special quiet excursions into the mountains, but even if I could go, I didn't want to. Most days I'm lucky if I have enough energy to just get out of bed. Ultimately, they didn't know how to deal with my emotions and eventually stopped coming. I miss them both.

I hear Caleb leave the house first. Then I hear the crinkling sound of Mom grabbing her breakfast bar before she and Dad shut the front door behind them.

That's when I emerge from my room. Despite my better judgment, I head straight for the fridge and open it, only to stand there. I look down at my stomach that's now getting bloated from all the excessive eating I've been doing. I shouldn't eat, *but what else am I supposed to do while stuck inside the house all day?* I ignore my stomach and grab a big container of yogurt, then throw a couple handfuls of M&Ms into it. I take it over to the leather couch warmed by the sun pouring in through the windows. Other than my bed, this is my favorite place to be. The tall windows on my left reach all the way up to the peaked ceiling and are surrounded by wooden logs that extend to the rest of the house. The house is way too large for our small family of four, but I love it.

The leaves outside the windows are changing colors in response to the cold air. The red and yellow leaf season right before winter used to be one of my favorites, but this year it discourages me. The summers are always short here in the mountains, and I didn't even get to enjoy this one. I'm not ready for winter again.

I turn on the TV that sits above the large fireplace in front of me and flip through the channels, stopping briefly on channel five for the morning news update. I hate watching the news, but recently I've fallen captive to the sad channel.

Of course, the first thing they talk about today is the war back east. It's still going on in the GreenLands. It's been five years since the war started, and it has no effect on my life whatsoever, so I try to move past the story. But I can't. The images on the screen show refugee camps based on the shore of a large island. There are thousands of refugees now, having been boated there with nowhere else to go. Large white tents are the only shelter they have. The image has been shown on the channel every day for the last month and pulls me in. I feel bad for the poor refugees. They look so lost and forsaken, much like how I feel.

Soon the anchors change the topic to another dead Pepp found. A warning flashes on the screen telling viewers that the images they're about to see might be disturbing. Man, either the attacks are becoming more frequent than ever before, or I just never realized how horrible and active the killers were. The warning is replaced with a picture of the gruesome letter S painfully carved into the dead Pepp's shoulder, obviously embedded with poison. The bulging veins around the wound are black and blue, looking like hungry claws spreading deeper into the skin. This is the same type of blackened wound I saw on the hunter's shoulder.

I swallow.

A video now flashes over the screen, of the authorities carrying the Pepp woman's body on a gurney and loading her into an ambulance. She was found overseas. Far away, but still too close. I stare at the screen. *How did the killers find her? Will they eventually find me?*

The face of the man leading the worldwide investigation comes into view with his name running across the bottom of the screen in big bold letters: Jaxxon Balac. Everyone knows him and his face. It's hard to forget with it always being so dirty and rugged, not to mention the scar that runs from the side of his mouth to his ear. It makes him look like he enjoys finding dead bodies.

His team is apparently the one that's in charge of finding the Pepp killers across the world, which has been a difficult task. There are never clues around the murder scene. No footprints, no fingerprints, not even a single eyelash. There are also never any witnesses—or none that will come forward. To make things even harder, the dead Pepps never have an ID on them, and nobody ever pipes up to claim them as a friend or family member. So, nobody can be questioned for clues as to why the Pepp would be attacked.

It's as if these Pepps live a completely disconnected life. *But why? To hide? To protect themselves from getting killed? To protect their mysterious power?*

I guess this is why Jaxxon Balac has become so popular. Twice he was able to predict where an attack would occur. He wasn't able to save the Pepp, but he was able to capture several killers in the process. He tortured them for information and found about a dozen more killers. That's where he learned it was a group ... of men. And, according to several of the men, they aren't killing the Pepps to find the source of their power. That power can't be transferred. No, instead, they're killing them for money, paid by someone they claim they don't know.

How do you not know who you're working for?

Jaxxon and his team have been praised ever since, and he continues to search.

The look of him chills my bones. But if he's finding the killers, then I sure appreciate him.

Raising the remote, I turn off the TV. I've had enough.

Looking outside, I grumble in disgust. The day is wasting away while I sit here on the couch with no ambition, no energy, no ... nothing.

The sun shifts slowly in the sky. I should probably get up and do something. Should.

I'm just dozing off to the humming sound of the refrigerator, when Caleb comes bursting through the front door. I raise my head off the couch an inch. *He shouldn't be back yet.* One glance at the clock tells me it's only two.

"Lenny!" He quickly finds me moping on the couch, his face full of excitement. Ignoring my obstinate glares, he sits next to me on the edge of his seat.

"Alena, I want to take you somewhere." His energy fuels a little flame inside me, but I quickly put it out. *I'm not going anywhere.* This no longer has anything to do with Mom and Dad's rules. I just have no energy.

Caleb ignores my languid expression and grabs my hand.

"Alena, another woman was attacked by the S group in Deadwood."

I clench my jaw. *Deadwood, that's close.* Caleb's voice is too jubilant for such a grim story, and I close my eyes. This information makes me sick, and I don't want to hear any more.

"She survived," he whispers.

My eyelids fling open, and I study Caleb's face. There have never been survivors from an S attack, at least none we know of.

"How?"

Caleb looks like he's about to bounce right out of his seat. "This says that after hearing about all the attacks on Pepps, she came up with her own antivenom. She used it quickly enough after the attack. It worked. How she managed to create that antivenom boggles my mind, but, hey, she survived."

I now see that Caleb is holding an article in his hand, and I snatch it.

"She's a witch doctor who practices at an old hunting lodge up in Deadwood," Caleb continues, pointing to the section I should read.

Too anxious to read, I move to extract what I want to know directly from Caleb. "Is she a Pepp?" I ask, a small amount of Caleb's excitement rubbing off on me.

Caleb shakes his head, and my spirits fall again.

But Caleb's excitement doesn't fade. "She doesn't have the mark, but she must know why they attacked her. She must know something about the Pepps, otherwise, why would they try to kill her? Or why would she create an antivenom to protect herself?"

I have to admit the story intrigues me, but any excitement I mirrored fades as I realize what Caleb wants me to do. Leave the house. Go searching for this woman.

I hand the article back to him. "No."

I'm not sure why I say it. Either I'm too afraid of *not* finding something, or I'm too afraid *of* finding something. Or because the thought of leaving the house makes me feel very uncomfortable. I don't want to go. I stand, ready to walk to my room. Caleb's enthusiastic expression crumples into the disappointed frown that seems to occupy his face most lately. I instantly feel guilty for letting him down, as always, but I just move past him to the hallway.

"Please, Alena." Caleb follows behind me. "If we leave now, we can be back before Mom and Dad get home from work."

His pleading tugs at me, but I don't want to back down. I reach my room and shut the door behind me in Caleb's face. I cringe at my own harshness.

Caleb doesn't retreat, though. He opens my door and comes inside. "This woman might have answers about the Pepps, answers about what that thing is and how to get rid of it. We have to go."

Caleb points a finger at the vine on my arm. He's angry with it just like me, but I take his anger personally. I hate that I'm different now. I hate that my family can no longer look at me without seeing the invaded deformity on my arm.

I walk to the window and pull up my white blinds, trying to hold back new stupid tears.

Caleb's resolve melts at the sight of my tears, and he sighs in frustration before gripping my arm.

"Alena, I hate watching you live this way. I hate being so helpless. If I hadn't insisted we go to the hot spring for our birthday, this never would have happened. I have to help you, and the only way I know how to do that is by searching for a way to get that vine off your arm. The Pepps are the only ones who know about the vines, and since we don't know where to find them, we have to go to this woman. She's our only lead."

I blink back tears. He's right; deep down inside I know it. But I hate it.

"I'll drag you out there if I have to," Caleb says quietly. "But I don't want to. I want you to make this decision on your own. Do you want to live the rest of your life this way?"

I meet his gaze for only a moment before looking out the window.

"Yes."

I say it just to be difficult, but the lie falls flat, and my lip begins to quiver. Of course I don't want to live the rest of my life this way. I would love more than anything to feel a smile on my face again. I slide my eyes back to Caleb, his face earnest and loving. Why is it so hard to tell him the truth? To admit to him that I hate feeling this way, but, even more than that, I hate the idea of doing something about it. It all seems so hopeless.

Caleb places his hands over mine, his love breaking down my pride. I decide to admit the truth. "I'm sorry, Caleb. I do want to be happy again."

His enthusiasm returns. "Then let's go."

Chapter 4

This is a bad idea. That's all I can think as we travel in Caleb's truck along the roads higher into the mountains. I've never been to Deadwood, but several patients from there hurt in hunting accidents have been sent to Dad in the past. Its location high in the mountains makes it even colder than where we live and very undesirable to me.

The concrete roads give way to dirt as we approach Deadwood, which slows us down measurably. I look down at my phone to see that I no longer have service, and two hours have already passed. If we're going to get back home before Mom and Dad, then we need to turn around now.

"Let's go back, Caleb," I say, wanting this whole draining trip to be over. I expect Caleb to respond in agreement but he doesn't.

"We've already come this far. We're not going back until we talk to her."

An all-consuming heaviness fills my chest, tensing every muscle in my body and making it hard for me to breathe. I grasp the arm of the door, hoping it will keep me from lashing out at my brother. Or keep me from panicking to death. One of the two.

Another hour passes, the sun sets, and the clock blares that it's too late to save myself from Dad's wrath. I clench my teeth. I can't even call Mom to ease her worries.

"There it is!" Caleb shouts, pointing ahead.

His words puncture my pressurized emotions, and my body sags in relief. Thank you. Still holding on to the door, I anxiously search the road in front of us.

An old gray concrete building with brown shutters and trim, hidden darkly between tall pine trees, sits just off the side of the road ahead. A chimney spits out smoke from the high peaked gables, and candles offer dim light in the few windows visible. The parking lot is full, with several old trucks and off-road vehicles parked outside. Thankfully, there's still a spot for us.

Caleb turns off his truck and gets out, but I stay in my seat, my hands suddenly shaking. What if the woman doesn't know anything about the Pepps? What if we came all this way for nothing? Or what if she does know something? What will I have to do to get this vine off?

A rush of cold air bites at my skin when Caleb opens my door, making me shiver. *It's freezing up here!* Surprised there's not any snow on the ground with how cold it is, I reach for the extra sweater I brought and put it on, pulling the neck upward to hide most of the vine on my jaw. Looking in the mirror, I can see a piece still exposed, but a person would have to be paying close attention to see it. Getting out of the truck, I grip Caleb's arm, both for warmth and support. When we reach the building, Caleb opens the door.

Dim light leaks from the lanterns placed sporadically along the dark wooden walls. The strong stench of cigar smoke mixed with liquor stuffs the air, and I struggle to breathe. Looking to my right, I see dozens of large, burly men in old camouflage coats sitting at the bar drinking and talking loudly. A couple of them, with heavy beards, turn just enough to see us enter before turning back to their more important ale. I sigh in relief at their disinterest. Caleb looks at me and tugs at the arm I'm using to pull my sweater over my nose.

"Alena, please, try to blend in." I let the material fall back down to my collarbones and take in a horrible, deep breath.

I look at the other half of the pub on the left that sits empty, several old wooden tables thrown about the room. The smell of raw meat drifting from the kitchen on the far side of the pub batters with the other smells, and I swallow, trying to force down a wave of nausea.

Caleb guides me to a table far away from the drinking men and sits me down. "I need to go to the bathroom. You stay here. I'll be right back." I watch as he walks away, suddenly feeling very vulnerable in the foreign bar. I try to distract myself by looking at the weathered menu sitting on the table but end up tossing it aside before burying my head in my hands.

"What are you doing here?"

A screechy old voice pierces my right ear and I jump, finding an old woman's face pulsing right next to mine. The smell of horribly bad breath meets my nostrils, and I turn my head away searching for inaccessible fresh air.

The woman repeats her question again, a little louder this time as she inches even closer to me. "What are you doing here?"

What do I say? Thankfully, I see Caleb walking back now, looking confused at the sight of the woman cornering me. I beg for help with my eyes.

The woman follows my gaze and turns toward Caleb.

After studying him, she quickly spins back to me, waving a long, pointy finger in my face. "Are you with him?"

She doesn't allow me to respond. "It's against the rules to mess around with non-Pepps! You ought to be horsewhipped! Out in public with a normal human?" Spit shoots from every word.

Non-Pepp? I look at her arms. They both lack the mark of a Pepp. Isn't she a non-Pepp too?

I turn back to Caleb, who's now trying to get her away from me as the woman pushes on him hard. "You stay away from her, you hear, or I'll make sure you never have another chance to be with a woman again."

The color drains from Caleb's face, and he holds up his hands in retreat, trying to avoid another push. "What are you talking about? She's my sister."

The woman freezes, fire still steaming from her eyes. "Sister?"

"Are you Issy?" Caleb presses hopefully.

The woman's back stiffens and her eyes narrow. "Who are you?"

"I'm Caleb. If you are Issy, we drove from Moose Pass to talk with you." Stepping closer, Caleb lowers his voice to a whisper and looks around hesitantly before proceeding. "We heard you were attacked. You were given the S mark? Do you know anything about the Pepps?"

The woman's eyes narrow tighter. "Are you another reporter? Trying to trick me into giving you information?"

"No, please," Caleb begs. "We need your help. We were in the mountains swimming in a hot spring, when this vine attached itself to my sister, Alena. It's the mark of a Pepp, but we can't get it off. It's making her really ... depressed. Can you help?"

I jump when the woman suddenly shushes him by pushing her gross finger over his mouth and looks around suspiciously. Then, with a tip of her head, she indicates we should follow her.

I stand and cautiously follow Caleb, who walks behind the scary woman. We quietly trail her past the kitchen and down a dark hall until we reach a doorway covered with hanging glass beads. The woman parts the bead curtain and leads us into a dark room filled with hanging dried plants and papers scattered all over the place. The room exhales a strong smell of "natural." Hundreds of glass bottles filled with what looks like herbs cover the shelves, lining every wall from the floor to the ceiling.

Two lit candles providing the only light cast several shadows over us.

"Let me see it." The woman, who stands several inches shorter than me, spits out her demand. Without giving me a chance to respond, she grabs my arm and drags me over to the light, where she pulls the sleeve of my sweater all the way up. I observe her quietly, thinking that the name Issy seems too dainty a name for someone as harsh and ragged as she. Her pinched eyes search the vine on my arm. She follows it up carefully, as one examining a precious diamond would do. Without even asking me, the woman grabs the neckline of my sweater and pulls it down to view the circular green hole just over my heart. I swipe at her hand, but she doesn't let go.

Finally, the woman looks up at my face, her nose almost touching my chin, and whispers with accusing eyes, "You got this at a hot spring?"

I have to clear my suddenly dry throat in order to speak. "Yes, near Falling Rock."

The woman lets go of my shirt and takes a step back, her eyes filled with shock. "Was it just sitting out in the open?"

I shake my head. "No, it was at the bottom of the hot spring. It attached itself to me when I touched the bottom of the pool."

Issy starts pacing back and forth in the crammed space of the room, no longer looking at me or Caleb. Then she goes to a desk in the corner and shuffles through the chaotic mess of papers there. Holding one up, she begins to rub her head, either trying to ease an approaching headache, like mine, or performing witch doctor stuff. I can't tell.

Caleb, unable to contain his question any longer, breaks the silence. "Can you help us?"

The woman speaks softly, "The vine attached to your arm is indeed a totem, the mark of a Pepp. But ..." She turns around and waves her arm toward me. "That one has been tampered with."

The woman rushes over to another table overflowing with objects and papers. "The boy, Mark, the hunter's son—his totem was defective too." She holds a piece of paper close to the candlelight to read.

"Mark?" My heart pounds at the mention of the familiar name. "Mark is a Pepp? Is he alive?"

"Of course he's alive," the woman exclaims, annoyed with the question. She reaches for a book high on a shelf.

"How do you know about the Pepps?" Caleb asks.

"Many years ago I was one," she says, laying a book out on the table. "I chose to leave, for reasons of my own, but I remain a communicator for them, telling them about stuff that goes on here among the non-Pepps."

"Is that why you were attacked? Because you used to be a Pepp?" Caleb asks.

Fire flickers in Issy's eyes. "Yes. Those men who attacked me are the scum of the earth. And now I've been bombarded by reporters, asking about those who tried to kill me, and wondering how I came up with the antivenom. You can only lie so many times without wanting to just tear your hair out. I've even been hounded by Jaxxon Balac, who wanted to drag me off to some protection unit." She scoffs. "I wish they would just leave me alone."

"*Do* you know who attacked you?" I ask.

Issy hunches down to get a better look at the pages of the book. "Yes, it was the Sybalt clan."

"Sybalt clan," I whisper. "Is that where the S comes from? The S they carve into the skin?"

"Yes, yes. Thankfully, the Pepp chief finally came up with a solution to their killings. He sent all the communicators some concentrated conglomerate of antivenoms. It's supposed to cover every venom out there. I don't know how they came up with it, but I sure appreciated it ... especially when I needed it."

"Why do they kill Pepps? Are Pepps bad?" I find myself asking.

"Pfff." The woman scoffs. "Houseflies are more dangerous than Pepps. Normal humans have always negatively judged things they know nothing about. They crave power, and since the Pepps have power, they attack Pepps, trying to steal it. They're awful men."

I open my mouth to ask how someone could steal the power, and whether or not I have power, but the woman hushes me.

"We need to get you to the Pepps. That thing on your arm"—she points to the vine again—"is dangerous, and the Sybalt clan will kill you if they find out you have it. I don't have any more antivenom yet, and even if I did, I wouldn't want to share it with you."

Waving her arm, she signals for us to look at the book in front of her. Stabbing the paper with her finger, she says, "You need to go here. This is a rendezvous point for the Pepps after they make a run. There is always someone there to guard the place. They will know what to do with you."

Caleb looks at the map, then straightens. "How do we know we can trust you or the Pepps?"

Issy waves her hand, indicating that she doesn't have the time to convince us. "You trust me, or you don't trust me. All I'm going to tell you is that either you get her to the Pepps or she dies by the hand of the clan."

Caleb stares at the woman for a couple of moments before looking back at the map.

"Isn't that straight up the mountain? I didn't see any other roads leading in that direction."

Issy shakes her head. "No roads. You'll have to drive an off-road vehicle."

Their conversation fades as I realize what I've just learned. *The Pepps aren't bad!* I now look at Issy's arm and see that it is void of any vine. She might have been a Pepp before, but she was able to leave them.

"Will they be able to remove it?" I blurt out, interrupting their conversation.

The woman's eyes turn to what I can only imagine is compassion on her strange face. She speaks carefully. "If it was a normal totem, then, yes, but I don't think they were able to get Mark's off."

My spirits fall, but Issy doesn't let me sulk too long. "You need to go now. It's not far from here. Take this map with you." The woman rips the map out of the book, rolls it up, and hands it to Caleb. Looking out the round window in the room, I can see it's starting to snow.

Great.

"The clouds are heavy. The snow is going to get worse," Issy says with certainty. "Come with me."

After grabbing an object from a broken drawer, and a lantern that's just outside her "witchy" room, the woman guides us to the back of the building where she shoves two coats toward us and opens a door to the freezing-cold air. The coats smell strongly of smoke and dust, but I can't get it on quick enough before the cold air whirls inside, seeping into my bones. Caleb gratefully does the same.

An old shed leaning to one side is only a couple of steps away. Issy swings the hanging door open and walks inside. The lantern sheds light on a four-wheeler with rust eating away at every inch of it. The woman climbs onto it, looking oddly out of place on the outdoorsy vehicle. Putting her hands on the throttle and kicking the gears, she tries to start the engine. The four-wheeler revs weakly but then dies. Issy aggressively keeps trying, kicking the old thing a couple of times before it starts up. *Is it safe to ride that thing?*

The gears clank, waking up the vehicle, and then the four-wheeler jerks out of the shed. After getting off, Issy hands Caleb a compass and shouts over the running engine, "Travel west. You'll run right into the cabin. When you see a heavy fog, know you're almost there. The totem is the key to getting through the fog, so you'll have to stick close to your sister. I'll let the chief know you're coming."

"Wait, can I use the phone too, to call my Mom?" I shout over the wind. I should probably connect with her before we head into the dark abyss.

"No, no phones here. I'm sending a message through my Magbaby. You must go, now."

My gut churns. *No phone? What's a Magbaby?*

She hangs her lantern on the handlebar of the four-wheeler and waves her hand, indicating we should go. Caleb looks back at me briefly. "You ready?"

I shrug. "I guess."

Following the arrow on the compass, Caleb takes us straight into the trees.

Chapter 5

Mom is going to kill us. Talking with Issy and getting information had clouded my mind. *I can't believe I let her talk me into this!*

"Are you sure we should be doing this?" I yell into Caleb's ear. "Mom is likely worried, and we have no idea where we're going."

Caleb shakes his head. "No, we need to find them."

We travel in silence for the next forty minutes, Caleb maneuvering the four-wheeler up the mountain. As the night creeps on, the tiny flakes of snow turn into large clumps of slush, wetting our borrowed coats and making them lose their warmth. We both shiver uncontrollably, and I hold on tighter to Caleb's body, hoping to share any warmth I can with him. His hands are probably freezing, gripping the handles without any gloves.

Just as I'm about to open my mouth again, to demand we go back, Caleb shouts, "I see the fog!" His frozen finger points straight up the mountain into the thick trees. I see it too.

"The slope is steep. I'll have to zigzag my way up there."

I hold on tight as he turns sharply to the right. We both lean the opposite way of the four-wheeler into the hill, keeping it from rolling.

After traveling several hundred feet, Caleb finds a spot to switch back the other way. The vehicle moves up the hill and then to the left.

The four-wheeler only travels a couple of feet, when the dirt beneath us begins to slip, wet from the slush. The wheels lose their traction, and the mud sweeps us sideways. Caleb revs the engine, searching for grip, flipping mud everywhere, but the vehicle leans to the left, the wrong way. I jump off just as the vehicle starts rolling down the hill. I try to bring Caleb with me, but he doesn't get off in time.

I scream when the four-wheeler rolls to the side, trapping Caleb's left leg underneath. Unable to free his limb, he's carried down the muddy hill with the four-wheeler until it hits a tree.

Jumping to my feet, I stumble down the slope through the mud until I reach him.

No, no, no!

"Caleb! Are you okay?" His teeth grind loudly in pain. He's pinned, crushed. I place my hands underneath the side of the vehicle and plant my feet, trying to lift it, but the movement only makes it slip again, putting more pressure on Caleb.

I look around in the dark. *I need help!*

Hoping the woman was right, and there is indeed someone behind the fog who can help me, I tell Caleb to hang on before climbing up the hill.

I soon realize that the pants and shoes I chose to wear this morning were a poor choice. I slip back multiple times, the mud now covering my face and body in several layers, with the old coat now pointless. The tree branches pull at me, scratching at my exposed skin, but I force myself into the thick fog. I wipe at the mud mixed with tears covering my face. Am I even going the right way? I don't have the compass Caleb was using. Do I just head straight up?

After what seems like an eternity of endless falls and wandering, I lose my footing again in the mud and slide down the mountain, out of the fog, almost back to where I started.

"Help," I cry. It comes out as a whisper at first, but then, finding more air, I push it through my lungs, mustering up a strong yell. "Help!"

"Shhh."

I jump to my feet when a man emerges from the fog, looking cautiously around as he walks toward me. "What's wrong?" he asks, trying to whisper.

"Please help me. My brother is hurt." I try to mimic his whispering, but I fail miserably through my trembling voice.

"Where is he?"

I turn my body down the hill and point in the direction of the lantern still miraculously lit on the four-wheeler. "Down there." Without a word, the man runs down the muddy hill. I do my best to keep up. Thankfully, going down is much easier than going up. He reaches Caleb first, finding him still crushed beneath the four-wheeler.

With the light closer, I stare at the man's exposed arms. My heart sinks. There's no vine there, just heavy snowflakes landing on his skin. Perhaps we're in the wrong place.

"Hang on," he says to Caleb. Then, placing his hands in the same spot I had earlier, he instructs me, "Stand over there, and help me lift."

I move to where he points.

"On three." He counts and I strain, lifting as best as I can, but when the vehicle flips, I know my effort was unnecessary. He lifted it entirely by himself.

How in the world did he do that?

Caleb screams in pain. The man looks around nervously as if worried about the sound.

"I'm going to pick him up and take you both back to my cabin," he whispers. "We're not safe out here. I have a friend that'll be here soon who can help you."

I look around, his anxious nerves rubbing off on me. *What's out here?*

With ease, the man picks up Caleb. "Grab my shirt once we get to the fog. I'll get you through it. And, please, try to be quiet." I stare at his arms again. They're big but not monstrous. *How is he so strong?*

I stumble up the hill after him, slipping way more than he does.

When we reach the fog, I grab his shirt. It seems too intimate, grabbing his shirt when we've only just met. But I appreciate having someone guide me through the dark fog. Unfortunately, my hand shakes harshly from the cold, and I slip several times, pulling on him. *How embarrassing.* He stops and waits patiently for me to find my footing again but doesn't say anything. And I don't either.

After what seems like forever, the fog thins, and we enter a large clearing.

I instantly release the man's shirt and follow behind, rubbing my freezing, wet arms. A large cabin sits in the middle of the clearing with candles lit in every window. I turn around to look at the fog behind us, but I see only trees.

The door to the cabin is cracked open, allowing the man to enter with a simple bump of his elbow. I pause at the door. The wooden floors are beautifully polished. And I'm covered in mud. *Does he really want me to follow him?* But the man doesn't turn around. He would have told me to stay out here if he wanted me to, right? So, I follow him down the dim hall, to the back of the cabin and into a large room. Tall glass windows span the entirety of the corner walls, revealing the snowy night. Three large leather couches rest beside a stone fireplace now alive with hot flames—the only source of light in the dim room.

The man places Caleb on the couch and I cringe, examining Caleb's right leg for the first time. It's twisted at an odd angle. I pull up his pant leg and see blue bruises forming on his shin and ankle. It's probably broken.

"I wish I could help you, but just hang in there. My friend will be here soon," the man says. Caleb's jaw tightens in pain as he stares at the ceiling. I grip his hand to provide some comfort.

When the man stands next to me, I look up to say thank you, but freeze. I see his face clearly for the first time in the firelight and recognize him from the newspaper article taped to my mirror.

It's Mark.

His face is muddier than in his picture and his hair more disheveled, but it's him.

My excitement quickly turns to confusion, though, when I eye his arms once again in the dim light. There's definitely no vine there. I thought Issy said they couldn't remove his vine? Was she wrong?

I'm about to ask him about it, when a pounding sound echoes outside. I look toward the back door across the room just in time to see it swing open, sending a gust of freezing air and cold slush into the room. I shiver, wishing I had dry clothes for Caleb and me.

Another man urgently enters the cabin, carrying someone over his shoulders. A dozen others, maybe in their twenties, follow behind, their faces streaked with worry.

"What happened?" Mark asks, walking toward them.

The man with brown hair and slanted eyes, straining under the weight of the big body, walks over to the vacant couch next to Caleb and heaves the body down. Compared to my brother, the injured body is ginormous. *How could he carry him?*

Out of breath, the brown-haired man talks. "We were ambushed. At least fifteen men knew exactly where our route was and caught us on the run." Looking directly at Mark, he says, "Thanks to Rusty, nobody was taken. Unfortunately, he was shot in the back. The bullet must have severed his spine. Scance tried to help him, but she couldn't get the nerves to cooperate. Medic is going to have to fix him."

I listen to the conversation, next to Caleb, switching between thinking about how insane it is to assume a severed spinal cord could be fixed and examining the newcomers in the room. My heart beats faster when I notice vine-like marks peeking out of their camouflage jackets and reaching up to their jawlines.

"Why didn't you send him in a toboggan?" Mark asks.

"We had to send Ling, who got shot in the head. Scance didn't have another one."

My hands start to shake. *Shot in the head? Who shot him in the head? Was it the Sybalt clan? Is he dead?*

"Did you send a message to the chief?"

"No, we didn't have time."

Chief? Issy had mentioned the chief.

The others in the room cover all the windows to block the light.

"We need to get you out of here," Mark says to the group, obviously not too concerned about the spinal injury. At least not as concerned about it as I am. "Get the aircraft ready—we can't wait until morning."

Aircraft? Up here? Issy said this was just a rendezvous point. Not where they actually live. Will the aircraft take them to their real home? *And where is that friend of Mark's that can help Caleb?*

The man runs from the room, obeying Mark's orders.

Turning his attention to a girl in the back of the group, Mark says, "Scance, I need your help with this man. He and his sister had an accident on the mountain, and he's injured badly." Mark points to Caleb on the couch.

A girl with long blonde dreadlocks pulled into a ratty ponytail steps forward. Her face is tanned and soft, and her dark eyelashes frame her big blue eyes. I've never been terribly fond of dreadlocks, but they look incredibly good on her. She walks briskly over to Caleb and me, kneels, and places her hand over his heart. My muscles tighten. I'm not sure what this woman can do to help Caleb here, without equipment. Maybe they can use their aircraft to get him to a doctor.

The woman sits there in silence for a moment before saying, "His leg is broken, but other than that he's okay. No internal bleeding."

I gawk at her. *His leg is broken?* She said it so assuredly, as if she had an X-ray to confirm it.

Looking up to Mark, who's now standing beside her, she says, "I can help him."

I hold up my hand. "Wait, help him? Are you a doctor? How are you going to help him?"

The woman ignores my questions and turns her focus to Caleb, who's sweating in pain. I look to Mark for help, more of an explanation, but all he says is "I'm going to send a message to the chief. I'll be right back."

I grip Caleb's hand protectively when Scance hovers her hand over his leg. "Do you have to set the bone? Can you make a cast here?"

Still no response. *What do I do?* Do I demand we leave? *Can she really help Caleb?* I stare at her, my hands trembling. I look at Caleb's leg. Then I watch Caleb's face. She isn't causing him more pain. So, I look back at his leg.

My jaw drops when I see it. The twist in his leg straightens, and the bruises lighten until the color of his skin is normal. I rock back on my feet in disbelief.

"H-how did you do that?" I stutter.

"Can I get more light in here?" Scance asks another Pepp, ignoring my question. The light in the room immediately brightens, but I'm too focused on Caleb to concern myself with how. Leaning back in, I observe the leg closer. There's no way she could have done that. Not without ...

Do they really have power? To heal broken bones, severed spinal cords? Do they have any idea how helpful this would be in my *non-Pepp* world? How many people could be cured, could still be living today if this power was shared?

I think of the hunter. I tried to save him. But couldn't. I felt so helpless. But this girl's not helpless.

I look at Scance. Her vine is on her right side in plain view and looks exactly like mine, except part of it is a bright-red color.

"I'm almost done. I'll try to explain ..." Scance glances at me for the first time, and I see her eyes drop to my muddied jaw where my vine is probably now visible in the lit room.

Her hands freeze. "Jase, were we supposed to get anyone new?" Her tone sets off little warning bells in the back of my head.

A woman speaks from the other side of the room. "No, the chief didn't mention anything."

Before I can even blink, Scance whips around, grabs me by the throat, and slams me against the stone wall beside the fire. I immediately bring my hands up to her unnaturally strong grip, trying to get free, but she tightens her fingers.

The room quiets, everyone's attention now focused on me.

"Who are you?" Scance demands.

Does she expect me to answer? With her hand pressed so hard against my throat? I kick my legs, trying to find some way to release my body, some way to get air.

Frustrated that I'm not answering her, Scance's hand tightens even more. "Who are you!"

"What's going on?" Those in the group draw closer, wondering what all the fuss is about.

"Look at her mark," the girl says through gritted teeth. She tears off my coat and pulls up my sweater sleeve with very little effort. The gesture reveals the vine running down my arm.

My ears are starting to ring, and my vision is darkening. *I need air.*

"Whoa." I hear Caleb's voice. Is he okay? I try to scream for help, but the only screaming I'm doing is in my lungs. Caleb quickly charges at Scance.

"Put my sister down!"

But another girl grabs Caleb by the throat and slams him up against another wall. "Sister? You don't have a mark. Pepps don't usually have siblings without marks. Do you work for the clan?" The girl, obviously not caring for an answer, turns to her friends, and asks, "Should we kill them here?"

"No, of course not," a boy quickly responds. "If they do work for the clan, the chief will want them."

I'm losing touch with the conversation, my mind fading to darkness. My fighting limbs weaken, and I stop struggling.

"What are you doing?" I faintly hear Mark's voice.

The hand around my throat is torn off, allowing me to fall into a heap on the floor. I gasp for breath, coughing. Black spots fill my eyes.

"They're spies! Look at the mark on her! We weren't supposed to get any new Pepps," Scance yells.

"We're not spies," Caleb croaks from across the room.

I'm about to turn my head to see if he's okay, when a strong hand grabs my chin, forcing it upward. Mark. I don't know what hurts more—the way his fingers dig into my skin or the fact that the man I haven't been able to stop thinking about the past few months is staring at me with hard, distrusting eyes.

He lets go of my chin, then grabs my arm, pulling me forcefully down the hall. I want to search for Caleb, but Mark's pulling keeps me from looking back.

The door to a dark room ahead opens, and he shoves me inside. I land on my hands and knees, turning just in time to see Caleb angrily enter the room before Mark shuts the door. The dark room lights up immediately, illuminating Mark's angry face that towers over me.

"What the hell?" Caleb yells. He comes to my side and tries to help me up.

"Where did you get that totem?" Mark shouts at me. He yanks Caleb away again, using an unseen force that sends him flying back into the wall. Wide-eyed, I stand frozen in place, unsure how to respond. Mark repeats his demand again, louder. "Where did you get it?"

I stammer, watching Caleb struggle against the wall, until I finally say, "Falling Rock. A hot spring in Falling Rock." I let the words rush out of my mouth, hoping they'll free Caleb. "Please let him go."

Mark's face turns from hard to confused. "Falling Rock?"

With Caleb still pressed against the wall, I rush to add more information. "Yes, the hot spring next to your father's cabin." I pause and let my eyes meet his. "You are Mark, aren't you, the missing boy, the hunter's son? I was swimming in the hot spring, when this vine latched onto me."

Mark's eyes are still fierce. "Why did you come *here*?"

I glance at my brother again. "We've been looking for the Pepps. Caleb heard about an old woman who was attacked a couple of days ago by the clan. He heard she survived. We wondered if she knew anything about the Pepps, even though she didn't have the vine on her arm. We found her in Deadwood, and she told us how to get here. She told us you would know how to help us. She also told us she would send a message to your chief."

"Who was the old woman?" Mark asks.

"Issy," Caleb heaves out this information from across the room.

Mark's body straightens.

Caleb clears his throat painfully, reminding Mark that he's still there. Without looking up, Mark removes the invisible force holding Caleb and drops him to the floor. Through coughs, Caleb starts talking.

"All we want is for the damn thing to be taken off. Can we get that done so we can be on our way?"

Mark shakes his head. "I don't think that will be possible."

My heart sinks, and Caleb spins on his heel, throwing his hands into the air. "Issy was able to remove hers! Why can't we remove this one?"

Mark ignores Caleb and instead looks at me, the fire in his eyes melting to something like sympathy. "In the middle of the totem, just over your heart, there's a hole. Can you tell me what color it is?"

I'm grateful he doesn't try to see that spot over my heart like Issy forcibly did.

"Green."

Mark shakes his head at my response. "It's the other half," Mark says to himself.

"What?" Caleb's usual patience is gone.

Mark sighs. "Normal totems can be removed easily, but this totem is not normal. We think it was created by an enemy, the Sybalt clan." Mark rubs his face in frustration. "They made it with millions of tiny hooklike contraptions that dig into the vessels like a fishhook would attach to a fish. Pulling it out, the way the other totems are pulled out, tears the vessels. It would kill you."

Caleb grabs my arm and starts hauling me toward the door. "Well, if you can't get it off, then we'll be on our way."

Quick as lightning, Mark blocks the door. "Please, sit down and let's talk this through." Mark suddenly looks exhausted.

"Talk about what?" Caleb demands. "You can't help us, so what's the use?"

"Word will leak out," Mark says, his tone now remarkably more kind than it was a few minutes ago. "If the clan finds out she has that totem ..." Mark's eyes find their way to mine. "We think they made this totem as a weapon, to attach to a non-Pepp, who would then carry it to Petrichor, where the Pepps live, and then activate it. But things didn't turn out the way they'd hoped. If they find out she has the other half of my totem, who knows what they'll do to collect her."

Other half of his *totem?*

"Collect her? Like a dog or an experiment?" Caleb yells, before trying to push his way past. "Well, we better just go hide like we were doing before."

Caleb tries to drag me along, but I eye Mark carefully. *Is he telling the truth? Can we trust his words after the way he just dragged me down the hall?*

"And they made the totem to hurt the Pepps?" Caleb fumes, still trying to find a way around Mark. "Well, after tonight I'm beginning to think the Pepps are worth hurting. Now let us go."

"The Pepps aren't who you think they are," Mark says quietly.

Caleb groans, not wanting to hear what Mark has to say. But I'm intrigued. I want to know what I am.

"Who are they then?" My voice is barely a whisper. "Who am I?" My cheeks burn when Mark's eyes land on me.

"Please sit down." Mark waves his hand toward the couch.

Stepping away from Caleb's glaring eyes, I walk to the couch, leaving sloshes of mud and water on the floor behind me. I sit on the soft sofa, trying not to get it too dirty. Mark grabs something from a desk under the window. When he finds what he's looking for, he drags a chair over and sits in front of me.

For the first time, I examine him close-up. He's even more handsome than in the picture sitting on my mirror. The dark mud on his body matches the color of his brown hair and enhances the strong features of his face. I suddenly become very conscious of the mud caking my own brown hair and clothes, sure that it doesn't look as attractive on me as it does on him.

"Have you ever been happy?" Mark asks me. The question catches me off guard, and I find myself looking into his eyes. They're brown, with a light-golden color speckled here and there. They're unique and light, so unlike the reddish-brown of my own eyes.

Caleb scoffs angrily, stepping toward the couch. "What does that have to do with anything?"

Mark ignores him, continuing to search me for an answer.

It's a simple question. Of course I've been happy in the past. But, right now, it seems like an almost foreign concept. What does happiness even feel like? I can't answer the question, so I just drop my eyes.

Mark proceeds when I don't respond, his voice turning soft. "Well, if you've ever felt happy, it's because of this." He holds up a clear flask in his hand. "It's called Peppate, a tiny element that's absorbed by every living creature, either through the air, water, or food, and it's the source of what ultimately makes us feel happy."

I stare hard at the clear flask. "I don't see anything," I say, trying not to sound too disappointed.

"It's too small to see, but it's there."

"That's stupid," Caleb interjects. "Happiness doesn't come from anything but ourselves. Plus, I've seen vials like that, they're usually filled with drugs. You're saying you distribute drugs?"

Mark drops his head and shakes it, clearly irritated with Caleb's comment. "They're not drugs." Then deciding to move on instead of arguing, he proceeds, "Anyway, the Pepps create this inside themselves, through the totem, and distribute it all over the world."

Caleb jumps in again, "The vine makes happiness? Pfff." Pointing to my vine, Caleb grits his teeth. "That thing does *not* make happiness."

Mark takes in a deep breath, rests his elbows on his knees, and rubs his eyes with his hands. He's trying to be patient. "Her totem is not a normal Pepp totem. Neither is mine." Mark lets out his breath and sits up, facing my distrusting brother. "*Our* totems don't create Peppate. Instead, they create the opposite of Peppate. Doler. Doler is normally created by normal humans in small amounts, but our totems create it in large amounts."

Mark's eyes come back to mine, but this time they're burning anxiously. "Does your totem make you feel like crap?"

I search him quietly, his question hanging in the air. I should pull away. The fact that I still see the golden color in his eyes means I'm too close, but Mark's gaze holds me in place, searching me earnestly. My answer seems important to him.

I nod.

Then I realize what he's saying. He feels the same way I do. Like crap. I don't know why, but the fact that someone else feels the same way I do and has the same defective vine or *totem* as me makes me feel ... better.

But I'm still confused. "You said you have a vine, but where is it?" I look at his bare arms.

Pulling down his shirt collar, Mark reveals his chest. My heart pounds, seeing his exposed dusky muscles, but then my eyes are drawn to the area just over his heart. There, embedded in the skin of his chest, is a vine with the same green eye that resides over my heart. Several tendrils reach out a couple of inches and terminate just before his arm. My heart leaps.

Mark *is* a Pepp.

"How did you get your vine?" I pause, but then correct myself, deciding to call the vine what he's been calling it. "*Totem*. Did you know it was different?"

Mark willingly answers my questions. "No. I didn't. My dad used to be a Pepp. He left them when he was in his twenties to marry my mom, who was a normal human, but he remained a communicator for the Pepps."

"Like Issy," I say, gathering the pieces of the puzzle.

"Yes. Like Issy. All communicators with children are given extra totems to store. If the communicators die before their children reach the age of eighteen, then the children can join the Pepps if they want. The child is told by their parents that if anything happens to them, they're to take the extra totem, attach it to their arm, and then go to the nearest rendezvous point where they meet up with the Pepps. The Pepps then take them back to Petrichor and look after them."

"So, there's a whole society of Pepps? In Petrichor?" I ask. "Where is that and how many Pepps are there?" This goes against everything I believed about the Pepps being isolated and disconnected.

"Yes, there are about fourteen thousand Pepps there now. And Petrichor is up north at the top of a very tall mountain. They live there most of the time for their own safety."

I bristle. *Fourteen thousand!* Then glance at Mark's bare arm. "And you're one of them?"

"Yes, I'm one of them." He sighs and rubs his jaw. "A year ago, I was hunting in the woods near my father's cabin, when I heard a gunshot. My father never shot his gun around the cabin, especially if he knew I was hunting close by. I ran back as fast as I could and found him in the bushes soaked in blood. He had large gashes on his arms, legs, and stomach."

I shudder, listening to Mark tell the familiar story. *I know those gashes. They're burned into my memory.*

"When I reached him, he was still alive but scared. He immediately told me to get the totem hidden under the floorboard, the totem he had only shown me once when I was fourteen when he explained who the Pepps were. I ran into the cabin while calling for help on my satellite phone, only to find the cabin ransacked. I ran to the floorboard where I had seen my father hide the box and found it still there.

"I hurried back to my father's side with the box in my hands and kneeled down to help him."

The anguish is unmistakable on Mark's face as he recounts this horribly traumatic memory. Even Caleb has come to sit beside me, his hard face softening a bit. Even he knows part of this story.

"I tried to cover his wounds, but he kept pushing my hands away, telling me to take the totem and go warn the Pepps. He told me I was in danger and that '*he*' would be coming for me. I didn't want to leave him. I had no idea who he was talking about, but as the emergency helicopter approached, he begged me to go."

My mind goes back to my own experiences that day. He heard the same helicopter in those woods. It's hard to believe that we were so close to each other. And so close to the clan.

Mark's voice becomes barely a whisper. "Leaving him there choking on his blood was the hardest thing I've ever done in my life. I've kicked myself every day, knowing I shouldn't have left him."

Taking in a deep breath, Mark shakes his head and proceeds. "But I did what he asked. I ran into the forest and opened the box, but instead of there being one long totem stick, like I remember there being, there were two short pieces. As if the totem had been broken in two. One of the pieces was brown and the other was black. There was also a black capsule in there labeled 'Toboggan.' It was totally different from what I had remembered Dad showing me, but I was in such a panic, I didn't care. The instructions on the box told me to grab the black stick first. You see, the totems are designed to attach the moment they touch live skin. So, I touched it.

"The black totem had just attached itself, when a bear came out of the woods, slashing me across the arm and sending the other totem and the black capsule flying away from me. I flung myself in the direction they landed, searching frantically for both objects but only finding one—the black capsule.

"The bear slashed me again across the leg, and I knew I couldn't waste any more time looking for the other piece, so I took my chances and activated the capsule, which took me to Petrichor."

Mark looks at me now. "I was standing close to the hot spring when the bear attacked. The other piece must have fallen in the water."

Staring at a seam in the wooden floor, Mark continues. "The chief examined me quickly when I got to Petrichor. He found that the totem I got was different, only internal. It runs through the blood vessels in my body but not through my skin. That's why you can't see it on my arm. The chief believes the clan somehow stole a totem from the Pepps, manipulated it, then exchanged it with the one my dad had hiding in the floorboards. They did this hoping I would carry it back to Petrichor and activate it, allowing it to do whatever it was supposed to do. But, instead, I only attached half of the totem, and the other half ended up in the bottom of the hot spring."

He says this guiltily as if he feels responsible for the conflict.

"We searched for the other half of the totem, but we couldn't find it. After several weeks we began to suspect the clan came and got it, and we've been bracing for its appearance ever since, but ..." Waving his hand toward me, he says, "Obviously they didn't have it. It looks like your totem is the other half of mine. The brown half."

I look at my defective totem. "What is it supposed to do?"

"We still don't know, but we do know that it's not activated unless we morph—change our shapes by becoming animals."

I swallow. "Animals? Like *real* animals?"

"Yes. When a Pepp turns sixteen, they participate in something called initiation. Where they're sent to survive outside the safeguards of Petrichor for three days. During this time, the totem becomes acquainted with the Pepp and their skills and matches them into a job in Petrichor. At the end of initiation, the sixteen-year-old Pepps get to morph for the first time. Into an eagle. That's how Pepps spread Peppate. By flying as an eagle across the world on what we call *runs*.

"I participated in initiation too. But when I morphed I dispelled large amounts of Doler. The Pepps were depressed for weeks." Mark chuckles softly. "Now they know how I feel. I just can't help but wonder what would have happened if I'd had both parts of the totem in me. Would I have been dangerous? Would I have caused more harm than just sadness?"

Without looking away, he changes the subject. "We need to get you to Petrichor. The clan has already attempted to capture me. I think they want to force me into doing what they sent me out to do. Maybe they have another brown half of a totem they want to attach. Whatever the case is, it can't be good. If they find out you have the second half attached to you, they're going to try to collect you and use you to complete the totem, finish what they started. Whatever that is."

"Wait!" Caleb's anger boils up again, realizing what Mark is saying. "You want to take Alena away?" He stands, shaking his head. "No."

"Trust me, it's much safer for her there than out here. Did you see the Pepps who just came in from a run? That's the work of the clan. Most Pepps think the clan is attacking because they want our power. Maybe that was true in the past, but I don't think it's the reason now. They've been especially brutal around this rendezvous point, the rendezvous point *I'm* stationed at. They're attacking us because they want their totem back. This totem back." Mark's voice is rising again.

Caleb shakes his head even more forcefully, but Mark turns back to me. "You're in the same danger I'm in. The chief can protect you in Petrichor. The clan cannot enter there. There are protective fogs and men working around the clock to watch the area. You'll be safe."

Protective fogs, like the one around this cabin?

Caleb is now pacing the room, tearing his hands through his hair. I sit quietly in front of Mark, who's watching me, patiently yet anxiously waiting for my response. I silently consider what he's told me. Then I open my mouth and state the most important thing I've learned.

"Your totem makes you feel bad."

Caleb stops pacing.

I raise my eyes to Mark's. He speaks softly, "It makes me feel awful. But, thanks to my friend Danny, I've learned how to control the crappy feeling."

Control the feeling? How would you control it? I search Mark's face, realizing in this moment that I do trust him. He might have roughly dragged me down the hall only moments ago, but something deep inside me believes him. And it doesn't have anything to do with the fact that I've been silently infatuated with him since I put his picture on my mirror.

No, it has to do with how he's treated me the last few minutes. Giving me answers to the questions I've been drowning in the past several months. And the way he's looked at me. Not once during our conversation have his eyes wandered to my muddy, disheveled hair, or to my *defective* vine. He looks at me as if he sees *me*.

"Are you happy?" I whisper.

The room is silent, and I search his eyes. They're soft and understanding. Slowly, he nods his head, the corner of his lips lifting. "Yes. It's a daily quest, but, yes. At least I feel like I'm living now—not just existing. We could teach you."

"Teach her? I could teach Alena how to be happy," Caleb interjects. But his words fall flat. We both know that's not true. This goes beyond what we know.

For the first time in months, a tiny light of hope glimmers in my heart. Maybe I don't have to be unhappy for the rest of my life.

Just then, a buzzing sound putters in through the window above the desk, breaking the silence. Mark jumps up and opens it, letting in freezing gusts of air. It makes me yearn for the old wet coat still in the other room. Mark quickly scribbles on a piece of yellow paper. Then, after folding it, he slips it into what looks like a black piece of coal. Soon after he pushes the paper into the coal, the object flies out of his hand into the dark night.

"Like I said, Petrichor sits in the mountains to the far northeast. It takes a couple of hours to get there in our flyer, and the group needs to get back, especially since Rusty is hurt so badly." Mark looks directly at me. "I know it's a lot to ask, but I need you to go with them."

The comfort I felt only moments ago quickly disappears, and fear jumps through every cell in my body. He's asking me to leave my family. My home. I still have so many questions. I can't leave now, can I? Tears begin to collect in my eyes no matter how hard I try to keep them back.

"Can I at least think about this?" I whisper. "Can I call my parents?"

Mark shakes his head. "I'm sorry, we don't use electricity or phones here."

I look around the room. He's right. The light comes from candles, not lightbulbs. Why don't they use electricity?

"I wish I could give you time to think about it, but I can't. It's too dangerous. I don't know how they do it, but the clan figures things out. Who knows if they saw you out there tonight with Caleb. They're always lurking around this rendezvous point. If they saw you, then they'll get to you. I need to get you to Petrichor. The chief will know what to do. He'll allow you to communicate with your family once you get there."

Caleb steps up. "I'm going too."

"No, I'm sorry, only those with a totem can get into Petrichor."

"Then get me a totem, dammit!" Caleb begins shouting again. "I can't send my sister with a bunch of strangers to a place nobody knows about!"

"It doesn't work that way. People don't just join the Pepps. Even if I wanted to let you go, I don't have the authority to make that decision." Mark's voice is equally loud.

Caleb grabs my arm and begins dragging me out, but I plant my feet, stopping everything in the room.

The battle rages inside me. I realize the two things I'm torn between. How am I supposed to choose between staying with my family and finding safety and happiness? Yet, as difficult as the decision is, I know what my choice needs to be. Tears escape my eyes, silently telling Caleb what I feel. I can't go back home.

As if sensing the fragile moment, Mark dismisses himself from the room, giving us some privacy.

Caleb shakes his head. "This is nuts!"

I agree, but through tears I add, "You can't protect me from the clan. I don't want you getting hurt because of me." Caleb starts to protest, but I continue. "I want to learn how to be happy again."

He can't fight that. I watch his resolve melt. "I want you to be happy too."

Then, as if accepting the new change, he sighs. "What on earth am I going to tell Mom and Dad? They're going to kill me."

I shake my head at the idea of leaving the comfort of my home and family. Caleb pulls me into one of his familiar healing hugs. I breathe him in until a commotion breaks outside the door.

"Are you kidding me?" It's Scance's high, shrill voice. My bruised neck throbs in response.

Mark speaks to her, but I can't understand his muffled words. After some shuffling down the hall, the door opens, and Mark comes back inside.

"Alena, they're leaving now. I need to get you on the flyer," he says, and then adds, "Please."

Looking back at Caleb, I silently plead for his approval.

He exhales, defeat clear in his voice. "I'll walk you out."

"Will you make sure Caleb gets home safe?" I ask Mark.

"Of course."

We follow Mark down the hall into the large room where Caleb had lain on the couch earlier. I recall the remarkable healing of Caleb's bone.

I shake my head. Issy had mentioned that the Pepps have power, but I never could have imagined ... that.

Walking through the back door and outside, I clutch at my still-soaked torso. Caleb puts his arm around me, trying to calm my shivering as we walk toward the buzzing sound.

Approaching the tree line, I see an aircraft hidden in the pine trees. With the back hatch lit up and open, it waits for me to enter.

"This aircraft will take you to Petrichor, where the chief will be waiting for you," Mark says. "I have to stay here as guard for the next groups, but I'll see you soon. I'll get Caleb back home safely." I try not to feel too disappointed that Mark isn't coming with me.

Turning to Caleb, Mark shouts over the noise of the propeller, "I'm sorry it has to be this way, but she'll be safer there."

Caleb suddenly grabs Mark's shirt and pulls his face close to his. "If anything happens to her, it's you I'm coming after. *You*."

Mark nods his head wearily. "I'll watch after her."

Caleb lets go of Mark's shirt, then gives me one last hug good-bye. My tears wet his soggy shirt, and then I let him go.

Placing his hand on my back, Mark guides me onto the aircraft to a seat near the tail, where nobody except the paralyzed severed-spinal-cord man sits.

I wave to Caleb, who's standing just outside the hatch, until it closes.

Then we rise into the air, leaving behind the only world I know.

Chapter 6

I keep my head down. Mark doesn't believe I'm a spy, but Scance definitely distrusts me, and so do the other Pepps in the flyer. I try to ignore their accusing eyes by looking down. Maybe this wasn't such a good idea.

Staring at my muddy shoes doesn't help either. They just remind me of how dirty I am. Why couldn't I at least look half-decent for their stares? I try to make myself very small, invisible, even though I need to shift my body repeatedly in the uncomfortable seat.

I'm just beginning to wonder if I'll have to hold still and stare at my shoes the whole way, when I hear someone snore. I look up. The Pepps are asleep. All of them. I sigh in relief.

I'm tired too, but I can't sleep—not with my mind spinning from the events of the day. Instead, I look around the dark cabin of the aircraft.

The worn seats, which offer very little comfort, line the walls, leaving the middle of the aircraft open. Dimly lit lanterns wired to the front of the aircraft are the only source of light, from what I can see, and even they've been turned down. Probably so the Pepps can sleep.

I count the Pepps—twenty-three including the lifeless man beside me. They're all from different lands. Some with darker skin, looking like they come from the cities southeast of the mountains I grew up in, while others have fair skin or wide-set eyes like those in the north.

My eyes fall to their exposed vine marks. Their totems are all different too. Some are orange, some yellow, and some blue. There is only one with a red mark—Scance. I wonder what the colors mean. And how did they get the colors?

The injured man beside me snores a little, and I examine him closely. He's tied to the chair from his ankles to his neck. They probably did that to keep him from falling over, but it makes him look more like a prisoner than a member of their group.

His bulky muscles peek out from under the ropes. His right arm, closest to me, has a bulging black sweatband but no totem. So I lean forward to see his other arm. His vine is on his left arm, just like mine. But his has two different colors wound around it—yellow and blue.

The aircraft shudders severely, tugging at my attention, and I peel my eyes off the man to look up at the source of the noise. I realize for the first time that the aircraft is made up of hundreds of pieces of scrap metal thrown together, and many are shaking violently from the wind. For as much power as these people seem to have, couldn't they have done a better job putting the aircraft together?

Leaning my head back against the shaking metal, I close my eyes and try to sleep in the uncomfortable position.

I'm just beginning to doze off, when a commotion breaks out near the back of the plane. Based on the light coming in through the windows, I must have slept. But as groggy as my brain is, it couldn't have been for long.

Two boys are rustling through a closet next to the paralyzed man, searching for something.

"Aha, here they are," one boy says as he pulls out two flat oval-shaped objects made of what looks like foam and fiberglass. He puts them on his feet while the other boy pulls out another pair. Growing up in the mountains, skiing was one of the more popular sports, something I mastered at a young age. Even though these plastic shoes aren't as long or as narrow as the skis I used, the look of them on their feet is similar. I wonder what they're doing.

The commotion wakes up some of the other Pepps, and they start gathering around the back of the aircraft. The first boy steps into an old harness, wrapping it around his torso. He then clips a rope to a harness ring just over his heart. I follow the rope with my eyes. The other end is tied to another ring on the floor.

"Hey, Jack!" he shouts to the front. "Open the hatch!"

Wind immediately whips through my mud-caked hair.

As soon as the hatch is fully open, the two boys leap out into the air.

What the...? I frantically jump to my feet when they disappear beneath the aircraft, but this draws attention from those standing around the back. Their glares force me back into my seat, making me silently vow never to move again. But once they turn their attention back to the boys, I can't keep myself from looking through the gaps of bodies to see what's going on. Slowly, the boys rise to my view. They're floating on the fiberglass things, holding on to the rope attached to the front of their harnesses.

I shake my head. They do tricks, circling, rising, and falling, leaving huge white puffy trails behind them in the warm air.

"They're air skiing." I jump at the accented voice that speaks next to me. It's the man with the severed spinal cord.

"You can talk?" I whisper in shock.

The man chuckles softly. "The problem's in my spine, not my head. Yes, I can talk." Then looking around at the vacant seats beside him, he says, "Unfortunately for me, I didn't have much of a say about who I got to sit next to."

The comment stabs at me, but the man laughs again. "I don't mind. *They* might think you're a spy"—he nods his head toward the others in the craft—"but I don't. You're too pretty." He adds with a wide smile, "And too emotional—much too emotional."

I gape at him. *Pretty?* He's mocking me in my mud-covered state. I immediately decide I don't care for him at all. Also, I thought he was unconscious the whole night. *How could he know I've been accused of being a spy or, even more, that I'm emotional?*

As much as I would rather not talk to him now, though, there's one question I have to ask. "Do you hurt?"

The man chuckles again. "I'm paralyzed, so, no, I don't feel any pain."

I stare at him. I had initially thought he was older, based on his size, but hearing him talk, hearing him laugh, I don't think he could be more than a year or two older than me. Which makes me feel even more self-conscious.

"Too bad I'm not able to get up now. I could show you how air skiing is really done," he says, changing the subject. "My name's Rusty, by the way. After the medic fixes me, I'll take you for another ride."

"After your medic fixes you?" I ask, not bothering to wonder why he would want to take me out for another ride. *He's so sure the medic can fix him.* A severed spinal cord? I wish I could witness that. Actually, I wish I could *do* that. I recall Caleb's broken bone being healed by Scance. *Unbelievable.*

"Not our medic—*the* medic, Jeter," Rusty says. "He can fix anything on a person's body."

"How?" I ask, incredulous.

Rusty nods in the direction of my totem. "When we morph into an eagle and spread Peppate, our totem fills up with power, in the hole just over the heart. It's a power that allows us to control the elements of nature. We wouldn't be able to do what we do without it. We each learn how to control different elements in different ways. Jeter has learned all the elements of the body and how to control them, making them do what he wants."

Control the elements of the body? My pulse thumps excitedly. *Is that really possible?*

I look down at the totem peeking out of my sweater. "The power is in the totem," I whisper. Looking back at Rusty, I ask, "Where do the totems come from?"

Rusty leans his head to the side. "The original Pepps were born with the power in their blood vessels. But then the Pepps started getting attacked and killed. Their numbers started to dwindle, eventually making it difficult for them to spread Peppate around the world. So they started adopting large numbers of abandoned non-Pepp children. When they brought them in, they had to construct something that would harness the same power they created within themselves, hence the totem was created. The Peppate generators, which create the Peppate we spread, were removed from the veins of the purebloods and put into the veins of an Aleshian tree, whose small vines and moldability made it a perfect fit for the job. The vines support the generators and act like the veins of a pureblood by collecting the power output by the generators. The plan was brilliant and has worked better than anyone could have expected.

"We haven't needed to adopt non-Pepps for a while, but we do occasionally have the children of communicators that join us. The totems can be added to, or removed from, any normal human if we need help."

My eyebrows furrow. I've never believed in magic, but after seeing what I saw ... I shake my head.

Rusty laughs out loud. "It's cool, isn't it? There's no way I could ever give up being a Pepp like others do."

This comment triggers a new question as I think about Issy. "Why *do* Pepps choose to leave?"

Rusty's face becomes somewhat sober. "Being a Pepp isn't easy. We work hard. We morph into eagles and go on *runs*—well, we should actually call them *flights* since we fly instead of run, but whatever. We go on runs to spread Peppate around the world. And then go on the humanitarian dropdowns. It can be exhausting. Not to mention the fact that we're often shot at by the clan." Rusty pumps his eyes up and down.

"Humanitarian dropdowns?" I ask.

"Yeah. When there's a natural disaster with a lot of potential injuries, we drop down as eagles from an aircraft like this one and help non-Pepps, using our power. We find trapped people in collapsed buildings, we heal them, we stop fires, etc. Even though we do a lot of good, we're not able to save everyone. There's a lot of death witnessed on the dropdowns, which is a big reason a lot of people leave."

That must be why Pepps are seen at natural disasters. They don't cause the disasters; they're there to help.

"So, you just spend all your time helping normal humans, spreading Peppate to make them happy, and helping out during disasters. Why?" I wonder why an entire species would dedicate their lives to non-Pepps.

"Well, we all need Peppate, so we aren't just spreading it for the normal humans. We're spreading it for us too. Some Pepps really do have the kindest heart and genuinely want to help others. But, personally, I love the power and can't give it up. Spreading Peppate and helping out at disaster sites is worth being able to create and control. The more Peppate you spread, the more power you get, and the bigger your blue power holster becomes. If you don't spread Peppate, you don't get power."

Blue power holster? I don't have anything blue on my totem, but I do have a green eye. Could that be where the power is stored on *my* totem?

"So, you get power after morphing into an eagle and spreading Peppate?" I say, "How do you morph?"

Rusty opens his mouth to respond, but then he shuts it. He's seemed so willing to answer my questions, until now.

"Maybe we should ask the chief if it's okay for you to learn morphing. After what happened with Mark, he might want to hold off on teaching you that." Mark hinted at the same thing. Maybe it's better if I don't know how to morph.

Rusty changes the subject. "I have a personal goal to get the largest power container in my totem out of all the Pepps. I'm close too. Only a few of the council members have a holster bigger than mine."

I watch the Pepps still gathered around the back hatch. So the Pepps go on runs, by morphing into an eagle to spread Peppate? They go on dropdowns by dropping out of the sky to help out at natural disasters sites? And they can increase the amount of power they hold in their power holster over their heart by spreading *more* Peppate? My body reacts to the possibility of harnessing this type of power, especially being able to heal. And I know it's a possibility even for me, one with a different type of totem, simply because I saw Mark's incredible strength. He has power too. *Imagine how much I could help Dad in the hospital. If I learned how to use the power ... and if it was safe to go back home.*

But then my spirits fall. *Dropdowns? Runs?* That part sounds overwhelming. "Is it possible to be a Pepp and not do all that dropdown stuff?"

Rusty laughs out loud again, pulling more glares from the group of Pepps, which he ignores. "If you are able, I don't think the chief will let you sit around. We need the help of every able body. But don't worry. Once you get your hands on the power, you'll realize the work is worth it."

"We're almost there." A shout reaches back from the cockpit, and the nose of the aircraft turns to the sky, sending us all sideways. I hold on to my seat and look over at Rusty, understanding now why they tied him down. Those who are standing immediately sit, and the boys outside on the air skis continue their sport from a different angle.

"Petrichor is located on the top of a very tall cloud-covered mountain, secured with a protective fog. We're heading straight up that mountain now," Rusty says.

I remember the fog around the cabin. "How does the fog protect you?" I ask. It doesn't seem like it would be very effective.

"It confuses anyone who doesn't have a totem. A normal human enters the fog and wanders around. The fog eventually spits them back out. It even messes with compasses, making them spin wildly. If the fog doesn't sense a totem, it doesn't let you pass."

I think about trying to get through the fog around the cabin. I guess I could have made it if I hadn't kept slipping.

The aircraft continues to climb until it plateaus. Then it hovers in the air, like a helicopter would, letting down until it thumps to the ground.

My ears ring when the loud rattling of the metal finally stops. The other Pepps gather around the open hatch, eager to leave the aircraft, but I stay in my seat, beside Rusty.

I'm not sure what I'm supposed to do when the last Pepp exits the plane. *Do I stay here? Do I leave?* I'm about to ask Rusty, when an old man enters the cabin and stops, waiting for his eyes to adjust. His graying brown hair is thick and full, reaching his neck in a neat yet carefree way. The same brownish-gray hair bushes over his piercing blue eyes and covers his face in a well-trimmed beard. He quietly searches the inside of the aircraft until his eyes land on mine. He walks toward me and kneels at my feet.

He doesn't talk, just stares intently at my totem, making me feel very awkward. I steal a side glance at Rusty, hoping for an explanation, but Rusty only seems curious about what the man has to say.

The old man's eyes follow my totem up to my jaw, where he reaches out to touch it. I withdraw slightly, forcing him to look me in the eyes.

"Alena Carlston," he says. He knows my name even though I don't remember specifically giving it to anyone. Especially my last name. Maybe Mark got it from Caleb.

"Mark sent me a message, telling me what's happened to you. He was right to send you here, where you'll be safe." The old man speaks to me kindly, his low voice making me feel as if he sees me as an old friend. *Is this the chief?*

Another middle-aged man, with the same sandy hair and hazel eyes as Rusty, walks onto the aircraft.

He's followed by a thin, graceful woman. At first her hair looks brilliantly blonde in the sunlight, but in the cabin, it darkens to deep auburn. Whatever color it is, it's captivating. Then I see her eyes. They're a deep green that almost looks chocolate brown. She's beautiful. Unlike anything I've ever seen. My eyes drift to her arms, where her sleeveless white top not only exposes her flattering muscles but also reveals the absence of a totem.

I don't understand.

"I've decided Alena's not a spy," Rusty says, interrupting my observations.

The woman's green eyes snap to mine, and I cringe. They may be beautiful, but they aren't kind. She glares at me, her jaw tightening. "We can't trust her," she says, her silky voice low and sure. Her words bite at me, and I sit gaping at her. *We haven't even met, and she already hates me?*

Ignoring the woman's comment, the middle-aged man drops to his knees and asks in the same accent as Rusty, "Do you mind if I see it?"

His hand reaches out for my arm. I raise it, allowing it to fall into his palm. Searching me quietly, he shakes his head.

"Extraordinary," he finally says, an exasperated look covering his face. "It's the exact partner to Mark's totem, beginning right where his leaves off and only winding through her heart, brain, and arm."

How does he know all that just by holding my hand?

Stepping back, he says, "The story fits. It indeed looks like she found the other half of Mark's totem."

The woman's eyes don't leave mine. "The clan knew very well Mark lost the other half of the totem near the hot spring. They could have found it, given it to a *little* girl, and sent her here so she and Mark could accomplish whatever the totem is supposed to accomplish."

I take back my initial opinion of her. She's not beautiful. In fact, her red-blonde hair is ugly, and her green eyes get duller with each word she utters. I hate how she talks about me as if I'm nothing more than an object sitting in the aircraft.

I look at the other two men, hoping for their defense, but they just nod in agreement, and I suddenly feel sick. *Was I wrong to come here?*

Talking to the woman, while still looking at me, the old man says, "Cordelia, we'll watch her closely for a bit. Gather the council together for a meeting tonight. We'll discuss this further then."

The woman raises her perfect eyebrows at me, proud to be given such an important task. Then, turning, she leaves the aircraft.

I drop my head.

"Ahem." Rusty clears his throat next to me, reminding us all of his presence. "Before you leave, Jeter, would you mind helping me out?" The middle-aged man, obviously *the* medic, moves over to Rusty, seeing him for the first time.

"Ah, that's right. You took a bullet to the spine." Jeter removes the rope holding Rusty down with one wave of his hand and catches Rusty on his lap before he can fall over. Placing his hand over Rusty's neck, Jeter scrunches his nose.

"This is pretty bad," he says, his expression turning concerned. "This might take a minute or two."

I curiously watch Jeter heal Rusty. I wish I knew what he was doing and how he was doing it. *How many lives would be made better if humans had this ability?*

"I'm told if it wasn't for you, the casualties from your team would have been far worse," the old man says to Rusty.

Rusty accepts the praise before glancing my way. He winks.

What's that supposed to mean?

"He's the chief, by the way," Rusty says, nodding toward the old man.

The chief holds out his hand in response. If we'd met under different circumstances, I might almost trust the kindness in his eyes. But I do take his hand.

"I apologize for not introducing myself. Alena, I'm sorry we haven't been more courteous to you. I hope you understand our hesitation. It's the Sybalt clan. They've been hurting and kidnapping our Pepps. At least we hope they're kidnapping them and keeping them prisoners and not killing them. Right now, we have seventy-five missing Pepps. We need to be cautious with you. I'll have you stay with Cody, one of our Pepps. You'll room with her in the dorms. I ask that you please not leave the room until you are given permission to do so. Do you understand?"

My heart thumps wildly. Mark didn't mention anything about me being a prisoner here. Tears well up inside me. *Did he really believe me when I told him I'm not a spy? Or did he just say what he needed to say to get me here?*

This isn't how I thought things would go. But I don't have any ideas on how to get out of this mess. Reluctantly, I nod, agreeing to do what they tell me.

"Thank you for understanding," the chief says kindly. "Rusty, will you please take Alena straight to Cody. Try not to let any others see her."

I turn my head to find Rusty now sitting up on his own, stretching his hands out in front of him as they regain their feeling. Then he hops onto his feet. "Of course."

He's standing. I blink hard, hoping to clear my head of the hallucinations, then look at him again. No, he's still standing. My eyes narrow, intently studying his body, trying to find the true culprit for this healing. *How? How is that possible?*

"I believe you, Alena," the chief says before leaving the aircraft with the medic. "We'll figure this out soon."

I stand cautiously, making sure to leave lots of space between me and the mysteriously healed Rusty. When I look up at him, I take another step back. Man, he's huge—both tall and muscular. I sink when he shoots me an attractive grin.

Again, I'm reminded of how I look with mud-dried hair and dirty clothes. The old Alena might have taken advantage of such a moment with a golden-haired man, regardless of how she looked. I have my father's friendly personality and my mother's beauty. I've never had an issue getting the attention of a boy. I miss that Alena. Not that I want Rusty's attention. He seems to be somewhat of a detestable man.

As if sensing my insecurity, Rusty laughs. "Come on, let's get you to Cody." Following him out into the daylight, I squint against the brightness of the sun, just as a wonderful smell meets my nose—the smell of rain. I take in a deep breath and close my eyes.

"Hey, Alena, watch this," Rusty says. I open my eyes just in time to see him pound his chest in an odd gesture, then ... change. His body puffs up, growing even taller and thicker. I squint, trying to make sense of what looks like long silky golden feathers emerging from his skin, swaying slightly in the breeze. A large golden beak replaces his sharp nose, and his hazel eyes turn black.

I step back, then stand frozen, unable to stop gawking at the unnaturally large golden bird standing in front of me. His enormous claws dig into the concrete below us. *So this is what Mark meant when he said they morph into eagles.*

The bird's head drops down in front of me, bringing its eyes to my level. I take another step back. Even though they're a different color, the eyes are the same laughing eyes of Rusty's.

I raise my hand and touch the head of the bird, just above its eyes. The feathers are so soft. As I do so, his eyes close and he pushes his head further into my hand much like a dog would do for a good scratch. I grunt a laugh. I'm not as intimidated by Rusty in this form.

This place is going to take some getting used to.

Rusty backs away from my hand before expanding his large wings. He moves them up and down, sending gusts of air around me. Gaining thrust he rises. Moving to the left, he circles around the airplane one time before he swoops down, claws me around my torso, and steals me into the air.

I startle at the movement, frantically gripping at his claws, sure that he's going to drop me. Rusty dips his eagle head to look at me upside down. His tightening grip seems to be assuring me that I'm safe. I hope he's right. As I take in a deep breath, I hold on as tightly as I can and look out over the land in front of me. The air swirling around me pulls tiny tears from my eyes, blurring my vision, while also releasing the mud chunks caked to my body. Soon my backbone relaxes. Am I flying?

I look behind us. Through my blurry eyes, I can see the aircraft that carried us here. It sits in the middle of a large concrete field surrounded by several other airplanes and gets smaller as we move forward. There isn't a runway, but we hadn't needed one. We landed like a helicopter.

I turn back to the direction Rusty is flying in. The land is laid out beautifully, covered in perfectly trimmed bright-green grass that stretches over the hilly terrain for miles, meeting with the green mountains in the distance. A gray stone path winds its way through the grass, crossing here and there, congested with various-sized groups of Pepps dressed in camouflage. The rich grassy terrain is interrupted by occasional groups of trees, some tall, some green, and some with the same red leaves as those close to my home.

Tilting to the left, Rusty heads to the large plush mountains in the distance with peaks going on for miles.

He approaches one mountain. *At least I think it's a mountain.* With its peak missing, it looks much like a pine tree with its top chopped off.

Rusty flies toward the middle of the mountain, his wings moving us at an increased speed until he descends in the direction of a large wooden balcony protruding from the side of the mountain. His wings shift position, allowing him to hover over the deck space. This must be where he's taking me. We're a couple of feet away when his claws release me, sending me flying down to the wood.

I try to catch myself with my hands but end up flipping ungracefully, landing with a thud. Standing with his claws on the railing surrounding the deck, Rusty changes back into his human form.

"Sorry about that," he says, leaping down to help me up. "I thought you were closer."

I only grunt in response. Pushing myself up, I try not to take the blunder personally.

Rusty waves to the mountain. "This place is called GreenGrotto, and it's where most of the unmarried Pepps live." On the side of the mountain are dozens of lit rooms carved into it, all behind large sliding glass doors. I cock my head at the one in front of me. Through the glass doors, the room seems odd. It takes me a moment to realize that it's made of wood, not rock, like I would expect inside the mountain, and it's perfectly circular, as if the room itself resides inside a very large hollowed-out branch.

Rusty slides open the door and walks inside, where a girl, maybe a year or two older than me, with long blonde hair pulled into a ponytail sits on a bed. "Cody!" he exclaims, apparently happy to see the girl. I watch his enthusiastic demeanor soften around her. When she stands, he gently wraps an arm around her slim figure, giving her a hug, which she gratefully accepts.

"This is Alena," Rusty says. Cody did have a smile on her face—until she saw me. I hesitantly walk through the door.

"Is she really defective?" Cody asks Rusty quietly, in a similar accent to his.

I can't help but wonder if she's referring to the totem or me.

"Yes, the totem is the perfect complement to Mark's."

As they whisper quietly, I observe Cody's features. Several strands of blonde hair have fallen loose from her long ponytail and softly frame her slender face and rosy cheeks. Her blue eyes are shadowed by gray shades of makeup, and her teeth are not just white but, well, perfectly perfect. In fact, everything about her seems perfect.

"Do you think she's a spy?" Cody continues to speak as if I'm not in the room.

"I don't," Rusty responds confidently but seriously. I don't know whether to be grateful for his trust or annoyed by it.

Looking at me for the first time, Cody says, "I'm not sure what I think yet, but we get to spend the next couple of days together, so hopefully we'll find out soon."

Wonderful. Not only am I an untrusted prisoner here, my prison guard is a beautiful girl who makes me feel uglier every time she looks at me.

"I better be off," Rusty says. "I have a lot of sleep to catch up on, but I'll try to visit you soon, Alena, just to make sure Cody is being nice." Rusty smirks at Cody, pounding her on the back.

Cody's not amused. She rolls her eyes behind Rusty when he walks through the only other door in the room, the one that leads into the mountain. With Rusty gone, the room is silent. I stare at the floor, unsure of what to do until Cody sighs.

"Well, this is your room for now. You can have that bed over there."

I look up and observe the room. Two twin-sized beds sit on curved frames to conform to the roundness of the floor. They're accompanied by two nightstands and two holes in the wall for closets. Old-fashioned oil lamps, resting on the nightstands with smoked-glass covers, suggest these are the main source of light.

I grieve, ever so slightly at the bareness of it. There's no TV, not even outlets for electronics. I sit on the bed and inwardly groan. The mattress is hard.

Cody enters the closet next to her bed and emerges carrying some clothes and shoes.

"You look like you could use a shower," she says with a disgusted side glance. "Why don't we start with that?"

***

I try to keep up with Cody as we walk through the dark wooden-framed tunnel. Parched torches buried in the wooden walls provide flickering light as we navigate the tunnel ... that branches into more tunnels. I glance back in the direction we came, hoping to memorize the route to my new room, only to find three halls staring at me with no way for me to identify which one is mine. I step closer to Cody.

The halls are congested with Pepps. Thankfully, my attempts at appearing invisible seem to be working. Nobody talks to me.

We round a corner, and a wall of mist slams into my face, forcing me to look up.

"Unfortunately, there aren't bathrooms in our room, so you'll have to do everything in here," Cody says.

We enter a dark, stifling room, barely lit, that emanates a pleasant smell of wet rock, like the scent in the air after a light rain on a sunny day.

In the middle of the room, a waist-high island with a double-sided mirror stands with sinks carefully placed on the counter. *Can anyone see themselves in those mirrors?* It's so dark in here.

"Those are the toilets," Cody says, pointing to the holes in the wall on the left. "There are no doors, but the darkness offers some privacy." I listen to continuous water sloshing in what must be the toilet. "Green-Grotto is made up of two large trees growing inside a mountain. They absorb water through their roots and bring it up where it's used in the bathrooms and kitchen. The water then takes the waste straight down to below the tree, where it's decomposed and used as fertilizer." Cody scrunches her nose at this last detail.

Pointing to the other holes on the right, she continues. "These are the showers, also lacking curtains, but there's also no light in them. You're about my size." She hands me the stack of clothes in her hands. "These clothes should fit you. Go ahead and shower. Take your time." She gestures for me to pick one.

I walk away from Cody, trying not to peek into a shower that's occupied, and find a vacant one at the end. I set the clean clothes on a bench in the hole and hang my dirty clothes on the hooks perched on the wall. I hold out my hand and touch the water. I sigh. It's warm.

I step into the shower, grateful to finally be rid of the mud caking my body. But cleaning my body isn't the only thing the water does. It triggers something inside me, and the tears I've been trying so hard to keep down suddenly ache to come through. Within the comfort of the shower I let them fall, crying quietly at first, until regret for leaving my family overflows, taking full advantage of the open floodgates. I stand in the shower sobbing with my face in my hands. Things haven't gone at all the way I pictured them in my mind. *Why was I so stupid to come here?*

How long will I have to stay here since they can't remove my totem? Why didn't Mark tell me this is how it would be?

I cry for a long time, but eventually my tears deplete, leaving me exhausted. I step out of the water with no towel, then put on the borrowed clothes that fit almost perfectly. With my muddy clothes in my arms, I make my way back to Cody.

Without saying a word, she leads me out of the bathroom and back to our room through the maze of tunnels. I try to memorize the way, but it's difficult. The tunnels all look the same, and there are so many of them.

When we get back to the room, I sit on my bed, ready to succumb to my prison. I ignore Cody, moving about the room, relighting the lamp, arranging her blankets, until I see her fiddling with a black band on her arm. It's like the one I saw on Rusty. She unwraps it like a bandage, and then a large black rock plops out and lands on her bed. Cody stretches her arm and rubs it in relief.

I want to turn away, but the black rock begins to move, and I can't take my eyes off it. It opens much like a roly-poly would, into a tiny black creature with a head, body, two arms, and two legs, then walks like a human. Atop its head, two long black tendrils swoop back, swaying as it moves from the bed to the nightstand. When it reaches the top of the nightstand, it closes back up into its rock form.

"What is that?" I squeak.

Cody scoots up her bed and grabs a book. "It's my Magbaby. It's how I communicate with Pepps in Petrichor when I'm down on runs below." Cody stops talking as if that should explain everything, but then after looking at my confused face she tries again.

"A couple of miles away from here there's a large magnetic mountain where these are born. There's an incredible magnetic force between the Magbabies and the Mother Mountain. And when you flip this switch on the bottom"—Cody points to a gray protrusion that can be moved back and forth—"the magnetic force is activated, and they fly off to the mountain at an incredible speed.

"Our communicators who live with non-Pepps each have one of these, and when they need to send us a message, we get it within an hour no matter where they are in the world. When the Magbaby crashes into the mountain, it falls to the base, where our messengers pick it up and take it to whoever is addressed on the note. Even though Magbabies are mainly communicators drawn to the mountain, they're also alive. My Magbaby can find me anywhere I am in the world, and I can send her on special errands if I need to."

I recall the black rock Mark used at the rendezvous point. Was that a Magbaby? And not only are they alive but they have genders?

"They're also great friends," Cody continues. "I'm guessing the chief will give you one so you can communicate with your family, once he learns he can trust you."

Her words stab at me. *If he can trust me.*

Suddenly very annoyed, I retort, "So phones don't work here, I guess." I pull my phone out of my pile of wet clothes. Cody's head raises, and her eyes flicker cautiously to my phone.

"Alena, may I see that?" Her reaction makes me want to hide the phone, but it whips out of my hand, into the air, and bursts into flames before I can say no.

Gaping at her in shock, I want to demand an explanation for what she just did. But Cody dismisses me completely by looking down at her book.

After a couple of minutes, she finally says, "We don't have any electronics here. No TV, no internet, no nothing."

I noticed! I want to scream.

Not sure what I'm supposed to do all day, I lie on my bed and examine the lines in the wood above me. I try to sleep but my mind races, recalling the events of the last twenty-four hours. My hands begin to tremble, the anger and frustration welling up inside me. There's no conversation, no entertainment, and no freedom. I might just go crazy in this place.

Chapter 7

The orange color seeping in through the window indicates the sun is getting ready to set. Cody is in her same position—sitting on her bed, reading in the dim candlelight. The position she's been in for the last three days.

I'm ready to be admitted to a mental ward. I never knew boredom was so emotionally and physically exhausting. All I want to do is sleep, but my body can't do it anymore. Instead, I lie on my bed staring at the ceiling. I can't even raise my arms, the energy completely drained from my being.

My mood is more than just black now. It's dangerous. My anger with the Pepps boils inside me, making me want to explode from the pressure. I long for the explosion. Maybe it would at least provide some relief from the constant squeezing and heaviness that has set in over my entire body. I had another panic attack last night, thanks to my new life as a prisoner, and it lasted longer than normal. Luckily, Cody was sound asleep and didn't wake up. But the event, and the lingering ache in my chest, has discouraged me even more.

I wish I had thought to bring the medicine Dad gave me. I could sure use it now.

I scoff at the thought of Mark telling me he could control the way he feels. How in the world does he do it? And when will he be coming to Petrichor?

A loud knock on the door startles me.

"Come in," Cody shouts. Her voice is tired, and I can tell she's getting antsy as well from staying inside for three days.

I don't bother sitting up in bed when the person enters. In fact, I turn my body toward the wall, hoping I don't have to notice them at all.

"How's my favorite defective Pepp?" Rusty's loud voice reverberates through our quiet insane asylum. I close my eyes and moan quietly. I don't want to face him.

"What do you want?" Cody asks, trying to act annoyed, but I hear the relief in her voice. She's happy to talk to another being.

"Cody!" Rusty responds excitedly, ignoring her tone. "I've missed you!" I turn around in time to see Cody swipe away Rusty's hand as he ruffles her hair. Despite her hostility, Rusty pulls her into a hug, which she accepts. I lower my eyes, uncomfortable with their intimacy.

"I was instructed to bring Miss Alena up to the courtyard to hang out," Rusty tells Cody. Then looking at me he says, "The chief thought you could use some fresh air."

I hear Cody mutter, "Thank you," and another pang hits my chest.

"I'll take her up, so you can go do whatever you want," Rusty says, giving Cody permission to escape.

Cody practically runs to the door without looking back.

As much as I want to get out of here too, I don't really want to go anywhere, not with Rusty and not to the courtyard.

Kneeling next to my bed, Rusty puts his hand on mine. I don't let it rest there too long before pulling mine away.

"Let's go get you some dinner. How does steak sound?" he asks.

I sigh. Nothing could have appealed to me more. Since Cody and I haven't been able to leave to get food, she's had to create it using her powers. But her knowledge of creating food is obviously very limited. Anything other than runny rice and biscuits sounds amazing right now.

Rusty takes my hand and pulls me to standing, then guides me to the glass door. I avoid my reflection in the mirror when we pass it. I'm pretty sure I look like a mess right now.

"I'm going to fly you like I did before. Is that alright?" he asks me. I don't even acknowledge his question, knowing I have no choice in the matter. Even though I'm expecting it, the morph still catches me by surprise, and I step back, waiting for him to pick me up.

His claws reach effortlessly around me and lift me into the air.

Rusty flies me up the mountainside, passing the many protruding balconies. The setting sun casts shadows across Petrichor while simultaneously drawing out the green pigmentation of the grass and trees, making the color bright and calming. I catch my mood softening at the scene, so I tighten my fists. I don't want to let go of my black mood. Not yet.

It takes us only minutes to fly the miles to the top of the mountain, and my ears pop from ascending so quickly. Finally rising over the top, I see why the mountain lacks a peak. A rectangle courtyard the size of a large sports field spreads out below us, packed with hundreds of Pepps mingling and eating food. The soft beat of music reaches my ears, and I instantly become overwhelmed with the scene before me. *Can I just go back to my room?*

After flying to the far end of the courtyard, Rusty sets me down, much gentler this time, and morphs back into a Pepp. I reluctantly look around. A bushy garden of flowers borders the entirety of the brick courtyard, expanding into lush gardens that climb onto wooden balconies. I catch a glimpse of a rock river in the garden next to me and watch as the water travels to the edge of the courtyard and disappears out of sight. If I wasn't so overwhelmed with being here, it might just look pretty.

Rusty puts his arm around my shoulders and guides me to large, crowded tables overflowing with food. While we wait in line, I observe two Pepps in front of me who are creating bubbles of ... what is that? Black ooze? With their hands in the air. They tease each other with the stuff, threatening to unload it on each other. I scoot further away, not wanting to be a part of it.

When we finally reach the table, I take a plate, and for the first time realize how truly hungry I am. I grab a piece of every vegetable, fruit, and cracker offered. By the time I reach the steak at the end of the table, I no longer have room on my plate, but Rusty hands me another one, and I fill it with the wonderfully aromatic meat.

With full plates, I'm not sure what to do now. I turn to Rusty, hoping he'll tell me where to sit, but I find him looking at the sun. In fact, the entire courtyard has paused, including the band, to watch the last bits of sun drop below the horizon. Only the top of it is visible now, and it doesn't take long, maybe seconds, for that portion to disappear, but that isn't what captivates me. It's the silence and calm of everything around us as the orange light fades. It's almost as if everything—the clouds, the trees, the birds—are saluting the sun, saying good-bye for the night.

I'm so captivated by the quiet peace that I jump when dozens of tiki torches burst into flame around the border of the darkened courtyard.

Five large bonfires blast sporadically throughout the space, and suddenly everything comes back to life, including the band, with their singers, and guitar players.

I finally surrender, allowing a piece of warmth to flow inside me. That was cool.

I follow Rusty through the crowds of laughing Pepps, past several large bonfires, until we reach a less occupied bonfire on the far end. Rusty points to one of the old, weathered logs sitting around the fire, indicating I should sit. The log is rough, but I almost don't notice, thanks to the comforting fire that warms the now chilly air.

Just as I'm about to take a bite of meat, a shout echoes behind me.

The consolidated groups hush, and I follow their gazes to face the sound. The chief is standing on top of one of the rock flower walls behind us. His white collared shirt hangs untucked. The top button is unclasped, exposing the graying hair on his neck. I haven't seen him since the aircraft. I don't even know what he and the council decided to do with me.

"Thank you," he says. "I won't take much of your time, but the council and I had a meeting tonight, and we've made some major changes to our runs due to the ongoing attacks on our teams the past few months. I wanted to come here in person to tell you."

The area hushes even more before he proceeds.

"The council and I have all agreed that we need to arm you with weapons to protect yourselves on your runs."

This piece of information causes an eruption of whispers around the courtyard. They seem both confused and excited.

"From now on, each group leader will be given one weapon and will be instructed on how to use it to protect the team."

The whispers grow louder, but the chief hushes them by raising his hand. “You know this goes against our most fundamental beliefs as Pepps. I must remind you of the severity of this action. Damage done by hurting someone depletes our power, and, right now, with all the Pepps we’ve lost, our power is already in jeopardy. This wasn’t an easy decision for us to make. But you are important to me, and your work is vital for everyone’s survival. We want you to be able to protect yourselves. The leaders of each group will begin training with Rusty tomorrow.”

I steal a glance at Rusty behind me, his face serious but not surprised.

Waving his hand in the air, the chief says, “You can proceed with your night. Thank you.” Then, just as Rusty had done, the chief turns into a large eagle and flies away.

The whisperings in the courtyard grow louder.

“Finally!” a boy across the bonfire exclaims. “It’s about time we’re allowed to protect ourselves!”

A girl in the group seems annoyed. “Don’t be stupid, Conrad. This is going to hurt us more than protect us. I don’t know why they would agree to something like this.”

Others around the group continue to argue.

I take a bite of my food, thinking, then tap Rusty on the shoulder. “Could you not use weapons before?”

Rusty sits up at my question, shaking his head. “No. Hurting another is something we’ve always been forbidden to do. Not only because we’re trying to help everyone by spreading Peppate, but because it sucks out our power. It makes us powerless.”

Sitting up straighter, he releases a long breath and interrupts the arguing by shouting, “Who’s up for a game of Mafia?”

I’m surprised by the sudden change in subject, but the worries of the Pepps melt into excitement at the mention of the game. Soon a crowd forms around us, forcing me to scoot closer to Rusty. Cody emerges from the crowd and sits on my other side, her shoulders more relaxed. The excitement tries to prick its way into my body at the mention of a game, but I'm too intimidated by the group to give it any attention.

Rusty nudges my arm. "Have you ever played Mafia?"

Of course I've played the game before, but I'm not going to admit that. I don't want to participate.

Rusty smiles. "You have."

I curse inwardly. *Is my face that readable?*

"Well, we have a few adjustments to the game." His expression turns mischievous.

Cody nudges me on my other side. "Rusty is the worst to play with. He cheats every time." Then, speaking to the rest of the group, she says, "Anyone but Rusty can be the Mafia."

Rusty groans as if these words hurt him, but he proceeds to explain the rules to me. "We have a host. I suggest that I be the host if I'm not allowed to be the Mafia." Rusty shoots Cody a ribbing look. "You all put your heads down. I'll walk around and choose the Mafia by tapping once on their head. Two taps for the constables. Since we're such a big group tonight, we'll have three Mafias and three constables. Everyone else will be towns people.

"After I've chosen the Mafias and constables, I'll ask everyone to put their heads down, then ask the Mafias to raise their heads and choose who they want to kill. Without speaking, they'll point to who they want to kill. Their heads will go down, and then the constables will pull their heads up. I'll ask them who they think the Mafias are. I'm allowed to indicate yes or no with my head, and then when everyone's head comes up, I'll announce those who've been killed. The constables will try to convince everyone else who the Mafia is. The goal is to all vote together and kill the Mafias."

Looking at me, Rusty searches my eyes to see if I understand. The game sounds the same as how I played it at home. "What are the adjustments?" I ask, but Rusty winks.

"You'll see." Then, shouting to the group, he says, "Everyone ready?"

I feel sick, suddenly wishing for the quiet room I've been a prisoner in for the last three days.

With loud affirmations rippling through the group, Rusty proceeds with the game by telling everyone to put their heads down. I hesitate, wondering if I could just get away with watching, but Rusty insists I play. I put my head down and close my eyes. My hands start to sweat against the plate I'm holding.

"I'm choosing the Mafias now by tapping once on your head." Rusty shuffles across the brick, stopping several times here and there, trying to confuse the group. I'm not chosen. I don't know whether to be relieved or not.

"I'm now choosing the constables by tapping twice on the head." Again, he shuffles around the entire area. My head remains untouched. I'm a towns person.

Clearing his throat, Rusty begins the game.

"Mafias, raise your heads. Who do you want to kill?" The group is quiet. All I can hear is my beating heart as I squeeze my eyes shut. I hear nothing from the Mafias that quietly peruse the group, picking out their prey.

"Mafias heads down. Constables, heads up," Rusty shouts. "Who do you think the Mafias are?" Still, I hear nothing.

"Constables, heads down. Everybody, heads up."

I lift my head, simultaneously, with everyone else and take in a deep breath, curious about what's going to happen. Just as I look at Rusty for further instruction, a burst of ice shoots straight toward me. I close my eyes and bring my hands to my face, bracing for the impact, when it hits right next to me. I open my eyes in horror to find Cody frozen in a large block of ice, the weight of the ice making her fall back. I shriek when she lands with a thud.

With wide eyes, I look at Rusty, who sends out another shot of power toward a boy on the other side of the fire, turning him into ice. Turning to the last victim, Rusty shoots something out, but instead of ice surrounding the girl, hundreds of bugs crawl all over her body. The girl starts to scream. The blood drains from my face. I look at Rusty, who's smiling along with all the other Pepps. Pointing to the girl, all he says is, "Fire ants."

So, these are the adjustments to their game. The deaths are brutally realistic. *Fire ants?* Rusty winks at me as if that's supposed to calm my shaking hands.

I don't want to play anymore.

"We know who is dead, so who do you think the Mafias are?" Rusty asks. The others begin to converse quietly, trying to figure it out, but I can't concentrate on their conversation. My eyes are frozen on the girl who's still running and shrieking in pain. I don't want fire ants on me!

The group finally accuses one boy of being a Mafia and decides to put him to death by hanging. I watch as the boy falls over apparently choking. *I can't believe anyone would be excited to play this game!*

After he collapses from lack of air, Rusty announces the boy is innocent. The boy gasps for breath once he's released and leaves the group, murmuring angrily about those who had him put to death.

I sit, trying to think of a way I can sneak out of the group. *Maybe when everyone's head is down, I can crawl away.* I look behind me, and my stomach tightens. I'm pinned in by onlookers standing there. I'll have to push my way through.

Rusty begins a new round, and my chest begins to scream in protest, but I obey when Rusty demands we all put our heads down.

"Mafias, heads up. Who do you want to kill?" I keep my eyes tightly shut even though I want to peek so badly.

I take in a deep breath.

Then everything goes black.

Chapter 8

"See, I told you so." I hear the soft murmur of several voices close by. The noise pulls me from my dark sleep, and immediately tears begin to flow from my eyes. I don't want to wake up.

I try to slip back into the darkness, but then I recall the event around the fire. *What happened?* I pull my eyes open, finding myself staring at a stone ceiling in a dim room. Large red and blue tapestries drape the walls, covering them completely.

I lift my head, only to lay it back down on the soft pillow beneath me as a painful pounding pierces through my eyes to the back of my neck. I moan.

"Alena." A familiar voice calls to me. I squint my eyes open again to see Rusty's hazel gaze in front of me. "Alena, I'm sorry I had to do that, but ..." Kneeling beside me, he wraps my hand in his. "I have good news. We know you're innocent."

I furrow my eyebrows, not caring much about what he's saying and more focused on asking, "What happened?"

I try to sit up again, but Rusty pushes me back down. "Lay there for a little while longer. Freezing is the only way I was able to disable you without depleting my power. Unfortunately, it shakes up the equilibrium of the brain. It'll take a minute for the pain to go away."

My eyebrows furrow more. "Freezing?" The events of the night slam into my recollection. "You froze me?"

"Yeah," Rusty says softly. "Sorry. The chief wanted to check your memories to see if you're innocent." The truth of what he's saying hits me like a punch in the gut. I sit up quickly, ignoring the pain in my head.

"You checked my memories?" Even though deep down inside I can understand their need to do this, I can't help but feel incredibly hurt. Tears build up behind my eyes. *When will this nightmare end?*

I look around the room. A group of Pepps are gathered around a table. The chief is among them along with the medic, Jeter, who I met on the first day. The chief reaches his hand to his right ear before leaning his head sideways as if trying to get something out.

"Did they all see my memories?" I ask, clenching my fists.

"Alena, it isn't as bad as it sounds." Rusty tries to reassure me. "Jeter has a bug that goes into the brain and sorts through memories efficiently. The bug only searched you for any memories with mention of the clan and your totem. Then it went into the chief's brain and showed him what it found. He didn't see all your memories, just those related to us."

This should relieve me, but I can't push aside the horrible feeling of betrayal in my gut.

The other members of the room start whispering until the chief's blue eyes meet mine. Unable to help myself, I thrust my anger at him. *I hate you*.

The chief seems to understand my silent attack. Waving his hand to those around him, he says, "Let me talk to her alone." I look at the blanket now, clenching my jaw. I don't want to talk to anyone, especially him. I ignore the eyes of the Pepps boring into me as they shuffle out the door and pull my hand away from Rusty.

"I am sorry, Alena," he says quietly before leaving.

I bury my face in my hands.

After the door closes, the chief sits beside me. My cries turn into sobs, which embarrasses me even more. Why do I have to cry?

Sitting quietly, the chief hands me a tissue, which I ignore. I pull my knees up under the blanket and turn away from him, willing the world to go away.

Unfortunately, I can't cry forever. Even if I wanted to. Eventually my sobs slow, and I wipe my nose with my hand.

The chief takes this opportunity to speak. "Mark told me that when you found him, you were hoping to get the totem removed."

Mark's brown eyes and concerned face flashes through my mind. Then a tingle in my back where he had placed his hand the night he guided me to the airplane. But the tingle is quickly replaced with stinging needles that weave up and down my spine. He betrayed me. Mark never mentioned any of this, me becoming a prisoner, getting my memories checked. Why did I let him convince me to come here?

"The clan has gotten closer to your hometown," the chief says quietly. "Issy said you went into hiding after you found the vine. Mixed with the Doler your vine creates and being stuck indoors, I'm guessing it has left you feeling ... crappy?" The chief sits quietly waiting for a response from me, but I don't want to be pulled into his conversation, so I keep my body turned away from him.

Unfazed by my coldness, he continues to talk. "You were right to seek us out, and you were right to come here. You're safer here from the clan." Leaning forward onto his elbows, the chief rubs his face in fatigue. "I'm still sorry, though, Alena."

The room is quiet for a long time, and I wonder if the old man has fallen asleep, but when I steal a look at him, his eyes bore into mine.

"You know, the clan wasn't always after us," he says. I still try to ignore him.

He leans back in his chair and continues to talk. "The Pepps and humans used to live and work together for the first thousand years of our existence. We need each other, we always have, and everyone seemed to know that then. But then somewhere along the way the humans became blinded and saw only what they lacked—power. They tried to get the Pepps to use their power for their gain. But we couldn't. We can only use our power to help spread Peppate. Otherwise, we lose it and become just like them—powerless.

"There was a man named Tadon Sybalt, who lived about seven hundred years ago. He was close friends with the Pepps and asked that they give him their power. This was before Pepps had created the totems out of necessity. The Pepps couldn't and wouldn't give him their power. He begged and begged, promising he would only use it to become a strong leader. Finally, after begging for several years, he disappeared. But not before he threatened the Pepps that if they didn't meet his demand, he would spend the rest of his life trying to eradicate them."

Nice. I guess my reward for being innocent is a history lesson.

"Security measures were taken to protect Petrichor from Tadon. But the Pepps weren't able to protect themselves during the dropdowns and runs. A couple of years after Tadon disappeared, Pepps started going missing. By the time they were found, it was always too late. They were always dead, slashed cruelly into hundreds of pieces. We lost many Pepps and a lot of power before the killer was caught. And the killer was, of course, Tadon. In his craving for power, he had captured hundreds of

Pepps and killed them while trying to figure out the source of their power."

My mind moves through his words. Tadon Sybalt. The initial S. "Is that where the S attacks came from? It stands for Sybalt?"

The chief nods. "Yes." Then he continues. "The Pepps' numbers became so depleted because of him that their ability to spread Peppate was becoming impossible, and it was taking its toll on the entire circle of life. It was during this time that the Pepps started collecting abandoned children to help here in Petrichor. They figured out a way to transfer their power to the orphans, through... the vine. It ultimately did what Tadon was trying to do." The chief shakes his head. "The only difference is that we're able to train the young orphans carefully, teaching them the importance of the Peppate. Teaching them not to abuse the power.

"Over the years, men with the same craving for power had adopted Sybalt's trends and tried to kill the Pepps, but they haven't succeeded. Thankfully the attacks finally stopped. Until recently. A couple of years ago the Pepps started going missing again, and some have been killed in the same way Tadon killed the Pepps. Large gashes, with the letter S engraved with poison. I thought it was just a fluke, that someone was picking up where Sybalt left off." The chief pauses before looking at me with those piercing blue eyes. "That is, until odd totems started showing up. First a piece of one on a Pepp named Danny, and then one year ago another on Mark."

Danny. Was that the boy Mark mentioned? His friend? He has a bad totem too?

"When I saw Mark's bare arm, I knew something was terribly wrong. For the first time it looks as though someone has not only found out our secret about the source of our power and how it works but they manipulated it against us. I can't tell you how grateful I am that Mark didn't attach the other half of the totem. Because if he had … Well, I guess we don't know what would have happened. But I'm guessing it wouldn't have been good."

I don't know at what point in the conversation I started looking at the chief, but I can see the burden of death weighing on him now, concern and worry woven into every crease on his worn face. His devotion to the Pepps chips away at the hate I felt for him a couple of minutes ago.

"We've done everything we can to examine the totem on his arm, but the moment we remove any part of it for examination, the vine turns to dust. The medic, Jeter, has spent countless hours trying to listen to other elements, other algorithms of the vine, but other than the fact that it produces Doler instead of Peppate, he can't tell what's different."

The defeat is evident in his voice, and he rubs his graying beard.

"Alena, I'm truly sorry for all you've been through this week—and the past several months. I hope you can forgive me. I just want you to have a little more understanding of why we did what we did. Lately, those Pepps who don't turn up dead are taken, and we are grieved every time we lose another. I think I told you before, but there are seventy-five missing Pepps, and they weigh heavily on our minds. I hope you can understand."

I do understand, and even though I still want to hate the chief, I nod.

"We're searching for answers. We've captured some of the clan members that have tried to capture Mark. We've searched their memories. Unfortunately, the clan members don't know much. They're just killing for money. We're hoping our Pepps are still alive." With mournful eyes, the chief pleads, "Are you willing to stay here and help us out while we look for a solution to both our problems?"

Tears begin yanking at my eyes again. Unlike before, I know exactly what I'm committing to now, something I don't want. A life without my family, in a foreign place where I may never be accepted because of my defective vine. I *don't* want to stay here.

But, at the same time, the truth tugs at me. I will never be able to safely go home until I can figure out what's on my arm and get it off. I must stay. I need more answers.

So, I nod. The chief taps my hand, and his eyes turn soft. "Thank you. I'll be meeting with your family in a few hours. They're very concerned about you, and they have every right to be. I'll try to ease their worries. I'll also try to arrange a time for you to see them soon."

My family. The mention of them both comforts me and saddens me. Oh, how I miss them. *Will they be angry with me for leaving?* The chief walks to the door and calls out for Rusty, who enters the room quickly, sending a concerned look my way.

I groan. Perhaps I don't want to stay here. The very sight of Rusty's golden hair and tanned skin recoils my commitment, provoking a bitterness that makes me want to punch him in the face for freezing me tonight. The old Alena would have. My cheeks flush. I wonder what memories they saw. I hope they didn't see any of my thoughts from the last couple of days. Of Mark.

The chief interrupts my seething. "Alena, in three weeks there is what we call an initiation game for the trainees who are turning sixteen this quarter. It will be the first time they are given a full capsule of power to activate their totems, and it's the event in which their totems will match them with a job here in Petrichor." The chief comes to my bed and holds out his hand, indicating I need to stand up. "I want you to participate in it."

My heart drops and my knees go weak. Mark had mentioned initiation, but I never thought I'd have to participate. *Sixteen-year-olds?* I don't want to have to do anything with kids who are two years younger than me. If Rusty wasn't standing in the room, I might have burst into tears again.

The chief picks up on my hesitancy. "I know you might not want to, but it will be a great opportunity for us to see how we can best use you here in Petrichor. I would like you to start training for the game tomorrow, is that okay?"

I bite my lip and tighten my fists. I already hate my decision to stay here.

"Alena, I need to tell you that at the end of the games we have a large dinner at the top of Training Mountain where each initiate matches into their jobs, and then they morph into an eagle. Because of your defective totem, it's very important that you do not morph. We aren't quite sure what your totem is capable of, and when Mark morphed ..." He glances warily at Rusty. "Bad things happened."

I remember Rusty being hesitant to tell me the secret to morphing. Maybe he was right to keep that from me.

"Your trainer will give you capsule power that you can insert into the hole over the heart of your totem since you won't be able to generate it yourself. You'll be able to practice with that." Then he turns to Rusty, "Will you take her back to GreenGrotto for me, Rusty?"

I bite my lip harder. *Why Rusty?*

"Before you go, I need to give you this." The chief places a package wrapped in brown paper into my hands. "It's your Magbaby. I'm sorry it's taken me so long to get this to you. Use it to communicate with your family. I will also be getting one to your mom and dad. Cody can explain how to use it."

I take the round object carefully. A Magbaby? One of those weird roly-poly creatures? I finally get to communicate with my family?

"You can go now." The chief dismisses us. I prudently avoid Rusty's gaze as we walk out.

The door gives way to a white concrete hallway lit with torches. The flickering flames cast shimmering shadows through the glass rooms lining the hall. I can see right through the glass to the dark night outside. As curious as I am about the rooms, though, I don't bother asking Rusty what they are. I don't want to talk to him at all.

Out in the crispy night air, after descending the stairs and emerging from the large structure, Rusty asks me awkwardly if he can carry me like before. I roll my eyes and look away from him, shaking my head.

With a sigh, Rusty morphs and effortlessly picks me up. I keep my eyes closed the entire flight, not wanting to see my new stockade right now, as beautiful as it may be. Before I know it, we're on my balcony. This time, Rusty puts me down carefully. Without a word, I start walking toward the door. But he grabs my arm.

"Alena," he says softly, his apologetic voice softening a sliver of my cold heart. I meet his gaze for the first time.

"I really am sorry." His hazel eyes pacify my anger for a split second, long enough for me to accept his apology with a nod before I disappear into my room, leaving him in the dark night.

Chapter 9

I was supposed to go to initiation training this morning. The chief had made things sound so easy last night when I agreed to it, but this morning I remembered I don't want to participate in anything. Cody left early, and when Rusty came to collect me for training, I just couldn't bring myself to go. Ultimately, he left me alone and hasn't been back.

My lap is now covered with letters from my family. I was finally able to communicate with them, thanks to the Magbaby the chief gave me.

Its name, or rather, *her* name, is Breccia, which I learned when I opened her up this morning. With her long eyelashes, a silver ring pierced into her tendrils, and a curvy body, she's definitely a girl. I never imagined rocks could have genders, but apparently here they do. She's also shy and nice. I don't know why, but this comforts me. Perhaps she can be my friend.

I glance at her now curled up on my pillow. It took her a while to find my family based on my instructions. I guess they use coordinates here, for everything. And I don't know anything about coordinates. But she eventually got there.

Communicating with my family made me feel better initially. Mom and Dad at least didn't kill Caleb. They said they had a long talk with the chief, that he told them about freezing me to search my memories. Even though they don't entirely trust him yet, even they admitted they feel safer with me here. They never told me before, but they've been terrified of the killers finding me since I got the vine. They knew they couldn't truly protect me. So they're glad I'm here with other Pepps. They made me promise to write every day, so they know I'm okay.

In the end, though, communicating with my family just made me more homesick and bitter. I wanted to tell them how *I* felt about all the bad things the Pepps have done to me. Keeping me a prisoner for three days, freezing me with their power, and checking my memories. But I couldn't bring myself to do it. As much as I hate it here, I know this is the safest place for me. Complaining to my family will only worry them more. And they're worried, I can tell.

But just because I didn't tell my family how I feel about what's happened doesn't mean I can't relive every awful moment in my mind. Heat rises in my face as I recall each encounter with the Pepps. I feel so betrayed and untrusted.

I hear footsteps approaching the door. My eyes flicker briefly to the glass shattered across the floor in front of me. I forgot to open the sliding door before flipping the switch on Breccia the first time I released her. She shot right through the glass, breaking it into a thousand pieces. I should care about the mess and try to clean it up, but I don't. Instead, I glare out the broken window.

Cody walks through the door.

"There was a book outside the door for you ..." Her voice trails off when she looks at the room, and then me. I'm sure my eyes are swollen and red, and I look a mess, but that isn't why she stops. My emotions are palpable in the room. I subliminally dare her to tag them, sure I will explode in a much-needed explosion.

"Are you okay?" Cody asks, her voice sounding truly concerned for the first time.

Oh, so you're going to be nice to me now? Now that you know I'm innocent?

I ignore her.

Cody doesn't come in any further but quietly turns and says, "I'm going to get us some dinner. I'll be back."

My body relaxes when she shuts the door, but the anger still burrows. I don't want her to come back. I lie on my bed, turning toward the wall, and pretend I'm asleep when she reenters. I hear her set something on my nightstand, but I ignore it as she quietly sits on her bed.

"Do you want to talk about it?" she asks.

I grumble silently. *Of course not.*

"Sometimes talking about things can help you feel better. Tell me what happened last night."

You know what happened. I remain quiet.

Cody clears her throat and begins talking anyway. "Nobody liked Mark when he first got here either. The Pepps were afraid of him, especially after his initiation when he morphed and rebutted all the Peppate in Petrichor. It took weeks for us to feel better from the absence of the element. The Pepps all treated him much like they treat you. But he proved himself and found something he was really good at." Cody's voice softens. "Everyone quietly loves him now."

The mention of Mark triggers a flutter in my stomach, but I quickly extinguish it with my anger. I hate him too.

Lying back on her bed, Cody calmly continues. "The Dino Games."

Unsure of what she's talking about, I turn my head to look at her for the first time.

"The Dino Games are what made Mark popular around here." Cody speaks to the ceiling.

"What are the Dino Games?" Ugh, I silently kick myself. *Why am I encouraging this conversation?* I turn away again.

Seemingly oblivious to my pushback, Cody puts her hands behind her blonde head. "The Dino Games were invented to help the extinct animals, refuged here, live a happy life. I'm sure you've heard about dinosaurs. Well, they used to live with the humans and Pepps, but then they started killing everyone. Stupid animals. So, the Pepps brought them to Petrichor, mainly to use if we ever needed additional protection. The dinosaurs were shrunk down to a bearable size. A safe size. But after hundreds of years the dinosaurs started dying off at earlier ages. So, the Dino Games were created. We take the dinosaurs to a lake down the mountain below Petrichor where they can roam—in their full size—for a couple of days, and then we bring them back. This foray into their semi-normal habitat has begun to extend their lives again."

My eyes widen more and more during Cody's story.

"There are dinosaurs, here?" The fact that they're shrunken doesn't ease my mind at all.

Cody bats her eyes. "If it was up to me, I would just kill the animals. But it's not up to me. Managing them on the trip takes almost all the dino trainers to maintain control. They're supposed to distract the dinosaurs, preventing them from hurting Pepps and promising to shrink them if they get cantankerous. Mark took on the challenge of partnering with our dilophosaurus dinosaur, the fastest and most dangerous of the dinosaurs. He not only prevented it from hurting other dinosaurs or

Pepps, he also got it through the entire trip without having to shrink it, something that's never been done before."

Cody stops now and twirls a piece of her blonde hair.

"How?" I can't hold the question back.

Cody shrugs. "He has this amazing ability to create fire, water, and ice, move rock, and control plants. He's what we call an environmental mover or an *enviro*. Some Pepps are good at controlling the elements of the body to heal or change form, but he controls the elements of land. He was also a hunter before he came here and learned how to think like animals." Cody turns to me. "But I think he's done something to entrance the dilo dinosaur. It obeys his every command." One of Cody's eyebrows lifts. "I have to say, he's a pretty amazing guy."

Her comment agitates me. She's already captivated Rusty. With her beauty, she could easily captivate Mark too. I hate that this bothers me, but it does.

Talking about Mark suddenly has me wondering, for the hundredth time, when he will be coming to Petrichor. Soon?

"You know, the main purpose of initiation is to know where to put you. The job you're placed in will give you a sense of purpose. Just like Mark was eventually placed with the dinosaurs and was able to prove himself, you'll be placed and have the same opportunity." Cody's face turns serious. "Your job is important. It will help you more than you know."

I want to stop talking to Cody, but the continuous mention of the word *job* churns my stomach. I want to know what job I might be cursed with.

"What jobs are there?" I ask, sitting up.

"There are many," Cody says, "There are those associated with the messages. This would include workers at Magnetic Mountain, messengers, and supervisors who keep track of where each of the Pepps are. They have orange totems."

I look briefly at Cody's red totem. "So, the color of the totem indicates what job is yours?"

"Yes. Another group would be the caretakers or mothers with white totems. When we get orphans, like me, who join us due to the death of previous Pepp parents, those orphans are placed in families where they can be taken care of. You weren't placed in a family because you're eighteen, but everyone else is. They all live at the Burrows.

"Then there are the educators, yellow totems. They take care of teaching all those under the age of eighteen the ropes of being a Pepp.

"Then there's the council, including the chief, who oversees the Peppate runs, humanitarian dropdowns, and any other major decisions for the Pepps. They have blue totems. There are those who guard and manage the rendezvous points down below. Mark does that on occasion to help out, but it's not his full-time job like dino training is."

Cody marks each job off on her fingers as if counting them.

"There are those who work with the totems, extracting them from the totem tree and training them in the language. They are the only group whose vine stays the natural color. And then there are those who work with the dinosaurs. The green group."

Mark would be a green then. I didn't recall seeing a ribbon wrapped around the totem on his chest, but maybe it's pointless to have a color on his totem since it isn't visible like everyone else's. I have a green eye on my totem, but that's just the power holster over the heart, right? The ribbon wrapped around the extensions of Cody's totem is much different, more visible than the eye of the totem.

"What's Rusty?" I ask. Much to my chagrin, I'm feeling a little better.

Cody laughs and shakes her head. "I don't know what Rusty is. He says he's a strength trainer for the younger groups, teaching them to build up their body muscle for runs, but I think he's also a serviceman for the chief. The chief always has him running *secret* errands." Cody emphasizes the word *secret* with her fingers.

"What are you?" I ask.

"Oh yeah," Cody says. "I'm a medic. I help at the hospital when I am not on runs, and then when I go on a run, my main job is to fix any injuries along the way." As Cody says this she points to her totem. "Medics are red."

Like Scance. I take a silent note of the medic's color. That's the color I want. If I get a color.

"A lot of Pepps have more than one job." Cody says. "You'll notice some of the council members have a couple of different colors, such as the medic, Jeter. He's both a medic and a member of the council, so he has both red and blue."

"How do the totems change color?" I ask, looking down at my brown mark now.

"The brand shop," she says. "After each initiate is placed at the match, they're taken to the brand shop, where a ribbon is wrapped around a portion of the totem on the arm. A needle is poked into the skin to get the ribbon under the vine. It's kind of painful, but the wrapping goes quick."

I've never really been afraid of needles, but as I observe Cody's arm, seeing the red ribbon wind all the way from her elbow to her shoulder, I shudder. That would be a lot of pokes.

The room becomes silent, my mood digressing again. I'm getting overwhelmed.

As if sensing my discouragement, Cody says, "Hey, tell you what, why don't we go for a walk? Let's go to Mossy Hollow. You need to get some things to prepare for initiation, and I could show you the dinos. An outing might do us both some good before it gets dark."

I don't really want to go, but the dark walls of the room are repelling me, and I want to get away from them. Lifting my weak arms, I put on the shoes Cody hands me.

Cody walks to the still shattered window and bends down. I blink twice, then stare wide-eyed when the tiny pieces of glass begin to float in the air, assembling together like a puzzle, until the whole window returns to normal. Man, she can't cook, but she can sure repair a broken window. Tapping my arm, she says, "I'm going to morph and carry you."

***

I stare in awe. In front of me stands what must be the largest tree on the planet, spanning at least a hundred feet wide and twice as tall. Its red and orange leaves stand out against the rest of green Petrichor.

Cody stands beside me, staring too.

"This is MossyHollow," she says. "This is where we get all the clothes and items we need for dropdowns. It's the coolest store you'll ever see." Sighing softly, she adds, "And it has the brightest red leaves. It follows the four seasons of the west and is my favorite tree in the world." Then, grabbing my arm, she pulls on me. "Let's go inside."

I try to stay out of everyone's way when we walk through the busy door. At least until I get a glimpse of the inside. Then I can't seem to move.

The bright, busy room reaches at least a hundred feet up. Tiny drops of water shimmering in the light fall from the canopy of leaves overhead and land in a rippling pool of water sitting in the middle of the room. Rocks of all sizes border the pool, blanketed in a bright-green moss that inches its way toward the water. A brick bridge arches over one of the rivers extending from the pool, almost completely covered in the same green moss. Several Pepps stand on it now, laughing, trying to make the falling water droplets float in the air.

Past the waterfall, on the other side of the room, black bars crisscross where a large portion of the trunk has been cut out, yielding to a beautiful but for some reason protected view of the tall grove of trees behind Mossy Hollow. The loud chatter of Pepps echoes throughout the store as they move through the endless supply of clothes and shoes.

"When we go on dropdowns and even for initiation," Cody says, "we have to take a lot of things—clothes, food, tents, etc. But we need to keep things light because we have to travel far. We could use our power to create these things each time we need them, but we need our power for other things in case we're in danger or get stuck." Pushing through the crowded space, Cody walks to a stand displaying black exercise pants and reaches into a box sitting below the display. "That's why these were created." She pulls out a silver capsule that resembles a shotgun shell. She shows me a red button on the end before pushing it. The capsule opens into the same pair of black leggings on the stand in front of me. I startle at the impossibility of pants coming from something so small.

"When you push the button, the item is released and you can use it, wear it, or do whatever you need with it. When you're done, you push the button again and it turns back into the capsule for easy carrying." Cody points to the bright-red button in the bottom hem of the pants. Upon pushing it, the pants wrinkle back up and return to their metal form. "We can buy everything in a capsule here, such as tents and even cabins. We carry the capsules in a carrier that wraps around our waist, legs, or arms."

Cody searches for something. "Aha, there they are." She walks to a stand close to the shoes and grabs a leather pack. Opening the top flap reveals several empty holes where the capsules could easily and safely fit. Cody wraps it around her waist, showing me how it can be carried. "They still need stored power to work, but it's a lot less than if you had to create the object from scratch."

I blink. The fact that the Pepps can heal broken bodies has been impossible to believe. Now to add that they can shrink objects with one push of a button? How does this power really work? I straighten my body, suddenly itching to learn how to use it. They'll teach me if I complete initiation, right?

I carefully observe the capsule she hands me and follow her around the store. Since her borrowed clothes fit me so well, I don't mind letting her pick out everyday clothes for me as she explains the different climates one has to get used to as a Pepp and the different clothes you have to have on hand.

"We need to go upstairs," Cody says, leading me to a staircase on the left. "Each of Mossy Hollow's branches house the different clothing and equipment capsules needed for different climates. We need to go to the cold room for your tent and sleeping bag."

As I approach the staircase, something in the wooden walls next to the staircase catches my eye.

Glass tubes, dozens of them at least two feet in diameter, weave their way up the wall of Mossy Hollow like a wild hamster cage. I walk closer to one as the familiar shape of an animal, known to be extinct to me, registers in my mind. I gawk in awe.

"These are the dinosaurs," Cody says, approaching the tubes with me. "The power in these tubes keeps them small."

I shake my head and step back, following the tubes with my eyes around all of Mossy Hollow. *There have to be hundreds of them in here.*

Cody points to the back barred part of the room. "Occasionally, the dino trainers will release the dinosaurs into the covert in their full size. There are probably a couple of them out there right now."

That explains the bars.

Grabbing my arm, Cody drags me up the stairs to the cold room. "You know, there's a Dino Game in a couple of months. You'll get to see how it works then. There's even a dance beforehand at the top of GreenGrotto. They throw a big party." Cody's eyes brighten when we walk into the room.

I stop.

The room is huge, filled with all sorts of items that immediately make me miss home.

"This room has items that are needed in cold climates. Coats, heavy tents, and thick sleeping bags. There's even a real iceberg in this room where Pepps can practice climbing ice using special shoes and axes." Cody leads me through the room, picking out supplies.

I follow her around, marveling at the endless selection of supplies. Canoes, kayaks, parasailers, hot air balloons, and even four-wheelers that can all collapse into the small convenient capsules. My body responds to the items in front of me, excitement budding at the thought of being able to own them someday.

Cody places several capsules into the leather band I'm still holding, loading it up with clothes, tents, jackets, shoes, sleeping bags, and food, the *basic necessities* according to Cody. We head to a checkout desk, and Cody hands all my equipment to the boy sitting behind it.

"The chief is giving you an allowance to pay for everything now," she says, pulling out several black coins. "Once you get your job, you'll be able to buy whatever you want."

I'm examining one of the coins she is using to pay, thinking that the first thing I would want to buy on my own is the four-wheeler, when a large crash explodes just outside the room. Startled, I look first at the opening and then back to Cody, who's already bolting toward the sound. The screams from below pull me toward the commotion, against my common sense. When I step onto the staircase platform with everyone else, I see the trouble. A dinosaur is growing bigger off to the left, breaking the glass tube that was housing it. With its large claws, it grapples the side of the tree trunk, its yellow eyes glued to the group of Pepps I've just become a part of.

"Alena, get back in the room." Cody pushes me anxiously. Just then the dinosaur leaps, grabbing on to the railing of the stairs.

I jump backward into the cold room, suddenly finding it very difficult to breathe. While I back away, the Pepps close in on the dinosaur, dispatching ropes to contain it. Someone shouts for the dino trainers.

The dinosaur leaps again, almost into the cold room and onto a girl, digging its claws into her back. She screams, falling to her knees. My heart hammers inside my chest as what I once thought could only be a fictitious creature suddenly becomes very real to me.

The dinosaur convulses, growing larger, and leans its head down to take a bite out of the girl. Thankfully, two large men come running into the room, one jumping onto the dinosaur's back without hesitation. In one swift movement he wraps an iron chain through its mouth and yanks it back, pulling the dinosaur off the girl. The other trainer hovers on the staircase, pointing a tranquilizer gun at the animal, then shooting it in the back.

The dinosaur convulses again, growing even larger and knocking the man off its back. Now drugged, it begins to sway violently, thrashing its head, carelessly approaching the edge of the stair railing again.

The dino trainers try to keep it from falling, but they're too late. The staircase cracks loudly and the dinosaur drops from my view, followed by a loud crunch below. I look at Cody, who's kneeling beside the girl who was attacked. She looks at me, her eyes on guard.

I step over to the stairs with everyone else and look below.

The dinosaur lies motionless on the floor below me. Dead. Or at least I hope it is. Several dino trainers come to collect it. I stand in shock until someone tells everyone to go back to their business. Slowly the sounds in the store get louder, and the Pepps continue with their shopping.

I simply try to slow my heartbeat. I'm not sure I'll survive the stress of this place. Moving out of the way of others, I stand against the wall inside the cold room.

"Are you okay?" Cody asks when she's done healing the girl.

I swallow. "Does that happen a lot?" I whisper, suddenly not so fond of the *fun* store.

Cody shakes her head and rolls her eyes. "The attacks by the clan are taking their toll. We've lost Pepps who can spread Peppate, hence we've lost power. We've had to cut back on the power we use to keep the dinosaurs at bay, hoping it wouldn't backfire, but obviously"—Cody points in the direction of the tranquilized dinosaur—"we need to figure out different places to cut back. Stupid dinosaurs. Did you know they don't absorb Peppate? Maybe they would be a little *happier* if they did." Annoyance flickers in her hazel eyes.

A solemnity engulfs the store, and the same fear that grips the Pepps oozes into me. The Pepps are struggling.

I grab my satchel of capsules and silently walk back to GreenGrotto with Cody. With the sun now set, the air grows chilly and the path is dark, lit only by an occasional torch. Cody morphs into an eagle at the base of GreenGrotto and carries me to our balcony.

After walking through the door, Cody eyes my untouched, cold dinner still sitting on my nightstand. "Are you hungry?" I want to tell her I'm fine, but my stomach growls loudly. Cody laughs. "I'll go get you some fresh dinner. I'm a little hungry myself." She quickly disappears back outside, leaving me with my thoughts of the dinosaur.

The sliver of compassion I felt while talking to the chief last night begins to grow, along with my fear. If the Pepps don't have enough power to keep the dinosaurs contained, does that mean they potentially won't have enough power to protect themselves in the future? Protect me?

While I sit on my bed, waiting for Cody to come back with dinner, I distract myself with the new clothes she got me, trying to sort through and organize it all. When she comes back, I eat quietly. Cody sits on her bed and examines the new capsules she bought for herself at the store. She holds her hand over one, and a ribbon of smoke floats into the air.

"What are you doing?"

Without looking up, Cody says, "I'm marking my capsules just in case some idiot decides to steal them." When she's satisfied with her task, she hands the capsule to me. The golden capsule now has a flower burned into it.

"It's the lotus flower. It stands for beauty," she says, batting her eyes. I chuckle and hand it back to her. When I sit back on my bed, Cody looks at me seriously.

"Alena, I'm sorry about the way I treated you. With everything going on, I didn't trust you. I hope you can forgive me." I stare at her for a moment before dropping my gaze to my food. A part of me enjoyed hating Cody, and I almost want to reject her apology just to revel in that hatred. But there is something I want more than that.

I want a friend.

"Thank you," I say.

"Can we be friends?" she whispers.

I study her eyes. They're no longer accusing but kind and sincere. I nod. "I would like that."

Then I lie back on my bed, happier than earlier. At least until I remember initiation. Sighing, I turn onto my side, trying to think ... Is there a way to learn how to use the power without doing stupid initiation?

Chapter 10

"Time to wake up!" A loud female voice blares into my ear, making me jump out of my bed. A woman with dark-brown skin and black hair slicked into a tight bun at the base of her neck shouts at me. Her stern expression looks particularly displaced against her beautiful features.

"If you want to learn in time for initiation, we start now!" The woman yells in a *don't argue* tone.

Without another word, she turns and stomps out the door. I frantically throw on the pair of shoes sitting beside my bed and scramble after her without a word, determined not to anger the strange woman.

I follow her through the maze of tunnels while she spits out the details of the game. "Initiation is in three weeks—not much time to train you. If you miss another day, you will not participate and you will not be able to match for another three months. The chief will not be happy about that." The woman stops abruptly, and I stumble into her. "I suggest you don't make the chief mad." She glares at me, and I step back. *I could care less about making the chief mad. This woman, on the other hand ...*

Upon reaching a spiral staircase, the woman grabs me with her thick arm and jumps. I bite back a squeal when we fall through the hole in the center of the spiral staircase. A rope simultaneously extends from her other hand and latches on to something above I cannot see. I cling embarrassingly to the odd woman, not wanting to bump my head on the stairs we fall past. When we reach the bottom of the staircase, the woman releases me before stomping to the sunlit door of GreenGrotto.

I try to stabilize my rapid heartbeat.

"The school is this way. You'll need to meet your team at the school every Tuesday and Thursday until initiation."

It's the first time I've seen the bottom floor of GreenGrotto, but I don't have time to examine it. I'm struggling enough to keep up with the woman.

"Initiation was created to put you in a place where you'll be tested and faced with hard things. We take you out of your comfort zone and allow your totem to assess how well you interact with others and how you react to distress."

We step through the door into the bright sunlight.

"This is not the only thing you will be evaluated on, though." The woman stops again, but I'm more prepared this time and stop before running into her. "The most important skill a Pepp needs to have is navigation." She turns and starts walking again. "On your dropdowns, it's possible to get separated from your group. You won't survive unless you know the most fundamental skill of using a map and compass to get to a rendezvous point. Since you have so little time, I'll give you a book to teach you the navigation skills you will need to know. I suggest you read and practice during every moment you're away from your team. You'll need to memorize the coordinates of most of the world, which will take years, but for initiation I suggest you at least memorize the coordinates of Petrichor and its landmarks."

Memorize coordinates? Oh boy.

I look up to see we're getting closer to another large mountain. This one is brown, though, instead of green. The woman continues.

"Initiation is on a Friday night. You will meet your team at the gym in GreenGrotto at six p.m. As a group, you'll make your way to the river, where you'll be given your first full capsule of power to activate your totem. You'll then board your boat with your team and travel down the river to the bottom of the mountain. You'll make camp there, and in the morning you'll begin your journey back to Petrichor."

Approaching the brown mountain, I see several younger Pepps scattered around the grounds.

"There's one important thing you need to remember about the game. The river takes you outside of Petrichor, so you'll be subject to outside weather and animals. These games are dangerous, so please prepare yourself. Your team will help you."

The woman walks to a group of younger Pepps, but just before reaching them she turns to me and says, "My name is Aba, by the way. I'm your trainer."

Unsure if I should shake her hand or introduce myself, I stand frozen until the woman begins speaking loudly to the group. "We have a new team member, Alena. She'll be joining you for initiation, so I suggest you get to know her and make her feel welcome."

There are five members of the group: two girls and three boys. One of the boys stands, crossing his arms, staring angrily at me. His hair has the same pattern as the mean red-haired woman on the aircraft. What was her name? Cordelia? I instantly feel the same hostility emitting from him that I felt from her.

"So, it's true," the red-haired boy spits out in front of the group. "You're giving us a deadweight, a team member who won't actually be a *team member* but a burden to us since she doesn't know how to use the power." I'm stunned at the potent hate gushing from the boy. I want to shrink back, but even I know that would be a terrible mistake. So I square my shoulders and stand as straight as I can, glaring back at him, hating him already. Amid my glares I can't help but notice that his arms are absent of a totem too. Just like Cordelia's.

Aba calmly replies, "Yes. She's your team member now, and if you want to survive the game, you'll need to make sure she gets back with you, so I suggest you learn to get along, especially you, Flint, since you're the leader. If you don't mesh well with her, then you'll be removed from the game." The boy's face squints in disgust at the trainer's threat, but Aba continues. "Today there's a prize waiting for you in Petrichor. I'll give you the coordinates to your first clue. What you find will help your team in the next training. I know some of you have classes in a few hours, so be sure to work quickly."

Aba holds out a white piece of parchment toward the group, and Flint snatches it. The group huddles together as Aba walks away, leaving me behind like a piece of dead meat for the vultures. One of the girls in the group, dark-haired, with a large pink flower stuck in her dark bun, eyes me curiously. I hesitantly shift under her gaze outside the group, noticing that she's taller than me with dark-olive skin and brown eyes. She leaves a gap in the tightly gathered group. *For me?* I get as close as I dare, still not taking my eyes off Flint.

"What does it say, Flint?" a tall, muscular boy asks. His neatly trimmed facial hair and smooth voice make him seem a lot older than a teenager. The third boy with dark skin, standing much shorter than the muscular boy, tries to peek at the paper.

Flint, refusing to let anyone else see the paper, reads out some numbers—coordinates.

Unaffected by Flint's controlling nature, the taller boy pulls a compass out of his pocket and lays a map of Petrichor on the ground to find his bearings.

"We need to head toward GreenGrotto."

How the heck did he figure that out?

With that, the group takes off running. I'm not sure what my purpose is here, but I follow them, forcing myself into a jog. At first, I purposefully keep a safe distance behind but soon find that I need to push my legs as hard as I can just to keep them in sight. When I reach them stopped at the bottom of the mountain, I'm heaving embarrassingly hard.

"Carlos, recheck," Flint demands, and I take note of the tall boy's name. *Carlos.*

Carlos takes out his compass and map again, redirecting us all a little to the right. Pointing, he says, "We go up."

The news makes my lungs ache. Running on flat ground was hard enough, but climbing up a mountain? I grieve silently, following the group, pressing my body forward. Stepping over the big rocks, my hamstrings start burning in protest. Carlos calls back to make sure I'm doing okay, and the olive-skinned girl watches me closely, but they all continue ahead, trying to keep up with Flint and the other blonde girl, who hasn't even bothered to look at me once.

Soon my sides start cramping, my lungs scream more, and my legs turn into rubber, forcing me to take too many breaks. The group ahead gets smaller and smaller until they disappear completely. I try really hard to keep up, but I can't.

How long have we been out here? Will they ever let me catch up? The only sign that I've been out here far too long is the sun that has reached its zenith in the sky.

Finally, I hear voices ahead. Making my way to the sounds, I find my team tucked away in some trees. "Ah, there you are!" Carlos says excitedly, his energy instantly annoying me.

Flint just rolls his eyes, plainly irritated by my slowness. Rising from the rock he's sitting on, he says, "Great, now that the slug is here, we can keep going."

I grit my teeth. Carlos thuds Flint on the back. "Don't be like that, Flint." But Flint jerks away. Then, turning to me, Carlos says, "We found the next clue. Coordinates to another site. We need to go back down the mountain."

What! I want to scream. *After all that effort, we're just going back down?*

Flint disappears through the trees, eager to move on, and the others follow. Carlos tips his head, indicating I should come. I move my wobbly legs, but when the group disappears again in the trees, tears tug at my eyes. I don't want to be here.

Just as I am walking past a GreenGrotto balcony, I slip on a root and begin tumbling down the hill. I flip until I hit my head on a rock. Sitting up, I cradle my head in my hands, waiting for the stabbing pain in my skull to subside. Thankfully, the group, too far away to have heard me stumble, can't see my tears.

When the pain dulls, I pull my injured body up and make my way back down. When I finally reach the bottom, my group is heading into a large green field, far ahead of me now, toward Mossy Hollow. Thanks to the openness of the field, though, I can see them clearly from so far behind.

My legs feel weird, my head is pounding, and my side still aches, even at my slower pace. The only thing that feels remotely good are the curse words silently flowing from my tongue. I throw every bad word I know at my team.

They finally stop ahead and begin digging into the ground. I slow my pace the closer I get and decide to stop short, to see where they're headed next. My heart beats faster when they make their way directly toward me. I brace myself, seeing Flint angrily in the lead with something in his hands.

When he reaches me, he shoves the item into my stomach, forcing the air from my lungs.

"We don't need a defective Pepp on our team. Just stay out of our way," he growls into my ear.

"Flint!" Carlos yells, clearly irritated. But Flint ignores him and stomps off.

"He'll come around, Alena," Carlos says, reaching my side. "You okay?"

I feel the urge to cry in this stupid moment, but I nod without making eye contact.

Flint calls out for the rest of the team.

Carlos taps my shoulder softly. "We need to get back to classes—we're already late—but meet back up with us on Thursday. We'll teach you how to use the compass." Carlos points to the package in my hands before walking away.

I stand there until I'm sure they're gone. Then I let the tears fall. The emptiness and loneliness I've felt since being here fills my whole body painfully, like a thorn in my side being twisted again and again. My tired, wobbly legs make their way back to GreenGrotto, the unopened package in my hands.

Keeping my head down, I avoid the curious gazes of the busy Pepps around me. I'm so lost in thought that I jump when someone steps out from behind a tree. My heart sinks when I meet Flint's green gaze. I look around for help, only to find that the path that was so busy seconds ago is now empty. I'm alone.

My throat goes dry. He closes the space between us, quicker than I can react, and grabs my shirt. I try to push him away, but he's stronger than he looks. I expect him to snarl some cruel retort, but he simply smirks mockingly at me. I don't quite understand until my skin burns under his grip. The smell of acid reaches my nostrils, and I watch the collar of my shirt disintegrate.

Frantically, I push harder, but Flint's grip tightens. "We don't need you here."

Finally, he lets go and leaves without glancing back. I fight to breathe, the pain of the acid searing my skin. Frantically, I search for a source of water and find a brook trickling through the green grass close by. Crying, I run to it, laying down face-first. The cold temperature immediately soothes the burning of my skin. I stay there, holding my head just above the water for a couple of minutes, sobbing, until I begin shivering from the cold. I push myself to my knees, only to find several Pepps gathered around with concerned eyes.

"Are you okay?" one asks, but I don't bother answering. Glaring at the ground, I pull myself up, grab my package, and slosh back to GreenGrotto, the acidic burn coming back. I need to find Cody.

I enter the hall of GreenGrotto with my head down, avoiding all eye contact, and head straight for the stairs. I'm almost there, when a loud bang echoes through GreenGrotto.

Looking in the direction of the sound, I meet the eyes of a young man standing by one of the tree trunks that must lead to the sleeping quarters.

His oily, stringy hair reaches his shoulders, and his clothes look too big for his body.

Odd whisperings start floating through the room, and I look around to find Pepps pointing their fingers and laughing at the boy. I slide my gaze back to him and find his deep brown eyes staring at me.

Looking down at his feet, I realize the loud sound came from the pile of books now in disarray on the ground. He dropped them. I'm about to step forward to help him pick them up, when the shaggy young man starts flinging his arms in strange movements, wailing in an unintelligible manner. The snickers and whispers get louder. They're amused by the grown boy throwing what looks like a two-year-old tantrum.

My surprise at his odd movements turns to compassion. He's different. And others treat him differently—just like me.

I hesitate, knowing that paying him any attention will not tip things in my favor, but then I step forward. Watching out for his flailing arms, I stoop to pick up his books. I hear the speculative whisperings behind me as a group gathers to watch me fall even further down my slippery slope. My blood rushes in response, but I take a deep breath.

The boy's breathing slows, and his wailings calm as I help. After stacking the books on the floor, I look up expecting to make eye contact, but his eyes wander around the room. I rise with the books in my arms, but before handing them to him, I thrust my hand forward and say, "Hi, I'm Alena."

A new outbreak of wails extends from the young man, and I take a couple of steps back to distance myself from his flinging arms.

"What's going on?" someone shouts behind me. I turn and see Mark running toward us.

Mark. My neck flushes at the sight of the one person I've been waiting eagerly to see here. But then I remember how I look and curse my wet clothes and bully wounds.

I should go.

But I can't move.

Mark slows when he sees me, his eyes glancing back and forth between the boy and me. I stand frozen watching him approach, until the wailing boy's arm knocks me to the side.

"Danny, what's wrong?" Mark asks, trying to calm him down.

Danny? The friend Mark mentioned before?

Danny doesn't answer, and Mark's confused look lands on me. *He's probably wondering what* I *did to his friend.*

But then Mark's eyes lower to my neck, and his expression turns from confused to concerned. "Are you okay, Alena?" The heat from the burn pales in comparison to the heat I now feel with Mark looking at me. And saying my name.

I don't want to respond, but I don't have to. Danny continues to scream and wail, hitting Mark several times. Unable to contain his friend, Mark looks torn between helping Danny and helping me. But I back away, toward the stairs.

"I'm sorry, I need to get to Cody," I say. The acid is starting to burn, and Mark needs to help the boy. "Will he be okay?"

Mark's concern deepens, but he nods, holding his arm out to protect himself from Danny. "Will you?"

"Yes, thank you," I say quickly before bolting up my stairs.

Chapter 11

Lying on my bed, I try to sleep. It's late and my body is tired, but my mind doesn't rest. Irritated, I sit up in the moonlight. The package Flint slammed into my stomach earlier sits on top of the nightstand, mocking me. I haven't wanted to open it, but seeing that I have nothing else to do, I snatch it and peel back the brown paper.

Unlike all the other extraordinary things I've discovered here in Petrichor, the compass looks rather ordinary. Like ones I've seen back home.

Shifting the compass from hand to hand, my mind continues to whirl.

I had to ask for directions several times earlier, trying to find my room, and by the time I reached it, I was in tears. Thankfully, Cody was here when I came rushing in. She was furious when she saw my burns and bruises, and after she healed me, she marched over to the school. She promised she would get Flint removed from the team, but I don't know if that's what I want. *Won't he hate me even more if he's not allowed to do initiation?*

What I do know is that I don't want to go back on Thursday.

Knowing that sleep is not going to come, I open my nightstand drawer and pull out the matches Cody gave me. I'm about to close the drawer after lighting my lantern, when I freeze. There's a rock, smaller than the size of Breccia, sitting in the middle of the drawer. That wasn't there earlier. I pick it up and turn it in my fingers; its smooth brownish color swirled with turquoise and orange reminds me of a sunset in the flickering lantern light. It's beautiful. But what is it, and how did it get in my drawer? Maybe Cody put it there.

I'm about to put it back, when it moves in my hand. I drop it nervously and stare at it on the floor, but it sits motionless. Maybe I imagined it.

Or maybe I didn't. A shiver runs up my spine. I pick up the rock, walk to the window, and toss it outside before sitting back on my bed. Whatever it is, I don't want it.

Taking in a deep breath, I pick up the comb next to my lantern and run it through my clean hair. My mind spins again, but I'm tired of thinking about Flint and initiation. So I force myself to think of something better.

Mark. And the boy downstairs, Danny. Is he the friend Mark had mentioned before at the cabin? Why was he acting that way? Is he sick? If he is, surely the Pepps can heal him, right?

Mark's strong, stubbled face dances through my mind, and my stomach flutters. Why am I always covered in grime when I see him? After talking to Cody yesterday, I'm sure I'm not the only one who finds him attractive. And seeing how I looked earlier, I'm no competition.

I sigh. Maybe that isn't something I want to think about either. I'm about to blow out my lamp in frustration and try to sleep again, when a knock interrupts the silence of my room. Cody said she had to work at the clinic until the middle of the night, so who is it?

I hesitate. Is it Flint? Come to finish me off? When the knock hammers a second time, I take in a deep breath and open the door. My body relaxes—and warms—when I find a very tired, distressed, and handsome-looking Mark.

"Mark?"

Leaning against the doorframe, Mark runs his hand through his hair like Caleb does when he's stressed.

"Hey, um, Danny, my friend you met earlier, hasn't been able to calm down since he saw you. He keeps calling out. I think he wants to see you. I know it's late, but would you mind going to him?"

I'm confused. Why would Danny want *me?* "Wouldn't a medic be more helpful? I don't know anything about his condition."

Mark shakes his head. "I really think he needs *you.*"

I can't ignore the desperate and tired look in Mark's eyes.

"Okay," I say quietly, stepping into the hall and shutting the door behind me.

It must be later than I thought because the halls are more still than I've ever seen them. Walking silently behind Mark, I descend the stairs, trying to ignore the muscles protruding through his shirt.

When we reach the bottom floor, we enter the boys' side, and after climbing more stairs and passing many doors identical to the ones on the girls' side, we finally approach one that Mark enters. Following behind him, my eyes are immediately drawn to Danny lying on a bed.

His body trembles, wet from sweat. His eyes are closed, but I sense that he's very much awake.

Mark closes the door and walks to him.

"Danny, Alena is here."

Danny's arms begin thrashing wildly, hitting the wall and nightstand next to his bed. Mark hastily moves the nightstand to keep him from getting hurt.

The scene is familiar. The sweating, the shallow breathing, the probable pain. It looks like a panic attack.

I'm drawn to the bed, moving cautiously until I kneel next to it.

"Hey, Danny," I say, taking one of his hands in mine. My voice soothes him, and his fight melts at my touch. "It's nice to finally meet you." His eyes flutter open, dancing wildly around the room, while his mouth moves to speak. But nothing comes out.

Then his body trembles again, as if he's crying. His shaking sobs tug at my heart, and I look to Mark for some explanation, but he looks as lost as I do.

"It's okay, Danny." I try to comfort him without knowing his troubles. He looks directly at me for the first time. His brown eyes look sad, as if he has so much to say but can't speak. He stares at me for a long time until his eyes grow heavy and finally shut.

Not wanting to wake him, I kneel there on the wooden floor captivated by the mysterious boy. I quietly observe his left arm that's tightly woven with a green totem. What job was green, again? Dino trainer?

His long hair is stringy and wet with sweat, but it's a beautiful chestnut color.

Mark moves quietly around the room, interrupting my thoughts. He goes to a corner, picks up a chair, and brings it to me.

Still holding Danny's hand, I push myself up and sit in it, the blood rushing painfully back to my legs.

Grabbing another chair, Mark sits on the other side of the bed. I distract myself from his presence by looking around the space for the first time. Their room is almost identical to Cody's and mine—two beds and two closets—except for the sundry collection of guns leaning against the wall and the absence of a very large body mirror.

"What happened to you today?" Mark whispers. "How did you get that burn?" I peer up at him, surprised at his concern ... and his closeness.

"It was ... uh ..." I sigh. I'd rather not talk about it. The last thing I want is for Mark to think I'm weak. And what happened today made me look *very* weak.

But I have to say something.

"It was just a run-in with one of my new friends; he doesn't like me very much." I play with Danny's hand and scrunch my nose.

"You know," Mark says softly, "I never got a chance to apologize for the way I treated you the night we met. Dragging you down the hall was not one of my best moments."

My eyes are pulled back to his. I wasn't expecting an apology from him. I'm so surprised by his comment that, before I realize it, I'm forgiving him.

"It's okay. I know you were all worried that night. I can't say that I blame you." Even I'm surprised at the kindness in my voice. Where's all that anger and hate I felt before? When I realized Mark sent me here to be a prisoner and not a Pepp? I kick myself silently. Weak.

Mark rests his elbows on his knees, bringing his face even closer, the muscles in his shoulders bulging in response. I swallow.

"Thank you for trying to help Danny earlier," Mark says. "He isn't exactly the most popular kid to be seen around."

I force my gaze away from his muscles and back to his eyes. "Of course," I whisper. I should add that I'm probably more unpopular than Danny, but suddenly I can't think about anything except his eyes. I thought I had them memorized after staring at his picture on my mirror day after day. But now I realize I could never look at them long enough.

"It's my fault they don't like you," he continues. "My morph at initiation caused a lot of problems."

I almost smile. "Yeah, that's why they don't want me to change form at initiation."

Mark tenses. "Wait, they're making you do initiation?"

Doesn't everyone know I'm doing initiation?

"Yes," I say. "I'm not allowed to morph, but I'm still supposed to do it to get my job."

Mark's concerned look deepens.

"Is something wrong?" I ask.

Mark studies me quietly for a moment but then shakes his head. "No, I just didn't think they were going to make you do it. But I guess if you don't change form, that's fine."

I sense he has more to say, but when the silence continues to permeate the room, I decide he's dropping the subject. And now that Danny's asleep I wonder if I should go. But I don't want to. Mark's simple presence has somehow made me feel more relaxed than I've felt since coming to Petrichor. So, I stretch my stay a little longer.

"What's wrong with him?" I whisper, nodding toward Danny.

A sadness sweeps over Mark. "We aren't entirely sure. I hear he was normal when he first came to Petrichor with Trevor, his brother. But then one day he and Trevor left without telling anyone. Danny returned three days later, like this. Unable to talk and unable to tell the chief what happened."

"*Nobody* knows what happened?" I find it hard to believe that the Pepps couldn't find answers.

Mark rubs the stubble on his face. "No. All we know is that he came back with half of an extra totem on his arm. It was the first manipulated totem, even before mine. On top of the totem he already had, the space in his brain became too crammed. The vine has interrupted his communication channels so he can't talk, and, of course, the extra totem can't be removed." Mark looks down at Danny. "Jeter did find a way to use a Magbaby for his *current* thoughts, though." Mark points to the black rock sitting on the nightstand Mark moved earlier. It stirs, opening into a Magbaby. Holding out his hand, he introduces himself as Gabbro. I touch his hand with the tip of my finger. His voice is surprisingly deep for something so small. I feel the vibration in my digit when he talks.

"We often use the Magbabies' tendrils to reach into our ears and play music for us. It connects to the brain to do that, but Jeter trained Danny's Magbaby to connect with Danny's thought center. Gabbro can see Danny's current thoughts and can then communicate them verbally so we know what Danny is thinking. In other words, Gabbro can talk for Danny."

Mark's face darkens. "Jeter doesn't understand, though, how Danny can have restored communication and still not be able to tell us what happened when he disappeared. Every time he asks Danny about it, Danny starts having one of his tantrums and Gabbro can't catch any of his thoughts. It's almost as if the memories have been removed or blocked somehow. Jeter eventually concluded that there's more damage to the brain than even he can see."

I recall uneasily the night my memories were checked. "The chief was able to use a bug to see my memories," I say. "Can't they use it on Danny?"

Mark shakes his head. "They tried, but they couldn't find anything."

Danny stirs, and we both sit quietly until he settles back down.

"What happened to his brother, Trevor?" I whisper once he's sleeping again.

"They never found him."

My heart suddenly aches for Danny. He lost his brother. I don't know if I would survive if I lost Caleb.

"How did you two become friends?"

My face warms when Mark's eyes meet mine. "He's technically my Pepp brother. I was placed in his family to be taken care of when I came here. But, to me, he was really my first friend, especially after initiation when everyone rejected me. He taught me about the defective totem since he had one himself. And then he taught me how to feel better."

I turn my attention to Danny. *Can he teach me?*

I observe his features in the comfortable silence, noticing that his strong pointed nose leans a bit to the left. His lips are soft. His jawline defined. His hands are strong in mine. And his muscles bulge in all the right spots from what I can see through the blanket. He's handsome.

I hold his hand tighter, deciding in this moment that I want to be his friend. If he'll let me.

"How often did you go up to the hot spring at Falling Rock?" Mark's whisper brushes against my face. His question catches me off guard, and I look at him. Nobody in Petrichor has asked me about my home or family life, let alone one of my favorite places to go. I realize in this moment how much I've been aching to talk about it.

"We went there several times during the summers," I answer. "Occasionally we would camp there for a night, but most of the time we just swam for the day. We all loved it."

"Did you ever swim in the river or just in the hot spring?" he asks.

The last experience at Falling Rock comes to my mind, and I both laugh quietly and shake my head in disgust, remembering Caleb and Rick. "I never swam in the river until ... well, the day I got the totem. Caleb and my friend threw me off the cliff into the water."

Mark chuckles. "Some friend. That water is cold."

I meet his kind and accepting eyes. I didn't realize talking to someone who could relate to my other life would make me feel so comfortable. Talking to Mark is easy, and I feel the old Alena bubbling up inside me.

I know what he's doing.

When I was fifteen, I had become increasingly frustrated that I couldn't make friends during the first week of junior high. It had always been so easy before. My mom sat me down after I came home from school one day and told me that the best way to make a friend is to build a connection with them. Talk to them about something *they love*. Ask them questions about it, and then build on the conversation.

All my friends after that were pulled in using this tactic. It worked. And now Mark is here, using the same tactic on me, and I can't help but respond to it.

I scrunch my nose and close my eyes, remembering how the bitter water reached to my bones and made me ache. "It was awful."

Mark chuckles again. "My dad once told me he would give me a hundred dollars if I would jump off the cliff into the water. I don't think the money was worth it."

A laugh ripples through my throat, the picture forming in my mind.

But then I realize I never saw Mark or his father at the cabin we so often passed. "Did you live there?"

"No, we lived down the mountain in Flake Pass, but my dad had the cabin my whole life. We spent a couple of summers there, but after my mom died, things got harder. I would come up on the weekends to hunt with him, but he would mostly go hunting during the day while I was at school."

The room grows solemn at the mention of his mother's death, but Mark tries to lighten it again. "It's amazing that we both visited the same hot spring and yet our paths never crossed."

My light mood suddenly falls, and I sadly raise my eyes to his. Our paths have crossed. In a way he doesn't know. I've wondered when I would have a chance to tell Mark about that day.

"What's wrong?" he asks, sensing the sudden change.

I swallow and bite my lip. "There's something I should tell you."

Mark's eyebrows furrow in response to my serious tone. I play with Danny's hand, trying to figure out how to say what I need to say.

"My family was headed to the hot spring the day your dad was attacked," I say past the lump in my throat. "We saw the emergency helicopter in the sky on our way. My dad, who's a surgeon, followed it and found your father lying in the bushes."

I finally brave a look at Mark. His face is pale. I immediately feel the sorrow that materializes at the mention of his father.

"Your dad was alive when we reached him. We helped him get into the helicopter, and my dad tried to stabilize him. I thought he could save him. But..." I shake my head, recalling the blood and poisoned cut. The emotions I felt that day in that helicopter surface, and my throat catches.

"He kept calling out for you, Mark, asking me if you were safe." I look back down, my eyes suddenly blurry. I had seen how desperately worried the man was about his son. I've often wondered if Mark knew how much he'd meant to his father.

"He loved you very much," I whisper the words. As awkward as they may sound coming from me, he needs to know.

The room is quiet. I don't look at Mark, hoping to give him the space he needs.

"Was he in a lot of pain?" he finally asks.

I sense the grief this question has caused him. He mentioned before that he hates himself for leaving his father. I wish I had better news for him.

"Yes, the venom seemed very painful. It attacked his nervous system. He kept trying to reach for his head as if it was hurting. Then his whole body started to shake until the venom finally paralyzed him. He died before we reached the hospital."

"You rode with him? You were there?" He stares intently at my face.

"Yes." Sometimes I wish I hadn't been.

The room is quiet. Even though I'm looking at Danny's hands again, I can see Mark wipe the tears from his cheeks. My heart aches, and I wonder if I shouldn't have brought up the subject.

"I'm so sorry, Mark."

He merely nods.

Blinking back my tears, I retrieve my hand from Danny's grip and stand. "I should go," I say, turning to the door. I'm about to reach it, when Mark jumps up and grabs my arm.

"Alena." His brown eyes are misty. "Thank you. I can't tell you how many times I've wondered what happened to him and whose hands he ended up in. It gives me more peace than you'll ever know, being able to talk to the person who was with him when he died. Thank you for telling me."

My shoulders relax. At least he's not angry with me.

"I want you to know," he says, "that nobody's going to get away with hurting you, okay?"

His concern comforts me. Maybe he can help me fit in here.

"Thank you, Mark, that means a lot."

I hear a low-pitched shout from the Magbaby still sitting on the nightstand. "Good night, Alena!"

I had completely forgotten about the little guy. "Good night, Gabbro."

Almost reluctantly, I leave, looking back one last time to find Mark still watching me.

I get lost on the way back to my room and end up wandering the halls for thirty minutes, but I don't care. Regardless of the grim topic Mark and I ended on, I feel good. Better than I have since getting my totem.

Well, I feel good until I get back to my room and look at myself in the mirror.

"What is all over your face?" Cody asks, staring at me with wide eyes. Apparently, her shift at the hospital is over.

What the ...? I stand mortified to find that, regardless of my shower only hours ago, black dirt is smeared across my face and arms. Normally I wouldn't mind, but I was just with Mark!

Cursing under my breath, I grab a cloth to wipe it off. I must have picked it up from the walls of the tunnels.

"Where were you?" Cody chides mischievously. I try to keep the experience to myself, shrugging off her question, but Cody somehow extracts the truth. I tell her every stupid detail. When I finally look at her, I find her staring at me with her mouth open.

"What?"

"Alena, Mark doesn't talk ... to *anyone.* Except Danny and the dinosaurs. The fact that you had a full-on conversation with him is a big deal."

I try to hide the grin tugging at my lips. It felt good talking to Mark. He made me feel accepted and not because he was *forced* to accept me, like Cody.

But then something pricks at my thoughts. Maybe he wasn't forced to accept me like Cody, but is he being nice to me for another reason? I swallow, remembering his promise to Caleb before we left. That he would protect me. Is that all he feels toward me? Responsibility?

The thought only dampens my spirits a little bit. Maybe he really does feel responsible for me, but that doesn't have to keep me from reliving the good night in my mind. At least for a bit.

Chapter 12

I sit on my bed, the night darkening outside. Between getting acquainted with the compass Flint slammed into my stomach yesterday and thinking about my visit with Mark and Danny last night, I kept pretty busy today.

I hear a tap on my window and look out into the darkness. A floating light bobs into the glass repeatedly as if trying to get into my room. Confused, I walk to the window and open the door warily, looking around for its source. When I don't see anyone, I carefully grab the floating light, noticing a piece of paper attached to it.

I read:

We're sorry, Alena. Can you come down to the lobby so we can talk? – Your team.

I approach the railing of the balcony and look down. Four Pepps standing at the base of the mountain are waving large lights, trying to get my attention. I can't see their faces, but I can guess who they are. My team.

I grumble. I don't want to go down and talk to them.

I'm about to shake my head no or somehow send them a message that I'm going to bed, but then I pause and look down again. There are only four of them. Does that mean Flint isn't there?

Maybe I should at least check things out. Not wanting to go alone, I grab Breccia off the nightstand. I find myself pulled toward the stairs, curious about what happened to Flint. But by the time I reach the eighth floor, my hands are shaking nervously. My last experience with my team didn't go so well. Even with Flint not there, I'm not sure I want to face them.

I'm about to turn back, when Breccia calmly puts her tiny hand on my neck and shakes her head with a look that makes me pause.

She's right. I need to do this.

By the time I reach the bottom floor, my hands are sweaty. *What am I supposed to say to them? What if they're angry about Flint being removed?*

There are two rooms on the bottom floor I didn't notice before, a library and a gym. The noises coming from them overwhelm my already troubled mind, so I keep my head down and hurry to the front door.

I'm barely outside, my eyes adjusting to the darkness, when my body halts. My team is there, waiting patiently for me.

I hate that I'm so afraid to face four sixteen-year-old kids. I hope that my nerves aren't as loud as they feel. I scramble in my mind for something to say, but thankfully the brown-haired girl, with a different colored flower neatly reposed in her bun, speaks first.

"Hey, Alena," she says, casually waving her hand.

I wave back, eyeing each of them cautiously.

"Thanks for coming down. We have some things to tell you," the girl says kindly, looking at Carlos, who's standing next to her.

"First, Flint has been removed from the team," Carlos says. He tries to hold back a sly grin, but I catch it, and relief floods my body. Carlos doesn't seem to be angry about Flint's removal. But then a part of me becomes terrified. I may not have to see Flint at trainings now, but he could still make my life here a living hell. I glance again at Breccia, who looks concerned. *What did Cody say to have him removed?*

"My name is Leinani, by the way," the brown-haired girl says. "And this is Bapoto." She points to the dark boy who stands several inches shorter than me. He grips my hand and bows to kiss my knuckles before flashing me a white but wild grin that stands out against his dark skin.

Carlos pushes him away, annoyed with his antics, but Bapoto just chuckles, saying, "We're sorry for what happened yesterday, Alena. It won't happen again."

I smile at their exchange, then Carlos speaks again, much softer, "And this is Nadia."

Nudging the blonde girl with his arm, he gets her to look up just long enough to nod before turning her attention back to her more important fingernails.

"It's nice to meet all of you."

"We only have a couple weeks left before initiation," Carlos says. "We need to prepare you as best we can. We're going to the river now, where initiation will start. Will you come with us?"

I shiver in the cool night, wishing I had brought a jacket, but I nod and follow them across the grass. Up ahead I can pick out the shadow of a bridge crossing a black rushing river. Each of my teammates patters across the bridge until they reach the middle, where they all sit. I stand awkwardly until Leinani pats the wood beside her, indicating I should sit too.

"This is where initiation will begin," Carlos says. "We'll board a boat in the water, and the river will take us out of Petrichor."

I sit and listen. Carlos does most of the talking, telling me about the games. I can only guess that with Flint now gone he's the new designated leader. I find myself captivated by Carlos's smooth voice and confident descriptions of initiation. Even though he's only sixteen, he seems to know a lot about the game.

He tells me how we're going to be challenged in the five most dangerous areas of runs: weather, health, navigation, wildlife, and strength.

Then each of them boasts about the areas they're good at. Leinani is good with health. Carlos has strength and is good with navigation. Bapoto raves on and on about how he isn't necessarily good at any of the five areas, but he's incredibly good with power.

This triggers a question.

"How are you good with power?" I ask as quietly as I can.

Everyone hears my question. I know because their eyes turn to me in the darkness. But they don't answer. So I clear my voice to clarify. "The chief said we will be given our *first* capsules of power at initiation, but you guys already seem to know how to use the power. Have you used it before?"

Carlos takes over, now understanding my question. "Yes. We've never had a full capsule of power, so our totems have never been 'activated.' But during our time at the school, we've been given little tiny samples of power, encased in glass, to practice with. We pop it into the hole over the heart of our totem. It's how we've discovered the different areas we like. It doesn't necessarily mean that we'll match in those areas, but it's given us a good idea of what to expect."

I nod as I remember something else the chief said about initiation.

"So, we'll all be given a full glass capsule of power the day of initiation for the first time. That will activate our totems and help the chief see which job is best for us. And then, after initiation, you will morph for the first time? Is that when you start collecting power for yourselves?"

"Yes, that's correct," Carlos says. "Up until initiation, the power samples we're given come from other Pepps who've collected it during a morph. But after initiation, we'll be able to morph and collect it for ourselves. I have to admit, I'm excited to morph. Everyone says it's amazing." Carlos tosses a rock into the river.

I almost feel jealous. They'll be able to morph and collect power for themselves. But I won't.

Regardless, it makes sense, so I nod and encourage them to continue with their other explanations.

Next, they talk about the different weather they can encounter.

"Petrichor sits in the middle of an extremely cold climate," Leinani says, breaking through Carlos's words. "Power is used to keep Petrichor and the mountain below warm, but sometimes the council allows it to get a little colder than normal." Leinani shivers as she explains this. "I hate the cold."

Me too.

"And then there's the lake," Leinani adds solemnly.

Bapoto catches my eye when she says this and speaks with a lowered voice. "The lake. It sits right at the border of where Petrichor and the cold climate meet. Because of the drastic change in temperature in that spot, the way the wind blows and the amount of moisture there, it's the place where the most lightning storms occur near Petrichor. And we'll have to pass it."

I look at the serious expression on each of their faces. "Is it that dangerous?" In the mountains where I come from we experience our share of lightning storms. They're scary, but the fear in the eyes of my teammates goes deeper than that.

"Lightning kills us, Alena," Leinani whispers quietly.

"Doesn't lightning kill any kind of person?" I ask, trying to understand.

Carlos shakes his head. "Not like it does us. Lightning is drawn to Peppate, particularly the Peppate generators that reside in each of our totems. It doesn't matter if a lightning storm is miles away. It finds its way to us very quickly." Carlos pauses and then adds, "It isn't just lightning. It's all electricity of any kind, including batteries. Any spark pulverizes a Pepp."

I remember Cody burning my phone to ashes my first night in Petrichor. I thought she was just being mean.

"We have to be very careful," Leinani says. "If a lightning storm does occur, the Pepps won't be able to stop it. We will all just have to get away as quickly as possible. Caves are the best place to hide."

They continue talking, but I can't help but silently wonder why the council would put a new team of Pepps right in the path of a common lightning storm if it's so dangerous. *Is the match really that important?*

My mood slips, the grim topic hanging in the air. I felt unprepared before, but now I can see why Flint called me deadweight. Even though they all seem mature and more than able to help me, I realize I won't be able to contribute anything at all. I'll have to rely entirely on my team to get back.

Leinani skillfully changes the subject to their lives before Petrichor. She explains how she used to live on an island, before her family died from a sickness aboard a supply boat that docked there. Carlos talks about how he lived with his parents before a hurricane whipped through and killed them. Bapoto has been here the longest, coming when he was five after his father died from an accident involving an elephant. His mother had died while giving birth to him.

Nadia is the newest of the group to come to Petrichor, her parents dying only six months ago during a car accident. Perhaps that explains her distant demeanor.

My heart breaks a little for each of them as they share their stories under the starry sky. I'm far away from home, but at least my family is still alive.

With the night drawing on, Carlos finally stands. "We better be getting back to the burrows now, but, Alena, we want you to know that we're happy to have you on our team." Holding out his hand, he helps Leinani up before tapping me on my shoulder to say good night.

"We'll see you tomorrow, right?" Leinani asks, her kindness melting any reservations I had about their friendship.

I nod. I'll be there.

***

I'm getting better at finding my room. I get there in record time and find Cody back from the hospital getting ready for bed.

"You know, you really should clean your face more," she says when I enter. Confused, I walk to the mirror again and find it covered in dirt. What the heck! It's starting to feel impossible to stay clean here in Petrichor. And why doesn't anyone tell me I'm dirty? I walk to my nightstand, open up the drawer, and pull out a sock to wipe my face with. My hand pauses in midair.

That creepy colorful rock is sitting in my drawer again. I pull it out and eye it closely, unnerved.

"Cody?"

Cody grunts in response as she pulls on her night clothes.

"Did you put this in my drawer?"

Cody looks up, confused. When she sees what I'm holding, she shakes her head. "No, why?"

"I found this in my drawer last night. I threw it outside. Now it's back in my drawer."

Cody moves closer and takes the rock from my hand. Examining it closely she says, "It looks like a Morgan."

"What's a Morgan?"

"It's like a Magbaby, but when it's mined off the Mother Mountain, instead of being filled with magnetic rock like other Magbabies, it's filled with this blueish rock called Morgan. They're quite beautiful but useless for us because they aren't drawn magnetically to Petrichor. They also have a hard time functioning during the day. The sun does something weird to them. So we usually just throw them away."

"Are they alive like Magbabies?" I ask, remembering the way it had moved.

As if answering my question, the rock ripples in Cody's hand, then flies into the air and out the door.

The color drains from Cody's face, and she swallows. "I think we need to go see the chief."

Chapter 13

Our visit with the chief made me more unnerved. He was angry and confused at the mention of the Morgan in my drawer. He said nobody is supposed to keep those, and the fact that it was in my room and flew out like that could mean that someone put it there to spy on me. He said Morgans are usually listless creatures that might roll around occasionally, but they don't fly.

It's daunting knowing that someone might be spying on me. This only adds to the violated feeling I still have from my memories being examined so rudely. *But this spy rock—who was it spying for?* What kind of information was it trying to obtain?

The chief had a council member search our room, and they found one more rock hidden in the mattress of my bed. *How long had it been there?* The chief has ordered that all Morgans in Petrichor be turned in to him. Not that this is going to solve the problem, of course. The person behind this is likely not one to obey the chief.

He's also having the memories of everyone in Petrichor checked. If there is a traitor here, he will find them. So he says.

I try to think who it could be. Problem is, I don't really know anyone yet. Or trust anyone. Everyone is a suspect to me. In the meantime, I'm not to communicate with my family. He doesn't want my Magbaby being followed to discover where they live. This news made me nauseated, thinking that someone might want to know where my family is. The only thing that made me feel better was knowing that I wrote my family during the day. When the sun was out. The chief assured me that the rocks could not have followed my Magbaby then. But that doesn't mean they haven't obtained other information. Cody seemed particularly quiet after learning all this, as if she was extra worried about something, but she didn't tell me what. She just assured the chief she would check daily for any new rocks in our room.

Today she seems better, though.

"Take only what you need for the game," Cody says, standing beside my bed as she patiently helps me pack my satchel for initiation.

Training the past week has gone well with my team. Thankfully, I haven't run into Flint again, but I still brace for his attack every time I walk alone.

"You start with the smaller items on the left and then gradually progress to the bigger ones on the right," Cody says. I watch her put the last of my supplies in my satchel—my tent on the far right and my warm clothes on the bottom left row.

Looking at the satchel, I'm grateful for Cody's help. This morning my supplies were so disorganized that I had to look at the symbol on each of them to identify them. Cody saw my frustration and decided to help me out so I could know where each supply was without pulling it out.

I take the packed satchel and tie it shut, then lay it on my bed.

"Now let's go get something to eat," she says, looking at the setting sun.

I've gotten used to Cody carrying me up to the courtyard for dinner in her eagle form, which is what she does tonight.

After grabbing plates of food, we sit in front of a warm fire and eat quietly for a couple of minutes before Cody mischievously nudges my arm. "I told you Mark likes you."

I raise my head to see what she's talking about. She nods in the direction of a table off to my right. My heart flutters when my eyes land on Mark. He's sitting with Danny, slouching down in his chair. And looking right at me. The plate of food in front of him looks untouched.

I haven't seen him since the night with Danny, although I've found my thoughts often wandering to him.

He doesn't look well, though, and my heart sinks. His disheveled hair and tired face worry me.

I pull my eyes back to my food. "He looks awful."

Cody laughs softly amid her bites. "He's stressed about you participating in initiation."

"Why?"

Cody sits quietly, her eyes darting back and forth between Mark and me, until she says, "There haven't been any attacks on the Pepps this last week from the clan."

I knit my eyebrows together. "Isn't that a good thing? What does that have to do with the game?"

Cody's expression turns grim. "The council thinks the clan has found out about you and your totem. They think they've withdrawn all their attacks in an attempt to plan a big capture."

"They found out about me? How?"

Cody shrugs. "How do they find out about the locations of our runs? They have spies everywhere."

Then I realize what she's saying. "The council thinks they'll capture me while I'm outside Petrichor during initiation?"

"No, Mark is the one that thinks they'll try that." Cody's voice falls, and she looks at her food. "He's been especially worried since we found the Morgans in our room. He's really angry that Chief is still making you participate when someone is obviously spying on you." Cody shakes her head and looks back up. "But the council doesn't believe the clan will take you during initiation. Instead, they think they're plotting to take you when you have your first dropdown. The clan would be stupid to come to our territory. The game is closely monitored by Pepps. With our power, the clan doesn't stand a chance." Cody pauses, then adds, "I agree with the council."

My uneasiness grows.

"Don't worry, Alena. I don't think the chief will let you do drop-downs now. You'll be safe," Cody says kindly.

We eat in silence for a couple of more minutes before Cody nudges me again. "You want to know a secret?"

Cody doesn't give me a chance to respond before continuing. "Mark never matched in the game."

"What?" I look back at Mark, who's still staring me down. "Why not?"

Cody shrugs before saying, "The nasty stuff the defective totem makes acted like a fog. It made it difficult for the totem to establish Mark's true character. It couldn't see him, so it couldn't place him." I suddenly remember the night in his room when he was surprised I was participating in the game.

"But he placed later," I say, knowing he's now a dino trainer.

"Yes, he matched two months later, but it wasn't until Danny started showing him how to get rid of the Doler."

"So that means there's a chance I'm not going to match?" I ask. *Why would the chief make me participate in the game if I'm not going to match?*

"You *are* going to match, Alena, because of Mark. I went to tell the chief about Flint after seeing the burns he gave you," Cody says. "He was upset, but he wasn't going to remove Flint from the game. It wasn't until Mark stormed in later the next morning, telling the chief that removing Flint was the only way you were going to match, that they decided to take him out of the game. And then Mark marched into the school with the chief and pulled out each of your teammates with Aba. He told them how important it was that you matched, and the best way for that to happen was for you to feel accepted, for you to have friends. I guess the Doler, the bad stuff inside you, hates friends."

I know this news is supposed to comfort me, but it makes me feel worse. "So, they were all *forced* to be my friends?" I say, looking at my now unappetizing food.

"Alena, knowing Leinani and Carlos, they wanted to be your friends. It was just hard to do that without angering Flint. Everyone is kind of afraid of him. His family is part of the pureblood line, and they haven't been nice for a while."

I drop my head, recalling Flint's bare arm, understanding for the first time why it's bare. He's a pureblood. Just like Cordelia.

"Why does he hate me so much?" I ask.

"He doesn't hate you, Alena. He hates your totem."

I look at her, not understanding.

"When Mark morphed at initiation, he dispelled high doses of Doler. It affected each of the Pepps in Petrichor, but not as badly as it did the purebloods." Cody hangs her head. "The rest of us are all normal humans. We naturally create small doses of Doler within us. In a way, we were used to the feeling it creates. Not to such an extreme, but we had experienced it somewhat before and were eventually able to get rid of it. Flint's family, however, was not used to so much Doler since they're purebloods, and they haven't been able to handle it. The chief has tried over and over again to convince them to do the things that get rid of the Doler, but they're too proud to believe it will work. It's easier for them to hate Mark—and you—for making them feel awful instead of trying to do something about it. They've turned into horrible people." Cody shakes her head. "When I first came here, they were really nice. And happy. Even Cordelia, which I thought was cool considering the terrible accident that had taken her husband and most of his family. But then after Mark's morph, it was like they all changed."

So, Flint lost his father? Great, now I feel guilty for hating him.

"And now Flint is going to hate me even more," I mutter, "since I've ruined his chances of matching."

Cody chuckles. "Alena, purebloods don't match."

I look at her even more confused. "What?"

"Flint has been a Pepp since the day he was born and morphed at the age of five, obtaining power way before any Pepps do. Things are different with purebloods. They don't really match but instead train from a very young age in every field. That way, when they go through initiation, they can choose which job they want to work in. For Flint, initiation is just the opportunity for him to choose what he's decided to do."

I recall Flint using acid on me. He has power. And knows how to use it.

"What is he going to choose?" I ask.

Cody shrugs. "I don't really know him well enough to answer that. All I know is that he is irritatingly good at everything."

We remain quiet until Cody breaks the silence again. "All I'm saying, Alena, is that Mark is doing everything in his power to make sure you match and stay safe. You have a better shot at this than he did, and he's pushing to have you protected. He made the council promise that they would help your team put up fog walls at each of your campsites. He's also made them promise to have a team of flyers circle the area to keep an eye on you, something that's never been done before. He's watching out for you."

I'm eager to learn how to use the power, but it sounds like an awful lot of effort for me, a defective Pepp, to participate in something I can't even really participate in.

I glance at Mark. He's throwing his untouched food in the garbage. He meets my gaze one last time before leaving with Danny. Little Gabbro sits atop Danny's shoulder, waving at me. I wave back.

Why is Mark going through such great lengths to make sure I match? Because he feels responsible for me?

And what if Mark is right? What if the clan somehow knows where Petrichor is, and what if they come after me? What if they know more about us than we realize?

Chapter 14

I stand dressed in the wet suit Cody helped me pick out at Mossy Hollow. The sleek material hugs my body all the way from my ankles to my wrists, with water shoes and gloves covering my hands and feet. Supposedly the river water is quite cold. The wet suit is supposed to help, but I still shiver thinking about it. Tonight, I'll have to feel it. My hair is pulled into a high ponytail, and even though I look several years older than the rest of my team, I feel ten years younger. They're much more prepared for this than I am.

Thankfully I have Breccia harnessed to my arm. I might not know how to use the power once I get it, but it comforts me to know I will at least be able to send a message with Breccia if something happens.

The past two weeks have flown by. I crammed in as much studying as I could, or as much studying as my nerves would let me. Everyone has heard I'll be participating in this initiation, and according to Leinani the crowds will be bigger than ever since everyone wants to see if anything happens to the *defective girl.* Some of the runners have organized a party at the top of Training Mountain, where the Pepps will be able to view the game through their special field glasses. This of course worsens my jitters. For me, this is no party. Why does everyone have to come?

Ever since my conversation with Cody, I haven't been able to ease my mind about participating in the game. I'm torn between matching and becoming an active part of Petrichor and keeping my friends safe. Keeping myself safe.

Regardless of how many times Leinani has told me that the Pepps need help and don't want to wait for me to match in a couple of months, I still feel wary. Is it really worth going through all this trouble? According to Leinani, the Pepps need more help than I understand due to their struggling numbers, and taking me out of my comfort zone, like the game will do, is the quickest way for me to match.

I still have so many worries though. What if the clan does show up? What if someone gets hurt or taken … or killed? My stomach hurts. I would never be able to forgive myself if something happened to my new friends.

Grabbing my satchel filled with my carefully placed capsules, I push all thoughts aside and head down to the gym on the bottom floor of GreenGrotto. My efforts at trying to calm my racing heart are unsuccessful as other Pepps slam into me trying to get to the river too … to watch. The bottom floor isn't any quieter until I step into the gym. I shut the glass door behind me, lean against it, and take in a deep breath. The room is empty except for the other four members of my team, and Aba, double-checking satchels and supplies.

Once I step up to the group, Aba begins to loudly explain the details of the game one last time. "You will travel down the river. It will take you a couple of hours to get out of Petrichor's protection fogs, to the bottom of Training Mountain. Dock the boat when you see the river splitting into three smaller rivers, make camp, and then in the morning you'll begin your journey back to Petrichor. Use your map and compass and choose your direction wisely, taking into account all obstacles. You have two days to travel back, so do so quickly but carefully."

Pulling out a ring, Aba continues. "This is a toboggan. It's to be used only in the worst of circumstances. It will fit two Pepps in it, so if someone becomes severely injured, you send them back in this. It will go straight to the hospital." Aba pushes the black jewel, and the ring expands into a large object resembling a casket made up of vines and branches woven together like a bird's nest.

Finding the black button on the bottom, she collapses it again and hands the ring to Carlos. "Keep in mind, though, that using it will cost you points and may keep the person sent back in the toboggan from matching. Also, keep your Magbabies with you at all times. If something happens and you need help, simply send your Magbaby. Don't worry about writing a message. The messengers have all been informed that any Magbaby from your team will summon an automatic visit by the chief."

Breccia wiggles in her harness at the mention of her.

Aba continues. "You will be given points based on how quickly you get back and how well you work together. The more points, the bigger your prize of power will be." Bapoto bounces at the mention of power.

"Last, just a reminder of the adjustments to this quarter's game. A fog is needed at each of your camps to protect you. Please be aware of where it is, and do not step outside it. A team will descend every night at dusk to make sure you're all okay. A team of flyers will also keep an eye out for you during the day." Aba's tight face relaxes. "Be careful out there, but have a little fun too. Use your power wisely, but use it all. It's your gift."

A loud horn blows outside the gym, and I see the sun dropping in the sky.

"It's time," Aba announces, her voice softer than normal.

We step out into the last few fingers of sunlight and head toward the river that gurgles at the base of the mountain adjacent to GreenGrotto. My hands tremble when I spot the large crowd that has gathered like a massive flock of sheep. Their blended conversations and laughter bounce through the air, at least until they spot us coming. Then their conversations dull to curious whispers, and their eyes cast analytical glances in my direction.

Carlos leads us toward the riverbed where the long bridge crosses the water. Walking beside Leinani, I lower my eyes to the ground.

When we reach the middle of the bridge, my team stops, and I raise my eyes. The river banks are lined with thousands of Pepps on both sides.

A simple wooden boat bobs in the water below us, a lamp attached to the front.

Someone clears their throat behind me, and I turn to see the chief standing there, Aba behind him. I expect the chief to speak to the crowd, to indicate the start of initiation, but he doesn't. Instead, Aba holds out five glass spheres with a yellowish liquid swishing inside. Is that the power? This alone hushes the crowds.

Aba carefully gives each of my teammates one sphere. I watch as they pull the neck of their suits down and place the spheres over their hearts. I eye her curiously when she gets to me. Her soft eyes look entirely foreign on her usually stern face. Pulling the neck of my wet suit down, I expose the empty green hole in the heart of my totem.

"This is your first vial of power, Alena. It will help your totem place you in a job."

Aba places the sphere over the hole and pushes it in. It fits perfectly and stays put when Aba steps away. I don't know what I expected from my first vial of power, but I definitely didn't expect to hear major ringing in my head. My eyes squint in response to the painful high-pitched noise, and I cover my ears with my hands to muffle the sound, but it doesn't help. I open my eyes to find the chief, Aba, and my teammates all staring at me. It feels all wrong, but then I see a smile spread across Aba's face. I strain to hear her words over the throbbing in my head.

"Can you hear it, Alena—the ringing?" I nod, wanting it to stop.

She pulls my hand away from my ear. "That's a good thing. It means you can hear the elements around you, and your totem can hear you. It means you'll match." I want to groan. I don't understand. *How can this sound be a good thing?*

I drop my hands, trying to adjust to the sound just as the chief sends out some sort of fireworks overhead. This elicits a roar from the crowd.

Wonderful. More noise.

The explosion obviously means that it's time to board the boat, so I follow Leinani across the bridge. Beating music from the crowd adds to the commotion and agitates my unease even more. I strain to breathe, the sounds crushing me, but I keep moving forward. *Just get to the boat.*

Carlos gets there first and stabilizes the canoe, then holds out his hand to help the rest of us board. Bapoto ignores Carlos completely, but the girls take his hand willingly. I practically tear it off when the rocking boat almost knocks me off my feet. I sit in the middle next to Nadia, whose face is blank as always. Carlos takes the front, with Leinani behind him. Bapoto takes the rear.

Carlos, fueling the commotion around us, raises his oar up into the air, and the excitement grows. The Pepps lining the riverbank send more fireworks into the sky.

Taking my oar, I help push us off the shore. I row through the water, hoping to get us out of the commotion as quickly as possible.

My team, unfortunately, is not in such a hurry.

Each of them waves emphatically to their Pepp families and friends tucked among the crowds. I search for faces I know: Cody, or Mark, maybe Danny. But there is only one face in the crowd that I recognize, and it makes my heart sink.

Flint. And he doesn't look happy. His mother is there with him. I cringe even more. Cordelia.

Swallowing, I look away.

With the sun now set behind the shadow of the mountain, the Pepps on the shore light candles and hold them high in the air to light our way. But after a mile or so the crowds begin to dissipate, and the culminated fireworks cease to explode. I sigh in relief. *Thank you.*

"Well, guys," Carlos yells back to us, paddling in front. "You ready?" Bapoto and Leinani both holler in excitement. I grasp the oar tightly and push it harder into the water.

Let's get this over with.

Eventually, the calm river gets rough, forcing us to paddle and steer more carefully. I expend every ounce of energy trying to steer the boat away from the edges and rocks. It doesn't take long for the cold, spitting water to soak my wet suit. Thankfully, it does a great job of keeping my body warm. The lantern up front provides little light to us in the darkness but is bright enough to make us stand out.

I search the dark tree edges as water splashes my face. After passing through the safety of Petrichor's fog, I can't help but feel like a sitting duck out here.

Suddenly, we hit an unseen rock in the middle of the water that sends the front of our boat flying into the air too much to the left, tipping us all over the edge.

My body falls into the water, and I whimper at the iciness of it on my face. Unable to touch the bottom of the deep river, I do my best to keep my head above the water that's swiftly taking me downstream. Where's my team?

I cough wildly, swiping in vain at the water in my eyes. I can't see anything! Where's the tree line?

"Help!" I try to shout to tell my teammates where I'm at, but the word comes out only as a gurgle from all the water in my throat. I need to get to the river bank. Struggling to keep myself above the water, I mentally gauge the direction the river is taking me and swim in the direction I think the bank would be.

I don't hear anyone else. Are they okay?

I laugh in relief when my legs scrape against the rocks beneath me, telling me I'm close to the edge. I desperately push myself further, then crawl out of the water.

I try to catch my breath, the rocks digging into me through the wet suit. When I can finally breathe again, I pull myself to standing. I'm about to turn and shout out again for my teammates, when I freeze.

Two very still yellow eyes stare at me from the trees. My cold heart pounds, and my tired muscles tense.

"Alena!" Leinani shouts behind me. Immediately the two eyes disappear from sight, and I hear the snapping of branches as whatever it was scuttles off.

"Alena, are you alright?" Leinani asks. I turn around to see the rest of the team coming up behind me with the boat in tow.

Shivering wildly, I search the trees again, Aba's warnings becoming more real to me now. *Watch out for animals.*

"Let's get going," Carlos says. He tries to keep his voice upbeat, but I can tell the flip has taken its toll, even on him. Thankfully all our supplies are in the satchels still tied to our waists. The only thing Carlos has to do is light another lantern.

Still keeping my eyes on the tree line, I get back into the boat. We brace ourselves again, all shivering and cold.

We quickly slip away from Petrichor's mountains and approach new mountains. The river takes us past two on the right. I look at the valley on the left and see a large lake in the middle of it. I eye the clouds above, looking for the lightning storms I've heard so much about. So far it looks pretty calm.

Our silent tension eases to fatigue. Our muscles are sore from paddling, and we anxiously wait for the end of the river. Finally, the water branches into three smaller streams up ahead, and we begin steering for the left bank. "This is the valley where the river ends. We'll get out here and camp for the night," Carlos says.

I sigh in relief. *Thank you.*

Carlos ties up the boat, while Leinani starts a large bonfire in the moonlit night.

"Everyone," Carlos says, "I know you're cold, but while Leinani starts the fire, get your tents set up and change your clothes. Bring your wet suits over to dry by the fire. Then we'll eat some dinner."

I'm exhausted. The thought of still having so much to do makes me even more tired, but I trudge to the area next to the fire and pull out my wet satchel. I retrieve my tent and expand it. After stepping inside, shivering violently from the cold, I change my clothes, so grateful the capsules kept the rest of my clothes dry. By the time I emerge from my tent in sweatpants and a sweatshirt, the fire is blazing, and the others are hanging up their wet suits to dry. They're efficient at making camp. I'm a deadweight, just like Flint called me. This isn't going to be as fun for me as it is for them.

I pull out my camp chair and sit by the fire. For the first time this whole night the air is quiet, except for the calming crackle of flames.

The ringing in my head, originating from the power placement, is gone. *Thank goodness.*

Nadia bends over the fire, cooking something brown and mushy in a large pot. I don't care what the food is. I'm so hungry, I'll eat anything warm.

The food doesn't take long to cook, and soon we're all eating chili.

"So, Mark made me promise," Carlos says, "to encircle us with fog every night before we go to bed." He stuffs a spoonful of food into his mouth. "If you could all help me with that after we eat, that would be great."

Bapoto complains next to me. "The fog takes up so much power."

Carlos ignores his griping and continues with his dinner. Everyone cleans their utensils when they're done and then stand to make the fog around the tents, while I just sit.

I'm staring at the fire, wanting to just go to bed, when I hear the soft plucking sounds of a guitar in the air. Confused, I look in the direction of the music. A deep bass joins the guitar, pounding through the campsite. Carlos starts to move his body smoothly, spreading the fog in front of him. Looking closer, I realize the music is coming from Carlos's Magbaby, who is now sitting on his shoulder. Leinani, who is close to Carlos, begins dancing in unison. The beat gets louder, and other instruments skillfully join in the song. I'm surprised that a tiny Magbaby can create and amplify music so loudly. The vibrations reach me even where I sit. I look around. Is it good for us to be so loud?

Carlos starts singing foreign words to the extremely buoyant song. Bapoto seems to know the song too. I watch him join in the dancing. They all soon drop the task at hand and move with the song around the fire, except for Nadia. I watch them through skeptical eyes, jealous of their ability to liberate themselves from the crushing worries that seem to preoccupy my mind.

Reminded of why I can't dance, I glance around now, searching for any sign of intrusion. I look behind me, and my heart drops when I see two people walking toward our dancing group. I jump up, terrified. It doesn't take long for me to see it's only Rusty and Cody. Unfortunately, this does nothing for my racing heart. I now want to disappear, knowing I look like a terrified soaked rat with my hair still wet.

I sink into my chair and bury my face in my hands.

"Looks like you all made it safely," Rusty shouts to the group, pounding me on the back. "How did it go, Alena?" Rusty kneels beside me. The music fades and everyone stops dancing.

"Good," I murmur into my hands.

This humors Rusty and he chuckles. I peek out the side of my hand to see Cody quietly continuing with the fog wall around the campsite. Her hair is down tonight, straight and silky in the firelight.

"Well, we've watched you all from above," Rusty says, "and have only found a few animals close by. A bear seemed to be following you further up the river, but now he's gotten distracted. Other than that, the area is quiet. You look pretty safe to me."

I lift my head, listening to these details. The yellow eyes. They must have belonged to the bear.

I have to admit I'm grateful for Mark's extra precautions. If only to keep us safe from the bear.

Once Cody is done with the fog and satisfied with her efforts, she turns to me and says, "Good luck, Alena. We'll be flying overhead tomorrow, watching you."

I nod, grateful.

A solemnness settles again over our campsite once Rusty and Cody disappear. With exhaustion evident on each of our faces, Carlos finally gives in. "Let's get to bed. We have a big day tomorrow."

The fire is put out before we separate. I enter my tent and pull out my sleeping bag, then slide inside. This is going to be a wasted effort. There's no way my beating heart and alert ears are going to let me rest tonight.

Chapter 15

The rustling outside my tent wakes me shortly after finally falling asleep. What a terrible night. I hear my teammates now up with the sun, and I moan in frustration. I can already feel the fatigue settling in. *How am I going to climb a mountain today?*

Regardless, I pull myself up. At least I didn't die last night. I shiver as I slip out of my warm sleeping bag. The temperatures dropped in the middle of the night, and the wind picked up. I'm grateful I at least had a warm sleeping bag, even if I didn't sleep much.

After changing my clothes and pulling on my hiking shoes, I crumple everything back into capsules and step outside the tent, finding everyone else awake.

"Good morning!" Carlos greets me with a large smile that shouldn't be allowed this early in the morning. I just grumble, making him laugh.

After compressing my tent, I walk over to Nadia, who's now cooking a delicious breakfast of chili again. I don't mind. We pack up our camp quickly, and Carlos gathers us in.

"Okay, guys, we need to figure out which direction we're going to take to get back up the mountain." Laying out his map on the ground, we all examine where he points. "We should aim to get here by nightfall. That would put us halfway back to Petrichor—that way we can finish the rest by tomorrow."

Nadia objects. "That's at least twenty-five miles away."

Carlos takes no offense to Nadia's grumbling. "Yes. There are a couple of routes we could take. If we follow the river, it will take us to the far side of the mountain, just below the halfway spot, and then we can climb up."

Leinani pitches in now, her hair in a loose ponytail, absent of the usual flower. "The river switches back and forth too much. If we follow it, we'll waste time."

Carlos nods. "Yes. The other option is to travel straight to the left from here, but it will take us directly up the mountain and over some high cliff walls. Once we're about halfway up, we straddle the mountain to the other side. It'll be much more strenuous and taxing on our bodies. Plus, we'll probably have to rock climb, which will slow us down, but it will be about ten miles shorter than following the river."

Looking up at the sky, he adds, "Climbing the mountain on this side will also keep us farther from lake, at least until the end when we straddle around it. The clouds already look bad. Let's vote. Those who want the river, raise your hand."

Nadia raises her hand and then groans when she sees she's the only one.

"Those in favor of going up and over the mountain, raise your hands." Leinani, Carlos, and Bapoto all raise their hands. I don't vote, but it doesn't matter. The majority agrees with his plan. As if that settles everything, Carlos picks up his map and loads his satchel. Then, looking at his compass, he leads the way. "Once we get there, we'll make camp, and then tomorrow we'll zip-line directly over to Petrichor Mountain."

I follow behind him, with Leinani, tension growing between us all. Carlos shouts back to us, "Let's keep up our pace so we can reach our goal before dark."

Nadia trails behind me in the rear. Bapoto hurries ahead to walk by Carlos.

When we reach the base of the mountain and begin our ascent, a very cold rain begins to fall. Standing on the outskirts of the thick brush and trees, we all pull out our raincoats and hats. "We're going up?" Nadia gripes.

"It's the quickest way," Carlos says. "Come on."

Stepping into the woods, we follow Carlos, winding our way through the pine trees that provide very little protection from the rain. Despite my coat, I still shiver as the cold seeps in. The slope of the mountain sharpens, and my thighs strain as I push forward. I'm thankful when Carlos begins switching back to lessen the strain on our legs, but he and Bapoto are now far ahead with Leinani close behind.

Even Nadia eventually passes me, but not without verbalizing her opinion of this trek.

"This is stupid. They're going to wear us out before we even get halfway. Flint never would have led us this way."

Nadia then proceeds without giving me a chance to respond, but I can't help but agree with her. I'm already tired. *How am I supposed to do this all day?* Soon the light-blue color of Nadia's raincoat begins to fade.

I sigh. This seems an awful lot like the training.

I use my anger to push me forward, trying to close the distance between Nadia and me, but after another hour of hiking through the woods the cold rain begins to seep into my bones. My body is exhausted, and everyone is still far ahead of me.

Trying to scale a generous rock, I slip and fall to a rock below. The rough surface bites into the skin of my back and buttocks, extracting a curse from my lips. *Why am I even here? Why did the chief think it was okay to include me without proper training? Why didn't anyone tell me this was going to be so hard?*

I sit on the rock, tears threatening my eyes. *Why am I so weak?*

I look up to see an eagle Pepp passing by, the clouds in the sky much darker than earlier.

Pulling myself up, I look back in the direction I last saw Nadia. As angry as I am, I need to stay with my team in case the storm gets worse.

I soon see the colors of everyone's jackets, but then I make out the form of a large rock wall ahead of me, extending at least thirty feet high. My mood slips further. They had mentioned a rock wall in the beginning, but I had completely forgotten. *How in the world am I supposed to make it up that now?*

"Carlos is trying to scout a way up the wall, so just sit tight," Leinani says when I approach the group. Nadia and Bapoto are sitting under a rock overhang, shivering from the cold, trying to get a fire started.

Standing in the rain, Carlos examines the wall in front of us. Nadia sits in the corner of the overhang, her face reflecting my mood. I never thought I'd be drawn to the girl, but in this moment, knowing that she hates initiation as much as I do, I am.

"The rain has made the rocks too slick to climb with our bare hands." Leinani says to Carlos. "Besides, everyone is tired. We could just make a ladder to climb up."

Carlos looks down to the heart of his totem. Keeping his voice low, he says, "We need to be careful with the power. We still need to create the camp fog tonight. Luckily, we haven't had to use it too much for other things, but just in case something happens, we need to try to preserve it."

The jab hurts. Their lack of power is my fault.

Carlos and Leinani continue to talk, but I no longer want to listen to their conversation. Instead, I scrunch down next to Nadia and pick up a stick to draw lines in the mud at my feet.

Coming back to the group, Carlos announces, "We're going to send up a rope to the top of the mountain. I'll go first. When I reach the top, I'll send down another rope you can tie around your waist to support you all as you climb. The rocks look very slick, so we all need to be careful." Looking up at the sky, he appears more concerned than I've ever seen him. "The weather is also getting worse. I know you're all tired, but we need to keep going. We have a couple of hours left until we reach our goal point for the day, and we might not make it if the weather turns bad." None of us like this news, but looking up at the sky even I sense the urgency. I can't blame him for pushing so hard. He's just trying to keep us safe.

Bapoto gives up on the fire, while Carlos prepares for ascent. He sends a long rope up to the top of the mountain, securing it on a tree above. How he does that, I don't know. Then, stepping to the rock wall with the rope gripped in his hands, he climbs effortlessly. As promised, he sends down another rope and Nadia takes it, then wraps it around her waist. Holding the rope in her hands, she props her body away from the wall and walks up. It takes her longer than Carlos, and she slips several times but makes it to the top.

Bapoto goes next. His heavier weight adds more strain to the rope, and I can see it cutting into the muddy edge at the top. Several chunks of mud drop and Carlos steps back, avoiding the collapsing ground.

With Bapoto at the top, Carlos sends the rope back down.

It's my turn.

Nervously I wrap it around my waist. I look up, only to have the rain splatter into my eyes. I grip the rope and prop my feet against the wall, but the rope tears into the skin around my torso and the muscles in my legs start shaking. Man, I'm out of shape. The strain is far more than I imagined, especially in my shoulders and arms. I have a hard time seeing what's in front of me, and the rocks that seemed sturdily jammed into the mountain are slicker with mud than I realized.

My feet slip and I slam into the wall, my shoulder taking the brunt of the hit. I yelp, channeling all my strength into not letting go of the rope. Placing one foot in front of the other, using all the muscles and strength I have left, I push myself until I reach the top and allow Carlos and Bapoto to pull my shaking body up over the edge.

I lie on the ground next to the cliff and breathe heavily, trying to get air, while Bapoto and Carlos send the rope down one last time to Leinani. She starts to climb. I sit up to move, when the ground beneath me begins to slip, the mud sliding toward the edge of the cliff. I roll away from the edge just in time to see the whole piece of rain-softened mud around the cliff give way. Carlos and Bapoto hop back just in time to avoid slipping down, but the rocky cliffside disappears. Leinani's scream is shortened by a sickening crunch. I scramble to the new jagged edge and see Leinani on the ground below us, her limbs bending in odd angles under the mound of mud.

Carlos swears as he and Bapoto create several vines with their power. It's amazing how they control the vines, get them to wind around her body from up here. Once she's secure, they pull her up.

Carlos lays her down far from the edge, and we all gather around, trying to examine her body. She groans.

"Does anyone know anything about the body?" Carlos says, worry in his voice. "Leinani knows about the body, but does anyone else?"

I'm pulled toward the injuries. She has an obvious wound in her thigh that runs deep and is bleeding profusely. I kneel down next to her in the mud and take a shirt capsule out of my satchel. I expand it and press the cloth against the wound. Leinani screams when I make contact, but then falls quiet again. She might have a broken bone. It looks bad, but that might be the least of the injuries. I can't tell what's going on internally, especially in her head.

"How bad is it?" Nadia asks Carlos, her disdain for the trip now replaced with worry for Leinani.

"I don't know." Carlos pulls out the ring that was given to him at the beginning of the game. He fidgets with it—the toboggan, which is supposed to be used only in emergencies. To use it will cost us points. Plus, if we send her back, Leinani may not match if her totem hasn't had a chance to sense her place.

"Let's get her over to a tree where she'll have some shelter," Carlos says. "If she doesn't wake up within a few minutes, we'll send her to Petrichor." The four of us step around Leinani, lift her, and move her to a tree. The movement sends a jolt through her, and she screams. When she opens her eyes under the pine tree, she scrunches her face in pain.

"Nani, tell me where you hurt," Carlos says softly, kneeling next to her. I don't miss the nickname he uses tenderly.

"C-Carlos," she grinds her teeth, pain contorting her face.

"Can you tell me where you hurt," Carlos coaxes again.

Leinani draws in a sharp breath. "My leg—it-it hurts a lot."

I peek at the gushing blood seeping through the cloth in my hand. "Do you think it's broken?" I ask.

Leinani squeezes her eyes shut. "I think it's just a simple fracture, but it sure hurts."

Carlos nods. "Do you think you can repair it?"

Lifting her head, Leinani braves a look at her leg but then drops it, exhausted from the pain. “No. I don’t know how to repair bones yet. I’m so sorry.” Sweat collects above her brow, her body arching in pain.

“It’s okay. We’re going to send you back in the toboggan. Okay?”

Leinani lets out a sob, either relieved or grieved by the news. I’m not sure.

Before I can stop it, my mouth opens. “Wait.” Everyone in the group looks at me. “Is your leg the worst of your pain? Do you feel okay internally? How’s your head?”

Leinani focuses on my questions, and I see her thinking. “Yes, it’s just my leg.”

“Can you heal skin?”

“Not very well.”

“Can you take away the pain somehow?”

Leinani’s eyes get wide. “Of course. I’ll take away the pain. Then I should be able to go on, right?”

Adrenaline kicks in now as I realize what I’m about to do. “I don’t know if you’ll be able to walk, but we might be able to help you continue on so you don’t have to be sent back. Listen, my dad is a doctor. I helped him out in his clinic many times and watched him stitch up open wounds like this. He even brought home supplies to let me practice on a medical dummy he had. I know how to do this. It wouldn’t be with power, but I can stop the bleeding. We could then carry you. It’ll slow us down, but at least we won’t be penalized for using the toboggan, and you could still have a chance of matching. If it doesn’t work, or if you get worse, then we’ll send you back.”

Carlos and the rest of the group consider this carefully. “What do you think, Nani?” Carlos asks.

“I’m down for it if you’re willing to carry me,” she says.

After another moment of thought, Carlos says, "Let's do it."

"Okay, I'll need a needle and a thread, if you could make that for me?" I ask Carlos.

"That's easy." Bapoto pitches in and takes responsibility for that task. Within seconds I have exactly what I need.

Looking at Leinani, I ask, "Can you numb it now?"

"Yes, I'll disable the pain receptors. If you can just stitch it up." Leinani pants through her words and tries to sit up with Carlos's help.

"Okay," I say, wiping the rain from my eyes.

Leinani holds out her hand, squinting in pain as she does what she needs to do. After a couple of minutes, she leans back exhausted but more relaxed. "That's the best I can do." I touch Leinani's skin, asking her if she can feel it, but she shakes her head.

I pick up the needle and thread and begin the repair. I see the muscle is torn and needs to be sutured before the skin. Leinani's body stiffens when the needle enters the muscle and she clings to Carlos, but she doesn't make a sound. I pull the thread through and poke the other side, going back and forth. I don't think an artery was cut, thankfully. The blood and rain make it much slipperier than the dummies I'm used to working on, but I'm able to find the edge of the muscle and sew it shut. Once the muscle is holding, I begin stitching up the skin, using the same pattern I used with the muscle. My stitches are too far apart in some spots, and they don't look nearly as perfect as my dad's, but I know they'll at least keep her bleeding at bay. Then grabbing two straight sticks and another shirt from my capsule, I stint her leg as best as I can, to at least keep the bone from moving if it is broken.

Suddenly, the buzzing noises I had heard the day before begin blaring in my ears again. I squint and shake my head, agitated with the overwhelming sound, but it doesn't do any good.

I look up and see the blood has drained from my friends' faces, and Nadia runs to a nearby tree and throws up. Probably from all the blood.

Carlos continues to hold Leinani.

The adrenaline I felt while stitching the wound vanishes, and the fullness of my limitation returns seeing her in pain. If I was a true Pepp, I would have been able to heal her completely, but I'm not.

"You did well," Leinani mutters.

"Can you sterilize it?" I ask, now realizing how muddy her wound looks.

Leinani holds out her hand. "I'm not great at that either, but I'll try."

I don't see anything change. I just hope that any bacteria that got in is now dead.

When Leinani is ready, we carefully place her in the stretcher Bapoto made and proceed up the mountain, Carlos and I taking the first turn carrying. I'm not strong, and my arms and legs tire long before Carlos's. Bapoto sees me struggling and takes the stretcher from me. As I walk behind, recovering my strength, I look at my group. *Is this how initiation normally goes?* I can't imagine being in worse shape than we're in.

The wind picks up, blowing against us, and the sky darkens, making our progression slower. We pull out our lanterns. Soon Carlos tells us we no longer need to climb. We just need to hug the side of the mountain.

There's no more complaining among us. I suddenly feel bad for the things I thought about Leinani and Carlos earlier and find myself worried about Leinani. She's shivering like the rest of us, but other than that her body isn't moving. We laid protective plastic over her to keep the rain off, but she's still cold. I also worry about infection in her leg. Was she able to sterilize it thoroughly? We might end up sending her back in the toboggan anyway.

"We're almost there," Carlos shouts into the dark over the sound of the heavy falling rain, when something rumbles in the distance.

We all freeze.

Thunder.

Carlos looks around, his eyes darkening in fear. Frantically he pulls out his soaked map and compass and tries to look for a place that will give us refuge. I look up at the sky, seeing the dark shadow of an eagle flying high above us. *They'll pull us out of the game if the storm gets too close, right?*

"Here," Carlos shouts. "There's a cave not too far from here. It should be big enough for us to hide inside. We can block it with rocks if we need to. Lightning can't travel through the rocks. It's about half a mile away. We need to hurry."

Half a mile!

Carlos picks up the front of the stretcher while Bapoto picks up the back. They run with Leinani while Nadia and I stumble in front, carrying the lanterns to light the way,

"I think I see the cave up ahead!" Carlos shouts after several minutes. "Alena, take the stretcher. Bapoto, take Nadia to start setting up the fog. We're right behind you."

I take the stretcher from Bapoto, with Carlos still on the other end, then hand Bapoto my lantern. My tired limbs object loudly when I lift, but I force every ounce of energy to respond within me. I'm much slower than Bapoto, but we move forward. The distance seems to stretch on forever. My legs and shoulders are giving way. If we don't get there soon, I'm going to drop Leinani.

Just before my body gives out completely, I see a thick fog forming up ahead of us and my body sags in relief. They must have found the cave. Now I can see our target.

Running straight through the fog, we find ourselves at the mouth of a deep cave. Both Carlos and I collapse in exhaustion. Bapoto and Nadia, done with the fog, pick up Leinani and carry her into the cave.

"We need to block off the entrance before the storm gets here," Carlos says. I nod and stand to walk inside with him. I need to check on Leinani's leg too, to make sure it's not infected. It's going to be a long night.

I step forward, when something catches my eye to the right. Relief floods me when I see Danny's familiar form stomping around in the mud. "Danny!" I move my sore body toward him. *Why is Danny here? Are there others?*

I approach him, ready to bring him inside the cave with me where the rest of my team is waiting, when he stomps more. Before I can call out to him again, he bolts into the line of trees, past the fog. I stop and look around. Where are the other Pepps? Did Mark come with him?

"Danny!" I call out after him, but I can no longer see him. Another rumble echoes around the rocks, and I panic. I have to get him into the cave. With the wind pulling at my hair and the rain pattering my face in the dark, I run after him, pushing through the trees. I call out his name. "Danny where are—"

A large gloved hand slams over my mouth from behind. Someone twice my size, with incredible strength, pulls me to their body. I grip at the hand, struggling to get free. I scream. But the glove is thick. Nobody's going to hear me. I reach my hands up, ready to claw eyes out, when I make out Danny's outline. He's kneeling on the ground with his back turned to me. I try to scream louder, confused that he can't see what's going on. But then I freeze. His hand reaches up to his hair, and he pulls off a wig. When he turns around and faces me, I can see that this man, even though he so strongly resembles Danny, is not Danny. I blink in horror.

"Quickly, get her power, tie her hands, and get her in here. We don't have much time."

After lighting a lantern on the ground, he fumbles with what looks like a capsule. A large bed expands in front of me with a wooden cover. *A toboggan?* I try to scream and fight, but the man holding me picks me up and slams me face-first into a tree behind him, crushing me into it with his body. The bark of the tree tears at my skin, and his weight pushes the air out of my lungs. I can't even scream.

The man pulls my hands behind my back, still crushing me, and ties them quickly. Then he reaches for the heart of my totem. He pops out the cylinder glass vial of power and crushes it against the tree, right next to my face. Letting go of me for a brief second, he stretches a piece of duct tape over my mouth and rips off my satchel that was tied around my waist. Then, picking me up, he heaves me into the toboggan, where the Danny look-alike ties my legs with rope. The cover begins to shut. No! I kick my body, screaming with all my might, but I'm too weak.

Just before the cover closes, though, something collides with both men. With the cover still half open I sit up, trying to pull at the ropes on my hands, stealing a glance at the scene in front of me. I freeze.

There's a large black bear attacking the men. It slashes the large man with a knife and throws him into a nearby tree. The man doesn't get up. The bear then turns toward the Danny look-alike and jumps, landing on him and pinning him down with his weight. I'm just thinking that there's no way the man will be able to get away from the bear, when the bear is thrown into another tree with an incredible force. The *crack* of the tree ripples through the air. Did my team hear that? *Will they come help?*

Breaking free from the harness on my arm, Breccia stares briefly at the scene before slicing through the air toward Petrichor for help. *Thank you, Breccia.*

"Dammit, Trevor, get away from her!" the Danny look-alike says.

Trevor? The bear's name is Trevor?

"No, *Case,* don't do this!" An oddly deep voice responds. *Is that the bear talking?* Something tells me it isn't. The low voice sounds remarkably familiar. Whose is it? I don't see anyone else.

I shake my head. I can't think about that right now. I need to get out of the toboggan. I roll out and toward a tree, when I stop. Trevor is now standing in front of Case, with his bear arms outstretched, blowing huge flames of fire toward him. His black fur ripples with the movement. Case waves the flames to the side before throwing Trevor with unbelievable strength into another tree.

They have power?

My mind spins as I look closer at Case, whose focus now turns to me. I see the totem in his skin. *He's a Pepp?* Scooting back, I try to escape his captive grasp. Thankfully, Trevor comes back, ramming into Case.

Just then an object slides on the ground toward me from my right—a knife at my feet. "Cut yourself loose!" the low voice demands.

Okay that's definitely not the bear talking. I squint in the direction of the voice but see nothing.

I scoot my body around so my hands can reach the knife, when the rumble of thunder, much louder this time, boils close by. I'm not the only one afraid of it. I can see the fear in both Trevor and Case. Seeing that they both have power, I realize they're in just as much danger as I am. I pick up the knife with my hands and begin sawing at the rope behind me.

"No!" Case yells in despair, "I need her!" An explosion of flames and heat erupts from him, pushing Trevor back to where I can no longer see him. Panicked, I saw faster, but Case stops the flames and closes the space between us too fast, then picks me up and throws me into the toboggan once more. I thud onto the wood, the knife behind my back slicing into my torso. The pain shoots through my body like thousands of tiny fires blazing through my cells. I scream into the tape, tears flooding my eyes. The toboggan is just beginning to close around me again, when the ground beneath us starts to shake so fiercely that Case loses his balance. The movement sends further shooting pains through my body, jostling the knife digging into me.

Another loud clap of thunder assaults my ears, and lightning appears overhead. I open my eyes just in time to see Trevor reappear. He throws Case to the side and pulls me out of the toboggan with his huge claw, then drags me away.

The knife. *I wish he knew the knife was in my back!*

I look back to see Case glancing at the sky. With such piercing anger, he eyes me one last time before hopping into the toboggan and disappearing.

Trevor drops me and tears the duct tape off my mouth with his claw, cutting my skin in the process.

"Alena." I open my eyes and see a tiny familiar figure sitting on the shoulder of the bear. *Gabbro? Danny's Magbaby?* That's the familiar voice I heard, but what's he doing *here* ... without Danny?

"Alena, I'm sorry, Trevor and I need to go," Gabbro says. Another clap of lightning appears in the distance, and Trevor grunts urgently. "Alena, your friends will be here soon, but I need you to promise me you won't tell anyone that you saw Trevor or me down here, okay?" Gabbro says.

His words seem very distant, but his begging voice and urgency call me back. "Okay," I whisper as best as I can. "I promise."

The bear quickly disappears. I try to watch, but the darkness of my mind is so heavy. I try to move and call for help, but the knife makes it hurt to breathe, let alone shout. Rolling onto my side to lessen the strain of the knife, I use my fingers to try to get it out. Suddenly a bolt of lightning strikes only a couple feet from me. The pressure is sucked from the air, and my ears ring from the deafening noise.

Just one more and I'm toast.

A strong hand grabs my shoulder and rolls me over. I scream out in pain when the knife stabs me further. But when I open my eyes, I see a kind and worried expression. Mark! *He shouldn't be here!*

But, at the same time, I've never been so happy to see anyone.

While picking me up, he sees the knife and pulls it out, quickly cutting the ropes still around my hands. My scream is drowned out by another strike. Then Mark runs. I watch his face for a second, which is illuminated by the bright light striking around us. It looks like he's saying something to me, but I can't hear anything. He drapes me over some kind of animal. And then my mind darkens.

Chapter 16

"Take his shirt off." A deep voice, mixed with the sound of shoes scuffing the floor, pulls me from my dark sleep. I open my eyes and look around the room. I'm no longer in the woods. Immediately my stomach churns. I'm in the same room my memories were checked in.

Whose room is this?

My eyes land on the group of Pepps gathered around a large table in the middle of the eerie space. It's lit by only a single torch.

"Who is he?" a familiar voice asks, and my heart thumps. I squint my eyes to see him.

Mark. Just the sight of him eases the heaviness weighing on me.

I move to sit up, my body responding to his presence, but then I freeze.

The Pepps around the table are examining something—a man. I look over the body quickly, analyzing him. My heart shudders. It's the man who had grabbed me and tied me up. The man who almost got me killed.

"He has the mark, and he's wearing the belt. Be careful." I now see Rusty on the other side of the table, a pair of scissors in his hand. His face is more serious than I've ever seen it.

"The clan knows about Alena," I can barely hear the chief's whisper, but his comment blankets the room in a bleak heaviness. Standing a whole head shorter than Rusty, the exhaustion is evident on his face.

"Not only did they know about her," Rusty says, "they knew how to draw her out. Why in the world did she leave that fog, Mark?" I'm shocked at the foreign fire in Rusty's eyes. "You said you wouldn't let her out of your sight. What happened?"

Mark's back stiffens, and so does mine. "I told you, Rusty, someone knocked me out." His hands tighten into fists, and I wonder if he will attack Rusty. Thankfully, the chief interjects.

"Rusty, please. Mark saved Alena and her entire team. We're lucky he was cautious enough to suspect this would happen."

Rusty's eyes are still burning in a searing way that makes me want to recoil, but at least he shuts his mouth.

"I find it curious he knew this was going to happen," a woman says. Standing next to Jeter is Flint's mother. Cordelia. *How does she do it? Manage to make each soft-spoken word feel like a knife to the chest? Why is she here?*

Hostility burns in my throat. I felt it that first day I met her, on the aircraft. But this time her venom is aimed at Mark. Picking up a capsule from the table, she continues, her demeaning eyebrows raised as high as they'll go. "Judging by the capsules in his satchel, we obviously have a traitor in our midst. Who's to say it isn't you?"

The tension in the room implodes. *Mark was the one who got me out of there. Why are they attacking him?*

Mark looks like he's about to pounce on the woman from across the table, like a cheetah ready to devour a gazelle. But the chief holds up his hands. "Please, let's just wait for Alena to wake up. Hopefully, she can help us understand what really happened."

The mention of my name makes everyone turn to where I'm half sitting up.

"Alena," the chief whispers when he sees that I'm awake.

He walks around the table, carefully approaching the bed. "Alena, how are you feeling?"

Sitting in a chair next to me, he searches my face intently. With the room now quiet and focused on me, all the events from initiation come flooding into my mind. Mark steps closer, ignoring Cordelia's attacking eyes.

"Alena, we almost lost you," the chief says. "I'm so sorry. We don't understand what happened. None of the Pepps overhead saw any other humans in the area. They say it's impossible for anyone to have been there without them knowing. We have no idea how they attacked you."

I observe his bushy, furrowed eyebrows. I think I know how the men got in and out so quickly.

"They had a toboggan," I whisper. "They were trying to get me in it."

"A toboggan?" the chief whispers. "They had a toboggan?"

Rusty and Mark are now standing behind the chief. "Why did you leave the fog, Alena?" Mark asks. "They wouldn't have been able to find you if you had stayed inside."

I squeeze my eyes shut. Talking about what happened brings all the images in my mind back to life. I don't want to relive it. I can already feel the fear creeping back in.

I open my eyes and look at the chief, hesitating, but his eyes beg for what I have to tell him, like a derelict begging for food.

I fiddle with the threads in the blanket. "Everyone was in the cave. I was about to follow, when I thought I saw Danny stomping around outside." My eyes meet Mark's, my stomach clenching. I truly thought it was Danny. The man had manipulated me. Somehow, he knew about my empathy toward Danny and knew I would follow him. *How did he know?*

"Danny wasn't there," Mark whispers, his face going white.

I know that … now.

"I walked toward him when … he disappeared past the fog into the trees." I furrow my eyebrows, still confused at what happened. "I didn't think anything of it, except that I needed to get him out of the storm. I left the fog and walked through the trees looking for Danny, when a man attacked me from behind." I point to the man on the table. "That man." My hands begin to shake, recalling the fight.

"I tried to get away, but I couldn't. Danny reappeared in front of me. He didn't seem concerned at all that I was being attacked by the man. Instead, he was focused on expanding a toboggan ring."

I meet the chief's eyes now.

"But it wasn't Danny, Chief. The man looked almost identical to him with his same brown eyes, but it wasn't him." The chief begins to shake his head, not understanding until I say, "His name was Case. I heard the other man call him that. Case."

The blood drains from the chief's face.

"It can't be," Cordelia says. "Case would never do …" The woman begins to babble, but she's cut off by Jeter, who places a silencing hand on her shoulder.

Still with his eyes glued to my face, the chief says, "Will everyone leave Alena and me alone for a moment?"

Nobody challenges the authority of the chief, but Mark hesitates long enough to conjure an authoritative gaze from him. His eyes are full of concern. I don't know exactly what happened tonight, but I'm grateful Mark was there. I meet his concerned gaze to assure him I'm okay. He nods before leaving the room, shutting the door behind him.

Once the door is shut, the chief leans forward, resting his arms on his knees. Clearing his throat, he begins to speak very carefully.

"Alena, did Case have a totem on his arm?"

"Yes," I say. "And he used it." I remember the otherwise inexplicable force I witnessed.

"That's why he was able to enter the fog to coax you out. He also had a toboggan on him, which got him in quickly and undetected." The chief continues putting the pieces together. "Was there anyone else there besides the man and Case?"

The pit in my stomach roils with a strong wave of nausea. The bear. I remember Gabbro's warning. *Why doesn't Gabbro want the chief to know about him and the bear? How the heck does Gabbro fit into all this?*

"No." I lie, but the chief doesn't sense it, and I hang my head. Gabbro better have a good explanation for this.

The chief rubs his graying beard. He's deep in thought, but I can't help but ask, "Who's Case?"

The chief's eyes rise to meet mine. I can see he's trying to process the information I've given him, but after a couple of moments he takes in a deep breath.

"Many years ago a Pepp lived here named Jose. He had a special knack for the body, similar to Jeter's. During one of his runs, he met a woman and fell in love with her. Because he couldn't bring her back to live with him here, he gave up his totem and began living with the non-Pepps. He continued his passion in science but remained a communicator for us.

"Jose had three sons: Case, Trevor, and Danny. It was during Danny's birth that Jose's wife passed away."

Danny. The pit in my stomach grows. *Danny, Case, and the bear, Trevor, are all brothers?* That explains why Case looked so much like Danny. And why Trevor's name seemed familiar to me. Mark had mentioned him.

"Jose was a good man." The chief shifts in his chair before proceeding. "When their oldest son, Case, was thirteen, a young boy came to live with their family. He had been abandoned by his parents and was a very sickly child. Jose gladly took him in and tried to take care of him, but everything he did to heal him made the boy remarkably worse. He communicated the details of the boy to me, wondering if I could help. Jeter and I both tried, but unfortunately our power made him worse too. Jose was determined to heal the boy, however, and asked for an extra totem to see if he could somehow find a way to use the totem's power to heal. He was convinced that it would help him find more answers."

A deep sadness emits from the chief as he looks down at the floor.

"The boy never got better and eventually died. Three years ago I received word that Jose had also died, bit by a venomous snake. I went personally to see what we could do for the three sons. I offered all three of them a home with us. The two younger boys, Trevor and Danny, chose to come with me. But the oldest, Case, decided to stay behind at his father's home, saying he wanted to carry on with his father's work since there were other sickly children just like the boy. He was almost eighteen, and I allowed him to make that decision on his own, something I've never done before. It causes too many problems splitting up siblings. I always collect them all."

I remember the confusion when I first met the Pepps at the rendezvous point. The girl had said that Pepps don't have non-Pepp siblings. This must be why.

The chief shakes his head in anguish. "I trusted him. He was exceptional like his father in science. Jose had bragged about him all the time and included Case in his experiments. Case knew more about the totem before he was sixteen than our own totem trainers here know now." The chief's voice grows louder. "Now he has started his own Sybalt clan? Is he the one responsible for our missing Pepps, hurt communicators, and the defective totem? Why?" The chief waves his hand toward my arm. "And I let him do it, all right under my nose?"

His voice is heavy with anguish. I put my hand on his. The room remains silent for a long time until he looks at me, confused.

"How did you get away?" he asks. "Mark found you lying there alone."

I edge around the truth in my mind, trying to find an explanation since I can't mention Trevor. I find one, and it isn't a lie.

"The lightning—Case was just as scared of it as I was."

The chief nods in understanding. "Case had a totem. Of course he was afraid of the lightning."

But then I'm confused again. The lightning had hit so close.

"How come I'm not dead?" I whisper.

The chief stares at me for a long time, and I examine his fatigued face. "I don't know. It didn't harm Mark either, which makes me believe it has something to do with your totem." He points to the vine on my arm. "I had never thought about it, but it makes sense. Lightning is drawn to Peppate, but your totem doesn't create Peppate. Instead, it creates Doler in large amounts, which repels Peppate. You must have been so full of Doler that the lightning couldn't strike you."

The totem saved my life?

"You also didn't have your power in, which probably helped. What happened to it?"

I tell him about the man crushing it against the tree, then taking my satchel. He shakes his head again.

"He not only had a totem, he had supplies. Toboggans that could have only been created here. The man that grabbed you had other capsules on him too." As the chief says this he stands, holding out his hand, indicating that I should follow. I take it, the pain in my legs angrily reminding me that I recently climbed a mountain. But then I remember the knife in my back. I already know it had to have been removed and my injury healed, but I reach behind anyway, sighing in relief to find only a hole in my clothing, not in my skin.

I'm moving toward the man lying on the table when a shiver runs up my spine. His chest is rising and falling.

"He's alive?" My voice rises.

"Yes," the chief says. "But we've tied him up and put him into a deep sleep. He can't hurt you." Then he adds. "He didn't have a totem like Case, so the lightning didn't kill him. But he did have capsules in a satchel draped around his shoulder."

The feet of the large man hang off the edge of the table, and his beard covers most of his face. Bile rises in my throat, and I turn my head to suck in some fresh air.

When I look back, I see that his coat and gloves have been removed, and he now lies exposed from the waist up. My heart sinks. The last time I saw the mark of a clan member, it was carved into the skin of a man who didn't deserve to die. Here, though, this same mark is tattooed proudly into this man's bicep, as a sort of trophy earned. The letter S. I try to look away, but my eyes are drawn to a belt attached tightly around his waist with several thick disabled wires dangling out of it. I want to ask the chief about it, when he hands me a capsule sitting on the table.

"These were found in his satchel," he says. Curious, I bravely walk forward and take the capsule. I turn it over in my still trembling hands, noticing that it's a simple equipment capsule. But then something catches my eye.

A black lotus flower is burned into the metal next to the red expansion button. I gulp back more bile. I pick up another capsule lying by the head of the man and study it, finding the same symbol. Frantically, I look at all of them. They all have it, the symbol Cody puts on all her capsules, the symbol of beauty.

I drop the capsules, feeling very sick.

"Are you alright, Alena?"

I blink firmly a couple of times, my mouth suddenly dry.

"These capsules ..." I whisper, "I think they're Cody's."

The chief stiffens. "What?"

I pick up a capsule and show him the lotus flower. "Cody burns the lotus flower into each of her capsules. Unless someone else does the same thing, these have to be hers." *Oh, how I hope I'm wrong.*

"How would he have Cody's capsules?" The chief stares at me, but I don't have the answer. My stomach just burns.

He falls quiet. One look at his face tells me he's thinking. Unfortunately, I don't have time to sit around and wait for him to figure it out. I need to get out of this place.

"Chief, is it okay if I go?"

I don't look at him but start walking toward the door, bracing myself on the table.

"Sorry, Alena. I should have had Rusty wait and help you back to GreenGrotto. But he probably went up to GreenGrotto's courtyard for the end of initiation party, if they still decided to hold it."

"Wait, initiation is over? Did everyone match?" The question is too light after seeing those capsules, and my head is pounding. "Actually, it doesn't matter. I need to go."

But the chief arches his eyebrows. "Yes, *everyone* matched."

His emphasis on the word *everyone* has me looking down at my own arm. Even amid my roiling stomach and my aching head, I can't hold back the disbelieving wheeze. A part of the totem on my bicep is wrapped in a red ribbon.

A red ribbon!

"Your totem sent out a red puff of dust while you were unconscious, matching you. I had the ribbon-wrapper do his job while you were still out-cold so you didn't have to feel it."

I touch the soft material with my trembling fingers.

I'm a medic.

Chief takes my arm and helps me to the door, returning to the previous topic. "Alena, one more thing. While we try to figure everything out, please don't tell anyone about your ability to repel electricity. We could use it to our advantage. So far, only Mark, you, and I know about it. Can we keep it that way?"

My stomach churns again. I nod, swallowing hard.

He whispers a thank-you before letting me go. I'm disappointed to find Mark isn't in the hall, but at the same time I'm so grateful. I would hate for him to see me like this. I can't even calm my trembling hands.

I'm unable to pay attention to anything in the place. I don't even know where I'm going as I walk down the stairs and out the door. All I know is that I need to get outside. Fast.

Once I'm in the night air, I see a tree and start to run. I barely reach it when the contents of my stomach come up. It's mostly chili.

Drained of my energy, I sit, lean against the trunk away from the vomit, and try to stop my shaking.

"Alena?"

I force my eyes open.

Ugh, it's Mark. Crouching in front of me with a worried look on his stubbled face. I groan and close my eyes.

"Are you okay?" he whispers.

"Please don't tell me you saw that." I wipe my mouth with my hand, hoping more than anything it's not covered in vomit.

Mark chuckles. "It's okay, Alena. I threw up too when I got back."

I open my eyes and narrow them in disbelief. "Really?"

Mark's brown eyes bore into mine, filled with compassion and understanding. But then he looks away. "Well, no."

I scoff. Of course he didn't.

"But I was really nauseated."

I almost smile at his failed attempt to make me feel better.

His voice turns serious. "Are you okay, Alena?" This time I know he's not asking about my stomach.

I lift my eyes to his. Raising my trembling hand to wipe my mouth again, I nod.

"Yeah, I think I'm just a little ... shook up."

"I don't blame you." Then, looking around at the dark night, Mark stands. "Can I help you back to GreenGrotto?" He extends his hand out to me.

Is he really willing to touch me, even after what he just saw me do? Maybe I should decline his help, for his sake, but after looking at his hand reaching out, suddenly I become very aware of how tired and shaky my whole body is. Perhaps I do need his help.

I raise my clean trembling hand to his. His warm fingers wrap around mine, and he gently pulls me up. I'm lightheaded, and my legs wobble. It takes a moment for my eyes to clear, but when they do, I realize Mark is holding me close. I look up at his face, finding his eyes etched with concern.

I swallow, making sure to keep my mouth shut so he can't smell my breath, and then gently push away.

"Thank you," I whisper. Forcing myself to find my balance, I turn and walk in the direction where I think GreenGrotto is.

Chuckling, Mark steps next to me, places his hand on my arm, and turns me around to the stone path lit with torches. "This way."

Man, I can't even think.

After redirecting me, he lets go of my arm but stays close, his arm occasionally brushing against mine. I appreciate his presence.

When I brave a look at him, I find him watching me.

"The knife in your back. Did Case do that?" he asks.

I open my mouth to tell him no, but then shut it. How do I explain that it was Gabbro who gave me the knife to cut the ropes, but it somehow ended up in my back? I look at the ground. Keeping Gabbro's secret from the chief felt bad enough, but keeping it from Mark? I hate it. Still, I find a roundabout way to explain it.

"I fell on it. He was using the knife to threaten me, and somehow it ended up in the toboggan. It stabbed me when he threw me in."

"I'm sorry, Alena."

He doesn't seem suspicious. But my trembling increases. For some reason, his trust makes me feel worse. I don't deserve it.

"I was supposed to protect you," he says. "One minute I had you in my sight, ready to get you away from the storm, and then the next I was lying in a toboggan all tied up. That man got to me too. But ..."

He holds something out in his hand. My heart rushes with relief when I find Breccia tucked safely in his palm. I carefully scoop her into my hand.

I had forgotten about her. I look up at Mark, confused as to how he got her.

"Breccia was on her way to get help from the chief but found me knocked out cold, tied up in a toboggan by Case. She woke me and helped untie me so I could help you."

I stare at her. "Thank you," I whisper.

"You're welcome," she responds quietly.

Then I raise my shaking hand to touch Mark's arm, to tell him thank you, but instantly recoil. That's the same hand I wiped my vommity mouth with.

Disgusting.

"Thank you, Mark," I say, clasping my hands together instead. "You saved me. I'm really grateful you were there."

Our eyes link for a moment. He silently accepts my words before noticing that my body is really shaking now.

Why can't I stop shaking?

He reaches into his satchel, then pulls out a capsule. It expands into a large coat.

"Here. This might help a little." He drapes it around my shoulders. I don't feel cold, but I still accept it. Getting my arms through the long sleeves takes a lot of effort, and zipping it is even worse, but I eventually get it. It smells like Mark and not only warms but comforts me instantly.

"Thank you." Now, trying to come up with something else to talk about that doesn't involve the truth about Gabbro, I ask quietly. "So, did you carry me out of there on a dinosaur?" I put my shaking hands in the large soft coat pockets while looking sideways at Mark.

"Yeah. Her name is Dilo. Riding her is a little rough, but she really came in handy tonight."

I shake my head.

"What?" Mark asks.

"I never thought a dinosaur could be used as a horse."

This makes Mark laugh out loud, a sound that soothes my tired heart. "Don't let *her* hear you refer to her as a horse." Then, leaning closer, he whispers into my ear. "She eats horses for dinner."

His whisper tickles my neck, sending shivers down my back. I gaze up at him, finding an amused twinkle in his eye.

It's in this moment that I realize Mark hasn't been nice to me out of obligation. He's here because he truly wants to be with me. I don't know why he does, but that realization warms me from the inside more than a coat ever could.

Talking to Mark the night I met Danny, about home and the hot spring, was something I had needed. Talking to him now is something I need. But looking at Mark walking beside me with his hands in his pockets, I wonder if maybe he enjoys our conversations too.

"Well, thank you, Mark." I find myself saying again. I bite my lip and look at the ground. Those words don't quite capture how indebted I feel to him. I look back up, finding him watching me again. As sincerely as I can, I repeat, "Thank you for everything."

"You're welcome, Alena."

We walk in silence for a ways. Suddenly, GreenGrotto, the mountain that seemed so far away not too long ago, is too close. I don't want Mark to leave me. I'm comfortable and safe, and within the warmth of his coat my body has slowed its shaking. But that will change the moment he's gone. I'll have to relive everything that happened during initiation over and over again in my mind. Alone.

The grimness of the experience settles on me again the closer we get to GreenGrotto. Needing to confide in someone, I whisper, "I saw the equipment capsules on the man, Mark." Bile rises again my throat. "I'm pretty sure they're Cody's. She marks her capsules with a flower."

Mark stops next to me. "Cody? As in your roommate Cody?"

"Yes." I furrow my eyebrows, still confused myself.

"You told the chief this?"

I nod.

"Do you think she intentionally gave them to Case? Does she know him?"

I shake my head and squint past a threatening headache. "She never made me suspicious. I have a hard time believing that she would give him the capsules. Or information. There has to be an explanation for how he got her stuff."

"Do you think you'll be okay sleeping in the same room with her tonight?"

I hadn't thought about that.

"I can find a place for you to sleep at the Burrows."

I shake my head. The thought of spending more time finding me a place to rest makes me want to cry. "No, I'll be fine. I won't tell Cody about the capsules or question her. I'll leave that up to the chief. For now, I think I just need some sleep."

"Okay." Mark raises his hand to my cheek, running the backs of his fingers across my skin. His gesture surprises me, but his touch is so warm and soft, I can't help but lean into it.

"Do you want me to keep watch in the hall? Or out on your balcony?" he whispers, his breath brushing against my forehead.

I have to admit that I would feel safer knowing Mark was close by. But he's done enough for me today.

"I'll be fine, Mark. You need some rest too."

Mark nods warily. "Okay. You know where to find me if something isn't right?"

"Yes." The walk to Mark's room is one I don't think I'll ever forget.

"Okay." Mark steps back, walks the last few steps to GreenGrotto, and opens the door. Holding it for me, he places his hand on my back and guides me through. I don't know what time it is, but it's late enough that the bottom floor is empty. Realizing I'm about to part ways with Mark, I start unzipping his coat, but he puts his hand on my arm. "You keep it, Alena."

Normally I would insist he have his coat back, but tonight, I have to admit, I'm not ready to part with the warmth of it just yet. Mark walks me to the girls' staircase. I take the first step but then turn back.

"Good night, Mark," I whisper.

"Good night, Alena."

I hear his words just before I disappear upstairs.

Chapter 17

I can't sleep. I've lain in my bed for hours now since Mark parted ways with me. I thought I was tired, but I can't stop thinking about everything. I've replayed the experience with Case over and over again and recounted the chief's words. I've even replayed every interaction I've had with Cody. But I'm just going in circles, getting more and more confused. And now I'm especially worried.

I haven't seen Cody.

It's almost early morning, and she should be back from the hospital by now, but she isn't.

Did the chief find her? Is he questioning her? Does she know about the capsules?

My mind goes back to Case and what the chief told me about his family. I can't seem to get past the fact that he gave Jose a totem. To experiment with. I haven't lived here long, but even I know that totems aren't just handed out. Which makes me wonder more about the boy Jose was trying to heal. And why the chief would be concerned about him.

Giving up on sleep, I light my lamp.

As I pace the room, I look in the mirror. After parting with Mark, I wandered to the bathroom quickly to shower before getting in bed. But it was dark in the bathroom, and I didn't bother to look in my mirror when I got back. Now my eyes are drawn to my totem.

A red ribbon has been woven around it, following the vine in a unique and special design from my elbow to the tip of my shoulder.

I'm a medic.

I sigh. *This is what I wanted, isn't it?*

But when I sit on the floor in front of the mirror to study it further, I realize I'm not so sure anymore. Not after tonight. *What would have happened if Case had succeeded? Where was he going to take me? What was he planning to do to me?* Mark had told me those men would do anything to get my totem back, but I don't think I really believed him, until now. Those men want this totem back. Me back. *But why?*

"Hey." I jump at the voice behind me and quickly turn around. Gabbro is there, a serious look on his face.

"Gabbro?" I whisper. He comes to me, and I pick him up.

"Are you okay?" he asks.

I want to tell him no. I want to tell him I'm scared out of my mind. I want to tell him I don't want to be a Pepp or part of this anymore.

But, instead, I ask softly, "Gabbro, can you tell me what's going on? Why don't you want the chief knowing about you being with ... Trevor?"

"Alena, I'll tell you, but I need you to promise me that you won't tell anyone."

My eyes narrow. I don't want to make such a promise. Whatever he has to say is something the chief should probably hear.

But his urgency tugs at me. I nod, hoping I don't regret agreeing to this and that he'll answer some of my own questions along the way.

"Swear it. Swear on the life of your brother, Caleb, that you will not speak of these things to anyone other than me, including Danny or Mark or the chief."

My muscles tense at the mention of Caleb's name. Maybe I shouldn't agree. Maybe I should drag Gabbro to the chief right now, force him to talk there.

But what if he doesn't talk there? I don't even know the truth. How would I know if what he says is really the secret?

Staring at Gabbro, I find myself curious. I can promise him ... for now.

So, reluctantly, I agree. "I swear on Caleb's life that I will not tell anyone," I say, and then push the conversation. "Why were you there, Gabbro? I thought Magbabies were always supposed to stay with their assigned Pepp. Why weren't you with Danny?"

A sad look burdens his face. "I'm not Danny's Magbaby. I'm Trevor's."

I furrow my eyebrows, confused.

"Soon after Trevor came to Petrichor, he and Danny were called away by Case. Neither of them knew he had gotten involved with the Sybalt clan. I'm still not sure what he wanted from them, but whatever it was, it wasn't good. Trevor and Danny left Petrichor suddenly in the middle of the night while I was asleep. Trevor forgot to take me with him.

"By the time I woke up, they were both missing, and I had no idea where he was. I went in search of him, but it took me time. After several days I found him in the southern swamps but not in his normal form.

"He was a specialized morpher in Petrichor before he left, someone who learns to change into multiple animal forms easily. When I found him, he was in the form of a bear with a new half totem attached. Like Danny. He wasn't able to morph back into his original form ... at least not without incredible pain." Gabbro shakes his head at the memory.

"Danny eventually made it back to Petrichor, but *his* Magbaby had been destroyed. Trevor decided not to come back since he wanted to figure out what Case was up to. But he still wanted to know what was going on inside Petrichor, so he sent me to be Danny's Magbaby. To keep Danny from ever looking for him and putting himself in more danger, Trevor made me swear to him that I would tell Danny he's dead. Danny thinks Trevor is gone."

Gabbro lied to Danny?

Gabbro hangs his head in shame. "After learning Case's motives were to hurt the Pepps, Trevor began silently following him and the clan members. He followed signs that eventually led him to SilverDen, Case's hideout, where he keeps all the kidnapped Pepps. He's kept watch there ever since. Trying to collect bits and pieces of information, trying to understand why Case is doing this and learning about the hideout."

I narrow my eyes, my voice harsh. "You know where the missing Pepps are, and you haven't said anything?"

Gabbro hangs his head even more. "The chief can never know about the hideout, Alena. Trevor has learned that the entire hideout is surrounded by electrical currents, currents that would kill the chief if he ever tried to enter. We've seen many of the clan members misstep or get careless and die from these currents. Trevor has thought about using his totem power to destroy the place, but he can't. Electricity is drawn to Peppate power and anything it creates. It would probably lead a Peppate trail back to Trevor and kill him too."

Gabbro looks me in the eye, the sadness in it suddenly replaced with excitement.

"Alena, we didn't know how we were going to ever get inside to get the Pepps out, until after I saw what happened with you during the lightning storm."

Gabbro pauses, and I suddenly understand where this is going.

"I ran away from the storm with Trevor to another cave. Once we were inside, I looked back and saw you still lying there on the ground. I was terrified when I saw that the others still hadn't shown up. I was about to go back to help you, when I saw the lighting hit right next to you. I thought you were dead, but you kept moving and then Mark appeared. The lightning couldn't hit you or Mark."

His words sink in.

"Alena, you repel Peppate. Lightning can't strike you. You are the key, the key to getting those Pepps out."

Nobody is supposed to know what happened during the lightning storm! Tears threaten my eyes. I don't want to be the key. I just want to go home.

"What about Mark? He's the same as me," I say quietly but instantly regret it. That's not fair. To send Mark out where he could get hurt.

Gabbro just shakes his head. "Mark is too angry. He has a right to be, as he lost his father to the clan, but he lets his anger cloud his judgment. I've seen how he treats the clan members he captures around his rendezvous point. He's not thoughtful. He'll go in there looking for revenge, for blood, and that isn't what we want. We just want to get the Pepps out."

I want to plainly state that Mark can control his temper, but then I remember the night I first met him. The way he dragged me down the hall. The malicious look on his face is one I don't ever want to experience again.

"Can we go together? Or can't the chief at least help me?" I ask.

Gabbro shakes his head more emphatically this time. "That's exactly what Case wants. He wants you and Mark both, since you both make up the defective totem he's created. You would be walking right into his hands. We can't do that. And even if the chief agreed to let you help him, it's too dangerous. He's much too likely to die."

My face falls. Gabbro wants me to free the prisoners? His plan is impossible. How am *I* supposed to get prisoners out of a hideout? I was barely able to get through initiation. I remember the chief talking about the missing Pepps. He said there were, what, seventy-five? How am I supposed to get that many Pepps out, assuming they're all still alive?

"What would I have to do?" I whisper.

"You'll need to learn how to rock rappel, and you'll need to learn it well. The hideout is deep within the ground, and the only entrance is about a hundred feet down a hole. Since the electrical forces will fry any powers, you'll be on your own. You won't even be able to use capsules. Once you're inside, you'll need to find the source of electricity. Trevor thinks it's a generator of some sort that sends electricity through the silver veins of the mine. We'll find something to help you destroy the generator, maybe a small bomb. Then you'll need to get the prisoners out the same way you got in. Up the rope."

Gabbro sighs heavily. "The clan men are there, though. It's where they live. So we'll need to figure out a way for you to do all this without getting caught by them. You'll need to make your body stronger." Gabbro's eyes bore into me. "I want you to train with Rusty."

I remember the night the chief announced Pepps would start carrying weapons on their runs. Rusty was the Pepp assigned to train them on how to use them. I guess that, coupled with the fact that Rusty is muscularly huge, would make him an understandable pick by Gabbro.

"Will you do it?" Gabbro asks.

I sit back on my heels and eye my totem. I left my home months ago hoping to get this thing removed. When I learned it couldn't be removed, I ended up here for my safety, hoping to at least learn how to be happy again. I've tried to go along with everything the chief has put me through, but now because of the clan's obsession with this totem, I know I can't ever leave. I can't take off the totem, and I'll never get to go home.

I rub my head. But what if the clan was removed from the equation? No longer a threat. Then I'd be able to leave Petrichor, right? Maybe go home after I learn how to use the power. I could practice medicine with my dad while quietly healing the patients so they don't even know what I'm doing.

"Alena?"

I stare at Gabbro. I feel like I should tell the chief, but would the chief be willing to let me capture the clan without him?

Something has been eating at me since I got back from initiation, and it's now that I realize what. *How did the clan know about me?* I lived safely at home in isolation for months. It wasn't until I came to live with the Pepps that the clan learned who I was. How? And who placed those Morgans to spy on Cody and me? Someone in Petrichor is feeding information to the clan. Who's to say that isn't the chief? After all, he had Rusty freeze me during a stupid game of Mafia and then checked my memories. He told me to do initiation even against Mark's warnings and put my team in danger.

Even the way he's handled the Sybalt clan has me doubting his abilities. With his power, I'm sure he could find them all and kill them, but all he's done is give the communicators in danger an antivenom. A slap on the wrist for the horrible clan. He's not protecting the Pepps. *Why?* He mentioned before that hurting others depletes Pepp power. Is that really the reason he's not going after the clan? Wouldn't it be worth it to get rid of them even if it does deplete their power for a bit?

My legs are going numb so I shift my position and sit on my bum.

Gabbro is giving me the chance to go the hideout where the clan members live. Without the chief interfering. I can get in, get the prisoners out. And ...?

I stand and pace the room. "You want me to risk my life to save the prisoners." I stop. "What's in it for me?"

Gabbro raises his jaw, not surprised at my demand. "Well, what do you want?"

I grip my hands tightly. "I want to be free. Free to go home without having to hide. Free to wear this totem without worrying about being killed. But I can't do that as long as the clan is around. As long as Case is around."

"Okay, so you want us to kill the clan. Maybe we *should* allow Mark to go in there."

"No!" The word bursts out without warning. I clear my throat and try again. "No. I don't want anyone to die. I wouldn't be able to live with myself if the blood of a single person was on my hands. But maybe we could capture the clan somehow. Capture Case. Put them in a prison where we'd know they couldn't get out. Then I could leave Petrichor and go home."

Now Gabbro starts to pace the floor. "That's possible. We could send a type of sleeping gas into their tunnels. I'm sure I could find something among the non-Pepps, something without Peppate in it. Then we could tie them up and bring them back to Petrichor. There's a prison here: Algor. If we deliver the clan to the chief, he would have to put the men in Algor."

Hand them over to the chief? That doesn't sit well with me. I don't really trust any of the council members either. Whoever is working with the clan would just let them go.

But there's one person I do trust.

"Not the chief," I say, my hands shaking in anticipation. "Rusty."

Gabbro stops pacing. "Okay. Rusty, then. Look, I'll help you come up with a plan, but will you promise to free the prisoners?"

I swallow hard. "Yes."

As soon as I say the word, a heaviness settles over my body. I might be getting what I want, but this isn't going to be easy. Or safe. I'm going to have to get stronger and learn how to rock rappel. And imprisoning clan members? Can I figure out how to do that without hurting anyone? Is this worth the risk?

"Good." Gabbro sighs in relief. "But please don't tell anyone." Gabbro looks around uneasily as he lifts off my hand and hums in the air. "I'll be in touch. I trust Rusty to train you privately, but please don't tell him why."

I stand motionless. *How am I supposed to get him to train me without telling him why?*

Gabbro turns to leave, but I can't let him go without asking one more question. Ironically, a question I think I already know the answer to.

"Gabbro, was Trevor the same bear that prevented Mark from attaching the second half of the totem?"

Gabbro hums softly. "Yes, Alena. He's also the bear you saw at the river after dropping out of Petrichor. He's watching out for you."

That comforts me. A little.

Chapter 18

The morning sun shining through the window wakes me, and my eyes flutter open. Lying in bed with the blanket loosely covering me, I quietly examine the balcony. I hadn't ever realized how beautiful the balcony is with its wooden railing roughly patched in an attractive branchy chaos. Flower-loaded vines reach down from the branches above and wind themselves around the rails. I stare at the beauty. That is until the sun hits me right in the eye and I can't see anything. Turning over to my other side, I try to fall back to sleep.

Yesterday was an emotionally exhausting day. Between thinking about initiation, worrying about Cody, and hearing about Gabbro's plan, I was tired.

I'm determined to get home, and Gabbro's plan is obviously the only way. But I don't like keeping secrets from the chief, even if I don't trust him.

Also, what if Gabbro is right? *What if I'm the only one that* can *get in? What if the chief insists on helping like Gabbro said and ends up getting hurt? Will I be able to live with that?*

My left temple still aches from gritting my teeth all day. I wish I could send a message to Caleb. Get his opinion. But I'm still worried about the Morgans tracking my Magbaby and finding my hidden family. Or intercepting my messages and learning what we're planning.

So, I'm stuck.

Thankfully, when Leinani came by yesterday with lunch, she helped get my mind off things. Of course, her leg was all healed, and I was elated to find the red ribbon wrapped around her arm just like mine. Apparently, stitching Leinani up was what allowed my totem to see me. One simple moment. I'm glad I did it.

I also learned that what normally takes two days for the totem to establish true character only took one day for our team. I'm saddened, though, to find out that now we won't see one another much anymore. Since Leinani knows the basics of the power, she'll be trained in her respective area at the hospital. Once she's trained as a basic medic she'll start dropdowns and runs. Her excitement dimmed my spirits until she told me that I'm going to get special trainers to work solely with me, to teach me how to use my power, something that's never been done before.

And my trainers just happen to be Danny and Mark.

I bit back my elation. Hard. The last thing I want is Leinani teasing me about Mark.

We spent the rest of the time talking about the other members of the team who had matched as well. Bapoto has been summoned to help with the totem tree and will be creating equipment capsules for all the Pepps. This makes perfect sense since he's good with the power.

Nadia matched as a messenger, which seems to fit her quiet, reserved nature.

Leinani then talked on and on about Carlos, who is now a trainer for the students. I think she likes Carlos.

After Leinani left last night, though, my worries continued. I still haven't seen Cody.

Someone knocks on my door, pulling me from my thoughts.

"Alena?"

I curse. It's Mark's voice. He's probably here to start training.

"Uh. Just a sec." I jump out of bed.

I look in the mirror and mutter in frustration. My hair! It needs work, but I can't keep them waiting outside the door forever. At least I'm fully clothed, even if I am in my pajamas. Reluctantly, I walk to the door and open it.

I see Danny first, smiling back at me, with Gabbro sitting on his shoulder.

"Good morning, sunshine," Gabbro says, rolling his eyes in irritation. One of the tendrils on his head winds up to Danny's ear. Based on his expression, speaking for Danny must not be his favorite thing to do.

The corners of my mouth lift at the sight. At least until I find Mark standing behind him. Looking so handsome in front of me, I'm even more aware of my messy hair and puffy eyes. I inwardly moan. Why does he have to be so handsome?

"We're going for a run," Mark says. "Get your exercise clothes on. We'll meet you outside the gym downstairs." He turns to leave, but stops. "Oh, and bring your Magbaby. You'll need her."

A run? I don't want to go for a run. But my body responds anyway when I shut the door behind them, probably because of Mark. I change into a pair of leggings and a loose T-shirt, then pull my hair into a ponytail. I showered after initiation, but I never did anything with my hair. It's now crimped in odd angles from sleeping on it, making me frown. There isn't much I can do about it now.

I grab Breccia and her harness, then leave the room.

I reach the bottom floor of GreenGrotto and walk through the gym toward Danny and Mark, who are on the grass outside. Danny waves from his stretching position on the ground.

I wave back and then, against my better judgement, let my eyes wander to Mark.

He has on gray jogging pants and a red T-shirt that shows off way too many muscles. I gulp.

I study his face and my heart sinks. There's so much I want to tell him, about Gabbro and Trevor, and the place where the Pepps are hidden. But I can't. I can't even talk to him about the lightning fluke, at least not with others around.

"The Magbabies know millions of songs," Mark says, stepping to my side, pointing to Breccia. "I like to listen to mine when I exercise. The songs don't have words, but they have a good beat. Your Magbaby will need to learn what type of music you like to hear, so if she plays a song you don't like, just tap her and she'll play another." As he speaks, Mark pulls the tendrils out of Breccia, extending them into long cords. He pulls one up to his ear to show me how it sits and then places them both into my hand. I then pull them up to my ears and shiver. The tendrils slip into the space, feeling like little worms. I'll have to get used to that.

With Danny done with his stretches, Mark turns to the mountain behind us, which is adjacent to GreenGrotto. "This is Training Mountain. In order to perform well on our runs and dropdowns, we need to be as physically fit as possible, so we spend as much time as we can here. This mountain provides different obstacles that might be pertinent to runs, such as rock climbing, river rafting, tree-climbing, and hiking. We'll run along its path today."

I recognize the mountain from initiation; the river we floated gurgles at the base.

Mark puts his own Magbaby tendrils into his ears and begins running. Danny turns to run as well but looks back at me to signal I should follow.

I sigh and then move my legs.

The sun is bright as we head toward the bridge leading to Training Mountain. A soft song begins to play in my ears, reminding me of classical music.

No.

I tap Breccia. A different song comes on, but it's still too slow. After tapping consecutively, skipping at least five songs, she starts playing a very upbeat one. My muscles respond to the music, pushing me faster. My feet land to the beat of the song, generating more power in my legs. We run along the side of the mountain, the rhythm pulsing through my body, lightening my spirits. My chest swells with new energy. Running with Mark and Danny is already way more fun than climbing a mountain with my team.

Mark, who is ahead of us, begins to ascend diagonally up the side of the mountain, putting more strain on my hamstrings. Just as my body begins to sweat profusely and my breathing heightens, Danny stops abruptly in front of me and turns around. I stop alongside him, and he grabs my arm to point at something behind me. I take out Breccia's tendril and look back. He's pointing at a cloud of black dust floating in the air. *Where did that come from?*

"It's Doler," Gabbro says. "From you."

"Me? That came out of me?" I drop my gaze to my arms, where thousands of tiny black dots are smeared over my skin like dirt. *Is this the culprit for my unexplainable dirtiness lately?*

"You have a lot," Gabbro says. I look at Danny and see his face covered too. "It hates exercise, and music, which is why we're doing this." Danny pops his tendril back in and turns to the trail to catch up with Mark, who is well ahead of us now.

I take in a deep easy breath. I do feel better already. The anxiety that trapped me so much last night slips away, and I push harder with a new purpose.

The steep terrain eventually slows us to a walk. We pass several rock-climbing walls crawling with Pepps gaining strength in the sport. They all do it without ropes, though, unlike my experience.

We climb the mountain for a while, my body cramping up, forcing me to slow down. Mark and Danny slow with me, but their contented moods pull me forward.

The sun is heating up the air, and it peeks through the thinning trees ahead. As we approach the edge of a cliff shaded with shrubbery, the bright-green Petrichor hills appear below. Danny pulls me to a shady rock overlooking the valley.

"You two rest here," Mark says. "I'm going to run up a little further and then come back." Wiping at his sweat, he smears black dust across his face. He must do a good job of getting rid of his Doler because I've never seen it on him until now. I've never seen it on non-Pepps either. This must just be a defective totem thing. Too much Doler.

After he leaves, I sit on the long rock, thankful for the rest, still trying to catch my breath. I try to leave plenty of room for Danny to sit, but, regardless of the space, he sits right next to me, his leg brushing up against mine. My lips tug upward, and I push my leg into his.

"Isn't it beautiful?" Gabbro says for Danny.

Gabbro is going to take some getting used to for me. Not only because of his secrets I can't discuss but the fact that he speaks for Danny in first person.

I watch Danny's face as he absorbs the scene in front of us. It's almost as if he loves the scene so much it lights him from the inside out. I glance between him and Petrichor, trying to see what he sees, but he catches me staring at him, and I look away.

I distract myself with the band on my arm. The sweat has made it sticky and uncomfortable, so I pull it off, placing Breccia in my lap while I stretch it out.

"Magbabies are pretty cool," I say.

"Yeah, they are, but ..." Gabbro is still speaking for Danny. He pauses, shooting Danny an offended glance. Confused, I watch Danny stare at Gabbro, eyebrows raised. He must be silently communicating with Gabbro. Finally, Danny gestures for the rock to speak. Gabbro narrows his eyes bitterly but proceeds.

"However, they can be quite lazy and stubborn." Gabbro crosses his arms after delivering the insult to himself. I chuckle, looking at Breccia, who just rolls her eyes.

Danny points at my Magbaby. "You have bubbles," Gabbro says.

I'm not sure what he's talking about until he touches Breccia, where a couple of bumps have formed. "Those are bubbles."

I look at them closer, surprised I've never noticed the raised areas on Breccia's back.

"What are bubbles?" I ask, touching them softly.

"Bubbles form on your Magbaby when you do something good. Your Magbaby holds on to the moments, like memories, and when you're having a bad day, your Magbaby will detect it and open up the memories to you. They help you feel better."

As much as I want to snicker at the comment, I can't. Breccia is kind, but does she really see good in me? The fact that she's already observed three good moments intrigues me. *What did she see?*

Placing her back into the harness on my arm, I look out at Petrichor. Last night my mind was consumed with the events of initiation and Cody. Now, after running, I'm amazed at how peaceful I feel. Danny knew this would help me. Looking at him now, I wonder if I can finally ask him the questions I've had ever since meeting Mark.

"Danny?" He turns his attention to me. "When I first met Mark at the rendezvous point, he told me you taught him how to be happy again." I finger a loose thread on my black pants. "Can you teach me?"

I wait for his response.

"How do you feel right now, Alena?"

I think for a moment and whisper, "I feel good."

"That's because we just ran up a mountain together, listening to music." I look up and see the sly grin on his face as Gabbro speaks, but then he adds more seriously, "What do you hate the most about your totem?"

The question catches me off guard, and I think for a moment before responding. "I hate the way it makes me feel."

Danny's eyes hold mine. "How *does* it make you feel?"

I sigh. "It makes me feel sad and tired all the time."

"Why is that a bad thing?" Gabbro asks.

I pause. I've never thought about that. "I guess it's bad because it isn't how I want to be. I used to be so fun and outgoing. I used to love being outdoors. I loved playing sports and being around people. I used to love my life ..." I stop. The statement triggers something inside me, and my eyes swell with tears. "Now all I want to do is sleep my life away. I hate waking up and facing things. I hate ... living." I hate the words coming out of my mouth. I'm ashamed and embarrassed, but they're the truth. Expecting Danny to be disappointed by my response, I hang my head.

"Mark's answer to that question was that he hates the way it makes him act. It fills him with so much anger. He hurts people who don't deserve to be hurt, but he can't stop. For me, I hate the way it makes me think of myself. It makes me feel like I am, and always will be, defined by my differences. Like nobody will ever be able to see and accept me for who I am inside."

I had no idea the Doler affected Mark and Danny these ways. Hearing this makes me even angrier with the Doler. They deserve better.

As if sensing my anger, Danny puts his hand on mine.

"It's okay, Alena. Whether we like it or not, the Doler has a purpose and is very important in our lives."

My eyes narrow. I don't understand how something so bad could be important.

Letting go of my hand, Danny leans onto his knees while Gabbro continues to sit on his shoulder facing me. "Inside us, we each have things we care about, things we like, and things we want. They're closely related to our different personalities we've been given. The Doler, when inside us, latches onto those things we care about, like, or want, and it makes them bigger. In a way it projects them into our brain like an enlarging balloon, making it a priority at the time. For example ..." Gabbro stops talking and looks down mischievously at Danny.

"For example, Danny really likes pretty girls, like you."

Gabbro is going off-script. I can tell based on Danny's reaction. Danny sits straight up, glaring at Gabbro, warning him not to go any further, but Gabbro proceeds. "The Doler gets into him and blows that *like* up like a big balloon, making *you* the only thing he can think about."

Danny now pushes Gabbro angrily off his shoulder, scowling at him. Gabbro lands in the dirt at my feet. Wiping his little knees off, he stands.

I can't help but laugh.

"Actually, you are all either of us can think about. Even my head is swarming with thoughts of you because of him."

Danny now stands, grabs Gabbro from the dirt, and throws him far over the cliff. I sit in shock, watching the rock sail down below. Danny sits back down, shaking his head, but Gabbro comes humming immediately back, smiling.

I chuckle again and push my leg into Danny's, very aware of my heart flipping at Gabbro's words. *He likes me?* This pleases me. Not as much as Mark liking me does. But it feels good to be accepted. My spirits fall a little bit, though. What do I do? There's no way I'll tell Danny that I like Mark. Can I appease him while quietly having feelings for Mark? Is that even fair to Danny? Ugh. *I'll think about that later.*

Gabbro's teasing face now turns kind as he picks up the conversation again.

"But Danny doesn't just like you Alena. He *cares* about you. The Doler latches onto that as well, making him think of ways to help you. Between these two blown-up projections there is, throughout the day, what Danny calls the internal battle. These projections create many emotions. Every human experiences these emotions, even without a defective totem. Our course of life depends on which projections we decide to act on."

Gabbro pauses, climbs back up onto Danny's shoulder, and sits, his face now serious. "While the Doler has a good side, when there is too much of it within us, it not only blows things up too big, it begins distorting the truth."

Looking at Danny, Gabbro's eyes get sad. "Mark cared about his dad, and when he found out his father had died, Mark started to blame himself. He told himself that he shouldn't have left him lying there or gone hunting that morning. He felt that if he had done things differently, his father would still be here today. But, the truth is, Mark's father is gone, and it wasn't Mark's fault.

"The Doler in a normal human being makes the same distortions, especially when it comes to something so traumatic, but Mark's totem made it worse for him." Danny shakes his head. "When he first came here it was difficult for anyone to have a simple conversation with him. He would say such hurtful and mean things. I tried to tell him the truth, over and over again, that his father was killed by the clan, not by him, and he's not responsible for his death, but he simply didn't want to see or accept it. It takes effort to see past all the Doler.

"Thankfully, though, after months and months of anguish, I convinced him to try to get rid of the Doler. That's when we started doing the *wiggems* together."

"The wiggems?"

Danny tilts his head to the side, and Gabbro explains. "Yes. The wiggems—things that distract us from the Doler projections. If we don't pay attention to the projections, then the Doler just kind of melts away."

Danny picks up a stick and starts drawing letters in the dirt at our feet.

W. I. G. G. E. M. S.

"Work." Danny writes the word next to the letter W.

"Interaction" next to the I.

"Exercise."

"Music."

"Scenery."

I nod in understanding. WIGGEMS is an acronym. I notice that he skipped the two Gs in the middle.

"What do they stand for?" I ask, pointing to the Gs.

Danny glances sideways at me, a smirk on his face. "We'll get to those later. They're more difficult. There are also more than these, like service and other things. These are just the basics. Anyway, taking advantage of these things on a daily basis chips away at the Doler like a chisel to a statue, until you see the beauty that lies at the core of it: the truth."

I eye him curiously. "It can't be that easy. Listening to music? Socializing?"

Danny's eyes meet mine, examining my face. "Who said it was easy?" Gabbro says. "When you're full of Doler, I can tell you, the wiggems are the last thing you want to do."

I realize he's right. I remember how hard it became to just leave my house after I obtained the totem.

"Okay, so what happened to Mark after you started doing the wiggems?"

"Soon the Doler began thinning, and he started to see the truth like I saw it. His father is gone. And he won't ever come back. But that isn't Mark's fault. It wasn't until after the truth was free of the distortions and projections that the Peppate could step in. You see, Peppate, unlike Doler, doesn't project or distort the truth. It supports it, surrounding it for a brief moment. Feeling and accepting truth generates something I like to call happiness." Danny's eyebrows pump up and down proudly at this statement. As if he's the one who invented the word. I would normally laugh, but my mind is too busy reflecting on what he's said.

I look below. *What sort of distortions or projections has my Doler made for me the past several months?*

The concept makes sense in my mind, so why am I still so confused?

"How do you figure out what truths you need to see?" I ask, looking at his kind eyes again. "I can understand Mark needing to see that he wasn't to blame for his father's death, but I didn't lose anyone. What is my Doler distorting?"

"You might not have lost *someone*, but you did lose *something*. Am I right?" Gabbro says, Danny's sad eyes meeting mine.

Suddenly, I think I know what he's trying to tell me.

I did lose something. Many things.

"I lost my friends," I say softly. "I lost my chances at medical school, my confidence." Tears unexpectedly well up in my eyes as I grieve for my losses for the first time. "In a way, I lost the only life I wanted. And I lost it all because of the totem."

Danny places a hand on mine. I quickly wipe away the stupid tears that spill over. "Is that the truth I need to see? That the vine has ruined my life?" I whisper to him.

Gabbro doesn't respond immediately. When he does his voice is soft. "It's a start. It's important to understand the source of your grief. However, dwelling on those truths will only make you angrier. I think there's another truth you need to see. Unfortunately, nobody can know what that truth is but you."

I shake my head and stare at the dirt. *How am I supposed to figure that out?*

Danny squeezes my hand gently, pulling my gaze back to his. "But, as an outsider, if I was to guess, I would say the truth you need to see is that the vine is a part of your life now. You need to learn to *accept* it. Doler and all."

My heart drops and I stare at him, creasing my brows.

Danny laughs softly. "Yes, based on your reaction, I would say that's exactly what you need to do," Gabbro says.

I don't find the idea funny. "How? How am I supposed to accept something that I ..." I swallow, more tears threatening to spill over. "Something I hate?"

Danny leans into me, still holding my gaze as Gabbro speaks for him. "You try," he whispers. "Give it time, and you'll find it's possible. And as your new friend, I'm here to help you, if you'll let me."

Try? Try to accept something I hate? After a few moments, Gabbro breaks the silence again. "Alena, learning to accept the totem doesn't necessarily mean giving up on trying to find a way to make things better. Maybe there is a way to remove it, and if there is, then by all means let's find it. But in the meantime, while it's attached to you, try to accept it." I lean my elbows on my knees, realizing for the first time that there's a lot more to Danny than meets the eye.

"Where did you learn all this?" I ask.

Danny smiles. "My mom." Then Gabbro adds, "My *Pepp* mom. Sepharine. She's Mark's mom too, although he turned eighteen pretty soon after he came here, so he didn't get to spend as much time with her as I did."

Ah, that's right. They're Pepp brothers. That makes sense.

"By the way." Danny nudges my arm, but his face turns serious. "We're all glad you're okay after initiation. Sepharine was so worried about you when she heard you'd be participating. I'm glad Mark was able to get you out of there."

The fact that another Pepp in Petrichor was worried about me during initiation comforts me.

"Thank you."

I notice now how calm he's been during our conversation. No erratic movements or waving arms. This must be an easy thing for him to talk about.

Just then I hear footsteps behind us. As I turn around to see Mark coming toward us, my muscles cramp up.

"Are you ready to go back down?" Mark asks, trying to catch his breath.

I turn back to the valley, suddenly very aware of how out of shape I am.

"Danny, I don't think I can *walk* any further," I whisper.

Danny's eyes brighten. "That's okay. I'll carry you," Gabbro says for him, rolling his eyes.

"We're going to paraglide down," Mark says. "It should be easier on your muscles." Mark wipes the sweat off his forehead.

I gulp, trying not to stare too hard at his tight chest rising and falling as he breathes. Paragliding sounds much easier and fun. I rub my sore muscles. "I have a long way to go in order to get strong enough for dropdowns, don't I?"

"You'll get there," Mark says, then he holds out his hand to help me up. Should I take it with Danny sitting here? I study his gaze before giving in and place my hand in his. He pulls me up close but steps back when his gaze slides to Danny. He must feel the same hesitancy. *Does he know Danny's feelings toward me?* Mark reaches into his pocket and pulls out a silver capsule, then pushes the button to expand a large triangular piece of fabric. Sticks form on the sides, and a harness drops down in the middle next to Mark.

It's a paraglider. My pulse quickens in excitement. A paraglider!?

Stepping close to me again, Mark begins wrapping the harness around my waist.

"Are you afraid of heights?" he asks. His fingers brush against my stomach, but he doesn't let them linger.

I shake my head, aware of his strong hands moving to wrap the harness around my legs now. I swallow, trying to focus on his question. "No. I've always wanted to paraglide."

Mark nods. "Good." He grabs my shoulders, then turns me around. Danny, who has strapped himself in his own harness, steps behind me and attaches his to mine, his chest rubbing against my back.

"You'll go down with Danny," Mark says. Mark *does* know Danny likes me. This pleases me and saddens me at the same time. Does this mean Mark and I can't be ...? I push my worry down.

I'm about to paraglide.

After stepping into his own expanded paraglider, Mark asks, "You ready?"

I almost laugh in excitement and nod.

"On three, we're both going to jump. Sit in your harness as if you're sitting in a chair. Then just let Danny and the wind do the rest."

Gabbro whispers into my ear. "It'll be awesome."

I can't see his face, but he sounds happy. *Is he still talking for Danny?*

Mark counts, and I jump with Danny. The wind catches the chute and jolts us away from the mountain. My stomach rises at the dip of the jump and forces a thrilled shriek from my throat. I can't help but laugh now. Laugh. Oh, I'd forgotten what it's like to laugh. The wind whips around my body, pulling on my ponytail and shirt. Letting go of the strings connecting me to the parachute, I hold my arms out.

The view is breathtaking from up here. The sky, clouds, and wind all become a part of me as I float in their space. I suck the air in greedily.

Then with my arms still lifted, I let out a yowl. I can't help it. Danny chuckles behind me before joining in. For the first time in a long time I feel like myself—totally free.

I send a daring glance over at Mark, who hasn't joined in the yelling yet, and howl again. He laughs before cupping his hands around his mouth to shout. I lean back into Danny, determined to cherish every second of this experience. Danny gladly welcomes my closeness and wraps his arms around my waist. The peaceful stillness of the sun and the clouds around me neutralize my insides, and I grasp at the moment. I had forgotten what it feels like to be alive, and I don't want it to ever end.

Unfortunately, the wind can't keep us in the air forever, and our glider dips. Much too soon, we're hovering over the green field beside GreenGrotto. This precious moment is coming to an end.

Reluctantly, I brace myself and lean forward, expecting a rough landing in the approaching field, but when my feet touch the ground, Danny's arm wraps around my waist to keep me from falling. He collapses the paraglider behind us in one quick movement. After letting me go, he helps me out of the harness.

"What did you think?" Mark asks, unhooking himself.

"I loved it," I blurt, still unable to wipe the grin off my face. *Is paragliding a type of wiggems? Is my skin still covered in Doler?* I don't care.

"Good," Mark says, chuckling at my excitement. With the paragliders tucked safely away in his pocket, we head toward the door of GreenGrotto. When we reach it, Mark touches my arm.

"Alena, we're your new trainers. As much as I would love to end the day with that, we actually did all this so we could s*tart* the day of training."

I look at him, confused. But he just says, "You two go to the library, and I'll go get us some lunch."

Chapter 19

"This is the library," Gabbro says for Danny as he leads me into the other large room on the first floor of GreenGrotto, across from the gym. "It's through these books that you'll learn to harness and develop the powers in your totem. There is so much to learn here."

I can't believe I haven't been in here yet. The entirety of the library is bordered with windows, sending in swirls of light that dust the rock floor and books. I see pops of fire and water as the Pepps practice using their totem power at the rough tables scattered around the joint. Hundreds of thin tree branches peek through the rock in the ceiling and wind through, disappearing and reappearing lawlessly throughout the library.

Unlike the quiet libraries I'm used to, this library is hopping with activity.

Danny leads me to a table in the corner where a box of tiny glass flasks sits and plops into a chair tucked beside it.

"We're going to teach you the basics of the totem's power." Danny pats the seat beside him. "Pepps usually have a long time to learn about the power before they match, but you've already matched, so we have to teach you quickly so you can move on to the hospital to learn how to be a medic."

Excitement ripples through my body, and I scoot my chair in further. Do I finally get to learn how the power works?

"Learning how to use the power is very similar to learning a new language, mixed with chemistry."

I don't know much about learning a new language, but chemistry I do understand. Maybe this won't be so bad.

Gabbro proceeds. "The totems possess the power to communicate directly with the atoms all around us, so it's not us that controls the elements, it's the totem. We have to learn how to communicate with the totem to tell it which of the elements we want to control. Luckily, we have an incredible trainer that teaches each of the totems the language, so all you have to do is learn the language to communicate.

"But before you learn the language, you need to memorize the sound each element makes. Each element has a distinct beat and sound that you're able to hear when your power is in. Learning the sounds will especially help you as a medic. You'll use these sounds to identify what's wrong with a body and what needs to be repaired."

Danny holds out his hand now, a glass sphere full of yellow liquid in his palm. Power. I need the power to hear the elements around me.

"Thank you," I say, realizing I haven't had power since that man at initiation took mine. I push the power into the hole over my heart like Aba did, then straighten.

The buzzing sound I first heard at the beginning of initiation, and then again when repairing Leinani, explodes in my head. It's like my head is filled with millions of bees. Unable to focus, I pop the power out and look at Danny for an explanation.

"What is that?" I ask. A smile creeps across Danny's face.

"It worked," a voice says behind me. I turn to see Mark holding three plates of food.

"What worked?" I ask, still confused.

Mark takes over for Gabbro now. "When we put power in our totems, it opens up the communication between us and the totem and allows us to hear the elements around us. That's what you hear now. Unfortunately, Doler dulls the sounds so we can't hear them. The more Doler we have, the less we can hear the elements, and the harder it is for us to communicate with the totem."

I remember the chief's reaction when he saw that I could hear the elements at the beginning of initiation.

"Fortunately, you were cleared of Doler enough to match during initiation. I'm guessing you heard the sounds during at least some parts of it?" Mark asks.

"Yes, when I stitched up Leinani."

"That's why you matched. You could hear the elements, and the totem could hear you."

Suddenly, I'm grateful the chief made me go through initiation. I hated it, but I can't deny that it's great to have a place. To have a job. To be a medic.

W—Work. Isn't that the first part of Danny's wiggems?

"So, we ran up the mountain today, together, listening to music to get rid of the Doler for me to hear the elements around me," I state. When Mark and Danny both nod, with food stuffed in their mouths, I frown, rubbing my sore muscles. "Do I have to run up a mountain and listen to music with friends every day in order to hear this?"

Mark, Danny, and Gabbro all chuckle, and Mark leans back into his chair. "Yes, you have to work hard to get rid of the Doler every day. *You and I particularly* have to work harder than everyone else. But we will work together."

Danny pulls my chair toward him with little effort and faces me, placing his hands on his knees that are brushing against mine. With his face close, I examine his features. His eyes are a dark brown, almost black. His white teeth overlap attractively in two spots, and his jaw is strong. A lump forms in my throat. Danny's face is handsome. His life would be completely different if he hadn't gotten the second totem. My mind wanders, momentarily wondering what happened to him. *How did he get the extra totem? If Case really did create the defective totems, how could he attach it to his own brother?*

Pulling me back to the present, Danny points to the power capsule, telling me to put it back in. The noises bombard me again after doing so. I'm pretty sure my head is going to explode.

I hear Danny laughing at my expression over the noise. He gently places his finger on my chin and pulls my head up.

"I'm going to help you," Gabbro says. "To start off, let's listen to each of the elements. Listen for the beats and tones that make them distinct from one another. If you close your eyes you'll be able to focus better."

Feeling a little awkward, I close my eyes.

"Okay, I'm going to put a flask to your ear, and I want you to listen closely. It will be louder than all the other sounds. Try to memorize it."

I obey. Taking in a deep breath, I wait. A flask reaches my ears. Above all the confusion, a tiny sound rises above the rest.

"Describe the sound to me," Gabbro says.

Describe the sound? I try to focus, making my mind pay attention. Ignoring everything else, I say, "It sounds high-pitched." I peek out of my closed eyes to see Danny's response.

"Good, keep going," he says.

Closing my eyes again, I say, "It has a quick beat."

Danny stops me. "Do you have a favorite song the beat reminds you of?"

Confused by the question, I open my eyes. Pumping his eyebrows up and down, Danny forces a reluctant Gabbro to sing a song that must remind him of this element.

"Take me out in the sunshine ... Uh-uh." Gabbro pauses as Danny switches to another song. "Flying in the clouds, boom, boom." Danny closes his eyes and moves his head to the beat of Gabbro's tune.

I bite back a laugh.

"I'm serious, Alena," Gabbro says for Danny. "What song does the beat remind you of? Listen carefully."

I listen and skim through the song inventory in my mind. I try to put words into the beat that is still humming next to my ear, but they don't fit. Finally, I find one that works. Closing my eyes, I shrug, then bob my head to test it out.

"Sing it out loud," Danny chides.

"No." I don't look at Mark, who, I'm sure, is getting a kick out of all this. Danny's pleas get louder, drawing the attention of others in the room.

"Fine," I finally whisper, trying to shush him. I clear my voice, focus my eyes on a spot on the table so I can't see them laughing at me, and then open my mouth.

"Come on, come on, hear the love ring on ..." They all burst into laughter. Clamping my mouth shut, I glare at them. Well, I glare at Danny. I can't even make eye contact with Mark. Even little Breccia flutters on my arm.

"Keep going." Mark encourages me, making my blush deepen. Unable to keep my gaze from him any longer, I let my eyes drift over his face. He's smiling, his white teeth standing out against his scruffy face. It's good he doesn't do that too much because it's distracting.

"No," I say.

Danny finally gets himself under control and shows me the flask.

"It was carbon," Gabbro says, "I've found that the best and fastest way to learn each of the elements is to associate it with a song I already know. So, as you're trying to differentiate between them, you'll be able to pick out the ones that sound like the songs you know."

I hold the flask in my hand. That might help me a lot, as long as I don't have to sing anymore.

"Before we do that, though, let's eat," Mark says.

***

We spend the rest of the day listening to the elements. I pick out songs that work with each one, like Danny said, occasionally learning new songs through Breccia, when I can't think of any on my own.

I don't know what time it is, but it's dark outside and the library has been empty for hours when we finally wrap up our training. The sounds in my head have completely faded.

We gather up all the flasks, then leave the box in the middle of the table and stand to go.

Just then someone enters the library.

My body straightens. It's the chief.

Walking in our direction, he unbuttons his gray wool overcoat with his gloved hands. He looks tired and worried, and my concerns about Cody come flooding back to the forefront of my mind. *Does he know where Cody is?* He shakes his overcoat gently, dislodging drops of water.

"Hey, Danny. Do you mind doing me a favor?"

Danny looks as if he'd run around the world and back for the chief.

"I just got back from the GreenLands. I need to run upstairs to talk to a runner, but I also need to deliver this message to the council." The chief takes a piece of paper out of a coat pocket. "Would you mind taking this to Rusty?"

Without hesitation, Danny takes the paper and runs out of the room.

Gone.

I admire his eagerness.

I expect the chief to go upstairs like he said he would once Danny's gone, but he comes closer to me and Mark instead.

"May I speak with you two for a moment?" He settles into a chair next to our table and gestures for us to sit back down.

"I'm sorry I hadn't gotten to you earlier, but there are some things I need to tell you about Cody."

Even though there aren't any other Pepps in the room, the chief keeps his voice low. "I've talked to her, Alena. Those capsules on the clan member were indeed hers. But she didn't give them to him." Chief rubs his graying beard, dislodging more water. *How did he get so wet?* "Before Cody came to Petrichor, she used to live in the GreenLands. When the war started, Cody's family, along with her friend Abby, fled their home. Unfortunately, Cody's parents died in the process, leaving Cody and Abby alone. When I tried to get Cody after her parents died, she put up such a fight because she didn't want to leave Abby behind. After seeing how she was living, though, I knew Petrichor was the best place for her, so I brought her anyway. She hated me for it." He rubs his tired eyes. "It wasn't until several months later that I found out she was sneaking food, clothing, and equipment capsules to her friend using her Magbaby. When I found out about it, she promised she would stop, but I guess she didn't."

The chief stares at me now, his piercing blue eyes searching me underneath his bushy eyebrows. "I think the clan somehow intercepted her supplies. And now her friend is missing. I just came from the Green-Lands myself. It looks like the clan might have taken her."

My stomach churns into knots. *The clan took a young girl, Cody's friend? Why?*

"There's more I need to tell you, Alena." The chief looks at Mark. "Jeter checked the memories of the man who attacked you at initiation with a memory bug."

Mark straightens at this. I remember Gabbro mentioning Mark's involvement in trying to get information from captured clan men. He seems intrigued.

Not me. The mention of the clan man forces acid into my throat. I swallow.

"He had more information than any other clan member we've captured. The man knew about your defective totems. They are indeed a type of weapon, just like I thought." The chief pauses before proceeding carefully. "I'm going to tell you what I've learned, but you must not tell another living soul. Promise."

Mark and I exchange an uneasy glance before nodding.

The chief sighs and rubs his forehead. "I've debated whether or not to tell you. A part of me thinks you'd be safer not knowing, but I've decided you should at least know what you're capable of."

Rubbing his beard, the chief raises his eyes to ours. "When both totems are activated through morphing, they produce large electrical currents."

I stare at the chief.

"Like lightning?" Mark whispers.

"Yes. It produces the one thing that could kill a Pepp. The memories didn't indicate why the totem was split in two, or even why it was created in the first place. But I can guess it wasn't for something good, and it's clearer than ever that you two can't morph into eagles for any reason, especially not together at the same time. If you do, you'll produce lightning. I don't think it would hurt you two since you can't get hit by lightning. But it would hurt others."

My good mood from the day disappears.

Deep down inside I think I'd guessed that the totem was bad. But never could I have imagined how bad. Never did I imagine it could cause physical harm.

I suddenly want to hide, place a generous distance between me and any Pepp. Or any human, for that matter. I could bear that type of loneliness ... I think. If it was for the greater good. The only consolation I have is the fact that I was never taught how to morph. That alone should keep me from doing it, shouldn't it?

But then I realize, more importantly, I should probably stay away from Mark. To ensure the phenomenon never happens. I bite my lip. *Will my totem ever stop being a curse?*

"There's one last thing," the chief says seriously, fiddling with a knot in the table. "I've moved your family to a safer place."

My stomach churns more at the mention of my family. I hadn't even thought about them being in danger, which makes me feel even worse. "Are they okay?"

The chief nods, his graying hair brushing against the collar of his overcoat. "They're fine. I was worried about them after initiation and thought it was safer to take them to a rendezvous point where they could be protected by the Pepps. I don't want Case going after them to get to you. We've also set up other protections so they'll be safe. I would discourage you from communicating with them, though. I don't want anyone intercepting your messages."

I cringe. *My poor family*! Mom and Dad had to leave work? Caleb had to leave school ... and Jess?

"I'm sorry, Alena. I wish I had better news for you." He places his gloved hand over mine. "But I do want to thank you. Because of what happened at initiation, we know more about the totem. About what's really going on. Thank you."

I search his eyes that silently convey that we've also learned about my ability to escape lightning. Something potentially useful.

Now looking at Mark, Chief says, "I haven't told anyone else about your totems, and I don't plan to. Please keep this between us. We don't want others more afraid of you two than they already are."

We agree.

"Good. I need to get back." Then, looking outside at the dark night, the chief adds, "Perhaps you should get to bed too?" He doesn't wait for a response but leaves the library.

I stare at the table, running my fingers along the edge.

Cody's friend was taken?

My family was moved?

I rub my forehead and silently curse. *I'm dangerous?*

"Alena?" Mark whispers.

I shake my head, pulled from my thoughts. "Sorry, I guess we should go."

But neither of us moves.

"It'll be okay, Alena," Mark whispers as if my worries are blatantly etched in every breath I take.

I stare at him. "Do you really think Case made this totem to electrocute every Pepp here? Why does he hate the Pepps so much?"

Mark shakes his head and sighs. "I don't know." Then he runs his hand through his brown hair, making me miss Caleb. "I really don't know. I'm just grateful that bear kept me from attaching the second half of the totem. Although, that meant you got the other half. I'm still sorry about that."

I almost smile. Today was fun with Mark and Danny. It was the best day I've had in a while. The bad news we just received dimmed a lot of that fun, but I'm starting to grow a little attached to Petrichor. "Don't be sorry." I say the words quietly and know I really mean them. At least in this moment. I raise my eyes to Mark's. "Thank you, for the fun day."

Mark's face softens. "You're welcome, Alena." Then he stands and holds out his hand to me. I take it, cherishing his warmth and kindness. Once I'm standing, he releases my fingers but places his hand at the small of my back and directs me to the door to the library, sending tingles all up my spine. Man, he's warm. Or I'm warm, I can't tell. When we reach the stairs leading to the girls' rooms I stop and turn around, hoping my face doesn't reveal the deep blush I feel.

"I'll wait here for Danny," Mark says, his voice low, his fingers grazing my elbow. "I hope you can sleep tonight."

I glance up at him in the low light. "I hope you can sleep too, Mark. Good night."

Chapter 20

It hurts—climbing the stairs after our run earlier today. So, I go slowly, with a lot to think about.

Mark and Danny.

I'm tired now, but I don't think I'll ever forget how good I felt earlier today. It gives me hope, just knowing it's possible for me to be happy again.

I finally find the door to my room and go inside. As I get dressed in my pajamas, my thoughts turn to Danny. He's kind, just like Mark. So kind that I find myself drawn to him in a different way. His words about the Doler made me think today. Only a true, concerned friend would be so painfully honest. He told me what I need to do to get better. Now I get to decide whether I'm determined enough to do it.

In my pajamas now, I blow out my candle and sit on my bed. I frown, looking down at my red totem. Accepting this part of me seems impossible. The totem. Even more so now that I've learned its purpose from the chief. It's dangerous. It could hurt my friends. How can I accept something that could cause others pain?

But then Danny's words ring through my mind again. The totem isn't all bad. The Doler does have an important purpose.

My thoughts turn to Cody and her friend. I never knew Cody was a refugee, that she's been through so much. And now her friend has been taken by the clan. Why?

I'm so lost in my thoughts that I almost don't realize someone is opening my door. My heart rate picks up as images of the men attacking me at initiation flash through my mind. Rising to my feet, I hold up my fists, ready to put up a weak fight.

"Who's there?" I demand.

I hear a shushing sound on the other side of the door before it swings open. I sigh, relieved, when I see Rusty entering with a sleeping Cody in his arms. My fear quickly turns to worry. He lays Cody on her bed, and after pulling the covers up to her chin, he sits on my bed, his weight pitting my mattress.

"She's finally asleep," he whispers.

This is the first time I've seen Cody since before initiation. I'm amazed at how different she looks. Even in the dim light I can see that her usually perfect eyes are swollen, her pink cheeks pale.

"How is she?" I ask, sitting next to him.

Rusty shakes his head, rubbing his tired face. "Not so good. She blames herself for what happened to her friend."

The room is quiet until I whisper back. "The chief said her friend had been a refugee with Cody. I didn't realize Cody was a refugee."

"Yes. Cody's parents were supposed to have gotten on the same boat as her, the boat that took her across the Malacia Gulf, but there wasn't enough room. She was grateful she'd at least had Abby. Cody says Abby is the only reason she survived. But not too long after she left, her parents were killed, and the chief went to collect her and take her away from the war. You see, her mother was previously a Pepp. But Cody didn't want to leave her friend behind. She knew Abby wouldn't survive on her own. So Cody did what she thought was best. She joined the Pepps but secretly sent Abby food and weapons through capsules. She also sent her toboggans to keep her warm and safe at night." Rusty shakes his head. "I just can't figure out how the clan knew about Abby. *I* didn't even know she was sneaking supplies."

My heart starts beating faster. It's as if she was being spied on. I draw in a breath as realization dawns on me.

"I think I know." I reach out to my nightstand. I don't expect to find the weird rock there, but I open the drawer anyway. It's empty.

"The Morgans." I look at Rusty. "There were Morgans in our room."

Rusty stares at me, his face pale even in the dark. Swallowing, he turns back to look at Cody. "She told me about them, but I didn't think ..."

We had thought the Morgans were spying on me, but maybe they were spying on Cody. Why?

"When I found them, she seemed scared. But then she seemed to get over it," I say.

My mind pictures Cody's Magbaby being followed by a Morgan, and my gut writhes.

We sit in silence until Rusty whispers, "I need to train her in combat. We don't know why the clan went after her friend. If Case went after Abby, they could come after her. I need to teach her to fight."

Rusty's words worry me more. *What if Case and the clan do come after Cody? What if they try to hurt her?*

"I need to train you too," Rusty whispers. "If it wasn't for that lightning storm at initiation, you would have been toast against that man and Case."

I look at Rusty curiously. I didn't think about Gabbro's plan all day thanks to Danny and Mark, but now it comes back to my mind. According to what he said, I'm supposed to convince Rusty to train me. Even though I agreed to go through with Gabbro's plan to free the prisoners, it terrifies me. It's an impossible plan. Rusty's offer is exactly what Gabbro would want, which is probably why my stomach starts to hurt the moment he offers it. If I accept his help with training, it will be the first step in accepting our plan.

I sigh. As much as I want to, though, I can't turn Rusty down. He's right. Even if there wasn't a plan for me to free the prisoners, I still need help being a normal Pepp. Running up the mountain with Mark and Danny today showed me that.

"Thank you, Rusty," I say hesitantly.

"You could use some training in rock climbing too," he says.

I try to keep my face from flushing. He must have been flying overhead when I haphazardly climbed the wall during initiation.

"Alena, I was scared to death. Case almost got you, and it was under my watch. I can't let that happen again. I'll train you in everything."

"Thank you."

Rusty stands before whispering, "Please watch over Cody. She's struggling. I'll check on her tomorrow."

"Of course."

Rusty turns to leave but then stops, "I've started training Pepps in weaponry at five in the morning. But I could train you earlier at four. It's the only time I have. Can you make that work?"

I want to moan. *Four a.m.?* But I bite my tongue.

This better be worth it.

Chapter 21

"Do you feel like your head's going to explode?" Gabbro asks for Danny.

Danny sits in front of me at the library table like he's done for the past two weeks, quizzing me on the last few elements I need to memorize.

I've spent every day with Mark, Danny, and Gabbro, running and then working to master the sounds of all 120 elements. I've learned so many new sounds that I do feel like my head is going to explode. This means I'm one step closer to becoming a medic, though, right?

The only time I'm not with Danny and Mark is when I'm with Rusty, and I hate it. He's started me off with knife-throwing and lifting weights. He'll eventually lead up to hand-to-hand combat, but he says for me to be successful in combat I need to get stronger. If there's anything I've learned this week it's that I'm weak.

I'm not sure if knife-throwing is what Gabbro wanted me to learn. But I don't know how to redirect Rusty without making him suspicious. And talking to Gabbro privately is not easy. So I'm just going with it.

I just wish our training didn't have to be so doggone early. He's on a dropdown right now with Cody, so I haven't had to train for the past two days, thank goodness. But when he gets back, I know I'll have to get up again at four in the morning, then try to go back to sleep, only to get woken shortly after by Danny and Mark. I could ask Mark and Danny to move our training to a different time, but then I'd have to explain why. I can't do that. Besides, they're my favorite part of the day. I'll put up with my training with Rusty as long as I can see them.

It's been almost two weeks since Cody's friend disappeared, and Cody's not doing well. She's never in the room when I get back at night or in the morning. Rusty thought taking her on a dropdown would help, so their team left Petrichor a couple of days ago, promising to take strict precautions. They should be back sometime tonight.

Danny taps my leg, bringing me back to the room.

I return the tap. For the first time in a while, Mark and Danny were asked to help in the dino rink today, so in addition to not training with Rusty, I didn't get my morning run with Mark and Danny. Danny was finally able to leave the rink and meet me here this afternoon, but Mark had to stay behind a little longer.

I never thought missing our runs or training with Rusty would affect me so much, but I can feel the difference in my mood today. I feel ickier than I have lately. There's a certain empowerment that comes from getting rid of Doler and making my body stronger, especially after so many months of neglect. I miss that empowerment today. Since Danny introduced the wiggems to me, I've been hesitant to believe they could really be the cause for the difference in my mood, but after today I'd be stupid not to notice. Today I'm filled with Doler, and I hate it.

But do I really have to run up a mountain every day to be happy? *Can't I have one day of rest without feeling like crap?* It was nice to sleep in ... at least until I woke up.

"It only gets worse," Gabbro says. It takes me a minute to realize he's referring to mastering the sounds and not the wiggems. This, however, doesn't make me feel any better, and I remain quiet. I would've already given up on this task of memorizing sounds a hundred times if Danny had let me.

I look around the room. To add to my despair, Flint is in the library today. He's been sitting at a nearby table, doing nothing but glaring at me for the past hour. I can almost see the wheels in his head moving, planning a way to get rid of me. Somehow word about Mark and me having the ability to create lightning got out. I don't know how. I have a hard time thinking it was Mark. The chief seems furious, but he's supposedly the only other one who knew. It definitely wasn't me. I'm glad I didn't tell the chief about Gabbro's plan. How could anyone else have found out? Unless they overheard our conversation in the library.

The lack of trust I've developed the past several weeks only gets stronger.

Now, after learning that Mark and I are potential weapons activated by morphing, Flint's been hard at work, spreading rumors across Petrichor that I'm secretly learning how to morph. Mark assured me that most Pepps know not to believe anything Flint says, but the glaring eyes I see daily from others suggest a different story. I can't say that I blame them; I'm wary of myself. I'm just grateful that I don't know how to morph. *But can I really keep the totem from ever being activated? Nobody has taught me how to morph. But is it something that could happen accidentally?*

I eye my totem now, particularly disgusted with it today.

Sensing my mood, Danny puts his hand on my knee while Gabbro says, "It's okay, Alena."

I try to smile. I've never met a nicer person. I know how much Danny is sacrificing to be with me every day, teaching me things he's already mastered. He doesn't have to be here; he doesn't have to be patient with me, with my moods. But he is.

"How about we do something different today?" I hear Mark's voice behind me, and I turn around as he approaches our table. I quickly rip my eyes away from his handsome face, kicking myself silently. He looks too handsome. Since the night of initiation, he and I haven't had much time alone. As a result, I've begun doubting whether or not he still enjoys being around me. A big part of that is because of Danny. It's like we have this silent agreement that Danny comes first, which means Mark and I don't have many personal conversations. Usually I appreciate this silent understanding, but today I find myself aching to be closer to him. Aching to talk to him as a friend.

I still don't know if it's right to encourage Danny. He's been so good to me that I'll do anything for him. If that means cultivating a closer relationship, then so be it. Maybe someday I'll figure out what is ethically right.

After placing a heavy book in the middle of the table, Mark sits in a chair across from me, a tiredness hovering over his eyes. Perhaps the missed run is affecting him too.

"We've been memorizing the sounds the elements make in order to identify what's around you," Mark says. "Now let's start teaching you the language of the totem."

Opening the book to the first pages, Gabbro says, "We identify each of the elements with a single sound we can make. For example, the sound for hydrogen is made by clicking the tongue once." Gabbro clicks his tongue on the top of his mouth one time, and without realizing it, I mimic him.

Danny leans back proudly, settling his hands on his stomach "You can't see it, but you just spoke to the totem, telling it to collect hydrogen, and it did, in a little puff in front of you," Gabbro says.

Mark chimes in. "I like to think of each of these sounds as a letter in the alphabet. They're the foundation of anything you create. As you know, in chemistry, everything we see is made up of millions of large compounds of atoms, but they all arise from the basic elements. You'll learn how to string them together one at a time to start out with. Once you can do that, you'll learn the shortcut words that identify very long and tedious compounds so you don't have to make each individual sound every single time."

Gabbro cuts in for Danny. "I don't like to think of the sounds as letters of the alphabet but instead like the different notes in music. Each note combined with another forms a melody."

I smile at Danny. Over the past two weeks he's repeatedly used music as a way to teach me about the totem and the elements. Danny's passion for music is evident.

Nudging his knee with my hand, I say, "Danny, will you write me a song someday?"

I haven't missed the fact that Danny tries to touch my hands or knees any chance he gets. I enjoy seeing his body melt when I return the touch. This time, though, Danny's face goes white.

Mark's voice drips with annoyance. "He already has. And you can choose whichever way helps you the most, either the music concept or the alphabet concept."

I'm surprised by Mark's comment, and I look at Danny both seriously and teasingly. "You wrote me a song?" His blush confirms what Mark said, and I coax him further. "I want to hear it." Danny doesn't make eye contact but looks very uncomfortable. I decide not to press him further.

"Sometime," I say. Then, with a soft laugh and touch to his knee, I decide to change the subject.

Looking around the library, I watch all the other students using their power.

"So, I have to make the sounds out loud to talk to the totem? I haven't ever heard other Pepps talking out loud."

Mark rubs his face, something he does when he's tired. "After you train for a while with your totem, it'll be able to read your thoughts so you don't have to say anything out loud. It doesn't take long to master the communications."

"Well, you guys ready?" Gabbro asks.

I look at him confused.

"Ready?"

"We're going to the school," Mark explains. "We want to show you the Magnifying Element room. I think we could all use a change of scenery."

Leaving our box of elements, and a still glaring Flint, I happily leave the library with Danny and Mark and head to the school.

The large barren mountain, the school where I first met my team, is very different from GreenGrotto. Instead of being lush with greenery, it stands bald and gray. Walking inside for the first time, I notice the stone caverns and halls lack the plant life GreenGrotto harbors even on the inside. Without the trees to absorb and transport water, the air is drastically more humid than GreenGrotto's. I huff when a wall of moisture slams into me. The only similarity to the other mountain is the torches used to light the inside.

Mark leads us through the busy open hall and to the left into a large room. It reminds me of the football field we had at my high school back home. The floor in the middle is long and open, with rows of stone seats encircling the whole space and tapering upward. In the middle of the room are several Pepps practicing their powers.

"This is the skills room," Mark says. "As part of the trainings, Pepps usually have to perform certain tasks in this room in front of the council."

"It's terrifying, performing in front of the council." Gabbro says for Danny.

I bet.

We walk up the stairs to an overhang above the skills room and reach a door. Mark opens it.

I blink, letting my eyes adjust to the lighting. Even though the room is remarkably darker than the hall, several glass boxes, at least ten feet high and five feet wide, placed sporadically around the area, emit bright light.

We walk in, passing many of the bright boxes crowded with Pepps, until we reach a light box in the corner that sits alone. I stare at it curiously.

"Tiny mirrors, strategically placed, direct the light from above into the light box," Gabbro says.

Danny picks up three flasks sitting in a box at its base and shows their labels to me—two hydrogens and one oxygen. Guiding me to the far end of the glass box, Danny points out five sealed holes in the glass.

"Each of these flasks holds an element. We can't see them now in their normal form, but once we put them inside the magnifying box we will." Danny places the oxygen cylinder up against the sealed hole. A soft sucking sound hisses as the seal is reestablished, and something whips out of the cylinder into the large glass box. I look closer. A fuzzy contraption floats around, while a couple of other fuzzies bounce off the glass walls wildly at incredible speeds. The image reminds me of models in my chemistry class.

"Is that a single element?" I ask, stepping closer to the glass, sure there's no way we could really be seeing such a thing.

There's a touch at my left elbow, and I turn to see Mark standing beside me, his fingers gently brushing my skin. He nods, his face tired. He hasn't touched me since the night the chief gave us bad news about our totems. Probably for Danny's sake, but I've replayed that contact over and over in my mind. Now that he's so close again, my skin shivers. Unlike with Danny, I can't casually touch him back. Instead, I stand frozen.

Mark drops his hand and steps away when Danny comes back to us after releasing the other two atoms into the box.

"Yes," Gabbro exclaims for Danny. "Right now the atoms are moving around individually at their own speeds, but we're going to control each of these elements by speaking to them. We're going to help them bond."

Danny's excitement distracts me from my disorientation around Mark.

"Put your power in," Mark mutters in a low voice next to me. Placing his hand gently on my back, he nudges me forward, closer to the glass so I can hear the sounds. His hand lingers longer than it should, making it impossible for me to focus on what's in front of me.

I shake my head to clear my mind and do what he says. They're faint, but considering no run today I'm surprised I can hear the elements at all when I put the power in. Danny places his hand on the glass.

"I will still make the sounds out loud so you can hear what Danny is signaling," Gabbro says.

I watch the movements of the atoms change as Danny calls to them. The hydrogen slows and the oxygen speeds up until they beat at the same pulse. Before I realize it, they're sucked together like magnets, dropping to the bottom of the case in the form of a thoroughly magnified drop of water.

It's amazing— and, yet, as I touch the glass with my fingertips, my spirits fall. I knew this was the next step, but it seems more complicated now that I've seen it. It's taking me so long to master the sounds of the elements. Not only do I have to learn how to speak to them, I have to learn how to string the sounds together to form compounds. *There are trillions of compounds! How am I supposed to memorize them all?*

Danny pulls up some chairs for Mark and me to sit on while we watch him suck the elements back out and replace them with different elements, forming different kinds of compounds.

I'm so engrossed in the magical movements of the atoms that I jump when the door to the room bursts open and hits the wall.

A girl with the bright-orange totem of a messenger enters the room and runs toward us. Her petite form moves quickly and gracefully.

"The chief wants to see all three of you immediately, at the post," she says. Her voice is gentle yet commanding. Her eyes glide over each of our faces until they land on Danny, who is looking purposefully at the floor. Even though he towers above her, he seems to be trying to make himself very small. The girl's eyes don't waver, and I wonder if she has more to say, but she clamps her mouth shut.

Does Danny know her? I want to ask Mark about it, but he doesn't give me a chance. He's already headed to the door.

***

I follow Mark and Danny in silence. My thoughts about the girl have shifted to thoughts of why the chief might want us. Has something happened?

We approach the airport where I first landed in Petrichor. Off to the left is an open field of grass that extends to the edge of the cliff where Petrichor ends. A hole descends into the ground in the middle of the field marked by a single wooden sign that conveys the location: "The Post."

Mark leads us into the dark tunnels below that are choked with busy council Pepps moving with purpose. We wind our way through until we reach a long hall with a door at the end stamped with the chief's title.

Mark knocks briefly before opening the door. I warily walk in behind him.

The chief stands at his desk scribbling frantically on pieces of paper, with a very dirty and distraught-looking Rusty standing next to him. A worried couple stands against the wall earnestly watching the chief. My eyes are drawn to the woman with dark hair that barely reaches past her chin. Based on the cut, it's probably normally smoothed to perfection, but now it's disheveled and tucked messily behind her ears.

I look around the room again. There are other Pepps in here, Pepps I've never seen before. I glance at each of their totems. Some have colors I'm not familiar with, like camouflage green. But they all have one color in common: blue. Members of the council.

"Alena, Mark, and Danny, thank goodness you're here." The chief signals for us to shut the door. His solemn bearded face sends worry fluttering through my gut.

"I'm afraid I have some bad news," he says. "It's Cody. This morning her team found this note in her tent." The chief walks around his desk and hands me a piece of paper, encouraging me to read it.

Eyeing the chief warily, I take the paper from him.

Pam and Tom,

I want to thank you for taking me in after my parents died. I don't know what I would have done if you hadn't been there for me. I have enjoyed being a Pepp, but I can no longer be with you.

I hope that someday you can understand.

Cody

I'm confused and shocked. *What's going on?* The council members all stare at me, silently waiting to see my reaction.

Standing behind me, Mark reads the note over my shoulder. Danny starts having a tantrum in the corner, flinging his arms wildly and stomping his feet. I don't understand his outburst, and I look to Gabbro, who is hovering in the air, for an answer, but he's just staring at the note.

"Alena, did Cody say anything to you about leaving us?" the chief asks, studying my face.

"No. She hasn't really talked to me at all since her friend disappeared."

The couple against the wall shifts on their feet, but they don't say anything. *Are they her Pepp parents?*

The chief opens his mouth, ready to say something more, but he's interrupted by the door swinging open behind us. A group of dirty Pepps drag in a man whose hands and feet are bound with metal chains.

I step back. This man looks like the clan member from initiation with his bushy beard and dirty face. Even though I know that man is probably tucked safely away in prison, my brain can't seem to accept that, and my hands begin to tremble. Without a word, Mark slides his body in front of mine, creating a barrier that calms me ... a little. I grip the back of his shirt and look around his shoulder.

"Sorry to interrupt you, Chief, but we have an urgent matter." The lead Pepp tightly holds the man's arm. "This man snuck onto a returning flyer. They didn't find him until they were in the air. Their mistake for not performing a normal check. What would you like us to do with him?"

"Jax?" The chief approaches the man he apparently knows. "What's going on?"

Jax?

The door opens again and Jeter enters. He slips around the group to stand by the chief, repeating the chief's question. "What's going on?"

This is when I look closer at the man's face. My blood runs cold.

It's Jaxxon Balac. The man who was assigned the worldwide case of Pepp attacks. The one who captured clan men. *The chief knows him by name?*

His face is old and worn. The scar extending from the side of his mouth to his ear looks worse in person.

"Why are you here?" the chief asks again. Instead of responding, Jax's eyes move until they find me standing behind Mark. His look makes me rock unsteadily.

"You know it's not okay for you to come back here," Chief says. "If you need to communicate with us, you use your Magbaby."

Magbaby? Jax has a Magbaby?

"By the way," the chief continues, "the clan men are out of control. As a communicator you agreed to help us capture them, but things are getting worse." He points to the letter in my hands. "I'll be assigning someone else to that task. You'll need to step down."

Communicator? Jaxxon used to be a Pepp? And now he's been given the task of capturing the clan? The chief asked him to do that?

"Jax?" chief says impatiently, demanding a response.

Jax's eyes just stay glued to mine. Then for the first time he opens his mouth.

"I'm here to give *her* a message." His voice is low and powerful, silencing the room. A terrible darkness leaks out of him, like a shadow, spreading out across the floor until it reaches me.

"He's got Cody ... But he wants *you*."

Each cryptic word out of his mouth sends a jolt through my body, enveloping all my fears and blowing them up. The room suddenly comes alive. Rusty flings his body from the corner, reaching out to strangle the man. Even the chief runs to him shouting orders. It probably happens fast, but to me it's so slow. All I can focus on is Jax's dirty eyes that are fixed on me. That is, until they make their way to Mark just before Rusty reaches him.

"How's your father?" Jax says.

Then a cloud of smoke blows up in the room, sending Mark and me flying into the wall.

"Where is he?" I hear the chief shouting. Within seconds the cloud is cleared, revealing everyone fallen on the floor. Everyone except Jax.

He's gone.

"Find him!" the chief shouts to those in the room. Without waiting for the others to respond, he swings open the door and runs out. The others follow him, except Rusty.

I've never seen such a look of hate on his face. And it's aimed at me. Is he blaming me for Cody's disappearance?

For a brief second I contemplate telling him about Gabbro's plan, to give him hope about Cody, when a soft hum approaches me. Gabbro settles on my shoulder and places his hand on my neck, but it isn't for comfort. As if he knows what I'm thinking, he warns me, reminding me that his plan needs to remain a secret.

Rusty spins on his heel and leaves the room with everyone else. That's when I see Jeter. He's still in the room, and he's silently watching me.

Why is everyone watching me?

"Let's get out of here." Mark pulls me out the door. I look back one last time at Jeter.

Why isn't he searching for Jax with the others?

***

I can't stop pacing. The walk back to GreenGrotto was quiet. Mark kept trying to calm Danny down, and I kept trying to answer new questions in my mind. The chief asked Jaxxon to protect the Pepps by capturing the clan men. *So the chief* was *taking some action by assigning the task to Jaxxon*. Was it Jaxxon's fault then that the clan was able to get away so many times? He's obviously a traitor, working for whoever "he" is. Case? Does that mean the chief is trustworthy?

But then I think about the cloud of smoke. Jax didn't have a totem on his arm. Either he has some non-Pepp magic, or someone in that room helped him escape. *Who was it, and how did they do it?* I carefully list off each name I know in my head. Chief, Jeter, Rusty, Mark, Danny, Cody's Pepp parents. I don't know who to blame. Plus, there were others there whose names I don't know.

I groan in frustration. I'm definitely not ready to blame Mark or Danny. Or Rusty.

Mark walked me to my room and almost wouldn't leave. A big part of me didn't want him to leave either. Jax threatened me, and I don't know if he's still in Petrichor. But I need to talk to Gabbro privately. So I convinced Mark to go take care of frantic Danny.

I sure hope Gabbro picked up on my glaring looks as we walked. I want to talk to him.

But he still hasn't come.

Now, sitting alone in my room, the questions sweep me away.

Cody was taken by Case's men. *And they wanted her, to get to me?* Should I leave Petrichor and go free her? I don't know what her note meant, but I think Cody chose to leave, probably to help her friend. *Would I do the same? Would I be willing to let Jax trade me for Cody?* Even if I do hand myself over, would that make things safe for the Pepps again? I'm part of a weapon that could destroy them all. *Am I willing to put so many at risk?*

An incredible weight has descended on my shoulders, making it difficult to stand. I would probably leave Petrichor on my own to go look for Cody if it wasn't for Gabbro's plan.

And then there's the question of Mark's father. *Why did Jax mention him?* Is he the one who killed him?

Finally, something slips through the bottom of my door. It's Gabbro, walking toward me.

"Who is Jax?" I didn't plan on shouting, but my built-up emotions are ready to burst out.

Gabbro tries to calm me down, by holding out his hands and bringing his finger to his lips in a shushing gesture.

I repeat my question, quieting my voice only slightly.

Sighing, Gabbro finally responds. "Jax is a communicator."

I shake my head. "That's it. That's all you're going to tell me? I saw him on the news in my *non-Pepp* world. He was the man assigned to capture the clan men. Was that a lie all along? Did he ever capture them, or was he working with them?"

Gabbro's words are quiet. "I'm as surprised as you are, Alena. I didn't know he was working with Case. We never saw him around SilverDen."

"Where did he go, Gabbro? Is he still here in Petrichor? Why did he come here—just to deliver that stupid message to me?" I still can't lower my voice.

"I don't know, Alena. I really don't know."

"Well, let's go to the hideout now. They have Cody." I look for my satchel, determined to do this.

"No."

I had played in my mind how this conversation would go before Gabbro arrived. I knew he would be hesitant.

"No? Gabbro, they took my friend. I can't just sit around here and wait while the chief and the others blindly look for her. You know where the hideout is—she's probably there. I've been training with Rusty. I've gotten stronger."

Even as I say this, though, I know my new strength is not enough. It never will be. I take in a deep breath and kneel on the ground so he can see the desperation in my eyes.

"Gabbro, I could train for months and still not be strong enough to do what you're asking me to do. Please, why can't we just go now?"

"There are many reasons, Alena." Gabbro's voice is rising now. "If you're not strong enough to get out of there, he'll get you. He doesn't want the prisoners. He wants *you*. Don't you understand? Everything is about *you* and that damn totem."

"I don't care!" I try to keep my voice down, but my words crack. "I can't just sit by and let Case hurt others to get to me. I'd rather ..."

I press the heels of my hands into my eyes.

"You'd rather what? Hand yourself over? You'd be doing exactly what he wants you to do. And in return you'd be hurting more Pepps than just Cody or the prisoners."

I raise my head, set my jaw, and stare at the wall. I frantically search my mind to come up with another idea. I think briefly about convincing Gabbro to tell the chief. But then I remember that someone spilled the beans about the secret behind defective totems and their ability to create lightning. And someone helped Jax escape. I can't necessarily rule the chief not guilty.

So I switch gears and try to think of some way to push myself to getting this going sooner. It only takes me a few moments.

"I'll look in the library. I'll find a way to increase my muscle strength with power." I look at Gabbro. "As soon as I'm strong enough, then we'll go."

Gabbro's mouth hangs open. He wasn't expecting that.

"Okay. Five weeks."

"Five weeks! No! One week."

Gabbro shakes his head emphatically. "Five weeks. At the end of December. I still need to find sleeping gas. We need gas masks for the prisoners as well, otherwise they'll all be knocked unconscious too, and these things aren't terribly easy to find among the non-Pepps. I also need to make a pulley system for you, to help you get the prisoners out faster. You look for a way to increase your strength and learn how to rappel. I'll do all those other things. Then we'll go."

"Okay." Maybe he's right. I have no experience in rappelling. Maybe I do need a little time.

But having an actual date to aim for in saving the prisoners, and, hopefully, Cody, relieves me. A little.

Gabbro suddenly looks tired. "I should go, but please be careful. Keep your eye out for Jax—they still haven't found him."

His warning sends shivers up my spine. *What is Case up to?* It's terrifying knowing that he's going through such great lengths to get me.

What if he does find me?

Chapter 22

I walk through the trees on Training Mountain. My muscles are tired, but I ignore my protesting body and turn up the music pounding in my ears.

After my conversation with Gabbro two weeks ago, I went to the library and found a book on rappelling. Then I went to Mossy Hollow and traded in some of my equipment capsules from initiation for rappelling equipment. I have to learn how to do this, and I have to learn fast. With my book and equipment in tow, I've been going to a rock wall on Training Mountain every morning this last week. It's taken me time, but I've figured out how to tie the knots needed and connect the harness. I've even been able to descend the rock walls several times each morning. I always feel good, until I'm reminded that I have to not only go down, I have to go up as well. That's much harder.

I also found a book about muscle building. However, I still don't understand it. It talks about listening to certain sounds, but reading the description of the sound and actually hearing it are two very different things. I need somcone to purposefully point them out to me. I've asked Mark and Danny about a couple of the sounds, and they've been able to help me, but I don't want them to get suspicious of my very specific questions. So I haven't been able to increase my muscle strength. Which means I'm still weak.

I kick a rock. Training with Rusty the last two weeks has been torturous, and I loathe every morning I have to face him. He won't admit it, but he blames me for what happened to Cody and I'm sure he would have stopped training me altogether, except yelling in my face and kicking my butt seems to make him feel better. Since Cody left, he's become a completely different person. He has no patience with my lack of skill in combat, the new area he's training me in. Regardless of how hard I try and how much I practice fighting, I can't do it. My efforts don't seem to be making a difference.

I replay Gabbro's plan over in my mind again.

Drop down the long hole, find the prisoners, gas the clan men, find the electrical source ... blow it up. Then guide all the Pepps back to the hole and help them up the rope, all without power and without getting killed.

The deadweight of dread sitting in my stomach gets bigger every day. *How am I supposed to fight clan members if I can't even fight Rusty? How am I supposed to get dozens of Pepps up the rope when I can't even get up the rope myself?* Gabbro has three more weeks to get everything ready while I try to get stronger and lie to everyone's face, pretending like I'm not planning some super-dangerous prisoner heist. I want to pull my hair out. It's not enough time, but yet it's too much time. Every minute that passes is a minute that Cody might not survive.

I grunt out loud in the open air and squeeze my eyes shut.

Aside from the fact that my friend is missing, that I'm supposed to become immensely stronger, and that I'm a weapon that could destroy all the Pepps, there's something else that's been nagging at me.

Jax. Nobody ever found him. He just disappeared from the chief's office, which has me constantly looking over my shoulder. He didn't have a totem, so he couldn't have used power to disappear. And Mark confirmed that he's not a pureblood. Then the night after he disappeared I had a dream. It was a dream of Cody. She looked like she'd been beaten with a swollen eye and lip, blood dripping out of her ear. She was sitting on a wooden chair, her face twisted in pain. A cloudy ending to the dream revealed a green forested place. At first I thought it was just a stupid dream. But then I had it the next night, and the next, and the next. It was so vivid and scary that I felt like there had to be more to it. I felt like it had something do with Jax. But how? *How could he get a dream into my head? How was I seeing Cody?* I talked to Gabbro about it, who immediately told me to go see the chief. The chief sent me to Jeter, who found a memory bug in my brain.

I remember when I realized Mark's dad hadn't been attacked by a bear but by human beings. It was daunting that a human being could actually want to cause harm to one of his own kind. That's how I felt when they found the memory bug in me. It wasn't just a dream but a real memory of something that actually happened. To Cody. Knowing that another human not only hurt Cody like that but could also invade my mind hoping to collect me to hurt the Pepps is all-consuming. The dark shadow of Case and his men has descended on me. I feel their evil, and it scares me.

Is Jax still here? Is Cody still alive? Who is helping him? Who will they take next? I told Mark quietly about the dreams. He made me promise never to go looking for Cody. To leave it up to the chief, who is earnestly searching for the forested area I saw in my dream. He hopes that that's where Cody is, in the southern swamps.

There's something else that's been bothering me. Another question I keep asking myself. Jax told me that Case wanted *me*. But why didn't he specifically tell me where to go to find him? The only thing they showed me in the dream was the green forest, but that could be anywhere. It would be a lot more tempting for me to hand myself over if I knew exactly where to go. It's like an incomplete message was delivered.

The only thing that gives me hope is that Gabbro and I have a plan. Not only to free the prisoners but a plan to capture the clan so I can eventually go home.

Home. Saying the word sends a pang of sadness through me. Will I ever get there?

I push all my built-up confusion and dread toward my muscles. Breccia turns up the music without me asking her this time. She seems to understand my needs now as if they're a palpable chemical seeping from my pores.

I look below at Petrichor. The place is pretty dead. A large group of Pepps, including Rusty, Mark, and Danny, got in late last night after a humanitarian dropdown in the GreenLands. Hundreds of Pepps have spent the last several days there trying to help the wounded refugees safely escape.

The war has taken the Pepps' gossip off me and I've tried to listen, finally learning what the war is all about.

I guess Verdure, the country adjacent to the GreenLands, claimed land on the other side of the GreenLands to expand their vegetation trade. In order to get to it and develop it, though, they've had to travel around the GreenLands to the other side. To make things easier for themselves, they asked Sacka, the leader of the GreenLands, if they could travel through their country. Sacka gave them permission.

But then the Verdure workers started causing trouble—harassing the people and stealing chemicals they produce for trade. Eventually Sacka closed their borders, refusing to let them through. That started the war.

When I first heard about the war a couple of years ago, I thought it was stupid. The GreenLands are well known for their chemicals, produced and shipped all around the world for land-improvement projects. *Why would Verdure be so stupid as to attack a population that can just bomb them?* The GreenLands did too. They bombed them several times.

But even though the GreenLands had chemicals, they didn't have the one thing Verdure did: massive numbers of men. And smaller deadly weapons. The strength they had in numbers to cross the borders and sneakily attack the civilians eventually put Cody's people in a very bad spot. Their civilians couldn't even protect themselves, so they started fleeing their land. Cody was one of those who was forced to leave her home for her own safety.

Earlier this week, Verdure finally advanced its troops to Actinic Point, the biggest chemical plant the GreenLands has. And they overtook it, now giving them access to dangerous amounts of bomb chemicals.

So now the Pepps are trying to help the refugees with food and supplies and healing. It seems silly for the Pepps to be helping with such miniscule things when they could destroy Verdure and end the war. *Wouldn't that be more helpful?*

Everyone was called back last night, and now they're all asleep.

When Mark and Danny wake up, I'm supposed to meet them for our daily training, which will be soon.

I breathe in deeply. Mark and Danny. They're the only reason I've survived the last several weeks. They still don't know about my trainings with Rusty, but I think Mark is suspicious of something. He pointed out how the muscles in my arms have mysteriously gotten more defined.

I couldn't tell him the reason, so I attributed it to the runs we go on. He dropped the subject but didn't seem to buy it, which is why I now wear long-sleeved shirts every day. Trying to act normal and not give away how confused and scared I am is getting harder and harder. I want so badly to tell Mark about everything. But aside from Gabbro's warning, I really don't know who I can trust. This makes me angry. I shouldn't have to doubt the integrity of someone good just because of everyone else's bad decisions. Regardless, I want to trust Mark, and I'm grateful he's with me all day every day until late in the evening. The only time he's not with me is nighttime, which is when I worry the most about Jax. But that's when a council member sits outside my room. So far I've been safe.

My pace quickens as I run down the mountain. I lean back so I don't tumble forward.

Mark and Danny have been teaching me more about the totem language. I've even started stringing together different elements to create compounds. Since I'm a medic, Danny has helped me create the backbone of blood cells, proteins, enzymes, and tissue cells all within the walls of the micro box. All that stuff comes easily to me. Well, a lot easier than other things, like fire. For fire, I can hear the elements needed in the oxygen and fuel, but it's difficult for me to hear the difference in temperatures. Supposedly, according to Mark, elements that are heated move at a higher rate and faster beat, but I have a hard time controlling that rate. And then there's ice, and plants and metal. Pretty much anything outside the body is impossible for me to command.

Even though the elements of the body are easier for me to understand, when Danny quizzes me on what to do in the event of a human injury, such as a bone break, my mind gets all foggy and the compounds start mixing together. I forget how many of each element is in each compound or what order they go in. I'm getting better at the language, and I know the science behind it, but I can't seem to put it all together correctly. Danny keeps reminding me that it's only been two weeks since learning the language, but I was hoping to be farther along than I am.

Looking down, I see the bottom of the mountain just ahead of me and I race toward it, staggering into the grass clearing next to the gym. Sweat covers my body along with the usual Doler, and I slow to a jog. I look at the sun again. I should have enough time to shower before my training with Mark and Danny.

When I look up toward GreenGrotto, though, I stumble over my feet when I see two figures standing on the balcony just above the gym.

It's Mark and Danny, leaning on the railing, their eyes on me, both smiling widely. Mark raises his fingers in a wave. I grumble. *They're early.*

I run to the bottom of the stairs and then walk up, my legs cramping. I meet them on the balcony. Mark's gaze warms my already red face.

"We all love watching you run, Alena," Gabbro says, smirking. Danny and Mark chortle beside him.

I roll my eyes, wiping the muck off my forehead. "You're early," I say, aware of Mark's eyes still on me.

"Today we're going for a ride," Gabbro says. "Mark has an idea of something that might help you with your power."

I sigh and follow Mark and Danny down the stairs back to the grassy field. *I stink, and I'm covered in sweat. I don't want to go now.* But Danny ignores my reluctance. He pulls out a capsule from his pocket, then expands a vehicle that resembles a four-wheeler. Oh, how I miss four-wheeling.

Danny hops on and pats the seat behind him. "Come on," Gabbro says.

I plant my feet. "Danny, I stink. And I'm really sweaty. I'm going to get you grossly wet."

Gabbro's lips tighten as he relays Danny's reply. "I wouldn't have it any other way."

Shaking my head, I swing my leg over and scoot up behind Danny. I try not to get too close.

After Mark pops open another vehicle for himself, we move forward down a bumpy path. I find it more comfortable to lean back and brace myself on the rack, but to appease Danny I rest one of my hands on his waist. When I steal a glance back at Mark, he winks, making my heart flutter.

He's in a good mood.

I turn my attention back to the green hills in front of us, watching them quickly pass. I've never been past GreenGrotto in this direction. We're in different mountains.

I'm so absorbed in the scenery and the hum of the four-wheeler that I almost don't notice what eventually appears in front of us. A large meadow of bright-purple wildflowers stretches out until it comes to an abrupt halt against a wall of snow at least ten feet high in the distance. The clouds darken on the other side of the meadow, and I shiver. I had heard that Petrichor sits in the middle of a cold climate, but to actually see its defined border is somewhat disturbing. It's as though summer and winter meet here and are separated only by what looks like a single piece of glass.

"This is my favorite place in the world," Gabbro says for Danny.

When the four-wheeler stops, I get off the back and follow Danny to the grass, where he pats the ground next to him. I'm grateful the sun is shining brightly on this side of the snow wall. Mark sits on the other side of me with a basket full of food.

Pointing to the dark snow area, Gabbro says, "The prison is out there. Algor."

I remember Gabbro mentioning the prison here in Petrichor. Is that where that man from initiation is being held?

"Who is sent to prison here?" I ask.

"Those who betray the Pepps, like the clan men, and ..." Mark pauses as he pulls out some apples and sandwiches from the basket, then hands them to us.

"And?" I ask when Mark doesn't continue. He remains quiet, so I turn to Gabbro, who is lying in the warm grass with his eyes closed, his hands behind his head.

Gabbro's expression is smug, but he also remains silent. I look at Danny, whose cheeks are bright red.

"What?" I ask, confused.

Mark continues quietly on my left. "The other way you get sent to Algor is by having ... *intimate* relationships with humans." Mark emphasizes the word *intimate*, and I understand their hesitancy, but I still don't understand what it means.

Danny clears his throat, and Gabbro finally speaks again. "If a Pepp falls in love with a human, they have to give up their totem. If they don't, and have a child together, then the Pepp is sent to Algor."

I remember the day I met Issy at the old hunter's lodge. She had threatened Caleb because she thought we were "together." Now it makes sense. The Pepps aren't allowed to have those kinds of relationships with humans.

"But why? Why not just have the totem removed and send the Pepp away from Petrichor? Why do they have to be sent to prison?"

I look at Mark for an answer to this.

"It has to do with the mixed blood babies that come from mixed relationships. They come out ..." Mark searches for the right word. "Sick. Most babies don't live very long, but the ones that do suffer from terrible illnesses. I've never seen one, but I've heard they really struggle. Jeter and Chief have tried to help the babies with our power, but it only makes them worse." Mark stops, and I recall the boy the chief had mentioned before. The boy that Danny's father, Jose, tried to heal but couldn't. Did he come from a mixed relationship? Is that why the chief was willing to give Jose an extra totem to find a way to heal the boy? Because the boy's sickness stemmed from a Pepp-human link?

I guess that's a good enough reason to threaten prison.

Danny clears his throat, evidently wanting to change the subject. "Over there, hidden in the trees, is my own secret flyer," Gabbro says. Bringing a finger to his lips, he adds, "Don't tell anyone. I'm not supposed to have it, but I found it abandoned on one of my dropdowns. I had Ching shrink it and brought it back here." Wrinkling his nose, he adds, "If the chief found out, I would be dead meat." I chuckle and bite into a sandwich. I don't think the chief could ever hurt Danny.

Danny then pulls out a capsule that he expands into a guitar and begins softly plucking the strings.

"You play the guitar?" I ask quietly. *Of course he does.* His soft pluckings turn into a steady melody, his fingers gracefully skimming the strings like flat rocks skipping across a pond. The tune sweetly echoes through the mountains around us, and I drop my hands to my lap, mesmerized by this new and unfamiliar song ... at least until Gabbro tries to sing the words. He hates doing it, I can tell, but Danny forces him. Unfortunately, it comes out as more of a screeching. I reach to cover my ears until I realize what Gabbro is saying.

A simple smile, a calming hand, is what you offered this strange man.

An enlightening word, a tender touch. To you, it might not have meant too much.

But to me you aren't just a dawning friend. To me, you are the change in who I am.

You're like a freeing light from the darkest of nights.

You're like a warming flame, burning fiercely and yet tame.

Setting.

Me.

Free.

From the shadows that threaten me.

I swallow past the lump forming in my throat. *Is he talking about me? Is this the song Mark had mentioned before?* The one Danny wrote? The words melt away the darkness in my heart. I should be singing the song right back to him. It perfectly captures the light he's been in my life since meeting him. The light he is to me now.

I gulp past the lump in my throat to speak again when the song ends. "That's a beautiful song, Danny."

"I have something for you," Gabbro says as Danny puts down the guitar and pulls something out of his pocket. He holds up a necklace made of old twine. In the middle of it is a round pink bead caged in three tiny strings of gold.

"I made this for you. It's made of MiraWax. Said to be lucky." Danny winks.

"Thank you, Danny," I whisper again while pulling my hair aside so he can put it on. "For being my friend ... and for the luck."

Mark stands, breaking the moment, and walks back to the four-wheeler. We aren't leaving yet, I hope. I finger the bead on my neck and take a bite of my sandwich. When Mark comes back and sits, he's holding something in his hand. I make eye contact with him briefly, wondering what he's doing, when he says, "You ready?"

Something is up. I can feel it, and I already don't like it. Furrowing my eyebrows, I swallow my bite and lean away from him, waiting for an explanation.

He doesn't offer it. Instead, he extends his legs out in front of himself and exposes the item in his hand—a knife—before stabbing himself in the thigh. The muscles in his neck bulge, and he bites back a yell as he pulls the knife out of his leg and drops it from his bloody hand. Lying back on the ground, he grunts.

"Close me up."

"Mark!" I yell in horror, my shocked body shaking as I drop my sandwich and rise to my knees. "Why did you do that? I can't heal you!"

"Just do it!" Gabbro says while Mark distracts himself with the clouds in the sky.

I want to punch him. The anxiety, inadequacy, and fear all slam a wall into my brain, blocking everything I've learned the past several weeks.

"I can't," I say, tears tugging at my eyes. "I don't know how."

Danny stands behind me, gripping my shoulders. "Alena, think of your anatomy. What happens when a knife cuts through skin?"

Images from my anatomy books and graphs push through the wall.

"The proteins," I say. "The proteins are broken."

"Good, now listen. You know what healthy tissue sounds like. Listen for the break—what does it sound like and where is it?" I focus on the sounds again. They've become more familiar and less overwhelming now that I wear my power all the time. We have only ever talked about the whirring sound that comes from broken proteins, but I can now hear it for the first time. My ears take me right to the broken tissue and vessels, the sounds telling me the story. I reach to them mentally, then hold out my hands in response.

"Now, how do you complete the broken proteins? What elements do they need? Tell your totem."

The endless graphs and arrangements of proteins I've been studying come together. I speak hesitantly to my totem.

"Ah!" Mark flinches, his wound bleeding more at my mistake. I panic and my hands begin to shake.

"You've got this, Alena," Gabbro encourages from behind.

I try speaking to my vine again, focusing on both the sounds I hear and the sounds I speak. I rack my brain to remember which tissue compositions go where. It's like putting a puzzle together. A terribly confusing and complex puzzle. I watch Mark's face, looking for more grimaces, but his golden-brown eyes are trying to stay focused.

Slowly, while continuing to speak to the totem, the whirrings of the broken proteins fade, and I grin when I see the wound on Mark's leg stop bleeding. I pause and listen, then much quicker this time correct and redirect the totem to the other damage I can now hear. Before I know it, the muscles and tissue are all bonded, looking like ordinary skin, only a pink scar visible.

Sitting back on my heels, I wipe the sweat from my brow.

Mark's chuckle breaks the silence, and without a second thought, I punch him in the arm.

"Don't you ever do that again!" I say.

Sitting up, he grins widely at me. "You did it, Lena." I don't miss the nickname that slips through his lips. The sound of it softens my angry heart. *Why can't I just be around Mark all the time?* His presence does me good. And that smile. I can't stay mad at him with that smile. So I redirect my anger somewhere else.

I turn around to Danny, who's still behind me, and swing at his shoulder. "You're awful!"

He laughs, unshaken. "It worked. You know the stuff. You have a natural instinct to help people medically. You're a true medic."

Standing, Danny extends a hand to help me up. "We better get back. We're going to take you to the hospital. I think you're more than ready to start training as a medic with them."

This news stops me. "You can't train me to be a medic?" The thought of having to train with others I don't know makes me uncomfortable.

"No. Sorry, Alena. We don't know much about medic stuff. However, we will still train you a couple of times a week on the other things you need to know for dropdowns."

Looking at my sweaty clothes, I'm reminded of how filthy I am. "Okay. Do you think I could at least change my clothes before we head to the hospital?"

Chapter 23

After changing my clothes, we walk through Petrichor, past Mossy Hollow, toward the airport. Once past the flyers, we approach a mountain cliff that ascends above us. As the cliff looms in front of me, I realize for the first time that this is the place where my memories were checked and where I woke up after initiation. This is the hospital.

I observe the side of the cliff, my eyes widening. I can't believe I hadn't seen it before. It extends straight up above the airport, with hundreds of hexagonal compartments set into the cliff made of some yellow transparent material.

A beehive—that's what it looks like, with people standing in the compartments, looking very small from this distance.

I spot something flying in the sky toward the cliff—a wooden cylinder the size of a large tree trunk. It swiftly enters one of the compartments. A toboggan.

Since I've stopped walking to stare at the cliff, Mark places his hand at my elbow, gently pulling me toward the door at the bottom of the cliff, then guides me through.

The bright open area, with floors and walls made of gray concrete, hosts pillars strategically placed to prevent a cave-in. The place is busy with casually dressed Pepps, their roles identified with a simple nametag. Danny guides us to a staircase with a pulley. I have yet to learn how to use the pulley, but I can tell Danny is more than happy to oblige, taking me up the way Aba did the first day I met her.

The floor we rise to meets us with hallways. We walk down one very long one until we reach a door at the end. I know this room.

"Alena!" Jeter opens the door after Danny knocks. "I've been eager to see you here."

I haven't seen him since the night Cody disappeared and Jax threatened me. He doesn't seem as serious today as he was then, but I eye him warily. I realize for the first time that every time something bad has happened to me—Chief putting me in "prison," my memories searched, finding the spy rocks—Jeter was there. He probably knows an awful lot about me. This makes me uneasy, especially since I don't know anything about him.

We walk into the room, and for the first time I see it in bright daylight. The walls that were covered with tapestries the last two times I entered here now embrace large windows crisscrossed with light-brown wooden muntins that separate them into dozens of smaller glass squares. The glass wall leans outward at the top, allowing for a spectacular view below.

The left wall is also glass, but instead of clear squares it's the same yellowish color as the outside of the cliff, reminding me of honey. The yellow glass starts in the medic's room and extends down a bright hallway that travels parallel to the hallway we just emerged from, all the way across the mountain. Hexagonal units stretch past the glass, creating several distinct rooms down the hall that are transparent and visible from where I stand now. This is the cliffside I saw outside.

"It's good to see you again, Alena. Thank you, Danny, for bringing her to me. Is she ready?"

Danny nods but Mark speaks. "She closed up my leg about an hour ago." Looking at me, he adds, "She did a pretty good job." Mark shows Jeter his wound through the gaping hole in his pant leg.

Jeter examines it closely. "This is your first healing?"

"Yes," I say.

"Well done. That's pretty incredible for the first time without training. Mark, if you head down to the clinic, one of the medics there can redo it so you don't scar."

Looking at me, Mark shakes his head and whispers, "No. I think I'll keep this scar."

Heat rises in my cheeks.

"Well, I'm grateful to finally have your help," Jeter says. "After losing Cody and the other Pepps, we've been somewhat short-staffed here." His voice is too light for such a dark topic.

Jeter walks over to a large bookcase on my right and reaches for a book. My eyes are drawn to something sitting on the top shelf. My heart sinks.

The belt. The one worn by the man killed at initiation. Its wires are hanging down, and it brings the faces of Case and the man to my mind. *Why did Jeter keep that?*

"First, we need to get you some of this," Jeter says, walking back to me. I swallow and look at his hand. He's holding out a capsule full of yellow liquid. Power.

"I'll be giving you some every day you come help me. It'll take a lot of practice for you to learn more than just simple tissue repair, but I'm going to assign you to Mitch, who will train you."

Speaking directly to Mark and Danny, Jeter says, "I'll take it from here."

When Mark and Danny both look at me, I silently beg them to stay and not leave me here alone, but Mark encourages me with a wink.

"Well, let me show you around," Jeter says after they leave. He talks easily, leading me to the honeycomb wall. "These are the capsule combs. There is a hall of combs on every floor. If something happens on a run and a Pepp needs to be sent back quickly for medical help, they use one of these." Jeter pulls a ring off his finger and shows it to me. I recognize it from the one given to Carlos at initiation, silver with a black jewel on it. A toboggan. My heart beats faster, remembering how the man at initiation tried to force me into one of these.

"The injured Pepp is placed in the toboggan, and then it quickly makes its way here. It usually only takes these things a couple of hours to get the injured to Petrichor from the farthest place in the world. They're incredibly fast and durable." He opens the door to one of the combs. "The toboggan flies into one of the combs, where we take care of the injured Pepp. From my office back there I can see every capsule that flies into this top-floor section, and I can monitor and assign my helpers to take care of any newcomers. The worst cases come to me."

I walk into the empty comb. The space is only about ten feet by ten feet, and the far wall is completely open to the air so a capsule can enter. It's a strong contrast to the hospital rooms I'm used to that are loaded with monitors, beds, equipment, and IV fluids. That stuff is obviously not needed here.

"Each group of runners has a medic that goes with them. They can usually heal the simple stuff like broken bones and lacerations—unless they run out of power, which has been happening more lately. Those who get sent here are the ones in the most critical condition."

A girl passes our comb, and Jeter stops her.

"Scance?" I recognize the girl ... and the name. It's the girl with the dreadlocks whom I met at the rendezvous point. The one who pinned me against the wall with her obnoxiously powerful hand. I shrink.

"Will you take Miss Alena to Mitch? He'll be her new trainer."

Recognition dawns on the girl when her green-blue eyes meet mine. This time, though, they're not angry but kind. "Sure."

"Alena, Mitch will teach you the ins and outs of being a medic." Guiding me out of the comb, Jeter adds, "I'm grateful to have your help. If you have any questions, don't be afraid to ask."

I bite my tongue. I do have questions. What happened the day Jax disappeared? Why didn't you look for him with the others? Why did you keep that wire thing that belonged to the clan member? I doubt those are the types of questions he'd appreciate. So I keep my mouth shut and say good-bye, following Scance.

"I'm sorry about the way I treated you at the rendezvous point," Scance whispers to me. I'm taken aback for a moment, surprised by her comment. But then I nod.

"It's okay. I understand why you did it."

Neither she nor I have much else to say, so we walk along the hallway in silence. Finally, we enter a large room strewn with odd couches and tables. Several Pepps lounge in the sunlight leaking through the windows, studying books and talking softly.

Two boys, bickering loudly in the middle of the room, capture my attention. A scrawny boy, tall and lanky with dark fuzzy hair all over his body, holds his hands over his nose, shaking his head. The other boy, blond and muscular, is agitated.

"Come on!" he says.

The hairy boy's hand doesn't budge, and he takes a step back, and then his gaze catches mine. Apparently knowing who I am, he removes his hand from his bleeding nose and waves me over—a bad move. The other boy steps forward, then punches the exposed nose, spraying blood all over the table and down the boy's shirt. The hairy boy lets out a groan when the contact breaks his nose.

I cringe, but Scance beside me snickers. The hairy boy sits patiently, rolling his eyes, until his nose is repaired by the one who broke it. Wiping the blood from his face, he touches the bridge as if to make sure it's fixed properly, then pats the other boy on the back before turning toward me.

"Hey, Alena!" He grins, revealing a mouth full of crowded teeth.

"Hey, Mitch, can I punch you in the nose too?" Scance says.

The hairy boy—Mitch, my new trainer—rolls his eyes. "How does it look? That was the twelfth time he broke and repaired my nose. It better be perfect now."

Scance examines him closely. "Nose looks good, but maybe he can work on your eyebrows next."

I cough out a laugh. Apparently I'm not the only one to notice his excessive hair.

"Ha-ha." Mitch pretends to laugh before introducing himself to me. "I'm Mitch, and I'm probably the best medic here. You're lucky to have been placed with me." He nudges Scance.

She smirks. "Second best." Then she turns and disappears down another hallway.

"Whatever," Mitch says to her back before facing me. "I'm glad for the assignment. I don't want to get punched in the face anymore." Mitch rubs his nose while glaring in the direction of the boy, who is now reading a book.

"So, Alena, let's get started." Mitch rubs his hands together. "Let's go to the clinic. First, I'm going to teach you about each body system and how it sounds when it's healthy and when it's not. Obviously, there are millions of things that can go wrong in the body, so mastering them all will take time. We'll start simple."

I follow Mitch toward an adjacent hall. "The clinic is where all those with minor injuries in Petrichor are taken. Practicing how to use the power is not without danger. We have a lot of teenagers that come in with burns needing to be healed, lacerations needing to be closed, and sometimes concussions from falls. They can be gruesome, so please be aware." Mitch winks, mitigating the heavy topic. My shoulders loosen. He's serious but light at the same time. I think we'll get along great.

We reach the stairs and drop a few floors; I awkwardly hold on to Mitch as he uses the pulley. He then leads me to a well-lit room sectioned off into six private sectors, each with only a flat board bed. I barely have time to examine the room, when a woman comes in with a boy in her arms.

"Hey, can we get some help?" The woman, calm and collected, carries the teenager to the vacant bed next to Mitch. Mitch approaches the bed, and I try my best to stand beside him. My throat goes dry. The boy's entire right side is covered in deep-tissue burns, the clothing melted into his sloughing skin.

"He and his friends were practicing making lasers, when he was lit on fire by a girl in his group." The woman steps back, allowing Mitch to perform his assessment. He places his hand over the boy's leg.

"Listen to the sounds," Mitch says to me.

I close my eyes, listening to the high-pitched screech that rings through my ears.

"When something is interrupted in the body, the brain signals the white blood cells to the site to prevent infection. These cells have a high-pitched screaming sound. Do you hear it?"

I nod, and Mitch continues to speak while healing. "These are third-degree burns with severe tissue and nerve damage. You can hear the proteins breaking apart and changing from the heat. It presents as a blubbery sound—*blub, blub*—like mud boiling, as they die. I'm going to repair the proteins first, by changing them back into their original form."

Mitch continues talking to me, telling me what he's doing, describing the sounds with incredible detail that helps me identify them. He's a great teacher.

This is almost fun. I imagine myself standing beside my dad, secretly speaking to the elements of an injured body like Mitch is doing now. Healing. Imagine how much good I could do?

Soon the burned skin changes to a healthy pink color. "Now the nerves," Mitch says. "This is the hardest part for me."

He works quietly for a while. When he starts talking again, it's in a quiet whisper. I lean in to hear.

"These burns are pretty bad, but it could be worse. Several months ago some of our Pepps were attacked by a clan member who was wearing an electrical belt. The man grabbed one of our Pepps and held him while sending electrical surges through his body. The dead Pepp was sent back to us in a toboggan when his team found him. I was beside Jeter when he came in." Mitch is now sadly quiet, the anguish written on his face.

"I'm sure the electricity from the belt killed the Pepp, but the electricity ignited his clothes on fire, burning the kid to a crisp. I've never seen a body so ... charred. It was awful." Mitch continues to repair the nerves, but his face is angry. "The dead clan member was brought back to us as well. The belt was wired to him. Humans can't withstand the currents he delivered. He knew it would kill him too, and he still did it."

My body stiffens, recalling the man at initiation. That thing with the wires—was it an electric belt? *Are they really that desperate, to be willing to kill themselves for their cause, whatever that is?* My fear of the man returns, until something dawns on me.

An idea.

It burrows into my mind like a worm working through the dirt. Suddenly I'm eager to leave the room, but I wait. As patiently as I can.

When the burned boy wakes up, looking as good as new after a couple of hours, I speak in amazement. "That was amazing, Mitch."

"Aw, thanks!" he says cockily.

I almost leap for joy when he tells me I can go, but he doesn't let me leave without handing me a stack of books to study.

"I'll see you tomorrow," he says, slapping me on the back.

With my arms weighed down by books, I shuffle through the halls looking for a quiet room to sneak into. I find one downstairs and go inside, then close the door behind me. After setting the books on the floor, I pull out Breccia, who looks at me curiously.

"I need your help," I whisper, trying to formulate my thoughts. "I need to get into Jeter's room. You're small and discreet. Can you go keep watch and let me know when he's not there?"

A mischievous look spreads across Breccia's face as if she's excited to do something so sneaky. Giving me a nod, she rolls back into a rock and slips under the crack in the door. I pace the room, waiting for her return as my hands begin to sweat. Is this bad? Using a Magbaby to spy? No. It's not like those Morgans planted in my room. At least I don't think it is. Then my thoughts redirect. *Could this work*?

Breccia is gone for an awfully long time, trapping me with my thoughts. Just when I decide I can't go through with this, she comes humming back.

"He's gone."

My heart pounds harder. "I don't know the way back. Can you guide me to his room?" Breccia nods, and I lift the books into my arms. I try to come up with an excuse along the way, of why I would be in there, in case someone sees me, but I can't think. My mind is all sludgy. And my palms won't stop sweating. I'm thankful that the hallway to Jeter's room is quiet. When I reach the door, I knock softly before peeking into the room. It's empty.

I close the door quickly behind me and stand there frozen until Breccia nudges me. I set my books on a side table, then grab a chair and step up to the bookcase. My hands start shaking as I just now realize I haven't thought this through entirely. What if the belt shocks me? What if initiation was just a fluke?

I close my eyes and gingerly touch the belt. I sigh in relief when nothing happens. I grab it and jump off the chair, then slip the belt around my waist under my shirt, tucking in the wires so they can't be seen. It's been disabled thankfully, but figuring out how to reactivate it shouldn't be too hard, right?

A smugness enters my veins at having come up with such a brilliant plan. I can't be shocked by the belt. But if I wear it, I could shock others. Like the clan men in the hideout.

Piling the books back into my arms, I open the door and freeze. I didn't even think to have Breccia check the hall before we went out. I panic when I see Rusty and the chief only steps away.

Unable to hide myself from them now, I walk out casually, trying to act normal.

"Hey, Alena," the chief says, eyeing me curiously. "What are you doing up here?"

My knees weaken. I try not to stumble over the words coming out of my mouth.

"I was looking for Jeter. I had some questions about my training today. I thought he might be in the honeycomb hall, but he wasn't there." Even I'm surprised at the smoothness of the lie, but to solidify it I shift the books as if they're heavily weighing me down.

"Ah, yes. I was told you started today. Congratulations," the chief says, patting my arm before moving past me. But Rusty stands planted behind him. His eyes are narrow and untrusting. I avoid them and try to leave.

"Is there anything I can help you with?" the chief asks, stopping me.

"It's okay," I say. "I'll just ask him tomorrow when I see him."

"Alright, Alena. Have a good night."

I run out of the hospital, into the evening air, my chest tightening with each step. They're bound to notice something as dangerous as the belt missing.

***

Dropping my books on the floor, I lay facedown on my bed and take in a deep breath. My heart rate is just beginning to regulate, when I hear shuffling in the room. Jumping to my knees, I face Rusty standing in the dark.

I sigh in relief, silently telling my heart to calm down, until he lights a lantern, illuminating his stern face.

"What were you doing in Jeter's office, Alena? Why did you lie to the chief?"

I cringe. Oh boy.

"Does the chief know I lied?" I ask, acknowledging my guilty position.

Rusty shakes his head angrily. "I want to know what you're up to."

With Rusty towering over me, I try to come up with another lie. I'm trying to think of something, anything, when Rusty suddenly takes several steps back.

"What in the world are you doing with that?" I follow his pointing finger. Three stupid wires are peeking out of my shirt. I slouch in defeat, shaking my head.

"Rusty, I'm not strong enough."

"Strong enough for what?" Rusty shouts.

Gabbro is going to kill me. I shake my head again. I'm not supposed to tell Rusty. But I'm so tired of lying. Perhaps if he knows what I'm training for, he'll be a better trainer.

I sort through my thoughts.

"Alena, what's going on?" Rusty says, kneeling in front of me, a smidgen of kindness returning to his face after all these weeks.

"Rusty, at initiation there was a lightning storm."

"I know. I was there. It was a miracle you survived."

I shake my head. "No. It wasn't a miracle. I should have died, but the lightning *couldn't* hit me ... or Mark."

I watch confusion sweep over Rusty's face.

"The chief thinks it's because of the Doler created by our totems. It repels Peppate, which is what attracts lightning, making it impossible for it to hit us."

"Lighting can't hit you?" Rusty's hazel eyes lighten as he grasps this concept. But then he shakes his head. "But what does lighting have to do with you being in Jeter's office?"

I take in a deep breath, knowing Rusty is not going to like what I'm about to say.

"Gabbro, Danny's Magbaby, knows where Case is hiding the prisoners."

It takes a brief moment for this to register before he stands, his face burning red. "What!"

"The only reason he hasn't told anyone," I quickly blurt, "is because the hideout is surrounded by electrical currents. Currents that would kill any Pepp who comes close to it. He knew if he told the chief, there was a good chance the chief would go searching for it and get himself killed."

Rusty clenches his fists, breathing heavily. "Gabbro knows where the prisoners are, and he hasn't told the chief? Is Cody there?"

"I don't know, Rusty. Probably."

Rusty comes alive. "Let's go get her! Let's go now! Tell me where she is. I'm strong enough. I'll get them all out." He tries to pull on my arm, getting angrier when I don't move.

"Rusty, *I'm* the one who has to enter the hideout. I'm the one who has to rappel down a hundred-foot hole, and then I'm the one who has to climb back up the rope ... with the prisoners. I can't use power or capsules. And I'm not strong enough."

Rusty lets go of my arm and spins on his heel, running his hand through his hair. Yelling out loud, he angrily pounds my wall with his fist, which makes me jump, but then in defeat he comes and sits next to me.

"Why didn't you tell me?" Rusty's voice cracks in despair. "If I had known, I wouldn't have wasted so much time in our trainings yelling at you."

The room is quiet. I don't know what to say.

"I'll train you better," he eventually says. "I'll work harder. I'll get you stronger." Then, sighing, his eyes drop to my belt. "I'm guessing you want that on you to protect yourself from possible clan members. When activated it'll hurt them but not you?"

I nod.

"Jeter is bound to notice it's gone." Rusty rubs his face. "I have to tell the chief, Alena."

"No," I almost shout. "He can't know. I have to do this, alone, so nobody else gets hurt."

Rusty sits quietly for a long time. He grinds his teeth, and his fists tighten until they're almost white. I hold my breath and wait, hoping it wasn't a big mistake to tell him.

Finally, he expels a heavy breath.

"I'll create a replica of the belt and put it back in his office," he says. "Maybe together we can figure out how it works."

I fight the urge to give him a hug. Somehow, I don't think he'd appreciate it now.

"Can you lessen the electricity in this one somehow too. So it won't kill anyone, just give them a disabling zap?"

"All you have to do is turn down the knob, here," he says, pointing to a circular knob that apparently controls the amount of electricity produced. *Good. I'll experiment with it.*

Then Rusty's pained eyes meet mine. "Will you bring her back?"

His words are crushing. His ache for Cody diffuses through me. *How can I promise something like that?*

"I'll try," is all I say. "But, Rusty, please don't tell the chief."

Rusty sighs but agrees. Before he leaves the room, he looks back. "Meet me first thing in the morning. I'll teach you how to rappel."

Thank you. Maybe the real training can now begin.

Chapter 24

The rope in my hands is slippery from sweat, and I'm already breathing heavily. I look up to the top of the cliff where Rusty attached my practice rope, the dusky early morning sky a backdrop.

I was supposed to meet Rusty here this afternoon, which I thought was unusual since our trainings are normally so early in the morning that the sun isn't even up. But sleep didn't come, with so much on my mind. So I came here early. Alone.

I grunt.

Being around Mark has been even more difficult ever since I got the belt a week ago. Not that I see him as much as I used to. Now that I'm supposed to be at the hospital, we've only seen each other at dinner. I guess the Dino Games are coming up in a few weeks, so he's been preparing for that. But the number of secrets I'm keeping has grown into a wall that is now wedged between him and me. Every time I see him looking at me, I picture the look of betrayal that'll be on his face when he learns the truth. There's so much I want to tell him. It doesn't help that Rusty knows now. I wish it was Mark who knew the truth.

Rusty taught me how to rock rappel earlier this week, and I've worked on the skill every moment I'm not in the clinic with Mitch. I got up the courage to ask Mitch about increasing muscle strength with power, and he was more than happy to explain things to me with no sign of suspicion. So yesterday I tried it out, increasing my muscle strength with my power before rappelling, then repairing my tissues when they got tired and swollen. It worked. There was an undeniable power added to my body. It also didn't make my muscles bulge more like I thought it would, which is good. I don't want Mark getting suspicious. I just have to be careful not to do it too soon before I go rescue the prisoners. I don't know if the Peppate power in my muscles will attract electricity. I figure if I give my body a day or so abstaining from the power, the Doler will push any Peppate out, leaving behind only increased muscles.

Rusty has also worked with me more on knife-throwing. There's something oddly satisfying having the knife slip out of the palm of my hand and cut into the bull's-eye of the target. Thanks to Rusty's training, I hit the bull's-eye more often than not now, a great relief to both Gabbro and me. I'll have two weapons at hand to defend myself with. The electric belt and the knives.

Gabbro was impressed with my idea of using the electric belt. If there are any straggler clan members who don't get gassed and try to attack me, the belt will electrocute them, not me. He was upset about me telling Rusty the truth, but his anger eventually simmered down. He even said Rusty could come along to help, if he listens and doesn't tell anyone else. This has relieved me tremendously, and any relief is welcome considering how sick I've been about this whole plan.

But Gabbro is still worried. I can tell. Last night at dinner he was terribly distracted and couldn't translate for Danny very well. I wonder what he's thinking about.

My arms begin to shake as I grip the rope almost twenty feet above the ground. I need to focus. I bring my feet up to clamp the rope beneath me and straighten my legs, pushing myself upward.

The chatter of Pepps reaches my ears, and I look down to see a large group walking toward the cliff wall. Panic rises in me. I don't want people watching me or around me while I'm doing this. I curse under my breath. *Keep moving up.*

Breathing deeply, I look up. I'm almost to the top of the fifty-foot wall. I remember what Rusty said about not wasting my energy, so I force myself to move quickly the rest of the way. Huffing heavily, I climb upward until I finally reach the top, grip at the dirt, and pull myself up. I heave my body over the edge, then lie on the ground. I did it. My chest puffs out in pride.

Now I just need to be able to climb a rope three times as long and be able to pull prisoners up with the pulley system. My chest deflates. This is impossible.

Rolling over, I grab at the rope and attach it to the harness around my waist like I learned in the book. The sun peeking over the horizon now sheds more light on the group below. More Pepps are arriving. Man, I couldn't have picked a worse time to do this. I'll just go down and then leave. Easy.

Standing on the edge of the cliff, I lean back against the rope and begin rappelling down, the rock crunching beneath my climbing shoes.

Steady.

I'm looking just below my feet, when the rope begins to vibrate roughly. I look up just in time to see something headed straight toward me. *Is that a rock?* It pounds me right in the heart, the force breaking my grip on the rope and sending me swinging through the air. I hang by the harness, flinging my legs, trying to stop, when the tightened rope, still tied around my waist, detaches from above.

I don't have time to scream. I brace myself for the impact and land with a crack.

The air is yanked from my lungs. I arch my back trying to expand my chest, to breathe, only to grit my teeth in pain. Something's wrong with my back! Finally, my lungs pull in air, but only some. That's when I realize my fingers and toes are tingling ... a lot.

"What happened!" It's Rusty's voice. *Where did he come from?* Never mind. I don't care. He couldn't have had better timing.

His face hovers over me, but there's something off about it. The size. He seems disproportionately smaller.

"Alena? Is that you?"

Of course it's me. But I can't say anything; breathing is hard enough.

"What are you doing?" he asks.

I shake my head. *What does he mean?*

Rusty grabs my arm and pulls it into my view. My blood runs cold when I see it. Where there used to be skin, there are now hundreds of long reddish-brown feathers. It's monstrous too, almost as long as Rusty's body.

What's going on? That's not my arm. But I feel Rusty's touch.

"So it's true," someone from the gathered group says. "She really is learning how to morph." Rusty ignores them and looks at me urgently.

"Alena, how did you do it?"

I shake my head. It feels heavy, really heavy. "I didn't do anything. Something just hit me in the chest, and I fell." I grind out the words, pushing through the pain in my back, but the words come out of my beak as an odd birdlike sound. *Oh man, I have a beak? I can speak bird?* Fortunately, Rusty understands what I say.

He looks up the cliff to where my rope broke.

A head of red-golden hair catches the rays of the rising sun, mocking me.

It's Flint, with the severed rope in his hand.

Rusty has morphed into an eagle, grabbed Flint, and brought him down before I take three excruciating breaths. Flint stands in front of me with a rope pinning his arms to his side. He doesn't even try to get free; he just glares at me.

I briefly look around at the others. A mistake. Their eyes are untrusting and accusing me. I wheeze through the horrible pain in my back. Can't any of them help me!

"What the hell are you thinking, Flint!" Rusty's face is red, his chest rising and falling too quickly.

"She was bound to learn it sooner or later," Flint says. "Besides, everyone needs a little reminder of what she is." Flint's eyes come back to mine, narrowing into little slits. "Defective."

Soft murmurs hum through the group, making me want to disappear.

Rusty kneels next to me. "Alena, pound your heart twice to morph back." I close my eyes and hit my chest. "Harder," he says.

I feel it, the moment I morph back, and the freaky feathers disappear. It's like my body shrinks, and sighs in relief being back in its normal form.

"I just wish it had been my idea," Flint says, breaking the awkward silence around us.

"What do you mean?" Rusty demands.

Flint's expression shows he's annoyed. "I found a note in my room. It told me that if I force Alena to morph somehow, I would be greatly rewarded."

Flint scoffs at the word *greatly.*

"Do you have this note on you?"

Flint gives Rusty a bored look. "In my pocket. I'll give it to you if you let me go."

Rusty ignores the ultimatum and rips at his pockets, finding a piece of paper in his left one.

Rusty reads the note and then looks at the rest of the group. "Thanks to your friend Flint here, our training session this morning is cancelled."

I expect the group to respond happily. At least I would have at getting out of training with Rusty. But the group just stands quietly, looking solemn.

I must have dispelled Doler, lots of it. I think I'm in too much pain to feel it, but looking at the others, I sense the difference, see it in their eyes. My simple morph affected them.

Rusty grabs Flint's shirt from behind. "I need to take Flint to see the chief." Rusty shakes the boy and looks at the crowd. "Based on how Alena's breathing, she might have punctured a lung. Any of you a medic?"

Nobody responds. Even if one of them knew how to repair bones, I doubt they would do it on me. I don't have my power in either, otherwise I'd repair myself.

Rusty clenches his teeth. "Fine. I'll send her back in a toboggan."

Rusty pulls a ring off his finger, opens the toboggan, and carefully places me inside. Trying not to grimace or scream in pain, I bite my cheek, filling the inside of my mouth with blood. He closes the lid and sends me on my way.

I'm relieved to be away from all those glaring eyes, but I can't escape the embarrassment. Or the confusion.

I peek at the sky through the toboggan branches, forcing myself to take shallow breaths. *How could Flint do that?* In front of so many Pepps.

And what actually happened? Looking back at all the times I saw a Pepp morph, I recall them pounding their chest before morphing. I always thought it was a Pepp gesture. And it wasn't every time. Just sometimes. Stupid. *How could I be so stupid?* That's how you morph into an eagle. Pound your chest.

What disconcerts me more is my power wasn't even in. Knowing that I won't have power when I get the prisoners out, I decided to practice without it. I realize now that morphing can be done at any time with or without power. It was too easy. *Pound the heart? With the key to morphing in my mind, will I be able to keep myself from ever morphing with Mark, creating electrical currents that can kill?*

I grind my teeth. Do we even really create electrical currents? Nothing happened just now, except I expelled Doler. Is that man from initiation wrong?

I'm not sure I'm willing to find out.

My mind shifts to the note Flint found. Someone else in Petrichor wanted me to morph. *But why?*

I'm swimming in an ocean full of questions. If I don't get answers soon, I just might drown.

Chapter 25

A week later I walk toward Mossy Hollow during my clinic lunch break, shaking out my sweaty hands. Mitch told me yesterday about the Dino Dance coming up in a few days. I remember Cody mentioning it, but I had forgotten about it. Mitch said they do it a week before the Dino Games, and he suggested I find someone to go with. With everything going on, I have no desire to go to a dance. But I thought it would be a good opportunity to take Danny, since he probably won't get asked. But now I'm nervous to ask him. Stupid.

The chief was furious when Rusty told him about Flint and the morph. He demanded to see the note written to Flint. He took the letter to the head of the messengers, who is apparently very good at identifying handwriting—probably since he sees hundreds of notes every day. He pulled up some letters from past communications and found that it was Jax's writing.

Now everyone's worried. I guess I had secretly thought Jax would have left Petrichor when he disappeared, but now I'm not so sure. Is he still here? Is the chief involved? My new suspicion is Jeter. I recall the way he stared at me when Jax vanished.

I'm so tired. My body aches from the constant questions and worrying.

The chief finished checking everyone's memories for clues regarding who might be involved and came up with nothing. I find it odd that the memories of everyone in Petrichor have all been searched but *nothing* has come up. What if that's because the one whose memories need to be checked is actually the one doing the checking—Chief? Jeter? Could they really be helping Jax?

Because I seem to be in imminent danger, I now have to have someone with me at all times. During the day, Mitch is responsible for me, and at night I have to room with Scance.

Somehow Mark and Danny found out about the morph too. Actually, all of Petrichor knows about it. Thankfully, Mark and Danny aren't angry with me like everyone else; they're angry with Flint. Ever since learning how to morph, though, I've felt this need to stay away from Mark. *One pound to the heart.* That's how you fully morph. Rusty clarified this at our last training session. *And two pounds to morph back.* It terrifies me that Mark and I could potentially kill so easily.

Mark.

I rub the back of my neck. I wonder what Mark would think if he saw how good I'm getting at knife-throwing. I was able to hit my target several times in a row this morning. Rusty found some special knives that were made by humans, knives that don't have any Peppate in them.

He also got me some human clothes. I hadn't thought about it, but all my clothes now are made of Peppate. If I go down into the mine wearing them, they would probably get zapped, which would be very awkward. He also found me a nice bulletproof suit that fits perfectly. Not sure where he got it, but it works.

I'm even getting better at rappelling. My strength is increasing and it feels good.

The gas, though, has been tricky and the main reason we still haven't left. Rusty and Gabbro are leaning more toward a mustard gas, something that will disable the clan mentally. But it can be dangerous if they're exposed to too much. I told both Rusty and Gabbro that I won't do this unless they promise me nobody will die. So they're trying to calculate the potency, and then they have to find some, among the non-Pepps. I wish I could leave Petrichor and help them. I hate the delay.

I still haven't been able to communicate with my family because of the Morgans. I don't want to put them in danger. I'm still being watched. I can feel it, and I don't want to lead my enemy to my family. But it's been months since I've seen them, and I'm starting to forget what they look like. *What color are Mom's eyes? What does Dad's voice sound like?* I miss his jokes and the way his nose crinkles when he laughs. I even miss Caleb's annoying pestering. I don't even have pictures of them to look at.

The chief said he would stop by the rendezvous point where they're staying on his way to look for Cody again. He left a week ago, and I still haven't heard anything. The only thing that keeps me going is knowing that I'll get to see them soon. Maybe.

Walking through the grass, I reach Mossy Hollow. The red leaves that hung from the tree when I first got here are long gone, and now the tree is covered in snow. I shake my head. Other than the snow at Mossy Hollow and the giant decorated pine tree in the lobby at GreenGrotto, Petrichor doesn't have very much of a Christmas feel to me. They don't celebrate it here. Even if they did, it seems too green and warm to be Christmastime. Nonetheless, the season reminds me of home.

I walk in through the door and head to the back where the trunk opens up to the dino covert. Next to the opening I see a sign that reads "Trainers Only" in big, bold letters.

Looking through the window, I see Danny trying to hang an animal carcass in a tree with his back to me. I shout out his name, but he's too far away to hear, and I don't want to draw the attention of any big dinosaurs.

The open grass area sits empty when I look around, so I step through the door, suddenly dangerously exposed in the dino covert. Thankfully, Danny finally turns and sees me. His pleased expression instantly warms my heart. He drops the rope he's just tied and walks toward me.

Without thinking, my body moves toward him. Just when I'm halfway to Danny, the trees rustle to my right. I turn and see a dinosaur sprinting out of the thicket toward me, its beady yellow eyes focused on my face.

It's quick, too quick.

I turn to bolt, but I'm not fast enough.

It reaches me before I take two steps and slashes me across the arm, throwing me back several feet. Danny is by my side instantly. The animal towers over me, its quivering frills coming out of its neck. Dropping its head to my face, the dinosaur hisses before spitting out a thick mucus that covers my left leg. I would groan in disgust if I wasn't so scared. Danny yells at the dinosaur, pushing it back. Mark comes out of nowhere and wraps a rope around its neck.

I try to scoot my trembling body further away from the animal but look down in horror when I realize my left leg, covered in slime, is now completely numb. Lying on my back, I try to lift and shift it, but I can't. I try to scream, but it gets stuck in my throat. Mark shouts toward me.

"The dilophosaurus has a paralyzing serum that she spurts as a defense mechanism. Is your leg numb?" he asks, still pulling the dinosaur further away. My mouth is too dry to respond, so I just nod. Mark's eyes are kind. "It's okay, Alena. I'll help you. Just let me calm her down."

Danny jumps up and harshly tugs another rope around the dinosaur's neck. "Don't hurt my girl like that, Dilo," Gabbro says for Danny.

As soon as the animal is contained on the far side of the thicket, Mark comes to me. Bending down on one knee, he generates fire in his hand. He aims it over the white serum and starts to burn it. Seconds later the serum starts to steam.

"The serum hates heat. Burning it is the easiest way to get rid of it. With just a little heat in one spot, it starts to shrivel up." Mark explains this at the moment I witness it happening. The serum on my leg begins to wither in the spot the fire touches. Then, much like a rippling effect, the shriveled area expands until it's all gone.

My toes begin to tingle again.

"Are you okay?" Danny asks through Gabbro.

My eyes shift to the gash on my arm, my bone visible through the muscle and blood. My stomach churns at the pain.

"Yeah," is all I can say as I scoot myself and semi-numb leg toward the tall concrete wall surrounding the covert. The effort sends stabbing pains from my arm all the way to my head. *Why am I so stupid?*

Danny and Mark both slip their arms behind my waist and pull me to my feet, helping me hop the rest of the way. I breathe in deeply Mark's scent as he holds me. Today he smells like pine. My favorite smell.

They help me sit against the wall, then they plop next to me. I turn my attention to the gash on my arm.

I've decided I love healing. In the short amount of time I've spent with Mitch, I've learned so much. I've even been able to practice healing myself, especially with the injuries I obtain from training with Rusty. Which has come in handy, since those injuries would be difficult to explain. Danny says healing is my primary wiggems, the one that emits more Doler than anything else for me, just like music is his primary wiggems. Mitch makes fun of me at the end of each clinic day when I'm covered in Doler.

I'm just glad *something* works better than exercising.

I still haven't quite figured out what truth I'm supposed to see underneath all the Doler, but Danny says to be patient.

I work on healing my arm now, squinting. Pain itself has a very loud sound, and I have a harder time focusing when healing myself, but it isn't long before the gash in my arm closes up, leaving behind only pink skin.

Raising my head, my heart finally calm, I turn to Danny and nudge him, remembering his comment to the dinosaur.

"So, I'm your girl, huh?" I tease.

Mark chortles next to me, and Danny's ears turn a soft shade of pink. When Danny doesn't answer, I lean toward him and whisper, "I love being your girl." He's avoiding my gaze, but I still see him smile.

A pang of guilt hits me in my chest. I love being his girl, but I wonder if that means the same thing to both of us. Why am I here? Why am I really asking Danny to the dance? Is it because I want a deeper relationship with him?

I can't imagine my life without him. He's become the best of friends to me. But if I'm being totally honest with myself, the person I really wanted to ask to the dance was Mark. Why aren't I asking him? Because I know how much Danny likes me, and I don't want to hurt his feelings? Or because Danny is just easier to ask? No, I really do like Danny. He's handsome, kind, and fun.

But I like Mark more.

Ugh! What am I doing?

I lean back and turn my attention to the field in front of me. I'll figure this all out later.

Changing the subject, I ask, "What was that thing?"

"It's the dilophosaurus," Mark says. "It's one of the more dangerous dinosaurs since it can paralyze its prey to eat. Fortunately, we've learned that burning the serum stops the paralysis."

Is that the dinosaur Mark used to get me out the night of initiation? I don't want to ask him out loud with Danny here, so I ask him with my eyes. He understands, nodding.

I shake my head in amazement when Mark changes the subject again.

"What are you doing here, Alena?"

My heart rate picks up again when I remember why I'm here. Now it's my turn to blush. I had hoped to ask Danny to the dance alone. But Mark is here. Unable to think of something else to say, I shrug and sigh deeply.

"I want to ask you to go to the dino dance with me, Danny."

I brave a look at Danny, and his face pales, his mouth hanging open. It's the type of response I had expected, but for some reason I doubt myself.

"If you don't want to go, or if you're going with someone else, that's fine."

I wait tensely for his response, then his face brightens and he jumps up, punching the air. "Wahoo!" Gabbro shouts, trying his best to depict Danny's emotions.

"I'm going to the dance with Alena!" Danny runs around the rink, yelling to all the dinosaurs, who, thankfully, are hiding.

My throat swells.

Standing, Mark holds out his hand. I take it, allowing him to pull me up onto my good leg. My left one still tingles, but I can stand.

"I don't think he wants to go with you," Mark teases quietly, watching his friend.

Danny runs back, and I take the opportunity to tell him I need to get back to the clinic. Before I can take one step, though, he pulls me into a hug. Holding me tightly, Gabbro whispers for him, "Thank you, Alena."

My heart swells at his words, and I hug him back until Mark clears his throat.

"Danny, I need to talk to Alena for a minute. Will you go get the food for the stegs?"

I eye Mark curiously after Danny pulls away, wondering what he would possibly need to talk to me about. But Danny doesn't seem to question Mark's request. He waves and skips away, with Gabbro floating along beside him.

Once Danny disappears through the trees, Mark pulls me through the door of the covert and guides me to a private corner of Mossy Hollow. His serious face churns my stomach.

"Alena, there's something I want to show you." After looking around, he pulls a piece of paper from his pocket and shows it to me. It's an image.

"Cody," I whisper, seeing the picture of a girl badly beaten and malnourished. Despite her sunken eyes and frail face, it's unmistakably Cody. My heart contorts painfully in response, and I hold out my hand, carefully taking it from Mark.

"Is this the image you saw in your dreams?" Mark's voice is low. I try to ignore how close he's standing.

"Yes. Cody is thinner here, though, than she was in my dreams, her bruises more purple." My words fall. These past several weeks I've tried to focus on the task ahead, my training. But I'm reminded of how little time we have left.

I turn the picture over to find eerie words carefully written:

Come on, Mark. Don't make me kill her.

The threat may have continued, but the bottom of the picture is torn off. I furrow my eyebrows.

"It looks like someone tore off the rest." Mark's breath brushes against my hair.

I swallow and try to focus. "The location."

"What?" The sound comes from deep in Mark's throat. His face is inches from mine, and his eyes wander over my skin, making it warm. His closeness, his heat, his smell has me wanting to lean in closer, to bury my face in his chest and will the world to go away.

Instead, I clear my throat.

"He keeps asking us to turn ourselves over but never tells us where to find him. Do you think someone else in Petrichor did this to conceal the location? If so, why would they do that and not just destroy the threat altogether? It's as if someone wants us to receive the threat but not do anything about it."

Frustration wells up inside me, and I look back down at the picture.

"Where did you get it?" I whisper.

"It appeared on my pillow last night. Someone in Petrichor had to have put it there," Mark says. So, someone in Petrichor is still untrustworthy even after the chief checked everyone's memories, and now they're trying to get to Mark just like they've been trying to get to me. It has to be Jax.

Mark gently takes hold of my shoulders and levels his face with mine. I try to avoid eye contact with him, but I can't. His eyes are like a warm fire drawing my cold, scared heart closer.

"Alena," he says when I finally look at him. "Please promise me you won't go searching for Case to hand yourself over." His words are etched with worry, not just for what could happen but specifically for what could happen to me. Fortunately, this is an easy promise to commit to. I have no intention of turning myself over to Case. Not as long as I have Gabbro's plan to hope for.

"I promise."

Without warning, Mark gently wraps his arms around me and pulls me close. I should resist. Danny could come in here and see us. That would make things so awkward. But silently I've been longing for Mark's touch. I can't pull away.

Stepping into him, I bury my face in his shirt and let my arms cling to him. He's so warm, so strong, so gentle. I close my eyes and breathe in deeply. That breath. It's immensely satisfying, like for the first time in ages I'm able to break through the darkness that's been shrouding my heart.

"Alena?" My name vibrates through his chest. "There's a place I've been wanting to take you. Will you go with me tonight?"

I would go anywhere with Mark. But then I furrow my eyebrows and reluctantly pull away. My eyes wander over to the covert where I had just asked Danny to the dance.

As if reading my mind, Mark drops his hands. "Danny would come too, but he's supposed to work tonight. He said we should go without him."

My heart rate picks up. *He's already asked Danny? Just me and Mark going somewhere?* I should say no. I should tell him I'm busy. I can't trust myself not to relay the burden of my secrets anymore.

But I can't tell him no. Not when every cell in my body wants to be with him.

So I just stand there, frozen.

Mark patiently watches me battle inside. Finally, he brings his finger to my chin. "I'll pick you up at ten tonight. I think we could both use a good break from all this." He waves the picture in the air. "Oh, and bring your winter clothes. You'll need them."

He taps my arm before letting me go and disappears back into the covert.

I stand there. *Did Mark just ask me out on a date?*

Chapter 26

Unsure whether I am supposed to wear my warm clothes or just bring them, I tuck them into my satchel, ready to change if I need to.

I was able to drag myself back to the clinic after my conversation with Mark, but I was pretty worthless. My mysterious outing with Mark tonight has me very distracted. And nervous. He'll be here any minute.

Guilt pushes its way into my mind. I haven't thought much about Cody or the fact that we've received another communication from Case. Maybe my mind will be clearer after the outing.

Since getting back to my room with Scance thirty minutes ago, I've done my best to make myself look presentable, something I've tried to do ever since meeting Mark but have never quite been able to accomplish. I finally settle on wearing a pair of snug Levi's and a loose white long-sleeved shirt. Not knowing what to do with my hair, I finally pull it up into a high ponytail and add a beige ribbon, something Caleb always told me he loved.

I jump when Mark knocks on my door. Taking in a deep breath, I open it.

I want to moan. Mark stands in front of me wearing Levi's and a T-shirt just like me, but somehow he looks more amazing than normal, which I didn't think was possible.

"Hey, Lena," he says softly. *Lena.* I try not to blush at the nickname he's used again.

"Hey," I say, grabbing my satchel. I tell Scance good-bye, then step out into the hall with him and close the door behind me. Avoiding his eyes, I look at his chest, noticing, again, his muscles bulging through his loose shirt.

"Ready?" he asks.

I nod, trying to focus.

Fortunately, most of the runners are either in bed or in the courtyard, so leaving GreenGrotto is easy to do without being spotted. We walk in silence.

Without Danny here to act as a buffer, though, I don't really know what to say to Mark, but he doesn't seem to mind.

Once we're standing outside GreenGrotto, Mark pulls out his four-wheeler capsule and hops on. I expect him to pull out another for me but he doesn't. I awkwardly stand there until he gently tells me to get on.

Get on with him?

I touch his shoulder to brace myself, then swing my leg around. When I'm settled behind him, Mark starts up the vehicle and shouts back, "You ready?"

I nod but realize he can't see me. So I lean forward, very aware of my body brushing against his. "Yes."

He grins, and I lean back, gripping his shirt.

Just for balance, I tell myself, trying to ignore the hardened muscles beneath my hands.

We travel for a while, the air blowing through my hair. It somehow extricates my worries, just a little. The moon lights our way through the warm Petrichor air, acting as a silver guide, until we reach Danny's meadow. Upon driving up to the unique snow wall, Mark kills the motor to the four-wheeler.

I guess it's time for me to get off. I pull my leg around, relieving my strained muscles. It reminds me of home, four-wheeling with Caleb.

"Here we get our snow clothes on," Mark says and pulls out his capsules. I follow suit, trying not to get too distracted by Mark, who's stepping into his snow pants. I look out into the dark cold. *Are we going out there?*

Like a frog wrapped in a twisted balloon in my snow gear, I follow Mark through the protection fog of Petrichor and the cold instantly sweeps up against me. The warm clothes are remarkably good protection, but my face is exposed and feels the true nip of the weather. I slip several times climbing up the steep snowbank, earning me an outstretched hand from Mark. I take it out of necessity. We finally reach the top.

After expanding a snowmobile, Mark gets on and I follow. The snow clothes create a thicker barrier between us. It's not nearly as intimate as the four-wheeler, but I still hold on to him, this time more out of necessity. Mark motors forward, and we glide across the frozen ground. Snow dust floats over the white moonlit land in front of us, looking like millions of tiny diamonds traveling in the wind. It's beautiful, magical.

Soon, a patch of pine trees appears ahead, and Mark heads straight for it. Once we're close, he slows the vehicle, then brings it to a stop at the tree line. He kills the motor. The hush of the snow-laden land around us weighs beautifully in the air. Without saying a word, Mark dismounts the vehicle and helps me off. Then he pulls out a blindfold and indicates that he's going to put it on me. Growing somewhat suspicious now, I eye him curiously, but he just flashes me an encouraging look. So I take off my hood and allow him to cover my eyes.

Taking my mittened hand, he guides me through the trees, the snow crunching under our boots. I stumble. A lot. It's embarrassing, but Mark's chuckles move me forward.

Finally, we stop. Mark reaches behind my head to remove the bandana. I look at him briefly before examining my surroundings. The moon shines directly overhead, lighting the snowy clearing surrounded by tall pine trees heavy with snow. The scene is so peaceful. I love snow-laden pine trees, and in the moonlight it's absolutely beautiful.

Mark points to the trees, directing my attention.

"Watch," he says, indicating there's more I'm meant to see.

I look closer. I don't notice anything at first, but then I squint. Tiny little lights begin to glow on the tips of the branches, growing bigger and bigger until I see that there are hundreds of lit candles woven through the trees. The scene strongly resembles the tree by the hot spring my father wound with Christmas lights so many years ago. I follow the lights around the circle of trees, watching them sparkle through the icicles. I walk toward one, reaching out to the limbs, wondering how he'd lit so many candles at once without a single touch.

"It's beautiful," I say, hoping Mark will hear. When I look back, he's sitting on a log in front of a newly lit fire. I remember Cody saying that Mark was good at controlling the elements of the environment, including fire. He pats the space next to him, inviting me to sit.

I move forward hesitantly. That log looks short ...

I try to give Mark space when I sit, but my efforts are futile. My coat brushes heavily against his, along with my leg and shoulder. Mark only smiles wide.

Did he choose a short log on purpose? Regardless of being in the bitter cold, a warmth spreads through my body at Mark's closeness. I resist the urge to lean into him more and instead take my mittens off to let the fire heat my skin directly. It's so warm.

We sit in silence, mesmerized by the crackles and dance of the flames, until I break the quiet.

"One Christmas, when I was younger, my dad lit up a pine tree by the hot spring with lights like these. He took us up to see it on the snowmobile. I remember swimming in the hot spring that night, staring at the sparkling lights. There was something magical about the way the colors twinkled through the snow weighing down the branches. It was one of my favorite Christmases. Such a beautiful tree." I pause and look at Mark out of the corner of my eye. He's not surprised by the story.

"But you already knew that, didn't you?"

The corner of Mark's lip lifts. "I always wondered who lit up that tree. Some years, I even took a generator out there to plug the lights into since he never took them down. It wasn't until I asked Caleb what you might like for Christmas that I realized where they came from."

"You talk to Caleb?" My throat catches. Not only does Mark communicate with Caleb, but he also asked him what he could get me for Christmas?

"Yes. I use my Magbaby during the day, to keep it from being followed by a Morgan. Caleb threatened to kill me if he doesn't hear from me every couple of days." Mark chuckles before he quietly adds, "He loves you very much, Alena."

Mark's words open a floodgate within me, and all the homesickness, guilt from not telling Mark my secrets, and fear of the future surface. I bite my lip in an attempt to keep myself under control, but the tears slip out without permission. So I bury my face in my hands.

Without saying a word, Mark wraps his arm around me and pulls me into him.

Stupid. Stupid. Stupid. *Why do I have to cry?*

Mark tugs me closer until I bury my face into his chest. I don't deserve his gentle embrace, kind words, or meaningful gestures. I don't deserve any of it. Not when I'm holding in so many secrets. But I cling to him selfishly anyway, grasping for his comfort.

Finally, when I'm able to gulp back my emotions, I wipe my nose and pull away.

"Sorry, Mark. I don't know why I'm so ... emotional tonight."

I sit back up and stare at the crackling fire, trying to see through my blurry eyes. Mark's gaze is on me, but I don't dare look at him.

"I've been avoiding you, Alena," he whispers quietly. His words, laced with regret, surprise me enough to finally look up. Those are the exact words I should be saying to *him*. The words my guilt screams in my mind. *Why is he saying them to me?*

"You're beautiful, so beautiful," he says, his eyes wandering over my face. "For Danny's sake, I've tried not to show my attraction to you, but ... it's just been easier to stay away."

My brows crease. *Oh, Mark, if you only knew what I was hiding.*

Turning his body toward me, Mark gently wipes at the tears still on my face. "Alena, you need to know that I like you, a lot. Not only are you *distractingly* attractive, you're smart and kind. Watching you with Danny?" He shakes his head. "He's changed so much since you came to Petrichor. I've never seen him so happy."

My body warms, but not from the fire, and my volatile emotions start to build again. I blink rapidly, willing my stupid emotions to go away, hoping he won't see how much his comments affect me. But he cradles my jaw in his bare hand and forces me to look at him.

"I'm sorry, Alena."

What he's sorry for, I'm not sure. But I can't focus on anything other than his mouth that seems so terribly close. In one swift movement, he closes the distance between us, placing his lips on mine, pushing me back.

Oh, how I've longed for Mark's kiss. I melt into him, my lips responding through my tears. I reach up. I want to touch his face, let my fingers run over his jaw, feel his scruff. But my fingers are cold. Too cold for his skin, so I lightly run them through his hair instead, gently pulling him to me. Mark presses down harder, holding my face, letting my tears brush against his cheeks. I'm sure he can feel my pounding heart even through the layers of coats, but I don't care. My guilt surrenders for a moment, and my body takes over, my lips hoping for more.

"Lena," he whispers briefly against my mouth, before weaving his fingers through my hair to pull me closer, kiss me harder, again and again. I cling to him, finally allowing my cold fingers to graze his jaw, feel his muscles move, feel his pulse quicken.

My eyes water again. *Man, I really like Mark.*

Gradually his kiss slows, into something tender and lovingly sweet, until he pauses and rests his forehead on mine for a breath. "Lena." I gaze at his lips, slightly parted. "I'm sorry," he whispers.

Sorry? Confused, I look from his lips up to his brownish-golden eyes.

"I'm sorry about everything." He rubs his thumb against my temple. "You having to leave your family, to stay here where you're continually threatened. Sometimes I wish I hadn't convinced you to come."

I swallow, trying to refocus my attention. Then I shake my head, my nose brushing against his. The last thing I want is for him to blame himself for anything.

"Don't be sorry. We both know Petrichor is the safest place for me. Besides, I never would have gotten to know you if you hadn't convinced me to come. Thank you, Mark. For everything, including this night." I swallow again. "And, for what it's worth, I like you a lot too."

Mark's lips lift into a very distracting smile. Unable to stop myself, I lean forward, letting my mouth brush against it.

Oh, Mark. I think I actually like you more than a lot. Mark grips my head tighter, instantly responding to my kiss, bringing his other hand to my neck, setting my skin on fire.

Eventually I pull away just enough to get a breath, hovering my lips just over his.

"I have a gift for you," he says.

I stare at him. *A gift? As if the thoughtful trees and excursion wasn't enough?*

He pulls away, taking his warmth with him, and reaches into his coat pocket. He pulls out a large metal cylinder. There's an animal inside. A dinosaur.

"I promised Caleb I would protect you," he says, "but with everything going on, I realize I'm pretty powerless unless I'm with you all the time. And I don't think that would be a very good idea."

Heat rises in my cheeks. *Probably not.*

"This is the dilo dinosaur. The one that attacked you earlier today. When I saw her hovering over you this morning, I realized she might be the answer I've been looking for. I gave her a good talking to after she attacked you, and now she knows better than to hurt you. I would be more comfortable knowing she's with you."

Touched by Mark's kindness, I observe the cylinder with the tiny dinosaur inside. If I hadn't been attacked by the thing earlier, I might think she's cute. She looks at me oddly now, her face scrunched up into a scowl.

"So, I'm just supposed to carry this thing around with me?"

Mark chuckles. "For now. She really won't hurt you."

"How do you do it?" I pull my eyes away from the cylinder and meet his. "How do you train the dinosaurs? Cody says you're exceptionally good at it. What's your trick?"

"I wish I could tell you it's some special secret, but the truth is I really don't know. They just seem to bow to me. I think it's the Doler. It's the only thing that makes me different. It makes sense though. Dinosaurs don't create Peppate, so I'm like they are. I think I make them comfortable. Don't tell anyone." He winks, then goes back to poking the fire. "That's a big part of why I'm giving her to you. Because you create Doler too, I think she'll be responsive to you. I'm pretty sure she attacked you earlier just due to unfamiliarity, the way I've often been attacked at first sight. But now that she knows you, she should be more discerning."

I observe the cylinder in my hands and swallow, trying to find something nice to say about the terrifying dinosaur. *Will it really listen to me before attacking?* I turn the cylinder in my hand. That's when I find two syringes attached to the side.

"Those are filled with the dinosaur's serum. I've experimented with it and found that it can be injected into a subject and have the same paralyzing effect as if the dinosaur sprayed it directly. It might come in handy." Mark pauses before adding, "I also learned, the night of initiation when I carried you back to Petrichor, that she's immune to electricity just like we are."

His words register. That means the dinosaur can go with me when I free the Pepps. I look back up at Mark. He just gave me a bigger gift than he realizes.

"Thank you, Mark. I'm sorry I don't have a gift for you."

The firelight dances across his face. "Well, maybe you could save me one dance at the dino party."

Oh, how I would love to dance with Mark. But I'm going with Danny. I lower my eyes to my hands. "You'll have to ask Danny," I say.

"I will," Mark whispers without looking at me. My heart skips in response. I hope he does.

Winding my arm through his, I lean into his shoulder. "Thank you."

"You're welcome, Lena." We sit in silence for a couple of moments before Mark says, "You know, there's a hot spring not too far from here. It reminds me a lot of home. I almost took you there tonight, but swimming in the bitter cold didn't seem like a great first date. Plus, I realized you might not be too fond of hot springs now. But maybe someday."

My heart hiccups at the word *date*. "I would love that."

I enjoy sitting in Mark's quiet presence, watching him poke the fire. I wish we could stay here forever in this cold, but peaceful piece of heaven.

Unfortunately, the night ends too soon, and we have to head back. My guilt and worries return while we are on the snowmobile, trying to chase away the precious moment, but I hold on as best I can. When we get back to the meadow, we take off our snow clothes and get on the four-wheeler. I wrap my arms around Mark, tighter this time, thankful for the absence of our coats now. Resting my chin on his shoulder, I close my eyes and breathe in his comforting scent.

We travel much slower back to GreenGrotto, but it's still too fast. Eventually we have to part ways.

When Mark gives me one last hug, I cling to him. He'll never know how much this night has meant to me.

Chapter 27

I walk up the stairs, the heavy music echoing through GreenGrotto from the courtyard above. I'm still not great at using the pulley, but it's okay. I'm in no hurry to get to the loud crowd. Thankfully, the other Pepps have found other means to get to the top, so the stairway is empty.

The material of my dress brushes against my legs. Well, Cody's dress. Going through her closet and opening the lotus flower capsules hasn't helped my mood today, but all the dresses at Mossy Hollow were gone by the time I decided I was going to the dance.

I frown. It isn't right to be going to a party while Cody is missing. Shouldn't all life stop and focus on those who are really in need? It should. *Has the chief found anything?*

Life doesn't stop though—and neither does the need, I suppose.

Cody has great taste in clothes. The white summer dress, made of a thin material, gathers gently just below my chest and then flows down to my shins. It should probably fit snugger, but even with it hanging loosely over my body it pleases me. Looking in the mirror right before I left, I felt its endorsement of my new body. Thanks to Rusty, the muscles in my arms bulge in the right places. I wondered if I should wear a jacket to cover my arms tonight but eventually decided that I don't want to hide my muscles, not even from Mark.

I reach up to my neck and fiddle with the necklace Danny gave me. I've worn it every day since the day in the meadow. Whether it's lucky or not, it comforts me.

At least it *normally* comforts me. My heart weighs heavily tonight. It was a bad idea to ask Danny to the dance. Especially after my night with Mark. I clearly see now that I've been selfishly leading Danny on and it's not fair to him. I need to talk to him, but that conversation will change everything forever. I've enjoyed being *his girl.*

It's not right, though.

Doing my hair seemed like an overwhelming feat, but I curled it into a soft beach wave and then pulled it into a loose ponytail. After seeing it in the mirror, I'm glad I curled it. I haven't had much time to do anything with it lately, and it's grown halfway down my back.

When I'm almost to the top of the stairs, I observe the courtyard. The usual eating tables and bonfires have been removed, replaced with overflowing pots of brightly colored flowers. The air is warm, the sun is setting, and the food smells delicious. It's a perfect night for a dance. The excitement in the air is palpable, tugging at my shadowy mood, willing it to lift.

My eyes skim over the Pepps, looking for Danny, who said he would meet me here. I don't see him at first, but then I find him.

He's standing right beside Mark—I just didn't recognize him. His shaggy hair is gone, cut into a very handsome crew cut. His white collared shirt hangs attractively, untucked, over his Levi's. He meets my gaping gaze, and his cheeks flush. For the first time, Gabbro is not on his shoulder. I wonder if Danny told him to leave him alone tonight. I would have.

When I realize I'm still staring at him, I shake my head and collect myself. His arms are open, waiting for a hug, so I move my body into them.

"You look amazing, Danny," I whisper, wrapping my arms around his neck.

Danny's arms tighten around my waist in response, making me tingle in a way they've never done before. Man, Danny is handsome.

Even in Danny's arms, though, I feel Mark's gaze. After our night in the snow, I wondered if Mark would bring a date to the dance tonight. I'm relieved to see him standing alone, his gaze warming my skin.

Danny pulls away but leaves his arm draped around my shoulders.

I look around the courtyard. Dusk is falling, magnifying the beauty of the waterfall and flowers surrounding the courtyard.

I take in a deep breath, allowing the nervousness I've felt today to fade away for Danny. I want to give him a good time.

Someone at the end of the area sends out a welcoming shout to the mass of people, and the Pepps begin to gather in the large open area cleared of tables. A group of Pepps holding instruments stands against the wall. I hadn't even thought that they would need live music here, but it makes sense since they can't use amplifying speakers. Based on the music that echoed down the stairwell, they're really good too. They even have a singer, something the Magbabies' music lacks. I narrow my eyes. *Wait, I know the singer. It's Leinani?* Carlos is there too. I remember them singing the first night of initiation. Of course they would be here.

Danny guides me to the edge of the crowd, where we watch others dance for the first couple of songs. Danny's body moves softly, his itch to dance suppressed for me. I can't help but watch his face out of the corner of my eye. He really comes to life around music, and I enjoy the sight.

By the third pop song, I slip out from under his arm and tug him into the crowd. Danny responds, happily surrendering.

Once in the mix of dancers, I mostly watch Danny dance to the music while trying to move to the beat myself. He's amazingly good in hip-hop. He's catching the eye of everyone around him. A young woman with long curly blonde hair seems particularly fascinated with Danny. She stands gaping at his moves as he flings himself across the floor.

I'm watching her watch him when something tugs at the back of my mind. She's familiar to me. I try to think of where I've seen her before. It isn't until she turns her head to the side, letting me see her profile, that I remember. She was the messenger that came to get Danny, Mark, and me from the magnifying room. She seemed infatuated with Danny then, and she seems infatuated with him now.

Danny grabs my arm, pulling my thoughts back to him. Encouraging me on, he requests that I follow his dazzling moves. I try. But it's much harder than it looks, and we both end up laughing ... at me.

Three hip-hop songs play, leading into a slower island song with steel drums and slurred words. The beautiful dark-skinned girls, with their tight skirts and loose shirts, head to the center of the floor, eager to dance their song. I stare at the girls as they move their hips in rhythms I've only ever been able to imagine, perfectly in sync with the boys who stand behind them.

It's captivating but slightly risqué. I resist a little when Danny pulls me onto the floor, but his sparkling eyes reassure me. Once on the dance floor he steps behind me. Thankfully he leaves plenty of space between us, but his hands gently brush against my hips, trying to help me move. Standing awkwardly, I look at the other girls around me. I try to follow their moves, placing my hands over Danny's. I join the beat, finding a groove, bending my knees and moving my body with Danny's. His hands find my arms, leading trails of shivers up to my shoulders and back down. Oh boy.

I don't dare look at Mark. I sure hope he's not watching.

Danny pulls at my hand, spinning me around to face him. Back and forth, front and back, I move my hips with his until the song ends and the dancers send out a shout.

"I didn't know my hips could move like that." I nudge him.

Laughing, he drapes his arm across my shoulders and walks me back to Mark. I still can't look at Mark's face.

We stand and watch on the side, resting during the next song. Leinani and Carlos, taking a break from singing, dance by us.

My worries return briefly when I spot Rusty standing on the sidelines alone, staring at me. I try to ignore him, not wanting to think about the future. But time ticks loudly in my head. It sounds like Rusty has figured out the gas. Now we're just waiting on the pulley system Gabbro and Trevor are building. It should only take a few more days, then we'll go. I'm hoping I'll be strong enough.

I look away from him and sway gently next to Danny, letting the music reach into my body, relieving me of some Doler. Tiny black spots pepper my skin.

Aw, man! Not here. But I'm relieved when I find Mark and Danny dealing with the same phenomenon. After getting a napkin from the table behind us, I wipe my face.

I'm wiping my nose, when someone clears their throat in front of us. It's the quiet blonde girl I caught watching Danny earlier.

"Would you like to dance with me, Danny?" I stand frozen, trying not to gape at the girl.

With wide eyes, Danny looks at me. It takes me a moment to realize he's waiting for my permission, but then I don't hesitate.

"Go ahead," I say, reassuring him. Danny swallows nervously, but then moves forward, offering his arm to the girl. I watch him walk away, his frame towering at least a whole foot over the pretty girl. He looks back at me one last time before proceeding to the dance floor. Finally, he pulls her confidently into his arms, ready to dance to the new slow song. A small seed of jealousy rises in my stomach at the sight of another girl in Danny's arms, but then I stomp it down. It's perfectly fine.

Mark steps closer to my side, interrupting my thoughts, his hand brushing against my elbow. My heart rate quickens when his fingers trail down to the palm of my hand.

"Will you dance with *me* now, Lena?" he whispers into my ear, his breath sending goose bumps down my neck. "I got Danny's permission."

I nod.

His fingers slide to my pinky, and he gently pulls me toward the dance floor. It's such a tiny touch, yet it sends a wave of shivers throughout my body. I follow quietly behind him, trying to silence my heart, until he finds a less crowded spot, away from Danny. Then he turns to me. I can see the golden specks in his brown eyes, now, burning with an intensity that makes my body warm. Placing his hand at my waist, he pulls me against him. Close. I don't even fight it for Danny's sake. I've ached for him since our date. Leaning into his tender embrace, I drape my left arm over his shoulder and sway to the slow music with him.

Dropping his head to my ear, his breath caresses my cheek.

"You are *disgustingly* beautiful, Alena," he whispers. I half snort, half blush, my heart beating heavily against his chest. I look at his face, expecting to be met with a teasing look, but he's not smiling. In fact, he looks rather pained. I know the feeling. It's how I've felt every time I've been in his presence.

"Well, thank you, Mark. You are ..." I have to clear the catch in my throat. "Horrifically handsome." His pained look flickers to amusement, and a glint lights his eyes just before I let my nose brush against his chin. Extending my fingers, I touch his neck and jaw. His arm tightens around my waist, pulling me closer.

My lips long to brush against his again. But they can't. Not with Danny close by. So I swallow instead.

I'm about to run my finger through his hair, when my body freezes.

Past his face, in the sky, out toward the airport, a fleet of small objects approaches the hospital, like bees going to their hive. I know they're not bees, though, they're toboggans. I count. Five, ten, fifteen. Fifteen toboggans all at once. Never in my time here have I seen more than two or three at the same time. My body stiffens. Something's wrong. To confirm my suspicion, a siren blares out over the music.

"Mark, look," I whisper, pointing to the hospital. I hate letting go of him, but the urgent pull of need has me stepping out of his arms. Several other Pepps have noticed the emergency and have sent out shouts, stopping the music.

Suddenly, Rusty is by my side. "We need to get you to the hospital." Without another word, he morphs, ready to carry me. I turn to Mark, stammering, not sure what to say.

He just shakes his head. "I'll meet you there."

Grateful for his support, I allow myself to be carried away by Rusty. Thankfully, his claws are so big they cover my whole body, including my dress, pinning it down. We quickly approach the hospital, the toboggans now tucked within the top emergency combs.

Rusty drops me off at the front door, and I dash inside up to the seventh floor, the emergency floor, with the rest of the other healers.

Upon reaching the emergency section, my ears are met with a sound I've never heard before. The sound is drowned out by the screaming of patients who are now lying on beds inside the combs. I see Mitch already inside one, working on a young, scarily skinny teenage girl. He's leaning over her trying to listen while she screams in pain. I look down the line of combs, through the glass windows, at the other patients similar to this one. Each is accompanied by an experienced medic, but the medics' expressions all say the same thing. They have no idea what's wrong.

"Jeter!" One of the clinic workers starts yelling. "Jeter, we need help!" The place comes alive as several medics run down the halls in search of Jeter. I enter the room with Mitch and expect him to shout out the same thing, but time is running out. Even I can sense that. Without any instruments in his hands, Mitch begins to cut into the girl's stomach where the unfamiliar sound is the strongest. Blood spills out, but it looks different. Instead of running down her skin, like normal red blood would, it spreads only a couple of inches before it stops dripping and starts moving, as if it's crawling. Slowly, the red color fades to black. Mitch reaches for the substance.

"What the ...?" His voice trails off as the substance latches onto his skin. I stare in horror, watching it eat away at his flesh, spreading across his hand.

It's a bug. A flesh-eating bug.

The color drains from Mitch's face, and the groan he initially released turns into a scream. He falls to the floor in pain, his eyes reaching mine, pleading for help.

"Alena! You need to burn it! Burn it, please!"

I reach out, but I can't create fire. Thankfully, another medic hears his screams—Scance. She comes to his aid, producing a flame that burns the black areas. Mitch's screams shake my bones as he's burned all the way up to his elbow, but then my heart sinks further when I see the flesh on his neck starting to turn black. The bug is eating him from the inside out.

"His neck!" I shout above the crackling noise of fire. Moving her hands to his neck, Scance burns the skin there, trying to transmit the flames inside his body, but then I see his right leg turn black. The girl next to me on the bed continues to scream, and I see her blackened blood crawling on the floor. I try to avoid it while looking back at Mitch's begging eyes that carve his screams into my memory. Scance burns his leg while reaching out to the bugs crawling toward her on the floor. Death is closing in. Tears pour down my cheeks as helplessness blankets me.

Mitch's scream quiets, and I watch his face relax, his presence disappearing.

Backing out of the room, I hold up my hands, the burns of my friend searing my heart. I look in horror throughout the hospital, the other screams fading, each spirit lost taking a little bit of light with it, until all is quiet except for the painful cries of those left behind.

Pulling us all from the horrible scene in front of us, Jeter finally arrives with a sick-looking Chief. He's conveniently back.

"Burn the rooms!" Jeter shouts. "Shut the doors and burn them!"

The workers react instantly, shutting the rooms and setting them aflame.

"They're corpuscites," Jeter says. "The deadliest and rarest flesh-eating bug. There's nothing you could have done." Jeter tries to reassure the workers, but his words fall flat. We are the Pepps. There should have been something we could have done.

Over the crackling flames, I hear a familiar hum approaching me. Gabbro. If a black rock could go pale, Gabbro would.

"Chief." Scance whispers. "I think that was Casey. One of the missing Pepps."

Sweat beads on the chief's brow.

I look down the line of combs again. They're prisoners? Fifteen of them. Sent back here by whom? Case? Jax? As a warning?

I look at the young prisoner girl in front of me, her body deforming in the fire, but then I see the toboggan burning beside her. There, carved into the side, is my name. And Mark's, next to numbers that are glowing against the flames. I haven't been in Petrichor long, but if anything has been engrained in my brain from initiation, it's coordinates.

It looks like the message finally got through. The location of where we're supposed to go. Whoever has been somehow keeping this information from Mark and me must not have had a chance to get rid of it this time. I stare at the hall. The message blares from each of the toboggans.

"Coordinates," the chief whispers.

All our attempts to keep the prisoners' location from the chief were in vain. There's no way he's going to let us go without him now.

My eyes sweep the scene before me one last time, my heart exploding. Standing up, I run from the hospital, through Petrichor. I have to get away from this horrible place.

***

Unable to see through the tears, I stumble up Training Mountain in the dark. I'm lost, but I don't care. I hope I never get found. My legs hurt, and my body is full of scratches from the branches that pull at me. My dress is muddy and ripped, but I push forward. When I hear someone calling for me, I don't respond. I keep moving until arms reach around my waist to hold me back. I fight.

"Alena," Rusty cries out, trying to calm me, but I don't hear through my sobs. All I can see is Case's face. He did this. For the first time, I want to hurt him. No, I want to kill him!

"Alena!" Rusty pleads again as I claw at his skin. I gradually calm down, and collapse in his arms. He guides me to a tree where I sit and bury my head in my hands. Without saying a word, Rusty puts his arm around me.

"Alena, I'm so sorry," he says. I sob harder. "The chief wants us to go now. Those were some of our Pepp prisoners back there. Who knows how many more Case will kill tonight. Gabbro says the coordinates carved into the toboggans lead to the hideout. We have to go now."

The encumbered task I've been dreading suddenly becomes very real to me. I want to do this. I want to fight. My friends were just killed. I have to do something.

Rusty flies me back to my room. While he stands outside the door, I change out of my dress into the human clothes he picked out for me. The suit he found outside of Petrichor, made without Peppate. Its thick material is supposed to protect against weapons, but it also has secret compartments for knives. Through my tears, I separate my last few items into two separate satchels, placing the electric belt, dinosaur, and serum syringes in one, and then all my power and equipment capsules in the other, just in case.

When I open the door, I hand my Peppate satchel to Rusty. "Will you hang on to this for me?"

The halls are barren, the emergency Petrichor siren calling in the distance. We head toward the airport, where the chief is waiting in an aircraft ready to go.

Seems Rusty and I won't have to go alone anymore.

The chief is coming.

Chapter 28

According to Gabbro, Case's hideout is almost a thousand miles southwest of Petrichor in the humid tree-filled swamps. Petrichor is long since dark by now, but here the sun is just setting. Rusty is closing the distance quickly as the pilot but not quickly enough. My thoughts are sucking the life out of me, regardless of how many times I try to shake them away. The faces, sounds, and smells of earlier haunt my mind, surrendering to a hate for Case that vibrates through my limbs like a jackhammer. My hands tremble. *How could anyone do that to a human being, let alone fifteen?*

Gabbro found his way to the aircraft after the combs were burned. He told the chief about the hideout, how it's covered in silver and pulsing with electrical currents. Then he told the chief about our plan. I felt the chief's accusing eyes bore into me for the first thirty minutes of the flight. He's more than angry. He might just kill Gabbro and me ... after we save the prisoners.

Now that he's explained everything, Gabbro sits quietly. He hasn't even tried to convince the chief not to come along. But he's extra worried, I can tell. Too many things could go wrong.

I am too. *Nobody* can die.

I quietly observe the others in the craft. Four other Pepps besides the chief, with blue council totems, sit in the old seats. The only one without a blue totem is the older man sitting on my left. The chief hadn't wanted him to come, and based on their argument before he got on the flyer I gathered that he's Cody's Pepp father. I remember him from the chief's office, standing next to his wife when Cody went missing. Sometimes I forget that each Pepp is placed with a family. Even though he seems way too old to be Cody's father, I'd say she lucked out. He's nice. Which makes me agree with the chief. He shouldn't be here.

But he refused to stay behind.

I stiffen, thinking about Mark. Then I slump forward, burying my head in my hands. With everything that happened, I completely forgot about him. I must have left the hospital before he could get there. And now I've left Petrichor without saying good-bye. Next time I see him, he'll know about my lies. I close my eyes. I hope more than anything he can forgive me.

The chief and the other four council members ask Gabbro and me once again to go over the plan. Gabbro clears his throat and hums to the center of the craft. I listen to him quietly. I don't bother working on my muscles with power now. It's too late. Too much Peppate. Hopefully what I've already done will be good enough.

"We'll land a couple of miles away from the hideout," Gabbro explains, "to keep from drawing attention to ourselves with the flyer." He points to a map that's lying on the floor of the aircraft. He's already very carefully adjusted his plans to include the chief and the council.

"My guess is that Case is expecting Alena to come with council members. What he doesn't know is that we know about the hideout's electricity. It's extremely important that you follow my directions carefully.

This hideout is tucked within a silver mine, with a river of water flowing through it. The silver veins extend for miles, and some reach the surface, making it vital that you know where you're stepping. Once we're on the ground, you'll search the surrounding area to make sure it's clear of any clan members. The chief, Alena, and I will go to the entry point, which is here." Gabbro makes an X on the map over an area of trees. "The rest of you, surround the entry point but stay hidden in the trees. And don't use your power." Gabbro pauses and looks up at me. "Case will probably be waiting for us. But, remember, he can't use his power in this area either. I'm guessing he's planning to grab Alena. Rusty, you fight him by hand while Alena slips through the entrance. Hopefully he doesn't know about Alena's ability to evade electricity.

"Now, Alena." Gabbro speaks to me. "You'll go down as we've discussed. Try to figure out where the Pepps are and where the electrical source is. Then blow it up." Now looking at the rest of the council members, Gabbro says, "The hum of electricity is heard on the outside. You'll know when she's taken out the source. When that happens, you can use your power to move the ground dirt and expose the prisoners below. Get in there and pull everyone out."

I pitch in now. "I'll be dropping gas inside the tunnels to knock out the clan men. I don't want anyone to be killed, please. We've already lost too many tonight. Once the prisoners are free, we can take the clan men back to Algor. But please don't hurt them." I eye the chief, silently pleading with him. *And don't let them go.*

Gabbro didn't reveal Rusty's prior involvement in all this. He probably doesn't want to make Chief any madder than he already is.

I don't even bother mentioning Gabbro's pulley system. We won't need it now. Not with the council here to carry each of the prisoners out.

"We're here," Rusty shouts back from the cockpit.

Gabbro rushes to finish his instructions. "We don't know how many prisoners are still alive, but get as many of them onto the aircraft as you can. Rusty will fly them home. The rest will need to be loaded into toboggans. Any prisoners remaining will need to be flown physically by the rest of you to the closest rendezvous point, here." Gabbro points at the map. "Rusty will come back for them when he unloads the others."

I swallow. It's a good plan, but it all hinges on me destroying the electrical source. I push down the sickness burning my insides.

Rusty drops the flyer into the trees, breaking through the canopy. The closely grown branches resist the groaning flyer until finally it lands with a thud. When the back ramp opens, the humid air hits me like a wall of steam. I inhale deeply, trying to breathe.

The council members disappear into the trees to search the area. Gabbro sits on my shoulder, ready.

I stand and step off the aircraft, watching the chief cautiously move around the trees. Rusty is looking for the collapse button on one of the wings of the flyer, when someone calls my name.

I freeze.

That voice. It shouldn't be here.

I turn around, hoping it's not who I think it is.

"Mark," I whisper when I see him. His skin is red and his hair terribly disheveled. *Did he ride on the outside of the aircraft?* I search his face, cringing at the sight of his tight lips and set jaw. He's angry. With me.

"What are you doing?" he asks.

Rusty jumps down from the other side of the flyer, ready to attack, but with the wave of his hand Mark freezes both Rusty and the chief in a block of ice.

No! I look around. All the council members are gone, searching the hideout. I'm alone.

"Alena," Gabbro whispers in my ear. "He can't be here. Freeze him. And don't let him get me either, or he'll use me to get to the hideout without you."

I tense in panic. "I haven't learned how to freeze an entire body yet," I whisper, not bothering to clarify that I really can't freeze anything at all. But Gabbro just slips down the back of my shirt, out of sight.

"Can you disable his brain or something?" His voice is rising. I look at Mark without explaining to Gabbro that I don't even have my power in. I gave it to Rusty.

I stand locked in place, frantically trying to come up with another plan.

"What are you doing here?" Mark whispers. Betrayal leaks from his expression. He waves purposefully to the chief and Rusty as if to say *with them*.

I know I need to explain—he deserves that—but when I open my mouth all I can say is, "I'm so sorry, Mark."

He steps closer, shaking his head, demanding more of an answer.

"Mark, Gabbro knows where Case is hiding the Pepps, but it's surrounded by electrical currents. It can't be approached by *normal* Pepps." I keep my gaze steady on his face.

Mark stops walking, understanding dawning. "Gabbro knows where the hideout is? And he told you? Why didn't you tell me? I can help you."

The pain on his face tears me apart, but as much as I want to look away, I can't. I deserve this. "We can't both be here. You and I both complete the totem the clan created. Gabbro didn't want Case to get both of us if something went wrong."

"So, he chose to put *you* in danger over me? And ... wait ... Gabbro refused to let me come? Why would ...?" Mark's voice fades and the confusion slips from his face, as if everything makes sense to him now.

"Where is he?" Mark's voice has lowered dangerously. Gabbro squirms against the skin on my back as Mark speaks of him. I take a step back, but with a wave of his hand, Mark wraps me in vines, pinning my arms behind me. I close my eyes, but I don't resist.

When I open them again, Mark is looking at me with blazing eyes. He walks toward me, until he's close enough for me to hear his grinding teeth.

"Mark, please," I say as softly as I can. "Even if I did let you take my place, there's no time to explain the plan to you. I'm prepared for this. I can do it." I defend the plan, but one look at Mark's face tells me he isn't going to let me go.

My spirits plummet. We're wasting time. Case probably already knows we're here. But how do I stop Mark? I cringe when I think about stabbing him with one of the knives hidden up my sleeves. Even if I could stab him, though, he could easily freeze me with his power and then leave. I wish I hadn't given my power to Rusty. I could just disable his nerves.

Then I stop.

Disable him.

The serum. The serum Mark gave me for protection. He gave it to me in syringes. Syringes that are in the satchel on my waist. *Can I really use it on Mark? Is it even safe to use on him?* My mind runs through all the elements of the spine, identifying several spots in particular that would completely disable a body, should they be paralyzed. It would be less painful than a wound, but would it work? *Once in there, would I be able to get it out?*

A Pepp could get it out, right?

I stare at his chest, knowing that if I go through with this, our relationship will never be the same.

He slips his arm around my waist and pulls me against him, carefully watching me. I silently will him to trust me, to just let me go.

But then Mark speaks, and his voice is rough. “Where’s Gabbro?” When I don’t respond, his hands move up my back. I let him search for the screaming Gabbro while forming a plan in my mind.

Slipping under my shirt, Mark grips Gabbro tightly.

“Alena!” Gabbro cries. As soon as Mark grasps Gabbro and pulls him out, I slide the knife out of my sleeve and with one swift movement I cut the vines. But I keep my wrists together. I’m quietly grateful that Mark hasn’t moved away yet. I need him close. I can even see the perspiration on his face from the heat. He doesn’t know I cut the vines ... at least not until I slip my hand into my satchel for the syringe.

I almost curse when he doesn’t move away, even after seeing my free hands. I wish he would disable *me*, so I wouldn’t have to go through with this. But he hesitates ... just enough.

Without another breath, I pull him into my arms, hold him close, and quickly press the needle into the skin of his neck.

I squeeze my eyes shut, the tears falling freely now. I don’t want to see the look of betrayal on his face. I hold him in my embrace as long as my strength can muster, until his body grows heavy.

Laying him on the ground as carefully as I can, I finally look at him. Thankfully, his eyes are closed. I hover over him, my tears falling onto his face.

“I’m so sorry, Mark.”

Standing up, I search through my blurry eyes for the chief.

“What’ve you done?” Gabbro asks, now released from Mark’s grip. The shock on his face surprises me.

I try to control my quivering lip. "It's the dilo dinosaur's serum. I paralyzed him," I say guiltily. The gravity of what I've done presses down on me. I hope more than anything I can free the serum.

"Can it be undone?" he whispers.

Heat is what Mark said it requires. I just need to apply some heat to him. That can easily be done.

I explain what Mark told me. Then I wait while Gabbro goes to get another Pepp to thaw out the chief.

"What the hell is he doing here?" the chief yells when he sees Mark, his thick eyebrows furrowed angrily.

I wipe at the tears on my face, shaking my head. "He must have followed me."

The chief doesn't press me any further, knowing too much precious time has passed. I pull off my toboggan ring to send Mark back to Petrichor, but Gabbro interjects. "We need the toboggans for the prisoners and for you."

"What about our plan?" I ask, confused. "We can't have Mark here. Wasn't that the whole point of me disabling him? What if Case gets him? Gets both of us?"

"He's right, Alena." The chief rubs his gray beard. "I don't like it, but we'll be cutting it close as is to get everyone back. We need to get the prisoners back first. If there aren't as many prisoners as we think, then we'll send Mark back in one. For now, we'll bring him along. Rusty will keep an eye on him in the meantime." The chief looks at Rusty, who's been thawed and is now shaking out his cold limbs. I fiddle with the ring on my finger, an alarm going off in the back of my head. Gabbro was adamant that Mark not be here. And yet here Mark is, and *he's wanting to take him along?* I don't like it.

Rusty and the chief morph, then carry Mark and me through the trees toward the hideout. The setting sun darkens the trees. New shadows jump on the eeriness growing inside me.

The thick trees eventually open into an area of dead plants and dirt. A loud humming vibration travels through the ground. Gabbro was right. We can hear the electricity from up here. I swallow. *What if I can't find the source?*

"We're here," Gabbro whispers, waving to the clearing in the trees. I look around carefully. *Where's Case?* I expected him to be here.

"We need to hurry," he says. My mind reacts instantly, knowing what to do. I pull out the electrical belt and activate it, making sure it works. The chief, who is walking carefully around the clearing, freezes at the sound of the belt, eyeing me curiously.

"Here are some more human knives you can strap to your leg in case you need them." Gabbro pats the ground next to a tree, briefing me on where they're hidden. I dig into the dirt and find some rope, knives, a couple of hand grenades, and an extra bulletproof vest. According to Gabbro, the clan's favorite weapon is a gun.

"And here's the gas." Rusty holds out a metal spherical container. It looks similar to the grenade. "What you're going to do is pull this metal tab when you're ready and everyone has their masks on. Then throw it into the general area of the clan men. Try to throw it where there might be a lot of men, if you can."

I nod, putting it into the waterproof bag Gabbro gives me.

I'm strapping the electric belt to my body under the vest, when a low growl rumbles behind me. Turning around, I see a bear with bright-yellow eyes.

Trevor.

He sniffs my belt from a distance and steps back.

"Trevor still has a hard time believing you could be immune to electricity," Gabbro says.

I send a clipped nod toward Trevor, trying to assure him. "I'm going to be okay," I say before adding, "I never got a chance to thank you for saving my life at initiation."

Trevor can't speak but he accepts my gratitude with a simple grunt. I glance at the chief, who's staring at the bear.

"Trevor? Initiation?"

I gulp. We have a lot of explaining to do, but there isn't time. I look around. There's still no sign of Case. *Why wouldn't he be here? Shouldn't he be waiting for me?* After placing one last knife on my leg, I look for Rusty.

He's staring at the hole. He's keeping his distance from it, but I can tell he wants to get closer.

"I don't like this, Alena. I expected Case to be out here waiting, but he's not. Where is he? What's he planning?"

"It's a trap." The chief steps up behind us. "We should head back to Petrichor—this isn't worth the risk."

"No," I almost shout. "No, I have to go down, now. We lost too many prisoners already because we waited too long. I'm going down."

The chief and Rusty exchange a look but don't protest. I'm grateful they agree.

I ask Rusty for the satchel I gave to him earlier. I've changed my mind about him keeping my stuff.

"Just in case you get distracted and I end up needing my power, I'll put it here." I leave the satchel next to the tree, take the toboggan ring off my hand, and place it on top of the pile.

Last, I take the black band off my arm. Breccia watches me as I set her into Rusty's open hand. "I'll see you soon," I say.

Rusty holds up a large bulging bag. "Gas masks," he says. "I'll lower them with another rope once you've reached the bottom."

I take in a deep breath. Okay, I'm ready.

"The hole is right over there," Gabbro whispers, pointing toward the middle of the barren ground. "This is as far as we can go."

Rusty takes the rope from me and ties it to a tree before handing me the other end.

"Please be careful," he says.

I turn to the open area and walk forward, holding the rope, replaying our plan over and over in my mind.

I find the hole and look down. It's so black, I can't see the bottom. Taking a deep breath, I wrap the rope through my harness and carabiners like Rusty showed me and lean back.

My nervously sweaty hands make the rope slippery, but I hold on, carefully dropping myself down into the darkness. The hole shrinks above me.

After thirty feet or so, I hear the sound of the swift river Gabbro described—the one that flows through the hideout, pulsing with electrical currents.

Before too long, my feet hit the water. I sigh in relief. I feel nothing except the strong current that tugs at my pant legs. I try to follow the dark river with my eyes. It drops aggressively into the rock on my left.

I shiver, taking special note not to get swept into that hole.

As my eyes adjust, the light reaching down from the hole above starts to reflect off the silver walls. Random sparks burst from the silver, the only proof that electricity oscillates through it.

I look around, trying to find any sign of where I should go. A dim light shines through a tunnel across the water, and a narrow stone ledge reaches out underneath it.

Using the force of my body, I try to rock the rope back and forth to swing to it. But it's hard. And it's consuming my energy, especially without anything to push off of.

I look down. I'll descend the rest of the way into the water, give myself a little slack, then tie the remaining rope around my body. If I do that, I should be able to swim to the ledge, right? The rope will keep me from getting swept away by the river.

Without any other ideas, I drop into the warm water. It rushes into my body, instantly trying to pull me into the death hole. But I tighten my grip on the rope, wrap it around my body, and tie it in a knot in front of my stomach. Carefully, I let it go.

It holds.

I push back the panic that's threatening to consume me and swim as hard as I can to the ledge. I sure hope there isn't a guard pacing that tunnel. Probably should've thought about that earlier.

The rope tugs on me, keeping me from disappearing beneath the rock, but I quickly curse the bulletproof vest that weighs me down.

It takes all my effort to reach the edge, but I finally get there. Once I pull myself out of the water and catch my breath, I untie the rope from around me, remove my harness, and stake them on a sturdy branch sticking out of the dirt wall. I'll need them to get back out.

Then I look up at the hole above me. I tug on the rope twice to indicate I'm ready for the masks. The bag of masks appears quickly, somehow attached to the same rope I descended on so that it comes directly to me. I catch it with my hands and make a mental note to thank Rusty for his intuition. And good rope skills.

Man, the bag is heavy. It would have to be to have so many masks. I untie it and then make sure all my weapons are still attached. They are. My belt still seems to be working too, regardless of the water.

I take in a deep breath and move toward the tunnel with the bag over my shoulder. Man, I'm already exhausted.

Peeking around the corner, I notice the tunnel is empty except for a lit torch mounted on the dirt wall. Trying to stay quiet, I walk, careful around each bend. My feet are silent but my heart sure isn't.

The stench reaches me first. I bring my hand to my nose to keep myself from gagging. *What in the world?*

My hands and legs begin to tremble, and not from the swimming. I peek around the last bend. Also empty.

Something seems off.

Why would the tunnel be unprotected?

I take my knife out and hold it in my free hand before stepping into the tunnel, bracing for an attack.

The tunnel gives way to a large room below.

Inching forward, I look over the edge, pulling my wet shirt over my nose to lessen the terrible smell.

I freeze in horror when I see dozens of ghastly-looking people below. The clothes—or, rather, shredded rags—they're wearing hang unnaturally loose over their dirty bodies. Most of them are lying on their backs, their sunken, hollow eyes staring blankly at the ceiling. Flies land unthreatened on their skin. *Are they dead?* Others wander painfully around, one step at a time, as if that's the only act keeping their fragile minds from breaking.

I search the area. The room is huge. So why are they huddled together in the middle?

Then I see it. A circular moat around them. The reason for the smell. A moat of their own bodily waste, pulsing with the same electrical currents as everywhere else.

I frantically search their arms for totems, but they're all bare. *Cody's totem had been sent back.* Case must know how to remove them. Ten, twenty, thirty ... I count the humans. fifty-nine. Adding the fifteen that had been sent back in the toboggans, this is the exact number of Pepps that had gone missing.

Minus one.

I search the group for my friend. Cody. I don't see her. Hoping it's just because I don't recognize her now, I search the room for any guards but find none. Even the two tunnels leading out of the room seem quiet.

A narrow path emerges from the wall to my left, and I straddle it, descending into the room. Some of the prisoners sit up and look at me. Quiet whispers indicate that the sickly-looking humans are still alive. Holding my breath, still trying to not breathe in the stench, I put my finger to my mouth to shush them. Carefully, I make my way to the brown moat. The smell of human feces and rotten urine makes my stomach gurgle, and I can't hold it back any longer. I heave the contents of my stomach into the moat. Unfortunately, I still don't feel better. Closing my eyes, I walk through the icky water to get to the Pepps.

"How is that possible?" someone croaks in awe at my unharmed walk through the water.

My eyes land on one prisoner, one who has a little more meat on her bones than the others. "Do you know where the energy source is?" I need to move fast. The room is too open. Someone is bound to see me soon.

She points down a tunnel that leads out of the room. "I think it's that way."

"Are there any guards there?"

"I don't know."

"Are there any other guards down that tunnel?" I point to the only other tunnel I see. From where I stand now, I'm pretty sure there are vibrating voices coming from it.

"Yes, there are a lot of men down there."

"How many?"

She shrugs. "Maybe a hundred? I don't know."

A hundred. I swallow weakly.

"Do you know where Cody is?" I ask, still not seeing my friend in the large group.

The girl shakes her head. "No, Case took her out a couple of days ago. She hasn't been back."

My heart sinks. I drop the bag and look around, trying to think. "Here. Put these masks on. I'm going to gas the men down that hall, then I'm going into the electrical room to blow up the electrical source. Once the electrical source is disabled, the chief and the council are going to come through the ceiling to get you out."

The girl's bloodshot eyes cloud with tears. I don't have time to imagine what she's been through. "Get everyone up and ready, quickly but quietly."

I grab a mask for myself, put it on, then turn from them and trudge through the moat again to the tunnel with the voices. I peek into it. I can't see anyone but the voices are louder, and the flickering flames are bright. I look back to the prisoners, who all have masks on now. Nodding to them, I point down the tunnel. Then I walk. I hope Case is in here. And Jax. Quietly, I round one corner but don't dare round another. Hoping I'm close enough, I pull the gas grenade out of my waterproof satchel, pull the pin, and carefully place it on the ground. It hisses as I quickly walk back out, rushing past the prisoners to the other tunnel. I need to hurry.

I walk through the tunnel, making sure not to scuff the dirt and give myself away.

I peek around the corner and see a large room similar to the first, with tall ceilings. But in here the walls are completely covered in silver. The river, possibly the same one as at the entrance, runs in one wall and out the other. Sparks fly from the wall on the far end, and an electrical hum rumbles through the rock. I spot a generator with hundreds of buttons and switches. But it's guarded by a man with a black beard, greasy hair, and a sweat-stained yellowed tank top. He's leaning forward, polishing a long gun in his hands. I straighten back against the wall, hoping he didn't see me. I try to think.

How do I get rid of him? My knives. But if I don't disable him somehow in the first attempt, he'll send out a warning to the other men down the hall. I chew on my lip. They should be incoherent now, though from the gas. I don't have much of a choice. I just have to be sure to destroy the generator.

Reaching under my shirt, I turn the electric belt on. It buzzes to life. Then, filling the palms of my hands with two throwing knives, I take in a deep breath, hoping my training with Rusty has made me good enough.

I step to the middle of the tunnel in plain view of the man and throw the knife. It sinks into his left shoulder. Blood melts into the fabric of his old shirt.

I curse. Not good enough.

The man is frazzled, grunting loudly. But he's not immobilized. He stands and aims his gun at me without even removing the knife. Hitting him with my other knife will be harder now with him moving, so I sprint toward him. My feet enter the river of water, slowing me down more than I would like.

The sound of the gunshot rings through my ears. I don't even have time to cover my ears before I'm thrown back. The wind is knocked from my lungs, and a deep ache starts pulsing through my stomach. The vest kept the bullet from puncturing me, I'm pretty sure, but that doesn't mean it didn't do damage.

Loud shouts echo down the walls, coming from the other tunnel behind me. I curse again. I need to get up.

"Well, well, well." The man's rotten teeth show through his sneer. "What do we have here?"

Tightening my fists, I roll onto my feet and start running across the water. The man's so surprised I'm getting up that it takes him way too long to cock his gun and aim. Before he gets his finger on the trigger, I run into him, hoping the belt will take care of him.

His body thrashes wildly the moment I wrap my arms around him. I let the electrical currents shake him unconscious, then pull myself away. I reach down and sob in relief when a pulse throbs against my fingers. He's still alive. I try to drag his heavy body away from the generator, so the blast doesn't kill him. It takes me way too long. But then I reach into my bag and pull out the real grenade, moving back to the generator.

I stare at the generator for a split second. There are so many switches, and they're not labeled. Using both hands and arms, I decide to switch them all.

The sparks and hums promptly stop. The absence of energy is palpable.

Hopefully the Pepps above ground know this is their cue.

I pull the pin in the grenade, drop it, and run back through the river. I reach the entrance of the room just as the grenade goes off, sending me flying through the air. The explosion sucks the air from my already aching lungs, and the room begins to crumble through my ringing ears.

I need to get up ... but my body isn't responding. It's as if that blast disconnected everything inside me. Coughing from the smoke and debris that slipped through my mask, I look around to see the ceiling giving way. The faces of large eagles, with bright torches on their backs, appear in the dark sky and dive down toward the group of Pepps. Blasts of ice and fire come from every direction, further disabling the clan members that aren't unconscious yet. Goose bumps nip my spine. It's beautiful how the Pepps sweep in. The clan doesn't stand a chance. Not now.

That scene is enough to get my body working again. I push myself up.

I'm about to walk back into the cavern where the prisoners were, when I hear popping sounds behind me. I spin around. The exposed electrical source—a large metal box at least ten feet high and ten feet wide—is spitting out fire. I back up to get away from it, but then I freeze.

The electrical source wasn't the only thing hiding in the wall.

A woman with dark stringy hair coughs wildly, lying on the floor of a room now exposed from the absence of rock. Looking back to the main cave, I see that all the Pepps are gone and some of the clan members are lying dead on the rock floor. I search the sky for more Pepps, but all I see are trees. The woman looks at me in pain.

"Please, help me." I barely hear her voice above the crackles of fire.

I quickly observe her arm, looking for a totem, but it's bare. Unfortunately, I don't have time to think. The smoke thickens, and the ceiling begins falling in large clumps from my explosion. I need to get her out of here, into the trees. I reach under my shirt again, about to deactivate my belt, when I hear a shout behind me.

"Hey!"

My heart drops, and I turn around. Several scruffy-looking men stumble out of the other tunnel. I search the sky again for help, but I don't see anyone.

Dammit. The gas didn't completely immobilize them.

The best thing I can do is wait for the men to reach me. I pull out my knife and hold it ready. This makes one of the men laugh.

"Oh no, she's got a knife." But then his mocking expression disappears when another root falls from the ceiling. Skirting around it, he runs toward me, then tackles me with a force that sends us both to the ground. His blasted weight grinds my head into the rock.

But the moment he touches me, his body begins to shake. When he stops moving, I slip out from underneath his heavy form.

I've just escaped the first man, when my body gets side swiped by another. Idiot. The rocks dig into my shoulder and back when I land back on the ground. But the man stops moving. Finally, I stand, trying not to appear beaten, and turn to the third man. He's more hesitant and backs away.

Smart man.

I want to just leave him, trust him to let me go, but unfortunately I can't afford to do that. Taking in a deep breath, I send my other knife flying in the air to him. It lands deep in his thigh, making the man scream. Good. Now he can't walk, then I stumble to him and zap him just a little until he falls over unconscious.

I take in a deep breath. There are no more men around. I turn off the belt and return to the woman. I'm lifting her arm around my shoulder, when another loud explosion erupts overhead, sending down more clumps of clay. A burning root falls next to us, dropping embers into our faces. The woman coughs wildly.

Something's wrong.

I rip off my gas mask, sure I don't need it now that the cave has been exposed, and look out into the dark night. The trees are on fire.

"Let's go!"

I head to the same ledge I came down, pulling the woman along. It crumbles behind us.

I search the burning sky for Pepps but don't see them anywhere. All I see is the rope I used to get down. I let go of the woman and face her.

"I'm going up the rope. Once I'm at the top, I'll throw it back down. Wrap it around your waist, and I'll try to lift you." The woman nods, still coughing.

I don't have time to put the harness back on. Instead, using my legs to pinch the rope beneath me, I climb up as quickly as my trembling arms and legs will allow, grateful for all the rappelling training. When I reach the top, I pull myself over the edge and toss the rope back down. While the woman wraps the rope around herself, I search for help again. I blink, trying to see through the smoke. I don't see Rusty, the chief, or Trevor. *Where are they?*

The only person I see is Mark propped up against a nearby tree. *Why didn't they get him out?*

The woman tugs on the rope, indicating she's ready. I pull. As hard as my tired body can. But her weight is too much for me. I groan and fall to my knees. I need help.

Reaching into my bag, I find the metal case holding Dilo, Mark's dinosaur. I pull it out and open it on the ground. Dilo quickly expands into her full size, wailing in the chaos. I instantly regret enlarging the dinosaur. I talk to her, the way I saw Danny do. It takes a minute, but I'm eventually able to calm her down. She holds still while I tie the rope around her neck, and then I guide her away from the hole. I sob in relief when the rope moves and the woman rises.

When she reaches the top, I roll her onto the ground and untie the rope. Once I know she's safe, I run to Mark.

He's still unconscious from the serum. I curse under my breath.

Why in the world did I do that?

I search the tree next to him for my supplies and toboggan. I dig through the dirt, but my hands can't find the capsules or the toboggan. *It should all be right here!* My stomach plummets in panic. I'm sure I put it all here. *Where are they? Where's my toboggan?*

I close my eyes to ease the burning from the smoke around us. I have to wake him up. I have to release the serum in his neck. Opening my eyes, I drop to his side again and touch his neck. Sure enough, there's a bulge in the spot I injected. This is good, but when I realize what it is I need to do, my stomach churns. Taking my knife out of my boot, I run over to a burning tree and hold the knife out, covering my hand with my sleeve, coughing from the smoke. When I'm pretty sure my face is going to get burned and not just the blade, I run back to Mark.

"I'm sorry, Mark," I say. Before I can warn him further, I slide the blade into the bulge in his neck. His scream tugs at my heart. More than anything I want to stop, but I keep it there until the bulge starts to shrivel.

While I'm holding Mark's pained face in my hands, I see a figure step out of a ... *What is that? A shelter of some sort, made out of rocks?* I didn't see that before.

I don't have time to figure it out, not when I see who it is.

It's Case.

I jump up, pulling the knife out of Mark's skin and raising it in front of me.

My fear instantly turns to anger that bursts from every cell in my body.

I'm ready, ready to throw it, ready to kill him. But his gaze stops me. He stands frozen, looking at the woman coughing on the ground behind me.

"Lilly?" he whispers. He runs past me to her side, frantically—yet so carefully—taking her into his arms.

I stand, confused. *He's crying.* Where did all my anger go? I search for it, trying to fuel it more, but I can't. Something is off.

The sickly woman in Case's arms pushes him away so she can speak. "Your friend Cody, she's in danger."

The mention of Cody tugs me forward. "Cody?" I whisper.

The woman encourages Case to tell me where my friend is. His angry eyes bore into mine, but he finally points to the trees. "She's that way ... not too far." Case drops his hand, and I turn to run into the trees, but then he calls me back. He pulls something out of his pocket and tosses it to me. It's a ring, a toboggan ring. It's much bigger than mine, but a toboggan ring no less.

"Thank you," I whisper to him. Nodding, he pulls out another toboggan, loads the woman inside, and with one wave of his hand disappears under the lid before the toboggan flies straight up and out of the fire.

I turn to the trees and head into the smoke in the direction Case indicated. I have to hurry before the fire reaches Mark. I cough wildly, unable to catch my breath. I don't even know what I'm looking for, but then I reach a clearing and see something in the middle. My heart sinks. It's Cody, tied to a stump.

"Cody." I cough.

I run to her side and check her neck for a pulse. My fingers brush against something. *Is that a totem? Didn't she turn her totem in?* But then I feel her pulse. She's alive!

"Alena?" she croaks.

I pull out my knife and cut the rope around her wrists. "Cody, I'm here to get you out—can you walk?" I pull on her arm.

Cody's cloudy eyes meet mine, and the disorientation clears. Suddenly, she begins to thrash wildly against me. "No!" she screams. "No, leave me!"

Ripping her arm out of my grasp, she runs toward the fire. It takes me only a second to understand what she's doing. When I do, I run after her, grab her around the waist, and throw her down on the ground. Unfortunately, neither of us has much energy after that. Cody sobs underneath me, and I fight to think.

Up.

The only way out is up. I pull out Case's toboggan and open it, loading Cody in.

I need to get Mark out of here too, but I don't think I can pull the toboggan through the fire to him. We won't all fit anyway. As quickly as I can, I activate the carrier, shut the lid, and watch as it flies up into the sky, out of my sight.

Getting off my knees seems like a feat I can't win now, but I still have to get Mark and the dinosaur out. So, I force myself up.

I stumble through the smoky trees. I cry in relief when I see them ahead of me. When I reach Mark, he's moaning back to life. Crouching beside him, I pull on the neck of his shirt. I need power, so I reach for his, but his holster is empty. The flames are getting closer, singeing my skin. I search around the area for an opening, but I can't see anything. We're trapped.

"Alena?" Mark's voice breaks through the crackling.

I look back down. "I'm so sorry, Mark. We need to get out of here, but the only way is up. We're going to have to fly. I'll morph, and I'll carry both you and your dinosaur. Hang on." I look around one last time, hoping everyone else got out.

Mark doesn't have time to respond before I pound my chest. A tingling sensation spurts through my limbs, like little ants rushing into my muscles. Hundreds of feathers pop out everywhere, like hairs on a wooly mammoth. I wobble slightly on my odd claws but then carefully grab Mark and the dinosaur. I'm not used to the wings, or the weight of two heavy creatures, but I pulse my wings the way I think a bird would, as hard as I can. The space around me doesn't offer much room to fully expand my appendages. My feathers start to burn. But I continue to flap them up and down until I lift us off the ground.

We're only up ten feet or so, when a tree beside us cracks and begins to fall. Without much room to move, I send us straight into the fire on the other side. My feathers quickly go up in flame, burning down to my skin, making me lose my thrust. We start to fall. Mark slips out of my claw, and I let out an eagle cry, unable to regain control. I'm thinking we're going to die, when Mark appears above me in *his* eagle form. He grabs me with his claw, and I hold on to Dilo.

A loud bolt of lightning splits through the air, pounding my eardrums to a pulp. I close my eyes, swooning at the realization that we just morphed. Together.

Mark carries us upward, away from the fire. Two more bolts crack, and then everything goes quiet. I'm hoping broken eardrums are the culprit for the silence, but a part of me says that's not the case. I finally open my eyes.

The fire is gone.

The beautiful green trees ... gone.

Every leaf, every twig, every bug. Gone.

For miles.

I pound my chest twice to morph back while Mark slowly lowers us to the ground.

I gawk at the scene. I hope this is a dream. I hope that I wake up soon and realize that I didn't just destroy so much … so quickly … so efficiently.

Even more than that, I hope everyone got out.

When Mark changes back into his human form, he lies on his back, still coughing from the smoke. I rush to his side.

"Mark, are you okay?" I'm completely useless without the power. I can't listen to his body.

Mark grabs the front of my shirt, pulling me closer to him. "Where's Gabbro?" he croaks.

I search his frantic face. "I don't know." I look around, wondering the same thing.

Mark's cracking voice brings my eyes back to him. "Alena, he told me to come with you." My eyebrows furrow, unsure of what Mark is trying to tell me.

"You left the dance to go to the hospital. I searched everywhere for you, but I couldn't find you. I was about to go back to GreenGrotto, when Gabbro came to me. He told me you were leaving on a flyer, and that I needed to follow you."

I'm confused. *Why would Gabbro tell Mark to come after me?* The pit in my stomach deepens. Mark tries to clarify further through labored pants. "Gabbro told you I couldn't be here. But then he brought me anyway. Why?" Mark's eyes begin to close, and his head falls back. "Alena, we can't trust him."

The tremors in my hands increase. Mark becomes quiet.

"Mark?"

He doesn't respond.

"Mark!" I pound on his chest. I slap his face. I scream. But he doesn't respond.

His pulse is there, but it's weak. I touch his forehead. *He's burning up. Damn that serum!*

I search the area, now panicked. Mark's words play over and over in my mind. *Why would Gabbro betray me? If he wasn't to be trusted, why did he help us get the Pepps out? Wait. Did the Pepps get out?*

Frantic, I start looking for signs of life around me. *What if we killed them? What if they didn't get out in time before Mark and I morphed?*

Leaning to the side, I vomit. Bracing myself on all fours, I try to control my breathing. *Nothing makes sense!*

Is Case even the leader of the clan? The way he looked at that woman ... *Could this all be bigger than him? Was he used, just like me, in some bigger scheme? And the woman—who is she? And if Case isn't the leader, then who is?*

And why was Cody tied to that stump?

I don't know how long I stay on my hands and knees. Based on the terrible ache pulsing through them, I'm guessing it's been a long time. Finally, the familiar buzz of an aircraft breaks through the silence. I raise my head and watch as it lands. I need to know that all the Pepps are safe.

My muscles ache in protest when I stand, but I force myself up, stumbling as quickly as I can to the aircraft. I wait anxiously for the ramp to open. When it does, several council Pepps come running out. "Alena, get inside. We'll search the perimeter for survivors."

Survivors.

I let them pass, until I see Rusty getting out of the pilot seat. Then I burst into tears.

"Did everyone get out?" I ask.

Rusty's face is dirty ... and worried.

"We don't know. We're still trying to figure out who's missing. But ..." A bit of relief enters his face. "Cody is accounted for."

I swallow. My body battling between relief and terror. Cody is accounted for, but not everyone else. What if some Pepps didn't make it back? My knees give out, and I fall to the floor. *What if Pepps didn't make it back?* Rusty helps me to a seat, then goes out to get Mark.

I'm unable to hold myself together any longer.

I sob. My body trembles like a toddler's rattle.

I sit there. I replay every moment in my mind over and over again. Tears seep out of my eyes. I almost lost Cody out there. And Mark.

I should be relieved that I didn't end up losing them. But something deep down inside churns. This isn't over.

"All the clan members are dead." A council member comes back into the aircraft, a clan man flung over his shoulder, breaking my train of thought.

Then, looking at me, he asks, "What happened here?"

It takes me a moment to realize that several other council members have brought dead clan men back to the aircraft too, and they're waiting for me to explain how they died. My lips tremble when I open them. I try to speak. I can't.

"Let's give her some time," Rusty says, eyeing my shaking hands.

The council member's question echoes loudly in my head.

What just happened?

Chapter 29

Petrichor is buzzing with life. The sunlit hospital combs are hopefully full of prisoners being healed by experienced medics. That's where I should take Mark.

As soon as the aircraft ramp lowers, the council members deplane with the dead clan men. My body is beyond exhausted. My side hurts from the gun shot, and my ears still ring from all the explosions. My skin smells like smoke and my arms have deep burns on them from getting too close to the fire. But the adrenaline coursing through my veins drowns out the sound of pain. I need to make sure the other Pepps got out.

I'm helping Mark up, when a messenger comes on board.

"Alena, I need to take you and Mark to the chief, right away."

I lift Mark's arm over my shoulders ready to help him walk. "Can I take Mark to the hospital first? He's sick."

"No, the chief wants him too, no matter what."

Fine. Thankfully Rusty helps me with Mark, bracing him on his other side.

We descend the aircraft and turn toward the Post. I know what's waiting for me through those tunnels. Questions. Questions I'm not sure I have the answers to. As we walk, I try to figure out what to tell the chief. Try to make sense of everything myself.

As should be expected, the tunnels in the Post are busier than normal. We struggle to maneuver through the crowd and finally reach the chief's office. Rusty knocks loudly but doesn't wait for a response to enter.

"Alena." The chief drops the papers he's holding onto his desk and walks toward us. His beard and clothes are dirty from freeing the prisoners, and he looks worried.

"Come in, please. Rusty, you can go. I know you're anxious to get back to Cody."

Rusty eyes me carefully before releasing Mark and slipping from the room. Mark suddenly becomes very heavy.

The chief walks to me and puts a hand on my shoulder. "I'm glad you're both okay," he says. "It looks like we got most of the prisoners out, thanks to you."

I'm about to ask him if everyone else got out, but the door opens again, a dark-skinned man bursting into the room. He has the mark of a totem trainer and reminds me of Bapoto.

"Chief, you called?" the man says out of breath.

"Yes, Alena, please help me take off Mark's shirt."

Mark's shirt? What's going on? I quietly follow his command. Mark's arm tightens around my shoulders, and I brace him as well as I can while slipping my hands under his shirt. His skin is hot.

I'm so distracted by his temperature that I almost miss the color of the cloth.

My hands freeze.

He's wearing a plaid button-up shirt. I've never seen him wear plaid. I look down at his pants. They're odd too—khaki and much too short for him. Mark wasn't wearing this when he left Petrichor, or when he tried to stop me after getting off the aircraft. When did he change?

"I need you to look at his power," the chief instructs the totem trainer while removing Mark's shirt for me. "Tell me if it's different."

The totem trainer steps in front of Mark. I follow his eyes. When I see it, I gasp. The familiar green glow of his totem's heart is now replaced with a large sphere of black liquid encased in a hard gray shell. Mark looks at me for an explanation since he can't see it.

"It's black," I whisper. "The heart of your totem is black."

The trainer reaches for the power and pops it out.

I'm confused. Mark didn't have power when we were in the fire ... I had checked. So, where did this come from? Was it generated from our morph? Coming with its own protective shell? Is mine black too? I rub my chest.

As the totem trainer listens to the elements of the black sphere, his eyebrows furrow deeper and deeper. "It doesn't sound like our power." He cocks his head, then adds, "It is power ... but it isn't our power. It lacks ..." The man pauses for a long moment, closing his eyes, until he finally says, "Peppate. It doesn't have Peppate." Looking at the chief, the trainer asks, "How is that possible?"

I follow the trainer's eyes to the chief's now uneasy expression. Swallowing harshly, the chief looks at me.

"Alena, what happened down there?"

Holding on to Mark, with the totem trainer listening, I tell the chief everything. I tell him about finding the Pepps and blowing up the electrical source. I tell him about the woman hidden in the wall. About getting her out.

I explain that the fire had already spread around the forest by the time I pulled the woman up, and how Mark was still there, leaning against the tree. I tell him that my capsules and power were gone and how Case came out of the trees focused on the woman. I tell him how he gave me a toboggan and told me where to find Cody. Last, I tell him about morphing with Mark, and what it did to the area.

When I'm done, I see that little beads of sweat have formed on the chief's forehead.

"What's going on, Chief?"

The chief's mouth is dry. I can tell by the way his voice scrapes against his throat when he responds.

"Well, a lot is going on," he whispers. "For starters, Danny has been taken."

I stand frozen, unsure if I heard him right. "What?"

The chief grabs a piece of paper off his desk.

"Danny followed us down there, Alena. He followed us in some sort of flyer. As I was leaving the silver mine, SilverDen, with the prisoners, I saw it and dropped down to see what it was. That's where I found this." He gestures to the piece of paper.

This news makes my blood run cold. Danny was down there? I don't even want to think the question. Did our lightning hit Danny?

Chief rubs his bushy eyebrows angrily, then pinches his nose.

"He would have died from your morph ... if someone else hadn't been there to capture him." Chief's eyes bore into mine. "Jax. He took Danny and left behind a message. He wants the power. The power you created tonight."

Jax? So, he did get out of Petrichor? Is he the one behind all this, the one 'Gabbro the traitor' was working for? The one Case was working for?

My body sags. Danny was down there because of me. Now he's missing, because of me!

I'm fighting to breathe when Mark whispers something beside me.

"It was all a setup."

I look up.

The chief nods solemnly. "Yes, Mark. I believe so."

I gape at the chief. "What?" I ask with narrowed eyes.

"Alena, that fire was started on purpose, to trap you and Mark, so you would morph." The chief rubs his face and starts pacing. "I should have known something was up the moment we got there. Nobody was waiting for us. You just went right in without a fight." He shakes his head. "You said Case was there in the trees, in a mound of rocks? He must have been waiting for you to morph. He was planning to collect the power you created when it was all over. Power without Peppate."

I stare at the floor. "But he didn't collect the power. So Jax did what he had to do to get the power himself. He took Danny, knowing I would do anything to get him back."

Even give up the power.

Gabbro was probably down there too, helping Jax, maybe sitting on his cold shoulder.

My mind suddenly goes back to all the odd things that happened in Petrichor.

How the locations were missing from every threat I got.

The Morgans placed in my room.

Pepp memory searches coming up blank.

The note Flint found from Jax, encouraging him to teach me how to morph.

Each of these things could easily be explained if Gabbro was indeed working with Jax.

"This is all my fault. For falling for Gabbro's stupid lies." I grit my teeth, biting back tears. "I should have just ignored him and come straight to you when he presented his confusing little plan."

"He fooled us all, Alena," the chief whispers.

The air is quiet, and heavy for a long moment before the chief speaks again. "All along we thought your totem was created to be a weapon. But that's not what it's about, is it? It's about this power. How could I not see it before? How could I not see that this was so much bigger!" His convicted words make my body sag.

How could none of us see? I close my eyes.

The totem trainer clears his throat. I had forgotten he was in the room. "Do you think this has anything to do with the Mixed Bloods?"

The Mixed Bloods? Aren't they the ones born to both a Pepp and human parent?

"Possibly," Chief says. "Case was helping his father cure the Mixed Blood boy. He must have continued his work even after the boy's death, engineering this totem's power to heal those like him."

If Case did create this totem for the power, did he know about the lightning? Of course he did. But did he know how much it would destroy? I squeeze my eyes shut, thinking about all the clan men, dead. Because of me.

Mark almost falls to the floor in my distraction. I grunt under his weight and gulp back the horror of the night. "Chief. Sorry, I need to get Mark to the hospital."

"Of course," the chief mutters, frustration still written on his face. Mark and I turn and almost reach the door, when the chief says, "Alena, don't go looking for Danny."

I stop, catching a scoff in my throat. How dare he make such a demand? Even if I don't have the slightest clue where to look, he can't ask that of me. Danny is in danger.

I ignore his comment and continue walking.

"If you leave Petrichor, I'll put you in our prison, Algor." His warning hits my back. I grit my teeth and pause for only a second. Then move forward.

We're out in the hall, when another man comes rushing in. I try to block everything out, but the man's words, no matter how softly they're spoken, slam loudly into my ears.

"We've finished clearing the hideout. Every Pepp has been accounted for, except for one."

I stop walking. My heart squeezes.

"Tom. We can't find him."

No.

My knees give out, and Mark and I topple to the floor.

Please don't tell me I killed him. Not Tom. Not Cody's Pepp father.

I scream into my sleeve, unable to hold it back any longer.

I tried. I tried so hard. I wanted to free the prisoners. And I tried to do it without hurting anyone. But instead, I hurt everyone. I killed the clan men. I lost Danny. I ruined my relationship with Mark. Case and Jax got away.

And now I'm never going to get home.

Pepps move by Mark and me in a sort of blur. When my pained body can't stand kneeling anymore, I finally wipe my nose and pull Mark up. I need to get him to the hospital.

My eyes are blurry, but somehow we get there. I get the attention of a free medic and tell her to help Mark. I'm relieved to see him in her experienced hands. But she wants to keep me too. I don't know why. I'm not hurt, am I? She pulls me to a chair. I can't see her face clearly. Does she have brown hair? Is she easing pain? It doesn't matter.

I lean my head back. Nothing matters.

And yet … everything matters. So many people's lives have been forever changed.

Because of me.

Acknowledgements

Wow. I never imagined this journey would be so amazing ... and so hard. Fortunately, I have amazing people in my life!

To my husband, Rich. He probably doesn't know this, but he's the main reason I decided to start this journey. Unlike other writers, this wasn't about *writing* a trilogy. It was about doing something bigger than myself. And it was Rich that inspired this through his example of embracing challenging things. His experiences seem to refine him as a person, making him more resilient. And I wanted to develop that type of resilience. Rich has given me his unfailing support throughout all this and lifted me when I couldn't lift myself. I couldn't have done this without him.

To my amazing parents, who encouraged me to keep going when I was determined to quit. Their faith increased my faith. Their love increased my strength, and I'm deeply grateful for their support.

To all those first readers who gave me much needed feedback: Kathy England, Cloey Green, Carrie England and Rich England. You were the first to see my new world, and I appreciate your enthusiasm and kind words.

A very special thank you to Emily Ensign. You were an answer to my prayers, reaching out during a very fragile time to give me much needed guidance. I will always be grateful for your spiritual intuition.

To those who first read the entire series: Abbie Conley and Kymbree Mitchell, thank you! Your feedback and insights made the series better!

To my emotional support system: Mom, Dad, Kristi Green, Jessica Kendrick, Tess DiPiero, and Rich. You listened and lifted me when I needed it.

Thank you to my editor C.S Lakin, for your amazing critiques. Your specific comments were like guiding lights that allowed me to clearly see what to do to make the book better. Thank you for your time and encouragement.

And thank you to all my readers! You're just the best!!

Lastly, I want to thank my Heavenly Father and Savior, Jesus Christ, for always being there for me. I know they live. I know they love each one of us. And I'm grateful for their constant love, support, and comfort. They are truly the brightest light in my life.

www.ingramcontent.com/pod-product-compliance
Lightning Source LLC
Chambersburg PA
CBHW020601310726
48979CB00008B/1296/J

* 9 7 9 8 9 9 0 3 8 0 2 1 9 *